THREE
STEPBROTHERS
SAVE
CHRISTMAS

D. E. BARTLEY

BOOKS

By D.E. Bartley

O'Reilly Fight Club

Four Stepbrothers & I
Four Daddies & I
Faking it with the SEALs
Three Stepbrothers Save Christmas
Four Fiancés and I

To everyone who has been in a toxic relationship, whether with a parent, spouse, friendship or any other, there is light at the end of the tunnel. Remember, there is always someone, whether a friend or other family member, who loves you more than you will ever know. Let yourself heal and accept that you are loveable, no matter what you are told.

My inbox is always open.

Vinci Books

vinci-books.com

Published by Vinci Books Ltd in 2025

1

A CIP catalogue record for this book is available from the British Library.
Paperback ISBN: 9781036709686

Trigger warnings

This book does contain some scenes that may trigger someone who has dealt with the same issues as the main characters. Please read the warning list first and decide if you wish to continue.

Your mental health matters.

Toxic parent/relationship
Self-harming
Death of a parent (off-page)
Suicidal thoughts
Extreme low self-esteem
Daddy doms
Dom/sub-sexual scenes
Detailed sexual scenes
Restraints
Anal play
Choking kink
Use of sex toys
Cheating (not MMCs)

Chapter One

VERITY

"I'm glad to hear your father is *finally* coming home for a bit."

Looking up from my book, I find Danielle King taking a seat beside me.

"How do you know? I only found out this morning," I ask, picking up my mug and sipping my latte. I love this time of year; the coffee shop on the school grounds gets gingerbread flavouring, so I can drink gingerbread lattes whenever I want.

"Dad told me last night. He said Henry called to ask if he would be around as he wants to talk business or something."

Why did he tell someone else he was coming home before me? You would think that as his daughter, I would be the first person he told.

"I'm hoping that will mean he's home for a while, maybe even for Christmas. Otherwise, why would he be coming back next week?" I answer, trying to keep the hurt from my voice. I can't believe he spoke to Mr King before his own daughter. Then I remembered I texted him that I was exhausted, so he must have wanted me to rest. That makes more sense than him thinking of me last.

My father's work forces him to live in the States for most of the year. Which means he's away more than he's home. I've suggested several times that we move over there, but he doesn't seem to like the idea of me being out there. He's never let me travel with him; I've never been to the States, and I don't even know what he does other than make money through stocks and shares. Occasionally, he will invest the money he makes into businesses like Danielle's father's casino and racehorses. But otherwise, he spends everything he makes, ensuring that I have everything I could need.

"Wasn't he home last Christmas?" she asks, cutting up her baguette. I shake my head whilst picking at the fruit salad I picked up this morning. I will never understand how others can eat large meals hours before a performance. It makes me feel heavy and fat, distracting me from the dances, so I prefer something light with no carbs.

It's the first of December, so we're in the final month of our Christmas production. This year, we are performing *The Nutcracker*. Usually, we only perform in December, but with the rising costs of everything at the dance school I attend, we have been performing for the last two months, trying to sell as many tickets as possible to raise essential funds.

The whole company is physically and mentally exhausted and cannot wait to finish on Christmas Eve. We then have three weeks off to recover before returning in the new year to prepare for the summer production. We will also have our final exams for our degree in dance.

"Huh," Danielle mutters, catching my attention. "I'm

sure he was at my parents' Christmas Eve party," she frowns.

"No, he was in the States as something came up at the last minute, and then he couldn't get a flight," I explain. She must be mistaken because he wouldn't lie about being away, especially at Christmas.

Danni starts eating her food as I sit quietly, contemplating what it will be like to have Dad home. I can't remember the last time he was here for Christmas. Being in the States makes it difficult to travel at the best of times, but the holiday season makes it near impossible.

"What's your plans if he doesn't stay for Christmas?" she asks next to me. I shrug and look into my almost empty glass cup.

"Nothing, I guess. I'll just be on my own."

"You can't spend it alone!"

I look up at my friend and see the concern on her face.

"It's fine. It won't be the first time," I smile, hoping she'll drop the subject because, in all honesty, it's far from fine. But I hate the idea of her worrying about me.

It's crazy to think that this woman was a bitch to Jasmine and me just eight months ago. I think it's fair to say she hated us. We stayed out of her way, and she made it her mission to make our lives hell. All that changed when Jasmine was attacked seven months ago. Danielle found her and raised the alarm. Since then, they put the past behind them, and I gradually warmed to her as well.

Six months ago, she proved how good a friend she could be when my drink was spiked during a night out for Jasmine's twenty-first birthday. The night had been amazing until that point. We later discovered my drink had been spiked to ensure Jasmine's bodyguards were preoccupied so she could be kidnapped. The whole experience has brought the three of us closer than ever. The drugs they gave me were strong, and it took me three days to recover completely. Danielle didn't leave my side for the first night until the eldest of my stepbrothers, Travis, turned up and took over my care. Even then, she called numerous times a day and kept me posted with all the updates whilst people searched for Jasmine until she was rescued a few days later.

Danielle and I spent some time with Jasmine afterwards, helping her to heal and come to terms with a few things she learnt during her time with the kidnappers. Since then, we have been inseparable. We do everything together, and it's hard to believe we were anything other than best friends.

"Has Jasmine been picked up?" I ask, looking for a way to change the subject.

Danielle nods whilst finishing her baguette.

"Yeah, Maximus picked her up twenty minutes ago. He is taking her to her therapy session and then bringing her back to get ready for the show."

Poor Jasmine has been having therapy every week for the last five months. The O'Reilly's, her four fiancés, insisted on it after she was taken, not only for the fact she was kidnapped but for the truths she discovered during that time as well. There is nothing those four guys wouldn't do for her, and they have done all they could to give her the safe environment she deserves while she heals.

Jasmine is so lucky to have not one but four men willing to give her everything she needs. There is nothing they wouldn't do for her, and I have to admit I'm jealous of her for that.

I look down at my phone as it vibrates on the table with a text from my boyfriend.

Marshall: I'm on break. Call me if you are free. Xxx

"I'm going to make a call before we get into costume. I'll see you in a bit," I say quickly, grabbing my bag. Danielle l looks up and smiles at me.

"Okay, save me a mirror if you get there first."

Promising I will, I pick up my phone and head towards the courtyard, hoping for some privacy.

As soon as I'm out in the cold winter air, I pull my jacket tighter around me whilst looking for a vacant bench. Sitting down, I pull up my boyfriend's number and look at it momentarily. I promised to call him, and I want to speak to him. But something is holding me back, and I have no idea what.

Marshall is a lovely guy; he's sweet and says he cares for me and all the romantic things a boyfriend should say, but I can't help wondering if he means it. It probably doesn't help that he can be incredibly immature and likes to tell his friends he is with a tall, blonde, skinny ballerina. Sometimes, I feel he is with me because of how I look on his arm rather than who I am. Not that I think I'm anything special because I know I'm not. Especially compared to the likes of Jasmine and Danielle. But I have the typical innocent girl look, which men seem to find attractive. Marshall loves to tell me how jealous his friends are that he is with someone like me. Yet, he never comes to any of my performances to support me or even seem remotely interested in my dancing. Maybe I'm looking too deep into this.

There again, my own father hasn't seen me dance in years, but he will boast to all his friends that I will be the "next big thing", and I know he loves the recordings I send him of the productions. I wish it were easier for him to come and watch them in person. Maybe when he comes back next week, he'll be able to watch one of the shows? Then he could finally watch me like I always wish he would.

My mum was the one who got me into dancing. It was always something we shared. I used to love watching her dance, and I hope I look as graceful as she did. Dad always said she looked like a goddess when she danced, and he was right. We used to watch her together in the makeshift studio she created. She loved it when I watched her practice whilst sitting on my Dad's lap. I loved those times, too. I think that's why my father doesn't watch me dance anymore, as it reminds him too much of my mum.

Miriam Stevenson was a loving and caring woman; everyone who met her instantly liked and loved having her around. There was nothing she wouldn't do for anyone, especially me. In every memory of her, she is smiling, laughing, dancing, or combining all three. My mum became ill and died quickly when I was seven years old. She had a brain tumour, and there was nothing the doctors could do to help her. There were only a few months between her getting diagnosed and dying. I know now that it was a blessing, as she could have suffered for years. But I still miss her daily, and I know my dad does, too.

Around that time, my father started working away more, and I saw less and less of him. It's not like he neglects me. He ensures I have the best of everything; I want for nothing, and I get to live in a big house without paying any bills. I attend the best dance school in the UK and have wonderful friends whom I would do anything for. But even though I have so much, I miss my parents. When Mum died, a part of Dad died with her, and I don't think he will ever get that part back. He was left heartbroken by her death, and I thought he would never recover. Then, five years ago, he announced he was getting married to a woman he met through work.

Linda Donavon is a widow whose husband was killed in

a car accident, leaving her with their three sons: Travis, Ryan and Ethan. They are all quite a bit older than me. Travis is ten years older at thirty-one. Ryan is seven years older, and Ethan is five. I only met them once before the wedding.

I get along with my stepmother; she seems like she loves my father, but they aren't home enough for me to build an actual relationship with her. I am probably closer to her sons than I will ever be with her. I don't hear from them all the time, and I can go weeks before Ryan or Ethan message. Travis has been checking up on me more since my drink was spiked, but I'm sure he only does that because my father would have asked him to keep an eye on me. The Donavon brothers spend the odd weekend here and there at my house, but even then, they seem to go about doing their own thing. I wish sometimes we were closer, and then maybe they would visit a bit more often. I like it when they are around. They are fun, and we always have a laugh. It's nice not being the only person in that big house. I never admit it out loud, but it can sometimes get lonely.

I take a deep breath and look at my phone again. I have ten minutes before I have to start getting ready for the show, so I might as well do something during that time. I tap on the screen and hold the phone to my ear. Hoping to still catch Marshall on his break.

Chapter Two

VERITY

Exhausted and aching, I make the drive home. I am looking forward to having some company tonight, as Marshall messaged to say he is on his way around.

The performance went well, as it always does. No one would dare to mess up; otherwise, Mrs Florence would have us all back at the studio at the crack of dawn for extra rehearsals. No one wants that this late in the year; we are all exhausted as it is.

As I pull up in front of the house, I notice a car in the driveway and lights on inside the house. My body comes alive with excitement as I park next to the strange car and grab my keys before jumping out. Rushing to the front door, I unlock it with shaking hands, hopping from one foot to the other, desperate to get inside as quickly as possible. There's only one person it could be, and I can't believe he tricked me by saying he would be home next week.

"Dad!" I slam the door shut behind me. I listen out for any noise and hear something from the kitchen. Rushing forward, almost tripping over my own feet, I race to where I know he must be.

"Daddy, you're home!" I call excitedly, only to come to a screeching stop.

"Well, I can be your daddy if you want me to be, Baby girl." Ethan, the younger of my stepbrothers, grins at me as he stands at the counter, making himself a sandwich. I drop my bag on the floor as my heart breaks a little.

"I thought you were someone else," I murmur, trying to hide my disappointment but failing miserably as I grab a bottle of water from the fridge behind him.

"I'm sorry to disappoint," he replies, looking over his shoulder as I turn to face him. "Am I not even going to get a hello?" he asks with one arched brow. I smile slightly as I step beside him to kiss his cheek.

"Hello, Ethan."

"That's more like it," he winks before returning to his sandwich. "I filled the fridge for you, by the way. There was nothing in there." I can hear the accusation in his tone.

"Thanks, I've been eating out most of the time cause of the shows. I was going to go shopping tomorrow," I lie, trying to ignore how he's watching me. I wait for him to call me out but relax when he hums deep in his throat.

"How come you're here? Have I missed something?" I ask, walking around the other side of the counter he's standing over to build his chicken salad sandwich.

"Mum called last night saying they would be home next week and wanted to see us all. I have some potential clients in this area, so I thought I'd come early and kill two birds with one stone."

It's not the first time one of them has come to stay for business reasons. Ethan and Ryan are personal trainers with a high price tag, meaning all their clients are all super rich.

They do online sessions as well as one-to-one sessions. They are amazing at the job, and both helped me recover from a dancing injury a couple of years ago. They are both fully trained PTs and physios, specialising in sports injuries.

"So, the others aren't with you?" I ask, reaching over and grabbing a slice of the tomato he's cutting. He slaps my hand away and sighs before passing me the other slice as I smile sweetly at him. Ethan always gives me what I want, not that I ask for much. But if I ever do, he gives in quicker than I can blink.

"They'll be here in a couple of days; they are taking care of a few things first." He cuts into his sandwich while grinning at me. "So, sorry, you're stuck with just me for the time being."

I pick up my bag and sigh dramatically.

"Well, don't bug me, and I won't bug you," I say, walking out of the kitchen smiling.

"But, what if I want to bug you?"

"Tough!" I laugh. "I have someone coming over, don't tell anyone, especially our parents!" I call out nervously, rushing up the stairs to my room. I hear Ethan asking who's coming over, but don't bother answering. He will know soon enough as he should be here any minute.

I don't think any of the guys have met a boyfriend before, and now that I know Ethan is here, I'm not sure how I feel about him coming over. My love life is something I keep very quiet, and even the girls haven't met him. It's not that I'm ashamed of him or that he isn't attractive because he is. But my father has always told me to stay away from guys, and I find it easier to hide it from him if no one else knows either. I might be twenty-one, but I still want to ensure I don't upset my dad. He does so much for me; the least I can do is do as he asks, most of the time.

Dropping my bag at the bottom of my bed, I shrug off my jacket and place it on the chair. I'd been so excited when I thought Dad was home. As happy as I am to see Ethan, it's not the same. I miss my dad and having him around. When he's home, everything seems a little better with the world. Even if he is only back for a few days, those days mean the world to me.

I rush into my bathroom to brush my teeth and check my make-up. It's been a long day, and the performance tonight felt like it was dragging. I think we are all in desperate need of a break. Thankfully, I have tomorrow night off before the last three weeks of performances start. Marshall is staying tonight and tomorrow after we go out for a meal at his favourite restaurant. I know I should probably use the night off to rest, but it's Christmas, and it's not like I have anything else to do with my time.

Walking back into my room, I grab my phone from my bag and check the time stamp on Marshall's last message. I realise he should be here any moment as headlights light up my bedroom window. Throwing my phone onto the bed, I rush down the stairs, eager to get to the door before Ethan. I'm just getting to the bottom step when he comes out of the kitchen at the exact moment Marshall knocks on the door.

"Who's that?" he asks as I rush past him to open the door.

"Hi!" I call a little too loud as I throw my arms around Marshall. He chuckles to himself whilst hugging me back.

"Anyone would think you'd missed me," he says as I take his hand, leading him into the house.

"I have," I reply, smiling before turning to see Ethan at the bottom of the stairs, frowning at us. "Can we help you?" I ask as Marshall comes to an abrupt stop beside me.

"Oh, hi," he says nervously, looking at my stepbrother.

"Who's this?" Ethan asks, staring at him.

"Marshall. I told you not to bug me when I have company," I point out as I go to pull Marshall up the stairs, but Ethan blocks our way.

"Are you the boyfriend or gay best friend?" Ethan asks, staring at him.

"Boyfriend. And you are?" he asks, standing tall beside me. For crying out loud, are they going to get their cocks out and compare sizes too? There again, if it came to a fight, I know Ethan would win. He has a lot more muscle mass than Marshall, who is relatively thin in compassion.

"The one who will break your legs if you hurt my ... stepsister."

"Okay, enough," I snap, stepping between them. "Ethan, move," I order, pushing him out of the way.

"Actually, Ver, I can't stay for long. I'm heading to Toms. Do you want to come?"

I turn to Marshall, frowning. He knows I don't like going to his friends.

"His parents are away, and we are going round in a bit for a gaming session."

Ethan snorts behind me before trying to disguise it with a cough. Man, I want to kick him right now. Going around to his mates while they all play on their game consoles is not how I want to spend my evening. He knows this and is probably only mentioning it now, knowing I will say no.

"It's fine; why don't you go, and I can see you tomorrow." I can feel Ethan's presence behind me; I can almost see the stupid smirk he has on his face.

"Are you sure? I promised we could chill out tonight," Marshall starts. I hear Ethan cough as he walks away from us and back into the kitchen.

"It's fine; you go and enjoy time with your mates," I smile as I lead him back towards the door. He turns around and wraps an arm around my waist. "I love you," I whisper, smiling up at him.

"You're the best," he smiles before kissing me and turning around to almost run to his car. I wave as he drives off and close the door, letting out a deep sigh.

"What? No, I love you?"

I spin and glare at Ethan.

"We did say it!" I snap. One side of Ethan's mouth lifts as he smirks at me.

"No, you did, he didn't. I was listening in from the kitchen."

I roll my eyes and head towards the stairs, planning on getting as far away from him as possible.

"F.Y.I, you could do better." He turns and walks into the lounge as I storm towards my room.

What does he know? "*You could do better*," please! Marshall is loving and caring, and he does love me; I know he does. Just because he didn't say it that one time doesn't mean he doesn't care about me.

I walk into my room and slam the door behind me. Well, there goes my plans for the evening. It looks like I won't be getting what I hoped for, which is why I was so eager to get Marshall upstairs to my room. The truth is I love the feeling you get after a good orgasm. It's something I crave to the point I could probably say I'm slightly addicted.

People would never believe me if I told them. They all see me as the shy, quiet woman who probably doesn't even have sex. But it's a side of me no one can ever know about. It can be an issue because I've noticed if I go too long without one, I can get moody, and then people start asking questions I don't want to answer. To prevent this, I need to orgasm almost daily; otherwise, I get cranky and irritable, making it a struggle to concentrate when dancing. I usually handle it by getting myself off in the shower most of the time. But tonight, I needed more and had hoped Marshall could relieve some of my built-up tension. Not that he's amazing at the actual sex part; I rarely get off unless I'm on top. But he is good at foreplay, and if I give him a little help, I can usually get off. But I guess that's not going to happen tonight.

I realised about a year ago, when I was with my ex, that my constant mood swings and concentration issues were always better after we had a good night of sex. He is the only person I ever talked to about this, and he left me because I was too high maintenance. Since then, I have dealt with the issue on my own, having not found anyone who makes me feel the way he did during sex. I figured all I could do was try to make the most of a bad situation.

Looking at my drawer where my selection of sex toys is hidden, including my favourite vibrator, I consider getting it out, only to remember I have a houseguest whose bedroom is next to mine.

I open my door quietly and listen, trying to gauge where Ethan is. I can hear the TV in the lounge in the distance and know if he has a film on, he'll be down there for a while. Closing my door with a smile, I head to my bed whilst stripping. I can feel the aching between my legs building as I climb under the covers and pull my toy and lube from the drawer. I won't need the lube, but it will add to the pleasure as it tingles, meaning I come quicker than I do without it. Not that it will take me long tonight. I have been on edge all day.

I get myself comfortable in bed; I squeeze a little lube onto my fingers and rub it over my clit, it takes a second to start working, but when it does, I feel my eyes rolling into the back of my head. I love this lube; it's cooling and feels the best of the many I have tried.

I lie back on my pillow and just enjoy the feeling of the lube and my fingers around my clit. It doesn't take long to have a small orgasm, but as I predicted, it isn't enough. I pull out my vibrator and listen out one last time for any sign that Ethan has come upstairs before turning it on to the lowest setting and teasing my entrance with it. I bite my lip as the vibrations course through me. I run it up and down between my lips from my entrance to my slightly sensitive clit and back again. Slowly, I push the vibrator inside and sigh as it fills me. This is what I needed, to be filled to the point it nearly hurts. I love the whole pain-with-pleasure element. I long to find someone who will grab my hair, slap my ass, and choke me. I want to be fucked hard by some-one, as well as made love to. But it's hard to attract the kind of men I want when you are as quiet as me, and everyone expects you to be the good little ballerina.

I start moving the vibrator in and out of me, starting slow until I know I have to go harder. With one hand on the vibrator and the other rubbing my clit I pick up speed. It feels so good; why can't I find a guy to make me feel this way?

"Ahh god," I gasp loudly before quickly reminding myself I'm meant to be quiet. I stop for the briefest second, and when I don't hear anything, I carry on. I know I need to hurry up, so I concentrate purely on the sensation of the vibrator hitting every spot within me. As I start rubbing my clit, I feel myself heading quickly to that sensation I am so desperate to feel.

As my body tenses and the pleasure builds, nothing else matters but this feeling right here. God, I love sex, but when you can give yourself the most perfect orgasm, hitting just the right spots, who needs a man?

I cum loudly and have to slam my hand over my mouth as my release vibrates through my whole body. My pussy clamps around the vibrator, and I swear it nearly sucks it completely inside of me. I'm breathing heavily and know that if Ethan walks past my door right now, he will hear me, but I'm too relaxed to care.

Removing my vibrator, I lie still in the after-orgasm glow and enjoy the content and satisfied feeling that overcomes me. This is what I love, this feeling of being so satisfied I could curl up and sleep.

I reach for the tissues I keep in my top drawer and clean myself up before dropping them into the bin beside my bed to throw away in the morning.

With everything hidden away, I curl on my side and close my eyes, ready for a half-decent sleep. Pushing all my insecurities and worries to the back of my mind as I do every night. Tomorrow is another day, and I want to start it feeling refreshed.

Chapter Three

ETHAN

I look at my sports watch as I stop at the back door and see it's bang on seven AM. Perfect. I still have time to get in, stretch, and have a shower and breakfast before I have to meet with a potential client.

I toe off my running shoes, not wanting to walk any mud into the house, before entering the utility room that leads to the kitchen.

I hate this house, not the actual house itself; that's beautiful. But when I visit, I have to deal with the stuck-up housekeeper who wants the place to be like a showroom, and no one can leave any sign that people actually live here. It's no wonder Verity can be so quiet and subdued at times. She's forced to live in a glass house and forbidden to touch any surfaces.

There again, she wasn't so quiet last night. I know exactly what she was doing in that room, and fuck, it was hot. I couldn't stop myself from going to my room and taking my cock in my hand to find my own release whilst listening to her.

I come to a stop as I enter the kitchen, surprised to see Verity dressed and eating muesli. Her long blonde hair is poker straight as it hangs down her back, she has a little make-up on, and her skin is so fair it almost glows against the dark interior of the kitchen. She reminds me of a porcelain doll, just without the creepy factor. She's so beautiful; it takes my breath away whenever I see her.

"Good morning, Baby girl," I chirp, walking over to the fridge to get a cold bottle of water. "You're up early," I add, turning to look at her.

"I'm always up by six," she answers, pushing her cereal around in the bowl. Something doesn't seem right this morning; she didn't even look up as I entered.

"Why?"

Verity finally lifts her head and shrugs.

"Why do you run in the morning?" she asks.

"Because I want to. Plus, it means I don't have to go later in the day."

Verity shrugs again and goes back to pushing her muesli around.

"There you go then. If I'm up at six, I can stretch and practice. I'm always showered, dressed, and ready to face the day by seven."

I lean against the refrigerator and watch her momentarily as she continues to push her food around in the bowl, not lifting the spoon to her mouth once.

Something is definitely different about her this time. I can't put my finger on it, but she seems more fragile than usual. Is that prick of a boyfriend to blame? If he is, I'm more than happy to ensure he never upsets her again. It took everything in me not to send him packing for good last night. I know his type; I've *been* his type. I know if I hadn't been here, he'd have had no problem fucking her and then leaving to have a games night with his friends. He was here for a fuck, that's it. If he weren't, he wouldn't have come around in the first place. She deserves better. Surely, she can see he is just a child who thinks with his dick.

Pushing myself away from the fridge, I pull my running top off. It's wet with sweat and sticking to me, making me cool down too quickly. I still need to stretch before I seize up. When I turn my attention back to Verity, I catch her looking away quickly. Smiling, I walk past her, purposely tensing my back muscles. Teasing her in a way I know I shouldn't, but I can't help myself. Glancing over my shoulder as I head back into the utility room to put my top in the washing machine, I catch her looking again.

"Like what you see, Baby girl?" I tease. Verity jumps up and rushes towards the dishwasher, where she busies herself, emptying the contents of her bowl into the food bin before placing everything in the dishwasher to be cleaned. All while muttering that I need to keep my clothes on. I can't help grinning, knowing she's flustered because of me. I know I can't act on the way my body aches for her, but I can enjoy teasing her, at least.

"What are your plans for today?" I ask, walking back into the kitchen whilst sipping my water.

"I'm going out with the girls, then meeting Marshall." Verity turns around and stares at me with her hands on her hips. Where did those hips come from? She wasn't this curvy the last time I saw her. Not that she is curvy in the right kind of way, but she could actually do with putting on a few pounds if I'm honest. There had been next to nothing in when I arrived yesterday afternoon. I had to do close to a full shop before I could make myself a simple sandwich. The only thing in the fridge was some lettuce, 0% milk and bottled water. That was it. Do I buy the whole *"I was going to do a food shop tomorrow?"* excuse? I don't know. How much time does she spend alone in this big house? Is she really grabbing food when out rather than cooking for herself? I guess it would make sense. But something is telling me she isn't eating properly.

"When he comes around later, try not to scare him off like last night, please. I love him and enjoy his company."

I look at her with one arched brow. I don't believe that she genuinely loves him; she might believe that she does, but does she even know what it means to be in love? Has anyone ever truly loved her the way she deserves? I know that prick hasn't. Even if he says the words, he doesn't show it. He would never choose games over a night with her if he did. I know I wouldn't.

"Fine, I will stay out of the way so I don't hurt poor Marshall's feelings," I sigh as I walk past her, planning on heading to my room. "But I still stand by what I said; he isn't good enough for you, Verity. You could do better."

"What do you know? You only met him for thirty seconds," she sighs behind me. I turn around and cross my arms, not missing the way she eyes the tattoos on my chest. I take a step forward, closing the gap between us.

"I could tell you were uncomfortable, and it wasn't just because I was there. Plus, what kind of man invites his girl-friend around for a game night? The only games you two should be playing are the type that makes you cry out his name." I take another step closer as Verity finds herself trapped between me and the counter behind her.

"Can he make you scream his name? Can he make you moan at all? Or does he need the extra help in that depart-ment as well as lessons on how to treat a woman like you?"

Verity stares up at me for a moment, her lip between her teeth as her cheeks warm, and I know she is feeling exactly what I am at this moment. Aroused and desperate for a good fucking.

"You need to back off," Verity eventually whispers as I smirk and step backwards.

"Fine, but think about what I said. You could do better." I turn around and walk from the kitchen, still smirking to myself.

"And I suppose you could do better?"

I stop in my tracks and look over my shoulder at her.

"Baby girl, you have no idea what I could make you feel or the games we could play. None would require batteries, a controller, or leave you reaching for a toy." I hear her gasp as I walk out of sight and up to my room, hard as fuck and desperate to relieve even more pent-up tension. Considering I only came last night, my balls are hurting; they are so full. This is going to be a long ass few days if I have to spend a lot of time around her. I'm going to need to stock up on lube and tissues for the amount of self-pleasure I'm going to require.

Chapter Four

VERITY

I look across the table at Marshall as he scrolls through his phone. We've been in the restaurant for half an hour, and he's hardly looked at me, let alone said more than a few words. Why does he feel so distant suddenly? It hasn't always felt this way.

Since Ethan cornered me this morning and implied that I could do better, I've been unable to look past all the little things he has done recently that prove Ethan right. I could say he is the perfect boyfriend and that he messages me constantly. We spend time together, go to the cinema, out for drinks with his friends, and he surprises me by turning up at the house. But when was the last time he did any of that? Looking back at him now, he's still glued to his phone. The only time he's spoken to me was to ask if he could stay the night. Considering he's ignored me all evening, do I really want to take him home?

Ethan's voice keeps replaying: *"You could do better"*. Why did he have to say that? It's put doubts there which weren't there before. He may not be the best lover, but he tries; bless him. It's not all about the sex anyway; I enjoy his company when he remembers I'm there.

"Is everything okay?" I ask, trying to get his attention.

"Yep," he answers, looking up and smiling. "One of my friends is just having a rough time, so I'm just checking in on them," he adds before typing something on the phone, locking it and placing it screen down on the table.

"Sorry, I didn't mean you had to stop," I add, feeling guilty for coming between him and his friend. Marshall shrugs, taking my hand, which is resting on the table.

"No, I'm here and shouldn't ignore you. I'm sorry, Ver." He smiles, and I feel bad that I'm sitting here complaining to myself about him. He doesn't deserve that; he has a kind heart, and that's the main thing, right?

"Are you nearly finished? We could go back to mine, as you suggested," I suggest, smiling.

"Will your brother be there?" Just mentioning Ethan brings back an uneasy feeling I've been pushing down all day.

"*Step*brother," I point out. I don't know how I feel about him at the moment. He overstepped a mark today. Plus, I can't completely ignore how my body reacted to him. "I don't know, but I have warned him to stay out of our way." Determined to make it up to Marshall for all my doubts, I lean a little closer to him as I give him my best sexy smile. "If we leave now, we could have dessert at mine," I tease. A smile spreads across his face as he nods and lifts his hand to get the waiter's attention.

"Can we have the check, please?"

Pulling up outside mine and jumping from his car, we rush to the house. Marshall holds me from behind as I unlock the front door, and we walk in. I look around, expecting Ethan to come out and cause an issue again, but we are met with silence. Maybe he has listened and gone out for the night.

Marshall grabs my hand and drags me to the stairs. The difference in him in the restaurant is hopefully a sign that we will have fun tonight and enjoy time just the two of us.

The second we are in my room, he pulls me against him and starts kissing me whilst helping me out of my clothes.

"You are so beautiful," he moans against my neck as his lips cover me in small kisses. He grabs my breasts to start massaging them. I push my chest out, wanting as much stimulation as possible, whilst I undo his jeans, eager to get to the foreplay and sex.

Marshall turns us around, and we fall onto my bed, laughing. He stands, grabs a condom from the drawer, putting it on as quickly as possible. As soon as he is on top of me, his hand lands between my legs and starts rubbing over my sex.

"I can't wait to sink into you. I've been thinking of nothing else all day," he moans before thrusting two fingers into me.

"Slow down," I gasp as he starts working his fingers in and out of me hard and fast. I wasn't prepared, and it's certainly not a comfortable feeling. But even when he slows down a little, it still hurts. Realising it's one of those nights, I need to talk him through it.

"You like that, Ver?" Marshall asks as he kisses me.

"Yeah, but not so hard," I flinch as I feel his fingernail scratches me on the inside. "Can we take it slow? We have all night," I start, but Marshall's lips cut me off as he presses them hard against mine and sticks his tongue into my mouth, stopping me from talking. This is not going the way I wanted it to go.

"We'll take it slow later. I need you, Ver." Marshall starts to move, and I know what's coming next.

"Not yet, I'm not-"

Marshall thrusts his dick into me and starts thrusting his hips hard as he chases the orgasm he needs. I cry out from the discomfort, but he takes it as a moan of pleasure and picks up speed.

"Yeah, beautiful, that's it. That's what I needed. Fuck you feel so good," he moans; his face is against my neck, and I know this is the best I'm going to get. I try to move slightly, hoping to get him to rub against the right spot, but he speeds up further, and I know what's about to happen.

"Marshall, wait, I-"

"Fuck, yeah," he calls as he cums, pushing his hips so his dick is deep inside me. Or at least as far as it will go. He doesn't have the biggest cock.

Marshall collapses on top of me and gasps for breath, feeling happy now he's cum. All I can do is hope for a round two or at least a little more hand action if he actually finds my clit this time.

"I love you," I whisper, smiling at him.

"I love you too."

Why does it feel like he's saying it more out of habit than meaning it? I knew things were changing a few weeks ago, but tonight has been a wake-up call. Things are not right between us. Is it my fault?

Marshall lies beside me as he continues to gasp for breath and removes the condom before dropping it in the bin. I rest my head on his chest, hoping he will stay awake a little so we can talk.

"I love having sex with you."

"I hope you love me for more than just that," I only particularly joke. Maybe that's the issue? Is he here for the regular sex?

"Of course, Ver." He wraps his arm around my shoulders and holds me tight for a moment before they loosen again, and I notice his breathing slows.

"Marshall, are you…?" I look up to find him already asleep. Letting out a sigh, I go back to leaning against him.

I'm not remotely tired as I look at the clock on the wall. Five minutes have passed since we exited the car, and he's asleep. The whole thing, from start to finish, probably lasted a whole three minutes if I was lucky. I know there are times I don't orgasm when we have sex, but I don't ever remember him being this selfish before.

Marshall lets out a small groan as I climb out of the bed.

"I'm just cleaning up. I'll be back," I whisper. I'm unsure why I'm bothering, as he just hums slightly and goes back to sleep. He usually falls asleep straight after sex and is a heavy sleeper.

Heading to my bathroom, I make quick work of cleaning myself up. As I thought he must have cut me inside as there's a tiny bit of blood on the tissue, and I do hurt slightly. It's not the first time it's happened. Marshall is a nail-biter, which means his nails are rough. We have discussed it before, but he seems to have forgotten tonight. He seemed to forget about a lot.

Grabbing my dressing gown off the back of the door, I head out of the room, needing something to help me sleep and some painkillers to help with the throbbing between my legs. A couple of tablets and a little time, and I know it will heal quickly; it always does.

I'm so lost in my own self-pity that I don't notice Ethan

until I'm right behind him. My heart freezes as I go to turn around and hide from him.

"Don't bother, Baby girl. I know you're there," he teases, looking over his shoulder and winking. "I'm heading down for a cup of tea; do you want one?" he asks, nodding towards the ground floor. I nod, unable to look him in the eye. "Come on then," he says, putting an arm around my shoulders and guiding me downstairs.

"Go and sit over there; I'll bring one over." He walks over to the hot drinks station I set up last year. "Any particular one?" he asks, pointing to the varieties before him.

"Camomile, please," I answer, anxiously waiting for him to say he heard my disastrous sex life through the walls. There's no way he didn't unless he had headphones in. I'm so embarrassed. I can feel my cheeks burning. I should have gone back to bed. I'm still thinking of getting up, telling him to forget the tea and leaving.

"Here you go." Ethan places the cup in front of me and sits with his own. "Don't think I didn't notice you have more tea and coffee than food in. I hope you are eating properly."

I nod, not looking up from my cup.

"When I'm on my own, it's easier and cheaper to grab things as I need them. During show weeks, we get food from the deli across the road from the theatre between rehearsals and shows. Food goes to waste if it's here, as I'm always there."

"That makes sense. As long as you promise me you are eating properly."

I don't miss the concern in his voice, so I force myself to flash him a smile as I nod.

"I promise."

Ethan watches me for a moment before nodding in

acceptance, and I let out a silent breath, relieved to have avoided that conversation.

"So, want to talk about what just happened upstairs?"

My heart drops to my stomach as my whole body burns with embarrassment.

"No, Ethan. I don't. Especially with you," I sigh, getting up and pulling painkillers out of the medicine drawer.

"Did he hurt you?" Ethan demands, watching me. I shake my head, swallow the tablets quickly and look back at my tea as I sit back in the chair.

"I've had a headache all evening, which isn't getting any better," I lie smoothly. Why didn't I go back upstairs when I had the chance? "Please just leave it. It's not usually like that," I start, but Ethan stops me by putting his hand on my arm.

"I'm not saying a word. I have told you what I think of him, and I know if I push it, you will snap at me again. I'm just worried about you. Something seems different." Ethan reaches over and hooks a finger under my chin, forcing me to look at him. "You know you can talk to me, right? About anything?"

I can feel my mood shifting again as I start getting annoyed. What's the point in talking to him about anything? It's not like he is here for me or to help me. He's here for his convenience and his convenience only.

"I'm going back to bed. Thanks for the tea." I stand from the seat, but Ethan also jumps up, blocking my path to the stairs.

"Baby girl, speak to me." I wish I believed he was truly worried about me, but I don't. People say they want to help, but they really want to make themselves feel better.

"There's nothing to say, so drop it. I'm tired, and I want

to go to sleep. Good night, Ethan." This time, as I step to the side, he thankfully doesn't try and stop me.

I'm out of the kitchen and halfway up the stairs before the sound of a cup being thrown into the sink rings out, followed by Ethan cursing. Stopping for a moment, I consider going back to check on him, but instead, I continue up to my room, where Marshall is still sleeping soundly.

Walking over to my chest of drawers, I pull out an old t-shirt to wear to bed. I know I need to talk to him about tonight and the last few weeks. Things need to change, and I hope it isn't in a way that ends with me being alone again. If there is anything I hate, it's the amount of time I have to spend alone.

Chapter Five

VERITY

I wake up and look at Marshall, who is still sleeping soundly. Last night, after coming to bed, I lay here thinking about how the night had gone. He had been selfish, which left me feeling confused and, in all honesty, hurt. He hardly spoke to me at dinner, and the only time he paid me any attention was when we were on the way back here. He only came for the sex, and that was abysmal, to say the least. What makes the whole thing worse is that Ethan heard the entire thing. All three minutes of it. Isn't that just perfect?

I've hardly slept, which I will pay for all day. I look at my clock on the side of the bed and see it's already ten past six. I need to shower and get ready for the day ahead. I never stay in bed this late.

"Lose an hour in the morning, and you'll spend all day looking for it," my childhood live-in nanny used to say. She woke me up at six every morning, saying it was to ensure I could have a proper breakfast and stretch before dancing. She had me on a strict routine when it came to homeschooling and dancing.

I know I wouldn't be the dancer I am today without her. But sometimes I really wish I could sleep past six.

"What would your father say if he saw you lying in bed until the middle of the day? He would be terribly disappointed in you." Another thing she would throw at me whenever I asked why I couldn't have a lie in like everyone else.

She's been gone for a long time now, but Dad still occasionally asks if I get up early, so I continue to do so to make him proud. Everything I do is to ensure he is never disappointed in me. Glancing at Marshall sleeping beside me, the usual guilt of doing something my dad would disapprove of tightens in my gut. I need to ensure Ethan knows not to mention Marshall in front of my father.

My dad doesn't know many people in my life. I don't know if that's because I haven't introduced him to them or because he is never around enough to meet them. The only friends he knows are Jasmine and Danielle. Not that he approves of Jasmine since she went public with all four O'Reilly men.

"I never put her down as a whore. What does she think she's playing at being with all four of them at the same time? It's unheard of and uncouth," Linda had snapped when I told her about the wedding. Dad nodded in agreement and told me not to be associated with her anymore. It's probably the only time I have ever openly disobeyed him. He hadn't been happy with me at all when I told him Jasmine had asked me to be maid of honour at the wedding. But I stood my ground, and now he doesn't mention it, nor do I.

"What time is it?"

I look down at Marshall as he rubs his eyes.

"Sorry, I didn't mean to wake you; it's ten past six," I reply as he reaches out and takes my hand.

"Come back to bed; it's early," he moans, trying to pull me towards him. I chuckle as I lie down next to him.

"I need to get showered and stretch. Unless you can think of another way for me to exercise," I tease, kissing his neck. Desperate for any sign, the Marshall who cared is still there. There was a time when he couldn't keep his hands off me. Now, he doesn't even try.

"It's too early, in a bit," he mutters, shutting his eyes. I let out a deep breath and force myself to kiss his cheek as I climb out of bed and head to the room across from mine, which Travis uses when he stays. I use it to stretch when Marshall is still sleeping, which is most mornings he stays.

"Sorry, I have to leave so early. I know I promised a full day with you, but work messaged for me to cover a shift."

I quickly kiss Marshall's lips to stop him from talking.

"It's fine, I understand. I need to prepare for the next week of performances anyway," I say with a forced smile. "Come on, I'll see you out."

Marshall takes my hand, and we both walk out of my room and straight into Ethan. Damn, this is all I need.

"Oh, sorry, didn't realise you were in. We didn't keep you up last night, did we?" Marshall asks, pushing his chest out smugly.

"Marshall!" I exclaim. I can't believe he would say that to Ethan, my stepbrother of all people. Ethan shrugs as he takes a bite of an apple in his hand.

"Not really, I only heard you."

My breath catches in my chest as I see Marshall's face change.

"Yeah, luckily, Ver managed to keep the noise down; she knows when to be quiet."

A smirk appears on Ethan's face as he turns and walks towards his room.

"Or you just weren't doing it right. *Verity* made plenty of noise the night before with her vibrator."

"Ethan!" I cry out, turning to find Marshall glaring at me. "He's lying to wind you up," I start, but he shakes his head as he lets go of my hand and walks away. "He's trying to get a reaction out of you. Ignore him!" I call after him as I rush down the stairs. I manage to reach the front door as he goes to walk out of it.

"Don't let him get to you, please," I beg. He looks down at me for a moment and lets out a deep sigh.

"You're right, I'm sorry. I'll see you later, Ver." He kisses my cheek and walks out of the house and down to his car.

Why did that feel like goodbye?

I watch him drive away before closing the door and rushing up the stairs to Ethan's room. I don't bother knocking; I barge in to find him in his shorts while stretching his hips.

"What the hell was that?" I yell, pointing to where Marshall has just stormed off. "You had no right saying that!" I add, crossing my arms over my chest.

Ethan looks at me and smiles as he stands tall.

"I only told the truth, and you know it. You may pretend to be okay with how he treated you last night, but I know you're not. He is using you, and you can't see it."

I stare at him as he comes closer, his chest on display again and begging for me to touch it.

"What happens between him and me is none of your business, Ethan," I reply, hating the weakness in my voice, knowing he notices by the smirk on his face.

"Baby girl, I told you, you need a man, not a boy. If you decide you want to experience a real orgasm without the need for toys, you know where I'll be." Ethan steps forward and places his hands on the wall on either side of my head, caging me in so I can't run. He leans in and buries his face into my neck. His lips brush against the skin, causing my sex to come alive. "I think you secretly like the idea of a night with me." Every word causes his breath to flow over me, igniting the flames more until I know I'm a mess. Ethan pushes himself away from me and stares momentarily before heading towards his bathroom.

"He's lucky I didn't break his legs like I promised to. If I were you, I would ask your man where he was yesterday."

"He was at work," I reply, frowning. Ethan stops in the doorway.

"If he says so, it must be the truth."

"What do you know?" I demand, but Ethan just shrugs.

"Nothing for certain, ask him." He disappears into his bathroom and closes the door, leaving me standing in his room, lost, confused and horny.

Chapter Six

ETHAN

Throwing the TV controller onto the sofa beside me, I lean back, groaning behind my hands.

Fuck, I'm in a mood and can't snap out of it. All I can think about is the way Verity smelt as my nose ran down her neck or the way my cock automatically jumps to attention whenever she's around.

Even though I'd already been for a run, I've worked out in the gym, held two online fitness classes, and I still feel the need to find the fucker Marshall and beat the shit out of him.

How the hell doesn't Verity see he is using her? I know I shouldn't have listened last night, but in the time it took me to find my headphones, he had blown his load and finished. I swear the dickhead lasted less than four minutes. If that wasn't enough to put me in a foul mood with him, then there's the small matter of what I witnessed yesterday afternoon.

I have no proof, and I'm not even a hundred per cent sure it was him I saw walking hand in hand with a woman who wasn't Verity. I didn't see his face, but it was just a gut feeling I couldn't shake.

"Hey! Anyone home?"

I turn around to see one of my brothers, Ryan, walking into the lounge.

"Hey! You made it then," I reply, holding up my hand, which he grasps before dropping his bag on the floor.

"Yeah, Trav won't be here for a couple more days by the look of it. How's it going? Where's Verity?" he asks, looking around.

"Hopefully not with her loser boyfriend. She stormed out of here a while ago," I reply, sighing as my mood sours further.

"Uh oh, that doesn't sound good," Ryan remarks, sitting beside me. "What's been going on?"

I fill him in on all I have seen of Verity and the dickhead. Ryan sits and listens as I get it all off my chest. By the time I'm finished, I can't miss the smirk on his face.

"Looks like you've finally realised our little stepsister is, in fact, hot."

"I noticed that a while ago. I didn't think you had, though."

Ryan smiles and leans back into his seat.

"Oh yes. That woman's had a special place in my heart for a long time," he sighs.

"You do remember she is our stepsister, right?"

"Exactly, *step*sister, not blood-related, so no foul," he replies. "Look, as I see it, if anything were to happen, no harm would be done. She is a sweet little thing who, I bet, is hiding a whole level of sexy. There's something about her that calls to me, and I struggle to ignore it. I bet you know exactly what I mean."

I nod as I reach for my glass of water from the coffee table.

"Oh, I know there is a deeper sexual side to her. On my first night here, the dickhead left her for a games night with friends. I went upstairs a few minutes later to get my jumper and heard a distinct vibrating sound from her room. I soon heard her gasping for breath as she made herself cum with a toy. Fuck, it was hot as hell."

"Sounds it," Ryan sighs as he adjusts his cock in his jeans. He's not the only one who is now uncomfortable.

"What do you know about her life when we aren't around?" I ask, placing my glass back on the table and running my fingers through my hair.

"Not much," Ryan answers as he starts to think about it. "Only that it revolves around her dancing. Why do you ask?"

I take a deep breath and look around, checking she hasn't come home.

"I don't know. It's just the way she reacted when I first arrived. She was so excited when she thought her father was home. I think she may be lonely," I point out quietly.

"It wouldn't surprise me; she's probably here alone most of the time. When were Mum and Henry last back? It must have been a while ago now."

I nod, as it has to have been at least three months, if not longer. As far as I'm aware, there isn't any other family around for Verity, as she's an only child. She was also homeschooled, so she has no one apart from her friends at the dance school.

No wonder she has latched on to a guy who is no good for her. She's probably just glad to have someone to spend time with and show her a little affection, as I'm betting she doesn't get much from anyone else.

"You could speak to Travis. He speaks to her more than her own father," Ryan points out.

"You don't mean Travis has fallen for her too?" I ask, amazed.

"He says he hasn't and that he's just keeping an eye on her for Henry, but personally, something is happening there. He was furious when she was drugged a few months ago," he sighs.

"She was drugged? By who?" I demand sitting upright. "Why am I only now hearing about this?"

"Travis didn't want everyone knowing in case they mentioned it to Verity. The whole thing upsets her. I only know because he let it slip a few weeks later whilst ranting about the O'Reilly's. Apparently, she was out with their girl, and her drink was spiked. It was all part of a ploy to kidnap the O'Reilly girl. That's all I know on the matter. Travis was too angry to say anything else. I figured it was best to drop it. You know what he's like regarding anything to do with that family."

I know all too well how he feels about them.

The O'Reilly's and Donavon's used to be close. Our dads did business together regularly after they met through Travis and Christian's friendship when they boxed together. Ryan and I became close to the twins, who are closer to our age. But when Dad died, Christian was there. All I know is he fled the scene, and Travis is sure he caused the accident. Personally, I can't imagine Christian killing Dad, but Travis is convinced he was involved somehow, so we all parted ways, and the two of them have been uncivilised to each other since.

"So, what do we do about Verity? It's not like we can show or tell her how we feel. Do we sit back and let her carry on making a mistake with this guy she is seeing?" I ask, feeling more conflicted now than I did before Ryan arrived.

"Well, we could tell her how we feel; like I pointed out, she isn't our blood sister, so nothing is stopping us."

"Except that we obviously are all interested in the same woman. No matter how much of a hidden freak she is in the bedroom, I doubt even she would be interested in a polygamous relationship with her stepbrothers. We don't know how Travis feels about her either."

Ryan stands as he shrugs.

"Just wait and see what happens. I don't plan to tell her how I feel, but if the opportunity presented itself, I wouldn't say no." He walks to where he dropped his bag and picks it up before heading up the stairs.

"I'm going to shower and get settled in. See you in a bit," he calls, disappearing from view. What the hell do I do with all this new information? And how haven't I noticed before that my two brothers have feelings for the same woman? The only thing I know for sure is that the next few days will be interesting, to say the least.

Chapter Seven

VERITY

It's been five hours since Marshall left, and I haven't gotten hold of him. I went into his work in the hope of putting things right. But when I got there, they said it's his day off. Why did he tell me he had been called in? I couldn't ask them if they had called him because I didn't want to appear needy. But why did he lie to me?

I drive to his house and feel hopeful when I see his car in the driveway. Maybe work didn't need him after all, and he came home. Knocking at the door, running through all the excuses and things I want to say in my head as I wait, but there's no answer. I knock again in case he didn't hear me, but no sound comes from inside. I walk away from the house, constantly looking back in the hope that he will appear before sitting in my car for a moment.

Where the hell is he? Why is he ignoring me?

Ethan, that's why.

I drive home, my anger building as I ready myself to confront him. I was happy; I had a life and someone to share it with. But now I'm back to feeling alone all because of him. How dare he turn up, mess everything up, to disappear again in a few days. It's not like he will be around for long.

I pull onto the drive and notice a different car parked up. For the briefest moment, I get excited again, hoping it may be my dad, but then I remember he said he was still in the States last night, so it can't be him. If Ethan has a woman in my house, I'm going to kill him! If I'm not allowed to have people around without him causing trouble, then neither can he.

I jump out of my car and rush into the house as my temper gets the better of me.

"ETHAN!"

I charge towards the lounge, where I usually find him watching some rubbish action film, but he's not there.

"Ethan! I know you're here!" I shout, marching into the kitchen, but find it empty. I growl with frustration as I charge towards the stairs to come face to face with Ryan, quickly realising it must have been his car outside.

"Where's Ethan?" I demand.

"Well, hello to you too, little Kitten."

I roll my eyes and hug him, feeling bad for snapping.

"Sorry, how are you, Ryan?" I ask as he kisses my cheek and steps back.

"I'm good, thank you. You don't seem to be, though. Want to talk about it?" he asks as he puts his arm around my shoulders, leading me to the lounge.

"I would rather beat Ethan," I sigh, falling onto the sofa.

"Well, he's out at the moment, so talk to me about it."

I close my eyes and remind myself I can't cry.

"He told my boyfriend something, and now Marshall's ignoring my calls, and I think he's going to break up with me, and it's all Ethan's fault." I take a deep breath to stop myself before I say more. Ryan reaches over and takes my hand.

"He told me. Do you want my opinion?"

I look at him and shake my head.

"You will side with Ethan. You three always stick together."

Ryan reaches up and tucks some hair behind my ear.

"Little Kitten, we don't side against you. We have more life experience and can see a disaster before you can. That's what this relationship is: a disaster that will only end in tears. Your tears, to be precise."

I turn and stare at him before pulling my hand from his and standing.

"You haven't even met Marshall; how do you know anything about this relationship besides what Ethan told you? I bet he forgot to mention how he told me to go to him when I was ready to sleep with a real man, did he!"

Ryan bursts out laughing as he shakes his head.

"No, he didn't. The big-headed bastard, he's got balls, I'll give him that."

"It's not funny!" I snap, storming from the room. I hate it when people laugh at me.

"Kitten, wait!" Ryan calls, chasing after me.

"Why? So, you can laugh at me further? I bet you're all getting a right kick out of this. Stupid blonde little Verity is about to get her heart broken because her stepbrother doesn't know when to keep his mouth shut."

"It's not like."

"Don't you dare stick up for him. He had no right to tell Marshall what he did, and he certainly shouldn't have listened to what he did. It's fine because soon enough, you will go home again and leave me to pick up the pieces.

Once again, I will be the one left on my own. Well, you can all go to hell!"

I spin around on my heels and charge out of the house, ignoring Ryan calling after me. My anger has hit boiling point, which means I no longer have any control over it. I need to get out of here before I punch someone.

As I reach the car, Ryan grabs the door, stopping me from getting inside.

"I'm sorry, just come inside, and we will talk about it. I'm worried about you; we all are."

"Well, it's a good job I'm only your problem when you are here. Leave me alone, Ryan." I try to open the door again, but he stops me again.

"Little Kitten, listen-"

"No!" I yell as I reach up and push him away from my car. "You listen. Fuck you, Ryan, fuck you all!"

I take advantage of his shock and jump in the car before driving away quickly, only narrowly missing him. I can see him shouting as I look in the rearview mirror, but I continue to drive. Needing to get away from him as quickly as possible.

I don't get far before I have to pull over as the tears have started, and I can't see the road properly.

Why the hell does no one ever take me seriously? Just then, when Ryan laughed in my face, it hurt. Once again, proving that no one has my back when I need them. I'm so tired of being the one people think has it all together and doesn't need any help. Maybe I'm tired of people leaving all the time. Even Jaz isn't around as much now. I know it's not her fault; she is in therapy once a week and has anxiety when out and about after everything she went through, but I miss her.

I rest my head against the steering wheel as I take a

deep breath and try to calm down. I have a performance in a little over two hours. The last thing I need is to have red, puffy eyes. I take a few slow breaths and try to calm myself.

Breathe in and out, push it all down. Put all emotions away and replace your mask because no one cares enough to notice. Smile and pretend everything is just fine, as you always do.

After a few more deep breaths, I sit up straight and wipe my eyes. Pulling down the sun flap, I look in the mirror to check my make-up hasn't run and force a smile.

There, no one will ever know; keep smiling and being the happy, sweet girl they want you to be.

I put the car into gear and pull away, heading to the dance school, telling myself I have this. No one needs to know that inside, I'm drowning and can't see a way out.

Chapter Eight

RYAN

Shit. Me and my big fucking mouth.

What the hell was I thinking laughing like that? I should have known better. She caught me off guard with the comments from Ethan. He isn't like that usually; in fact, he's the complete opposite when it comes to the female sex; he never knows what to say to them. I should know I've been his wingman since he was sixteen. I've watched him make a fool of himself for ten years, so hearing him being so forward with Verity was hilarious.

I pace around the lounge for the umpteenth time, trying to figure out what to do. I know I need to check in with her, but when I tried to call her phone, it went straight to voice-mail. Usually, it does that when she is at school, so hopefully, she has gone straight there to prepare for her performance tonight.

"Hey!"

I turn to Ethan's voice and rush for the kitchen, where I find him chucking his keys on the counter as he walks over to the coffee machine.

"Do you want one? I need something to keep me going," he calls as he turns around to look at me. "What's happened?" he asks, his face dropping.

"I fucked up and upset Verity."

Ethan looks at me for a moment and smirks.

"Did you try it on with her?"

"No, you idiot. She came in here yelling for you. It seems her boyfriend is avoiding her, and it's all your fault. I told her she would probably be better off without him, and she blew up big style. Yelling about how it's fine for us to turn up and screw everything up, then leave again so she is on her own." I rub my face before looking at my brother. "When I tried to get her to calm down and come inside to talk to me properly, she flipped and screamed in my face, 'fuck you, Ryan, fuck you all,' before driving off like a mad woman."

"Shit. What the fuck did you say to make her flip like that? That woman never swears!" Ethan yells at me as he slams his empty mug on the side. He's right. I have never heard her curse before.

"I laughed when she told me what *you* had said to her about showing her what it's like to sleep with a real man. I wasn't laughing at her, but she took it the wrong way and then all hell broke loose. I don't know what to do," I admit, pacing around the kitchen as Ethan rubs at his face. "You are right, you know," I admit, turning to look at my brother.

"With what? That her boyfriend is a cheating dick? Because I know I'm right about that, especially now."

"No, but I will come back to that," I start, knowing there must be more to that story. "You're right about her being lonely. Everything she said came back to the fact that she would end up here alone while we all went off to live our lives. Everything boiled down to no one giving a shit about her." I lean on the counter and look at my brother, who nods.

"I know. I think she is spending more time alone than we realised. Something is going on, and I don't like it one bit."

"Well, if you don't like it now, you certainly aren't going to like this next bit of information," Ethan sighs. "I thought I saw him yesterday with another woman but wasn't convinced it was him. But today, there was no mistaking it was him walking hand in hand with someone who was not Verity."

I curse under my breath as I realise what that means. Verity will have her heart broken, and I'm not sure she'll cope. If today was anything to go by, she is already balancing on the edge of a breakdown.

"We need to tell her tonight when she comes home," I sigh as I look in the fridge for a beer. I sigh and grab some water when I don't find one.

"She isn't going to believe us," Ethan says as he reaches under the counter and pulls out a bottle of Whiskey.

"Probably not, but there is one way to ensure she listens. It's also one way of guaranteeing that she has the right support when she needs it, too," I point out as Ethan pours us both a drink. I pick up my glass and head into the lounge, where I left my phone.

I pick it up and check one last time to see if she has read or replied to the messages I have sent, but all are still showing as unread. I have a feeling that they will stay that way until she gets back tonight. Verity has never been reliable with her phone; she often puts it down and forgets about it for hours. She also locks it in her car when she has a production to avoid anything happening to it in the changing rooms.

I check the clock and see it's five in the evening. She will be getting ready now, so there is no way I can check in with her. But the one person who could help us to get through to her will be free.

I pull up his number and take a deep breath because I know I'm about to have my ass handed to me for upsetting his Sweetheart.

I hold the phone to my ear and wait for the call to connect. After it rings five or six times, I decide to try again later when he answers.

"Hey, it's me. I think you need to get here. Something's going on with Verity."

Chapter Nine

VERITY

I have no idea how I managed to get through that performance. I think I ran on autopilot the whole time. I smiled and laughed with the other dancers, but I could feel Jaz and Danni watching me the entire time and knew they would pounce the moment we were alone. But I'm not in the mood for them demanding to know what's going on. I need a stiff drink, and I know just the place to get it.

Sneaking out of the stage door with my bag over my shoulder, I head towards the pub at the end of the road with no plans of returning home tonight. I'll sleep in the car if I have to. I don't want to face either of the Donavon brothers right now. I'm hoping to get hold of Marshall to see if there is a chance to put things right, even if it takes all night. But when I check my phone, I see messages from Ethan and Ryan, which puts me in an even worse mood.

Heading straight for the bar, I order a vodka and coke. I've been in here a few times with Marshall and his friends. Hopefully, he'll turn up at some point so I can corner him and force him to listen to me.

I'm paying for the drink when a laugh rings out from the back. A smile appears on my face as I rush around, regretting it as soon as he comes into view.

There's Marshall with another woman on his lap as he and his mates laugh. Marshall looks up at the girl and kisses her, causing my heart to shatter.

Rushing away from the scene before me, I grab my drink and neck it before almost running out of the pub. I stand outside for a moment, numb and in agony all at the same time. Spotting an off-licence at the end of the street, I head in there for a bottle of anything that will help me forget the last couple of days.

The man behind the counter must see something's wrong. He warns me to be careful as I pay for a bottle of vodka. I nod once and leave, keeping my head down, desperate not to see anyone who may try and stop me.

Sitting inside my car, the realisation hit me. I have nowhere to go—no one to call. Jaz will be with her daddies, Danielle will be with the girls having a drink or whatever they do, and I'm drinking vodka out of the bottle in a car with no boyfriend, no friends and two stepbrothers at mine who are determined to ruin what's left of my sanctuary. Where the hell did my life go so wrong?

It doesn't take long before I'm halfway through the bottle, cold, drunk, and wishing I could just go home to sleep. I don't usually drink, so this vodka's gone straight to my head. I hear my phone vibrating for the hundredth time in my glove compartment, where I hid it earlier. Opening it, I see Jasmine's name flashing on the screen. My phone has over twenty missed calls, and her name is at the top of the list. She's not going to stop until I answer.

"Hello."

"Finally! Where are you?" Jaz yells.

"In my car," I answer, leaning back into my seat.

"No, you're not. Your car is in the car park."

"I know, I'm in it," I answer. My words slur a little as I realise I'm even more drunk than I thought. Oh well. I pick up the bottle and have another drink out of it, nearly spraying the contents over the steering wheel when the car door flies open next to me.

"Are you serious?" Jaz yells as she reaches in and takes the bottle from my hand.

"Hey, give that back!" I shout, reaching for it. I know I'm past my limit, so I might as well keep drinking. It's not like I have anything else to do right now.

"What the fuck are you doing drinking in your car?" Danielle shouts as she approaches.

"I would still be in the pub, but I didn't feel like watching my boyfriend kissing another woman," I answer, lifting my phone, which is vibrating in my hand. Ethan's name flashes on the screen. He's the last person I want to speak to. I drop it on the seat beside me, but Danielle is already at the passenger door and picks it up.

"We found her. She's wasted and caught him with another woman."

"Hey! Don't tell him fuck all!" I yell.

"Verity! I get you are upset, but this isn't you," Jaz starts. But I'm not in the mood to listen to her bullshit tonight. I climb out of the car, desperate to get away from her.

"Why don't you go back to your daddies and perfect life and leave me with my vodka and cheating boyfriend." I start to walk away, but a car drives up to us and comes to a stop. When I see who gets out, I curse under my breath. "Well, isn't that just perfect!" I yell, throwing my hands up, nearly losing my balance.

"Get in the car," Travis snaps, marching up to me.

"She isn't going anywhere with you unless you tell me who you are!" Jaz yells, standing in front of me.

"No need to ask who you are. Big mouth and think you rule the world and all in it. You must be the O'Reilly's slut." Travis only just manages to catch Jasmine's wrist to stop her from slapping him across the face.

"Get off me, now!" she yells.

"What? So, you can try to hit me again. I don't think so."

"Get your fucking hands off my wife!"

I spin around and see Christian O'Reilly running into the car park with his security guard, Terry, next to him.

"Last I heard, the wedding hadn't happened yet," Travis answers as he pushes Jasmine towards Christian, who stops her when she charges forward, no doubt to try and hit Travis again.

"Do you really think I need a piece of paper to tell me she's mine?" Christian stops right in front of Travis, so there is merely an inch between them. Both have their hands balled up, and I know a fight is about to break out. "If you so much as touch a hair on her head again, I will kill you. Is that understood, Donavon?" Christian warns. I look at Travis, who looks scarier than I have ever seen him before. He isn't backing down; if anything, he takes a step closer to Christian.

"Oh, I know exactly what you are capable of, O'Reilly," Travis growls through his teeth. Christian doesn't back down as he stares at him.

"I don't know what I need to do to get it through your thick skull, but I had nothing to do with it."

"And I'm meant to take your word on that, am I?" Travis asks before shaking his head. "You've got more chance of hell freezing over. Now take your stepsister, I mean *wife*, and fuck off." Travis turns his attention to me as I sway on the spot. He steps closer and takes my arm to steady me. When he looks me in the eye, his whole face softens.

"Come on, Sweetheart, let's get you home; you're freezing."

I go to step forward, but the ground moves underneath me, and I fall against him. Travis sighs but lifts me with ease before carrying me to the car. I can hear Christian laughing behind us and hide into Travis's top with embarrassment as he lowers me into the car and places a blanket over me.

"Something funny, O'Reilly?" Travis asks through gritted teeth as he turns and looks at Christian.

"You give me shit for being in love with someone who was once my stepsister. Pot calling the kettle black comes to mind," Christian laughs as he turns around to look at Jasmine. "Come on, baby girl, you can call Verity tomorrow to see if she's okay. Danielle, we will give you a lift to your car," I hear Christian call as Travis closes the car door. I don't hear their response as I'm huddling underneath the blanket he has placed over me.

Travis climbs into the driver's seat and turns his attention to me.

"Put your seatbelt on, Sweetheart." I realise how hard I'm shivering when I try to do what he says. "Come here, let me do it." Travis takes the seatbelt from me and clicks it into place before tucking the blanket around me.

"I feel sick," I whisper as the car starts to move. Travis reaches into the foot well by my feet and hands me a plastic shopping bag.

"That's what happens when you drink yourself into a stupor. We've all been worried out of our minds."

I watch the lights as they pass the car, knowing Travis is

driving slower than usual, probably to prevent me from throwing up. I heave a few times, but it's not until the car comes to a stop outside my house that I throw up. Luckily, I manage to get it into the bag and not all over Travis's car.

Travis opens the door next and helps me stand before carrying me into the house.

"Shit, she really is wasted," I hear Ethan curse as Travis carries me upstairs.

"Find me a bowl and some towels," Travis orders while walking into my room. I can feel the saliva building in my mouth again, and I know what's about to happen.

"Toilet," I yell, putting my hand over my mouth. Travis manages to get me beside it as the vomit escapes my lips.

"That's it, Sweetheart. Get it all up," he says softly as he gathers my hair up from my face and holds it out of the way.

"Why are you never that nice to me when I'm throwing up?" I hear Ryan ask as he hands something to Travis.

"Because you are an arsehole who should know better," he answers, causing me to giggle. "Here, wipe your mouth with this." Travis holds out a wet flannel, and I take it, giving him a small thanks you as he flushes the toilet. I see Ethan and Ryan looking down at me as I lean back against Travis, needing something solid to hold me up.

"You were right; he probably wasn't at work."

Ethan squats down in front of me and takes my hand.

"I know; I saw him today. I was going to tell you tonight when you got home."

"I saved you the job and saw for myself." I look up to Ryan and feel my bottom lip quivering. Quickly, I blink back the tears, knowing if I start crying, I will never stop. "I'm sorry for shoving and swearing at you."

"It's okay, little Kitten. We all have bad days. I think you have had the worst, from the sounds of it."

I nod as I go to stand but don't quite manage it.

"Come on, Sweetheart, let's get you into bed so you can sleep it off," Travis sighs, helping me to my feet. He supports me as I brush my teeth and wash my face before helping me into bed.

"Close your eyes and get some rest. I'll be right here, okay?" he whispers, running a hand over my head. I nod, closing my eyes and letting myself believe for just one night that they won't be gone in a few days, and I will be all alone again.

Chapter Ten

VERITY

I wake up at the crack of dawn to find a shadow sitting in the chair in the corner of my room.

"How are you feeling, Kitten?" Ryan asks, standing from the chair and walking over to the bed.

"Like I drank half a bottle of vodka, threw up and made a fool of myself."

Ryan chuckles as he runs a hand over my head.

"Yep, that about sums it up. What do you remember?"

I sit up and lean against the headboard.

"Everything," I sigh as I take my pounding head in my hands. I hear Ryan doing something, and look up in time to see him holding out a glass of water and two tablets.

"Take these, they will help."

I thank him before swallowing the pills, praying they will take away the pain. If only they worked on humiliation as well.

"Have you been there all night?"

Ryan shakes his head.

"Travis was here most of the night, but I sent him to bed just over an hour ago. He was worried you would be sick in your sleep and didn't want you to be left alone."

"Oh god," I groan, hiding my face in my hands. Why did I have to get so drunk? This isn't me; I don't mess up this badly, not to the point others notice anyway. The only two times I have been that bad were the first time at a party with a drink and when my drink got spiked. But to sit in the car and drink vodka straight out of the bottle is ridiculous. I don't even like the stuff.

I hear the bedroom door open and look up as Travis walks into view.

"I told you to sleep," Ryan sighs as he looks up at his older brother.

"I couldn't. Leave us," Travis orders. Ryan stands from the side of the bed and heads for the door.

"Shout if you need anything," he says before leaving me and a very annoyed-looking Travis.

Travis walks to the bedside cabinet and turns on the lamp, which instantly hurts my head, before sitting on the side of the bed and looking at me.

"I'm sorry," I whisper, looking down at my hands.

"For getting so drunk, you couldn't stand? Or for doing it in an unsafe environment?"

I shrug, not knowing what to say. I hate being in trouble, and the thought of Travis being cross with me unsettles me more than it should.

"Do you have any idea what could have happened to you in that car park? What if it wasn't your friends that found you but someone else?" Travis points out.

"I wasn't thinking logically," I reply, unable to face him.

"Well, that goes without saying. If you want to get

drunk, fine. You are a grown woman who is *usually* sensible enough to think for themselves. If you ever feel the need to repeat last night, you call me or one of the guys, and we will sit with you whilst you drink; that way, you can do so safely. Ideally, not vodka straight from the bottle."

I can't stop myself from chuckling as I shake my head.

"What?" I hear Travis ask.

"Nothing," I answer, too tired and hungover to have this conversation.

"No, I want to know what part of that amused you," he asks. I look up from my hands to look him in the eye.

"Like you would drop everything just so I could get wasted. You aren't even here that often, so tell me how that little plan would work?" I point out, shaking my head, which I regret instantly as pain explodes behind my eyeballs. "Let's face it, as soon as this trip is over, you will be gone again and won't come back for months." I go to get out of bed, but Travis is in my way. "Excuse me, please, I need a shower."

He looks at me momentarily before standing from the side of the bed, giving me room to get up.

As I walk past, Travis grabs my hand and pulls me to a stop.

"Maybe we have been away a lot, but that doesn't mean we don't care about you and what you are doing to yourself."

I look down at my small hand in his big one and sigh.

"But not enough to stick around, I get it." I look up and find his dark green eyes looking back at me. "It's fine, Travis; we all have our own lives, I get it. It's the way it's always been. Why change a habit of a lifetime." I reach up and kiss his cheek. "Thank you for looking after me; I am fine now. You can go back to bed."

I walk into my bathroom but hear Travis whisper as I close the door.

"Time things changed for you, Sweetheart."

Chapter Eleven

TRAVIS

How haven't I noticed how bad she is before now?

Last night wasn't about catching her boyfriend cheating; that woman is on a slow downward spiral, and I don't know how no one has noticed before.

Because no one is here to see it.

"How is she?"

I look up to see Ethan and Ryan walking into the kitchen, where I'm making a cup of coffee.

"Not good," I answer, walking past them to look up the stairs. "We need to talk, ideally, before she comes down."

We all walk back into the kitchen and gather by the coffee machine.

"You guys were right; she's not in a good place. There's more going on than we knew about. I don't think her father even realises how ill she's becoming." Taking a deep breath, I run my hand over my face. I'm exhausted; I haven't slept a wink all night. Every little moan or cough from Verity whilst she slept had me jumping to my feet to check on her.

"For the time being, I don't want her left alone. I'm

going to take her to her performance tonight and see how she is when she's there. As much as I hate to admit it, I need to speak to the O'Reilly's woman as I know they are close."

"Do you think you can be anywhere near an O'Reilly without fighting?" Ethan asks. I look at him with an arched brow. "Look, man, I get it. But the last thing Verity needs is you getting arrested or worse for fighting with her best friend, fellas."

I know he's right; it's the last thing she needs. Am I willing to put my feelings towards Christian to one side for that poor girl upstairs? For the time being, yes. Verity needs someone to look after her. I think it's been a long time since anyone paid enough attention to her to do it. Henry has always worked in the States but says this is his primary home. Before his wife died, he would only be over there one week out of four. That all changed when Verity's mum passed away; he started working over there more and more, and now, he's been there for months at a time. But even I've noticed that his time at home is getting shorter and the time between visits longer.

I can't believe I never thought to check on how she was *really* doing before now. I mainly contact her via text messages and phone calls. It's obviously been easy for her to hide what she's been feeling and going through.

"Leave it with me. I won't do anything to cause her more stress than she's already under."

The others nod, but I don't miss the look between them.

We all turn to look at the entrance to the kitchen as we hear footsteps on the stairs. I return to the coffee machine and start making up two coffees, which I'm just handing to the others when Verity walks into the kitchen.

"Good morning, Baby girl. How's the head doing?" Ethan asks cheerfully. Verity looks at him and groans.

"I'm never drinking again," she sighs, coming to a stop beside him.

"Ahh, the famous four words!" he chuckles as he puts an arm around her shoulders. For a moment, she stiffens before relaxing into him. When she looks up at me, I can see her eyes are bloodshot, and she looks exhausted.

I point towards the small table that's in here.

"Go and sit down; I'll get you a coffee. What time is your performance tonight?" I ask, surprised when she does as she's told without arguing.

"I need to be there for five. Any chance one of you can give me a lift, please? My car's, well, you know," she nervously looks down at her hands.

"I'll take you tonight, but I want you to try and get some rest this afternoon before we go. You had a long night and didn't sleep soundly," I tell her while making her coffee the way she likes.

"I don't sleep in the day," she answers. I turn and look at her, frowning, but it's Ryan who asks the question first.

"What? Not even if you haven't slept in the night?"

Verity shakes her head as she looks around at us all.

"If you lose an hour to sleep, you spend the rest of the day chasing it."

"Who told you that bullshit?" Ethan exclaims. Verity shrugs, and I have a feeling there are lots of little phases like that she was taught growing up, which she still lives by. I know she had a strict Nanny when she was homeschooled. It wouldn't surprise me if that's why she also gets up at six every morning.

"Well, today, you can curl up and have an hour on the sofa or in bed. No arguments," I tell her as I place a coffee before her. She doesn't argue out loud, just nods. But I have a feeling she isn't going to do as she's told, but I can at least try.

"I need to pop out for a bit to sort some shit out. You going to be okay with dumb and dumber here?" I ask, nodding towards my brothers, who instantly start protesting loudly. I'd hoped it would get at least a smile out of her, but Verity just nods and sips her drink.

"I manage on my own every other day."

I walk up to her and place a kiss on the top of her head. It's not something I usually do, but right now, she looks like she needs as much affection as possible. Plus, I need to remind myself she is actually okay.

"If you need anything picked up, message or call me."

Verity looks up and nods before going back to her coffee.

"Thank you for looking after me last night. I'm sorry I was so stupid," she whispers before looking back at me. I can see how humiliated she is, and it breaks my heart. I reach out and run a hand over her head.

"We all do it at some point. You have nothing to be sorry for. Like I said, be careful in the future."

"I will," she replies, giving me a small smile. I lean in and kiss her head again, breathing in her sweet scent at the same time.

As I turn away from Verity, I look to my brothers and mouth, "Watch her." They both nod subtly before going about making their breakfasts.

Grabbing my keys from the counter, I rush to the car and head quickly towards the main road.

When I received the call yesterday from Ryan to say that he was worried about Verity and Ethan having caught her boyfriend with another woman, I jumped in the car without a second thought. I don't have any clothes with me, my laptop to keep on top of work, or even a toothbrush. All I could think about was getting here and ensuring she was okay. I'm so glad I did, as I had only been at the house ten minutes when the O'Reilly's girl had called by looking for Verity because they had seen she was upset and couldn't find her. I'd been in my room when they arrived, and they left instantly, which is why she had no idea who I was. Ryan had rushed up to my room to tell me that something might have happened to Verity, and I'd jumped in the car and started driving around to find her. I never expected to find her in the state I did.

Verity is one of the most innocent, quiet and level-headed women I've ever known. But after seeing her last night, I think the whole innocent little girl act is something she can't stop playing. Is she being someone she thinks everyone wants her to be? Because if she is, it would explain so much.

I rub my tired face as I get onto the motorway and head towards home. This will be a flying trip as I want to take Verity to the recital and watch it. I've already booked a last-minute ticket. I want to watch from the audience and see how she reacts to others. Something tells me her performance is much more than just the dance.

Chapter Twelve

VERITY

Ethan places a blanket over me as I lie on the sofa, absentmindedly watching the TV. He reminds me I said I would try to sleep. Neither of the guys has let me out of their sight, and I have a feeling it's Travis's doing. Has he realised how much of an emotional wreck I am now? I know I need to do something about it, but I just don't know what anymore. I have no idea who to turn to, as I hate being a burden on others. This is why I've always dealt with everything myself. It's easier than admitting I am dying on the inside.

Since Travis left this morning, I have put on my mask and tried to play the happy, carefree Verity everyone wants to see. Something tells me that the guys aren't buying it, though. I can feel them watching me as if waiting for me to crack. Would they help me if I did? I think they would, but only because they are nice like that. They would feel obligated to care for me, and I don't want their pity. I also don't want to frighten them off, so they never visit again. I like having them here for the brief periods that they stay.

A knock sounds from the hallway, and my heart freezes. I glance at Ethan to see if he recognises the sound. Judging from the look he throws my way, he does.

"Oh, hell no." He jumps from the sofa and has the door open before I even get to my feet.

"You've got fucking balls, I'll give you that!"

Ryan and I share a look before rushing to the door. My heart's racing as I pray I'm wrong and it's not who I think it is. But one look and I know it was just wishful thinking.

Marshall stands in the doorway, staring at Ethan, who is standing with his arms crossed over his chest.

"Ethan, let him in," I sigh as I approach the door.

"Who is it?" Ryan asks as he comes to a stop between me and Ethan.

"Marshall," I answer quietly as I start to shake. Ryan looks between Marshall and me, and I see I need to defuse the situation quickly. I go to walk past the guys, but Ryan puts his arm out, stopping me.

"You have some nerve turning up here after what you've done," he growls through gritted teeth. Marshall frowns, looking at the guys.

"Who the fuck are you? What's with all the hostility, Ver?" he asks, looking at me.

"Don't fucking talk to her! And he's the one who's going kill you after I break your legs as promised," Ethan warns as he takes a step forward.

"Ethan, stop." I grab the back of his top, and he turns, staring at me wide-eyed.

"After everything he's done?" he demands, pointing towards Marshall, who still looks confused. He really has no idea I know, and why would he? He didn't see me in the bar last night. As far as he's concerned, he's still in the clear.

"What have I done?" Marshall asks again. "Ver, tell

them I haven't done anything wrong," he demands, expecting me to be the good little girlfriend and stand up for him.

"Leave me to speak to him, please," I say, looking between Ethan and Ryan

Ethan throws his hands up in the air and storms towards the lounge. Yelling that I'm a fool. Tell me something I don't know.

"Don't let him weasel his way in," Ryan whispers as he looks to Marshall, who's looking a little less comfortable. "You upset her again, and you'll learn it's not my brother you need to fear. Just be glad our eldest brother isn't here. You would already be six feet under," he warns, reassuringly squeezing my arm and heading back to the lounge.

"What the hell was that all about?" Marshall asks, walking into the house. He goes to reach out for me, but I step back, wrapping my arms around my waist. "Ver? What's going on?" He looks concerned, which only messes with my head further.

"Don't," I warn him as I shake my head. "Don't touch me," I add as he reaches for me again. I look up as I feel my eyes starting to burn. "I know Marshall. I know about her."

For the briefest second, he looks nervous as he rubs the back of his neck nervously.

"I don't know-"

"Don't lie to me," I snap before taking a deep breath and forcing all my anger back down. "I saw you in the bar last night."

For a moment, Marshall says nothing. He stares at me before cursing under his breath.

"Shit, Ver. I'm sorry, okay, it was a moment of lapsed judgment. What your brother said got to me, and I wanted to feel less of a failure. Nothing happened, though. It's you I love, you know that. I didn't take her home; you have to believe me." He steps forward again, and I step back. Doubt starts shifting away as I realise he could be telling the truth. I only saw him kiss her, not take her home. What if what I saw was the extent of it?

"I mean, let's face it, I wouldn't have done anything if it hadn't been for your brother. When he said that about the vibrator, I was hurt and confused. Sometimes you are so hard to please, and it can take so long to get you to cum, but you feel so good I can't last. That night was a prime example. Maybe I wouldn't have looked elsewhere if you were a little easier to please in bed."

My breath catches in my throat as I stare at him in absolute disbelief.

"So, it is my fault you cheated on me? Because you couldn't give me an orgasm?" I ask for variation. There is no way that is what he means, surely?

"You make me feel like a failure, Ver. I had to prove to myself I wasn't. So, I could show you that I'm not."

I look into his eyes and realise he really believes it's my fault. Is it my fault? Is my high sex drive to blame? I know I can take a while to orgasm at times; he must get fed up while trying to help me reach that point. But then it dawns on me: I never have issues when I'm alone. Plus, he didn't even try the other night. If he had, he would have lasted more than four minutes.

"So, you cheated on me to prove to yourself and me that I'm the problem in bed, not you? How did you manage that if you didn't take her home?" I ask before bursting out laughing. "That's why you are here now. Why you left the other day saying you were working even though you weren't. You spend time with her, but she won't sleep with you yet, So you come to me when you want to get laid. It's the only reason you keep me around!" I shake my head as I walk to the front door and hold it open.

"Enjoy your new relationship. I hope she knows what she is getting herself into."

When Marshall turns to look at me, I see a side of him I haven't witnessed before. He stares at me with such hatred in his eyes. When he steps towards me, I find myself scared of him for the first time.

"Why am I being made out to be the bad guy here? Do you know how hard it is to be in a relationship with you? I've put up with so much of your shit, yet I mess up once, and this is how you repay me? How many times have you cancelled a date to practice or because you are dancing? I did something wrong once, and you are throwing away the only relationship you will have? No one else is going to put up with your dancing shit and your little ways. I mean, who gets up at six every morning anyway?" he says through gritted teeth, stopping right in front of me. He grabs my arm and squeezes, pulling me closer to him. "I only put up with your continuous shit because you are a guaranteed lay. Bare that in mind for the next sucker who ends up with you, Ver."

"You're hurting me," I whimper as he tightens his grip tighter.

"You're lucky; that's all I'm doing."

A hand lands on the wrist of the hand he has wrapped around my arm. I look up to find Ethan's usual soft brown eyes glaring at Marshall.

"Get your fucking hands off her now!" he growls through gritted teeth as Marshall lets go of me and turns to face him.

"Or what? You'll break my legs?" he laughs in Ethan's face. Nothing prepares me for the look that appears on my usual calm, down-to-earth stepbrother. A grin spreads as he steps closer to Marshall.

"No," he replies, stopping when they are nose to nose. "I'll fucking kill you."

Ethan swings and punches Marshall so hard that he falls out of the door and down the front steps as Ethan launches himself on top of him.

"Ethan!" I cry out, attempting to get to them and break up the fight, but Ryan grabs me.

"Leave him," Ryan whispers, wrapping his arms around my shoulders and holding me tightly against him. Ethan punches Marshall once before grabbing him by the shirt collar and pulling him to his feet.

"You can't keep your useless dick in your pants, and that's somehow her fault? You pathetic piece of shit!" Ethan yells before throwing Marshall down hard onto the gravel, "If you ever so much as look in her direction again, I will kill you. Is that understood?"

"Whatever, man, fuck you!" Marshall growls, jumping to his feet and spitting out blood. He's bleeding from his nose and his mouth. Ethan charges towards him, but Marshall rushes to his car like the coward he is. He's quickly realised he's no match for the guy who works out daily.

"Ethan, he's not worth it," Ryan shouts as his arms loosen around me slightly.

"You're dead, mark my fucking words!" Ethan yells, pointing towards Marshall as he climbs into his car and speeds off.

Ethan storms up to where Ryan and I stand and cups my face. All the anger I saw in his eyes melts away as he looks into mine.

"Don't listen to a word he just said. He was the problem, not you. Do you hear me, Baby girl?" He looks deep

70

into my eyes, and I find myself nodding slowly. Ethan sighs and pulls me into his arms, holding me tightly against his chest. "No one speaks to you like that. You are perfect, just the way you are," he whispers into my hair. I don't know what to say, so I stay still, allowing myself time to enjoy being held.

"Thank you for defending me," I whisper after a few moments.

"He's lucky I didn't kill him like I wanted to," Ethan sighs before looking into my eyes again. "No one touches you. No one." The conviction he places into the last two words reminds me of how the O'Reillys speak to Jasmine. Like there is nothing in the world they won't do to protect her. I let myself believe Ethan feels that way about me for a moment.

"Come on, let's get out of the cold and chill out for a bit," Ryan says behind us before Ethan guides me back to the lounge. This time, though, when we sit on the sofa, he lies down and pulls me into his arms, holding me from behind.

"Try and get some rest," he whispers into my ear. I relax against him, very aware that it's my stepbrother holding me, as much as I'm aware I like it.

Chapter Thirteen

ETHAN

I'm lying on the sofa, watching the TV with Verity in my arms. After everything with her dickhead ex, I needed to hold her. It was the only thing stopping me from jumping in my car to go after him and beat the dickhead to a pulp.

It seemed like a good idea to hold her at first. But now, I'm trying to ignore the way her body is moulded against mine perfectly, her back pressed tightly to my front. Her ass is resting against my crotch, and every time she moves, I get that little bit harder.

"You need to try and get some rest," I whisper in her ear before looking over to Ryan, who's asleep in the recliner chair with his feet up. I don't think anyone had a decent night's sleep.

"I won't be able to," she replies quietly as she wiggles again, and I have to grip her hip to stop her before she feels how hard I am.

"Do you want me to move?" I ask, tightening my hold on her hip a little harder. When she shakes her head, I find myself smiling. Does she like being in my arms as much as I enjoy her being there?

"If you are comfortable, then why won't you sleep?"

Verity shrugs, but as I look down at the side of her face, I notice her chewing on her lip while looking at the screen. We are watching *True Blood*, and as always, there is a sex scene when I need to be thinking of anything but sex.

As the scene on the screen heats up, so does the feeling in my trousers. Fuck I need to move away, this isn't what she needs after everything she has been through. But then she wiggles back a little, and I hear her gasp as she realises I'm rock hard. I freeze, expecting her to jump up and run away. But instead, she wiggles again.

"Baby girl, you are not helping the situation," I whisper through gritted teeth. My hand rests on her stomach, hoping to hold her still. For the first time in days, I see the sign of a genuine smile on her face.

"I'm just getting comfortable, plus you are nice and warm."

Reaching behind me, I tug the blanket on the back of the sofa over us.

"Is that better?" I ask as I gently rub my nose against the side of her neck, unable to resist the sweet scent of her perfume.

"A little," she gasps. I place my hand on her stomach again, but this time apply a little pressure to pull her back against me.

"How about now?" My cock is pressed directly against her ass, and I notice a slight change in her breathing as she becomes aroused.

"Almost," she whispers. For the briefest moment, I am considering getting off the sofa and doing the right thing.

But something about this woman makes me feel more confident than I usually do with women.

"I think I know what will help you to sleep," I whisper into her ear. Moving my hand from her stomach, I slowly slide it down until I'm cupping her warm sex. I wait a second to see if she tells me to move it away. But instead, I'm greeted by her grinding herself against my hand.

"More?" I ask as I move to look her in the eye. She turns her head and looks me dead in the eye as she whispers.

"Please."

Fuck, how am I meant to say no to that? I brush my lips lightly against hers and am rewarded with the feel of her tongue lightly swiping against my lips.

I continue to look into her eyes as I slide my hand down into her leggings until I can run my finger over that sweet spot between her legs. I'm surprised to find her already wet and ready for me.

"Do you think an orgasm will help you sleep?" I start circling her clit and can tell I'm hitting the right spot as her breathing changes again.

"Ryan might wake up," she whispers. I look at my brother and know he's asleep.

"Even if he did, I wouldn't stop. I think he would love watching you cum." I notice an intake of breath as her breathing changes, and I know I've hit the nail on the head. I always hoped there was a kinky little minx under the sweet persona. Looks like I was right.

I continue to rub her clit, with just the right pressure and can feel her getting closer. I kiss her neck before nibbling on her ear.

"Would you like it if he watched? Or how about if he joined in?"

Verity's sigh tells me everything I need, and I chuckle into her neck.

"Oh, Baby girl, I think it could be arranged if it's what you really want."

"Yes," Verity moans as she grinds against my hand.

I look over to Ryan and notice his breathing has changed slightly. He's no longer fast asleep, and the fact he's sporting a boner tells me he knows what's happening.

"Then why don't you be a good girl and cum on my fingers before we let him join the party," I whisper as I take her earlobe between my teeth again and apply a little more pressure to her clit, causing her to moan as she cums. It's all the proof I needed that limp dick Marshall was the problem in the bedroom, not my Baby girl.

"Fuck," I groan as she shudders against my crotch, rubbing against my hard cock.

I look up from Verity's neck to find Ryan watching us, clutching his dick through his jeans.

"Shall we take this to your room, Baby?" I ask, not taking my eyes off Ryan whose are locked with Verity's.

She doesn't say a word; just nods her head. Ryan stands up from the chair and comes to a stop in front of her as I remove my hand from her leggings. He holds out his hand, which she takes so he can help her to stand. As soon as she's in front of him, he threads his fingers into her hair and kisses her.

I know he's fantasised about this moment for over a year, this is his dream coming true, and I almost feel guilty being the first to make her cum, almost.

Verity kisses him before he pulls back and looks into her eyes again.

"You don't have to do anything you don't want to; you

know that, right?" he says softly. Verity nods as she looks back at him, not even blinking.

"I want this."

Ryan picks her up so she can wrap her legs around his waist before kissing him again. We both take the stairs two at a time, eager to get to her room.

I open the door for us all, and Ryan carries her inside before placing her on her feet. He steps to the side so I can get to those sweet lips.

Gently, I cup her cheek before leaning in to kiss her gently.

"Tell us what you like," I whisper against her lips as Ryan stands behind her, wrapping his arms around her waist.

"Anything," she replies, taking me by surprise.

"Have you had a threesome before?" he asks whilst peppering her neck with light kisses. Verity leans her head to one side, granting him better access.

"No."

"Well, that makes three of us, so why don't we start slow and see where this leads," I whisper before kissing her sweet lips.

Verity becomes sandwiched between us as I kiss her lips and Ryan her neck. Our hands start roaming over her petite body, exploring every dip and curve. The moans and sighs that escape her are like music to my ears. The need to touch her bare skin becomes too much, and I step back, smiling.

"Can I stripe you, Baby?" I ask, trying to hide how nervous I am. But when she smiles and nods at me, the last of my nerves wash away, and I savour the moment as Ryan and I slowly stripe her bare.

As soon as she's naked, Ryan stands in front of her,

threads his fingers into her hair, as he did downstairs and kisses her firmly on the lips.

"What turns you on the most and brings you the most pleasure?" he asks, still gripping her hair at the scalp.

"I love head. Giving and receiving."

If I didn't already think she was perfect, I do now.

"That I am more than happy to help with," he grins. He glances at me, and I nod, letting him take the lead. He has fantasised about this for longer than I have, and he can set the pace this time. Because I know this is going to happen again. I'll make sure of it.

"Here's what's going to happen, Kitten. I'm going to drop to my knees right here and worship you the way you should be. I'm not going to stop licking that sweet pussy until you beg me to. Then, if you still want more, you're going to climb on that bed, and one of us is going to take you from behind whilst you suck the other's cock." Ryan presses his lips to hers as he whispers, "Protection?"

"Implant," she whispers back. "Marshall always insisted on using condoms as well."

"Do you have any?" I ask, kissing her neck from behind as I take her breasts in my hand. She shakes her head.

"Do you want to use them?" Ryan asks as his hand dips between her legs. Again, she shakes her head. "Are you sure? Don't say no for our benefit. This is about you," he asks to ensure it really is what she wants.

"I want to feel everything." That's all the confirmation Ryan needs as he kisses her hard once more on the mouth before dropping to his knees with the biggest grin I have seen in a long time. "Then open your legs, little Kitten and let me finally taste that sweet pussy."

Verity doesn't have time to open them far before Ryan

presses his head between her legs, and she leans back against me, moaning.

"Does that feel good, Baby?" I chuckle as I tweak her nipples slightly.

"Yes," she gasps as she leans further into me for support.

"We've got you, Baby. We will make sure you get just what you need," I whisper into her ear as she moans again.

Next time, we will do this with her flat on her back so I can see exactly what he's doing to make her cry out like this. Verity lifts her arm and wraps it around my head, which is nestled into her neck.

"Oh god, don't stop," she gasps before crying out as she cums. I take some of her weight as her legs buckle from underneath her, and she cries out through her orgasm. Ryan doesn't let up as she tries to move away from him. Instead, he grips her hips, and in seconds, she's crying out from a second orgasm as he continues to eat that sweet pussy until she is begging him to stop.

He looks up from the floor where he's kneeling in front of her and looks extremely proud of himself. Verity is now leaning nearly all her weight on me as she gasps for breath, her whole body still shuddering from the two orgasms. Placing an arm around her back, I scoop her into my arms and carry her over to the bed. Ryan makes short work of pulling the covers back so I can lie her on the sheets.

"Feeling better, Baby?" I ask, brushing some hair from her face as she smiles at me with heavy eyes and nods. "I'm glad to hear it," I whisper against her lips. She surprises me by reaching out and running a hand over my jeans, where my cock is rock hard and constricted.

"I think I owe you both a little something in return." She moves until she's kneeling on the bed in front of me and smiling with the most amazing fuck me eyes I have ever seen. She makes short work of undoing my belt and releasing me from my jeans and boxers. She then beckons Ryan closer and does the same to him as I pull my bottoms off completely.

For the last five years, I thought this woman was a shy little thing. But now I'm seeing her in a whole new light. Most women would be begging to be left alone after three orgasms, but not our girl. Instead, she's begging for more, and I'm happy to give it to her.

I watch as Verity takes Ryan's cock in her hand and runs her tongue from the base right up to the tip as she takes mine in her other hand. She strokes me as she sucks Ryan.

"Fuck, that mouth is perfect," he gasps as he threads his fingers into her hair and starts to pump lightly into her mouth. "Don't forget Ethan, little Kitten."

Verity removes Ryan's cock from her mouth and looks up at me as she slowly lowers her lips around mine.

"Fuck, Baby," I moan as my eyes roll to the back of my head before I glance at Ryan. "You weren't fucking kidding, that's one naughty mouth."

"Do you still want a cock in that beautiful pussy?" Ryan asks Verity, who nods as she continues to suck me. Ryan winks at me before climbing onto the bed. "Stay right there then, Kitten; let me give you what I think you long for."

Ryan kneels behind her as he positions himself at her entrance, and I'm filled with jealousy. It's only right that he takes her first, he has wanted this longer than me, but fuck I want to be where he is right now. I want to feel myself sliding inside of her. I bet it is just as amazing, if not better, than her mouth.

Ryan takes hold of her hips and asks her once more if this is what she wants.

"Yes! Please!" she calls as I know he's right there at her

entrance. He winks at me once before pushing his hips forward. Judging by the moan that leaves her, I know he is in, and she loves it. I watch for a moment as they both get lost in the sensation of him filling her, and I swear my cock gets even harder.

How can I watch my brother with the woman I long to make mine and be so aroused? Am I jealous, of course, but not to the point I'm mad, and that's confusing in itself. Should it feel this right to be sharing a woman with my brother in bed?

"How does he feel baby?" I ask, running a hand over her head as she looks up at me.

"So good," she gasps as Ryan picks up speed, but only a little.

"Tell us what you like. What do you want," I ask, leaning down and kissing her lips.

"Use me and control me," she gasps as Ryan slams into her a little harder than before.

"Do you want us to dominate you?" I ask, hoping I have finally found someone to let me do everything I want to try with a woman.

"Yes," she cries out as Ryan gets a little rougher again.

"Fuck you are too perfect," I growl as I thread my fingers into her hair and pull her head back so she has no choice but to look at me. Her body is being pushed and pulled by Ryan, and I plan on taking advantage of it.

"Slap my leg three times if it becomes too much," I instruct as she nods. I take my cock in my hand and move it towards her mouth. "Open wide and stick your tongue out." Verity instantly does as I ask, and I run my cock over her tongue and around her mouth.

"How does she feel, Ryan?" I ask as I wipe my cock on her tongue again.

"Like fucking heaven," he replies through gritted teeth.

"Can we both cum in you, baby? Or would you prefer on you?"

"In me. Please," she cries as she starts heading towards another orgasm.

"Please, what?" I ask, running the tip of my cock on her lips, smearing my pre cum all over them.

"Please, Sir. Fill me with your cum!" she licks the pre cum from her lips, and I know I'm not going to last long at all once I get in there.

"Fuck, you are perfect. Open wide." She immediately does, and I slide my cock into her mouth and almost blow my load as she moans around me, taking me to heaven with her mouth.

Ryan and I start using her body the way she has asked. Before long, I'm fucking her throat as he takes her pussy. Neither of us lets up as she gags and cries out. I count at least two more orgasms from her before I feel my balls tightening, and I know I'm not going to last much longer.

"Little Kitten, you feel too good," Ryan cries out, and I can see he, too, is close to his own release.

"I'm going to cum, Baby. Take what we give you," I cry out as I feel myself squirting my release straight down her throat. She starts to moan around it, which intensifies the feeling. From the sounds coming from Ryan, he is falling over the edge with us, and the three of us have the most intense orgasm together.

I don't know how long I stand, my eyes closed and gasping for breath. Verity lets my now soft cock fall from her mouth, and I can see how exhausted she is. I climb onto the bed and pull her into my arms.

"Lie down, Baby, I've got you," I whisper as she curls up against my side, and Ryan pulls the covers over us.

"Are you okay, little Kitten?" he asks. She nods against my chest as he kisses the top of her head. "Are you sure?" he asks again. She turns in my arms, so she is now leaning against his chest.

"More than okay," I only hear her whisper as Ryan chuckles, tightening his arms around her.

"I'm glad to hear it," he smiles as he kisses her head again. "I always knew you would be amazing. But you are more perfect than I ever imagined. I don't think I will ever be able to let you go now," he says into her hair.

"I'm fine with that," she whispers before I notice her breathing settling. I sit up and look down at her as she falls asleep in Ryan's arms.

"I take it you are okay with her there for a while," I chuckle quietly. Ryan looks down at the woman he has cared for from a distance, lying naked against his as he holds her and smiles.

"More than okay. You better wait for Travis. He is going to be mad as fuck," Ryan points out, looking up at me.

I nod once, place a kiss on Verity's head, and climb out of the bed. I grab my clothes and look to the bed to find Ryan dozing off, his head resting on hers as he savours having her there and content.

Chapter Fourteen

ETHAN

I sneak out of Verity's room, pulling on my t-shirt.

She had fallen asleep so quickly; it shows how much she needed to rest. If only she could let herself sleep when she needs to and not worry about what people think of her.

I saw a whole new side of our girl today. I would have never put her down as adventurous in the bedroom before the last few days. But she didn't even think twice about being with Ryan and me at the same time. When she said she was open to anything, she meant it. My sweet girl has a naughty side, and I can't wait to see her hidden kinks.

I grabbed my phone from the coffee table where I had left it before the Marshall incident. Finding a message from Travis saying he'd reached his place and would pop into ours to pack some stuff for us. Followed by a message telling us he's leaving to head back. I check the time stamp of the messages and know he should be here any minute. The man drives like a lunatic at the best of times. He made it here in record time yesterday after Ryan called him about Verity.

How I haven't noticed his feelings towards her before, I don't know.

Throughout the night, he wouldn't leave her. He moved the chair to the side of the bed and watched over her. I tried to get him to rest a few times, but he refused. He was terrified she would be sick in her sleep. He has it bad, and I have no idea how he will take what just happened. Should we have done it even though we know how he feels? Probably not, but I don't think anyone was thinking logically once things started progressing. I feel bad, though, even if she is completely worth dealing with his wrath.

Walking into the kitchen, I head straight for the coffee machine to make myself a drink and prepare it for his arrival. I stand by the machine as it does its thing and think back to the last hour.

When Ryan, Verity and I came together as we did, it was the first time I had seen a genuine smile on her face since arriving three days ago.

When was the last time she smiled properly? Not the fake smile I'm sure she has been flashing to everyone. But a real one that made her cheeks ache and her eyes sparkle. I know Marshall certainly never made her feel as Ryan and I did. Otherwise, there's no way he would have called her difficult to please. That girl came so many times I couldn't keep count. She sounded even sweeter than she did the night I listened to her masturbating. Whatever that prick was on about just showed she is better off without him. She was so sexually frustrated I know she didn't feel the release she needed until she came a few times.

When I heard what he was saying to her, I wanted to kill him. I tried to reach the front door a few times, but Ryan kept holding me back. I couldn't see that he had hold of her until she said he was hurting her. There was no holding me back then. If I hadn't gotten to him first, Ryan would have. There is nothing neither of us wouldn't do for that woman upstairs.

"Hey, how's it going?"

I look away from the coffee machine in time to watch Travis drop a couple of large bags by the back door.

"You got everything?" I ask, nodding towards his stuff. I notice he's changed clothes and showered, too.

"Yeah, got you guys some extras as well. I have a feeling we'll be staying a little longer than planned." Travis walks over to me, and I move away from the machine to let him make his own drink. No one can ever make it right for him. We learned a long time ago to let him do it himself.

"Everything okay whilst I was gone?" he asks, filling his mug.

"Apart from that prick, Marshall, turning up."

Travis spins around and stares at me.

"Are you fucking kidding me? Did she see him?"

I nod and proceed to fill him in on all that was said. From what he was saying, I don't think it was the first time he had cheated on our girl. How he could cheat on someone who sucks dick like that, I will never know. Fuck that was the best head I've ever received, and she took me fucking her throat better than any woman I have ever been with. From that blow job alone, I'm considering putting a ring on her finger and claiming her as mine forever. Okay, I may need to share her with Ryan and even Travis if he ever gets around to finally admitting how he feels about her.

"Do we know where he lives? I'm thinking we visit the arsehole and teach him a few manners," Travis says through gritted teeth. His jaw is so clenched I can see every muscle in it. If he were to get his hands on Marshall, there wouldn't be any chance of him daring to come near Verity again. Travis would destroy him emotionally and physically.

"No, and for now, I think we leave it that way. But we can find him easy enough if he does anything else to upset our girl. I think she wants to put the whole thing behind her for now."

Travis nods as he takes a few calming breaths, and his jaw finally relaxes enough for him to take a sip of his coffee.

"Where is she? Did you manage to get her to go back to bed?"

"Uh huh," I hum into my drink.

"Where's Ryan?"

"Sleeping," I reply, trying to avoid looking at him, but I can feel his eyes on me.

"As well?"

"Uh-huh," I reply, pretending to be busy with my phone, unable to look him in the eye as I'm racked with guilt.

"Where?" Travis asks as he puts his head around the kitchen door, where he will be able to see the chair that Ryan tends to sit in.

"Upstairs," I answer, climbing to my feet. "I'm going to get changed and head to the gym now you're back." But I get less than one step past him, and he grabs my arm.

"Tell me they are not asleep in the same bed."

"Okay," I reply, trying to get away quickly, but Travis keeps his hold on my arm and stops me from going anywhere.

"When I said keep an eye on her, I didn't mean fuck her. Can neither of you two do anything that doesn't evolve your dicks?" he growls through gritted teeth. "Don't you think she has been through enough without him adding to the problem?"

"Wow!" I call, shrugging his hand off. "For the record, she started it. We never planned on fucking her, but."

"WE?" Travis shouts and quickly lowers his voice as we look up the stairs to see if she has heard us.

"Yes, okay, *we!*" I snap, nodding towards the dining room, where I know we can talk privately and close the door so Verity doesn't hear anything.

As soon as the door closes, Travis stares at me with his arms crossed. Ah shit, trust Ryan to be sleeping through the bollocking.

"You want to know the details, then fine, here they are." I pull out a chair and make a point of sitting down. When I nod towards another chair, Travis ignores me and glares at me. I roll my eyes and proceed to tell him how things progressed from cuddles on the sofa to me getting her off, and then all that happened in her room.

"Verity told us numerous times not to stop, and when we asked if she had enough, she told us no. I'm telling you, that woman is a fucking vixen. I swear she has some serious hidden kinks. She just needs the right person or persons to help her find out what they are."

"And I suppose you guys are the perfect people to help her?" Travis asks sarcastically. I shrug and pick up my mug.

"You could as well if you would just give in and admit you like her."

Travis doesn't reply, but from the look on his face, I know that he isn't going to be doing any of that any time soon. Instead, he looks at his watch and sighs.

"Well, as neither of them will get up any time soon, I might as well unpack." He turns to the door but stops when he places his hand on the handle. "I don't agree with what you did, but if it makes her happy, then who am I to argue with it."

"You could always join in?" I suggest again, which earns me the side eye to end all side eyes. "Or not. Got it," I add, pretending to zip my mouth. Travis shakes his head and sighs deeply before walking out of the dining room.

I relax into the chair I'm sitting in and finish my almost-cold coffee. He might not want to admit it, but I saw the way his eyes darkened when I was describing the sex. I even went into a little more detail than was needed to get a reaction out of him. It was there. It's only slight, but I bet he will need to find his own release soon enough.

I stand from the table and take my empty cup to the kitchen before heading to my room. As I pass Verity's room, I can't help but smile, knowing our satisfied girl is in there, sleeping in my brother's arms. Am I a little jealous? A bit, but I also know I don't have time to lie about today. I need to reply to a few clients and get a workout in of my own. At least if I can't be there to hold her whilst she sleeps, it's one of my brothers, that is. I know they will give her anything she needs, even the one who refuses to admit that he has fallen for her like the rest of us.

I have never considered the possibility of sharing a woman with my brothers, but for some reason, with Verity, it is all I can think about. Not just in a sexual way, either. That woman deserves to be showered with love and worshipped. She needs to be shown daily that she is loved and wanted and needs more than just one of us can give her. But the three of us together could finally give her the love and affection she deserves and craves.

Chapter Fifteen

VERITY

"Come on, little Kitten. It's time to wake up."

"What time is it?" I ask, looking around, surprised to find it's dark outside the window.

"It's just gone three."

I've slept for at least an hour and a half. I never sleep in the day, no matter how tired I am. But there again, I was feeling so relaxed after the best sex I've ever had. It's no surprise I fell asleep.

"How you feeling?" Ryan asks, sitting on the edge of the bed in nothing but his jeans, holding a mug.

"I'm okay," I reply as he hands me the coffee once I'm sat with the duvet pulled up to my chest. I take it and can smell the freshly brewed caffeine my body's craving.

"Are you sure? Do you want to talk about anything?" he asks, taking my hand. Shaking my head, I give him a small smile.

"I don't have any regrets if that's what you mean." Suddenly, my usual insecurities flood my senses, and I start to panic. "Unless you do?"

"What? No! God no! I, I mean we, don't regret a single thing. We were just worried you would feel like we forced you into something you weren't ready for," he stammers, lifting his hand to cup my cheek. "I've had feelings for you for a while, and Ethan has too. We just never dreamt anything would happen like it has. That doesn't mean you have to do anything again if you don't want to," he adds quickly as I relax a little. I want things to happen again. I loved it, and it really was the best sex I've ever had. But I also know how quickly I can get attached to people, which is never good when things have a time limit. The guys are only back for a short while, and then they will leave, and I will go back to being on my own again.

"Thank you," I reply, not knowing what else to say. He leans in and presses a kiss on my forehead.

"Anything you want or need, we are here for. Whether it's amazing sex, a cuddle when you need one or even someone to make sure you get some sleep when you need it. Whatever it is, we are here for it; we all are in our own ways."

I nod before looking at the clock and sigh; I need to shower and stretch before I leave for the performance. Ryan touches the duvet over my knee and squeezes slightly to get my attention.

"Go and do whatever you need to do before the show. Travis is back and will take you. I'm going to come with you both and collect your car. Travis has something he wants to do and will finish at the same time as you so he can drive you home."

"Is that his way of ensuring I don't go on a bender again?" I ask, forcing a grin. Ryan rolls his eyes as he stands.

"Probably, you know what he's like." He leaves the

room, leaving me alone with my coffee and busy mind to prepare for the performance.

———

"Do you have everything you need?" Travis asks as we pull away from the house.

"Most of my stuff is in the car. I'm hoping it hasn't been nicked or anything," I sigh, running my hand over my bun, checking for any loose hairs. My best hairspray is in my dance bag, and I don't trust the stuff I just used.

"I'm sure everything will be there," Ryan says from the back of the car.

"Including my phone. I dread to think of the messages Jaz and Danni will have left on it."

Travis hadn't grabbed my phone when he picked me up last night, and apparently, Danielle had locked up the car and thrown the keys to him before he brought me home. My phone, purse, dance bag and make-up are all still in the car, at least I hope they are. The make-up alone is worth hundreds. I hope no one stole anything. I can't afford to replace or claim it on the insurance. I don't like the idea of asking my dad to help me out. He pays for enough, and I know he works hard to give me what I have. School and the house aren't cheap, which is why I appreciate everything he does for me.

"How close are you to the O'Reilly girl?" Travis asks. I look at him as I remember how he treated Jaz and Christian last night. I had no idea he even knew them.

"Very, which is why you owe Jaz an apology and Christian."

Travis gives me the side eye as Ryan laughs behind me.

"Yeah, good luck with that one," he laughs as Travis grunts something I can't make out.

"I'll apologise to the girl if it makes you feel better, but I ain't apologising to that prick, Christian." I notice Travis clutching the steering wheel so hard that his knuckles are white. I find myself reaching over to place a hand over his.

"I can guess something bad went down between you, and I know he has done some bad things over the years. But he loves my best friend and saved her life. I will forever be grateful to him for that."

Travis turns his head momentarily and looks at me before nodding as he returns to concentrating on the road.

"Fair enough. I won't ask you to stay away as I'll never tell you what you should be doing. But I will tell you to be careful." He turns to look at me as he stops at a red light. "If anything happens to you because of him or any of his brothers, I will kill them without a second's thought."

From the way his jaw clenches, I know he means it. I squeeze his hand slightly whilst nodding.

"Deal," I reply, unable to stop the small smile that lifts one side of my lips.

Travis looks at me for a moment before nodding once and concentrating back on the road as the light turns green, and he starts heading towards the theatre.

I don't know what occurred between him and Christian, when or why. But all I know for sure is that Travis is wary of him, and I'm sure there is a good reason for that. I make a mental note to see if Jaz knows anything. Christian doesn't hide anything from her, and I know if she asked about it, he or one of his brothers would have told her everything.

"Hey, Kitten. How many performances do you have left after tonight?" Ryan asks as he leans forward and places his hand on my shoulder.

"Three weeks worth. Why?" I turn around to find him grinning at me.

"Do you have a break then from classes and practising?"

I nod whilst frowning at him.

"Another three weeks."

I can almost see the clogs turning in that head of his as he smiles and nods once before leaning back in his seat and letting go of my shoulder.

"What are you planning?" Travis asks, looking at his brother in the rearview mirror.

"Nothing, just trying to get ideas on time scales and so on," Ryan replies, pulling his phone out of his coat pocket.

I'm about to ask who he's messaging when Travis comes to a stop, and I see my car beside us.

Jumping out, I rush over to it. Checking for any damage or signs it's been broken into. It looks like everything is intact; nothing seems different except.

"Damn it, a ticket!" I exclaim as I start trying to pull it off the windscreen. I hadn't even thought about the fact my ticket would have run out. I only paid until midnight. I dread to think how much this is going to cost me.

"Leave it. I'll sort it for you when I get back to the house," Ryan says as he moves me away from the windscreen. "Get what you need out of the car and head inside to get ready. Everything will be sorted by the time you finish," he promises. I lift onto my toes and press a kiss to his cheek.

"Thank you. There is a jar of money in the kitchen. Take what it is from there. It's just spare cash for takeaways and stuff."

Ryan nods and hands me the keys to get my things out. I gather my things before turning around to see him climbing in behind the wheel, with Travis saying something quietly.

Ryan nods and closes the driver's door, and opens the window. "See you all back at the house. Break a leg, little Kitten!" he calls as he backs the car out of its space and drives off as I wave to him.

I look back to Travis and find him watching me with a look in his eyes that I can't quite place.

"Have you got your phone now?"

I nod and reach into my bag, where I threw it a moment ago.

"The battery has died, but I have a charger, which I keep in my bag."

"Then go and get it charged and call me if you have any issues. I'll be finished in time to pick you up. I'll wait for you in the foyer once everyone has left. Call me if I'm not there, but I won't be far away."

I nod and turn to walk away, but he calls my name and stops me.

"Try to forget the last twenty-four hours, if only during the performance. Do what you love and what makes you happy."

Why do I have a feeling he isn't just referring to the dancing? He hasn't mentioned what happened between Ethan, Ryan and me, but I'm sure he knows.

"Thank you." I rush back and press a kiss to his cheek, giving him a small smile before turning around and heading to the stage door, trying to push all that's happened to the back of my mind so I can do what I love, just as Travis said.

Chapter Sixteen

TRAVIS

I don't think there is anything more beautiful than Verity when she's dancing. Why have I never watched her before, besides the occasional clips she has sent me or on social media? She is elegant, graceful, confident and beautiful. Her head is held high and proud as she moves across the stage. I might not know much about ballet, but she looked perfect to me.

When all the dancers come out for their curtain call, I don't hold back as I stand with everyone else, whistling, clapping and calling out, especially for my girl. For a moment, I wonder if she will know I'm there. But then she looks in my direction, and for the briefest second, our eyes meet, and a giant smile spreads across her face before she moves with the other dancers. Surely, she couldn't see me in this darkened corner? I hope she did, so she knows I watched her tonight.

I continue to clap with the rest of the audience until the last dancers leave the stage. As soon as the house lights go back up, everyone leaves their seat. Picking up my jacket and placing it over my arm, I slowly make my way towards the exit, eager to see how Verity is doing and what her reaction is when she realises I watched.

Ethan was right today; there is no hiding that I care deeply for Verity. If things were different, I would make her mine and never let her go. But they aren't. She is my step-sister and too innocent and pure to be with a man like me. I can be as corrupt as they come and know a lot of shit about the darker side of the world. That's why Henry told me to back off when I started getting close to her in the past.

Verity thinks I'm just an ordinary accountant for the higher class. She doesn't realise I do accounts for people like the O'Reilly's. Ones that need to keep where their money really comes from quiet and out of view of the tax man. The illegal shit, you might say.

Do my brothers know what I do? Of course, they are personal trainers to many of my clients, but I know they will be able to protect themselves if they ever need to. Not only are they trained to fight, but our dad also made sure we could handle most weapons, including guns. There isn't much I couldn't cause damage with, and it has come in handy on more than one occasion.

This is why I don't think we are good enough for Verity. She is too sweet and innocent to be dragged into this life. She doesn't even know what her father really does out there in the States. But I do, and it's because of me she doesn't go out there with him. I will not have her in danger because of him or me.

A couple of years ago, she started hinting about moving out there so Henry didn't have to keep coming back just to see her. She was willing to leave everything she has here and move to spend more time with her father. At one point, he seemed to be considering it. So, I made him see that it was a bad idea and that it was putting her in danger. He agreed, but on one condition: I stepped back and didn't pursue her like I wanted. I agreed, and we have been in agreement since. I won't date his daughter, and he won't move her to the States. Which is why I'm worried now my brothers have slept with her. Yes, she is older and able to make her own decisions, but her father could still try and control the situation. There again, will she let him? I don't know.

I rub my tired face and look around the now emptying foyer. Desperate to think about anything other than everything that could go wrong for Verity right now.

The building is beautiful and screams sophistication. Which is to be expected by the amount the school charge their students. But no matter the cost, everyone is leaving, smiling and chatting happily about the performance, and so they should; it was beautiful to watch. I spot some couches on the other side of the area and head for them, planning to sit and wait for Verity.

I'm exhausted after not sleeping last night. Other than dozing off in the chair for the odd five minutes here and there, I didn't get any sleep. I was worried something would happen to Verity, and I wouldn't realise until it was too late. So, I've spent the day drinking coffee and rushing around, not giving myself a chance to feel how drained I am.

As I reach the couches, a figure steps out of the washrooms beside them, and our eyes meet. There goes my good mood.

"Donavon," Jason O'Reilly snaps as he approaches me whilst shoving his hands in his pockets.

"O'Reilly," I nod as I walk past him, but he steps in my way. I Should have known he wouldn't let things be; at least if his hands are in his pockets, he can't punch me, for now anyway.

"If you think I haven't got anything to say about last night, you are royally mistaken. Especially after hearing you dared to lay a hand on my fiancée." The anger is evident on his face, and I wonder how far he will go to defend his woman's honour.

"Don't expect me to apologise to your brother. As I told Verity, it will never happen. But I was out of order to your girl, and I *will* apologise to her when I see her next." I keep my face as neutral as possible, hoping he sees my sincerity. He continues to stare at me with the same angry look. It's not the first time he has been furious at me. You upset one O'Reilly, you upset them all, and I'm not worried about him trying anything as I know it would be a pretty even fight.

"You'd better because whatever has gone on in the past does not excuse you from calling her a slut. I will not stand for it, and neither will my brothers."

Shame fills me as I remember how badly I behaved towards Jasmine last night. There was no need for it. I have never treated a woman with such disrespect before. All she was doing was protecting her friend. Isn't that something I should encourage? Knowing Verity has such good friends watching over her would certainly put my mind at ease.

"As I said, I was out of order, emotions were running high, and I was worried for Verity, which is no excuse."

"No, it is not."

For a moment, we look at each other; I can see a part of Jason still wants to fight me, if not worse. It's what I deserve. If the shoe was on the other foot and an O'Reilly spoke to Verity the way I spoke to Jasmine purely because of her association with me, then I would wipe the whole family out.

Fuck, I'm ashamed of myself.

"She means a lot to you, doesn't she." It's not a question; Jason obviously knows. I nod and take a deep breath. "You going to do anything about it?" he asks as he sits on the couch behind us. I know this is his olive branch, and I'm not foolish enough to ignore it. So, instead of walking away, I sit beside him and lean my elbows on my knees.

"My brothers already have. We don't need to make her life more complicated than it already is," I sigh. "The four of us together would be too much for her. Last night showed that she has been hiding things from us and how bad things have gotten."

"Her boyfriend?"

"Ex and a dead man. I'll kill him if I ever see him."

Jason chuckles, and I look at him with an arched bow. He is leaning back, looking relaxed, with one arm over the back of the sofa, his left ankle resting on his right knee.

"Do you know how many boyfriends the guys and I got rid of before we finally admitted our feelings to Jazzy? The last one took a nasty fall down a flight of stairs, and last I heard, he couldn't even be on the same street as her without wetting himself."

I shake my head as he grins. These guys have always been arrogant fuckers; I used to look up to them for that, and in a way, I still do. It only seems natural they would be protective of their woman.

"I'm sorry about the call I made when Jaz was taken."

"You mean the call when you tore Christian a new one for Verity being spiked?"

I nod as I look back to the open area of the foyer.

"I saw her the day after it happened, and she was a mess; I was furious. She didn't get out of bed for two days; when she did, she was still confused and drowsy. I lost it and felt bad afterwards when I heard about Jaz being taken. When Christian screamed it down the phone, I thought, … I don't know what I thought. I just lost my temper."

"You were protecting what's yours. That's only natural. But for the record, once Christian calmed down, he understood. He admitted he would have done the same thing if the shoe was on the other foot, and he didn't know what was happening on the other end." Jason sits forward and leans his elbows on his knees like me.

"I'm going to be straight with you. Christian had nothing to do with your father's death; it really was an accident. The only thing Christian is guilty of is running away from the scene, which he did for us. He knew if he got locked up, we would be left with Tommy, with no Christian to keep us out of trouble."

I rub my face before pinching the bridge of my nose. I know deep down he is telling the truth. Christian may have killed many people in his time, but he always showed respect towards my father, and I could never understand why he had done it. It was easier to blame him rather than accept my father wasn't as clean as he claimed.

I don't say anything; I just nod while trying to push back that last seed of doubt.

"I think I'm finally accepting that," I sigh. Jason squeezes my shoulder before sitting back again.

"As I'm being honest, there is one more thing I would like to add."

I turn to look back at Jason with arched brows but stay silent as I already have an idea of what he's about to say.

"Speak to Verity and be honest with her. I think you'll be surprised by what she can handle and what she wants."

I shake my head whilst looking around at the now almost empty room.

"If I do, her father might take her to the States and keep her there."

"Would she go?"

I shrug, as I have no idea.

"I don't know. She has mentioned it in the past. With how unhappy she seems to be, it's a real possibility. Plus, my brothers may have started something with her, and I don't know if I can handle sharing her, if that's what you are implying," I answer before sitting back so I can talk quietly. "They have acted on their feelings, and both seem happy to share her; Ethan even told me to be honest with her. But I don't know."

"Does it feel wrong?" Jason asks, and I shake my head.

"No. That's what makes it weird. If I were to share her with anyone, it would feel natural to be with them. But I don't know, the last thing I want is to make things complicated by being jealous of what they share," I admit before looking at him again. "Does that even make sense?"

"More than you realise," he laughs before looking around. "There's been times when things haven't been easy for us. After Jazzy was taken and treated the way she was, there were times she wouldn't let anyone near her but Christian. Even now, she can wake up from a nightmare and leave our beds to find him. The first couple of times it happened, I felt like I wasn't enough for her to feel safe and that he would always be the one she turned to for protection. I'm ashamed to admit it hurt my pride."

"Did it get easier?" I ask as this is the exact thing that concerns me about sharing Verity. I don't know how I would feel if she chose one of us over the others.

"Yes, because we sat down and talked it through like adults." Jason turns in his seat to look at me. "Jazzy is a brat, but there are also elements of a little in there, too. Which is one of the reasons we took control as we did. We are her daddies, and it's what she needs. But she has a different type of relationship with each of us. Seans is the dominating one, Maximus is the fun one, I'm the reliable one who spoils her, and Christian is her main daddy. She sees him the way I suppose my brothers and I do—the protector.

"Christian has always taken it upon himself to be the one who provides safety, escape route, and protection. You will remember how he tried to keep me and the twins out of the loop as much as possible. He's like that with Jazzy, which is why she knows she can be as vulnerable as she wants, and he will hold her together. She can be her inner little and know her daddy will protect her."

"So, she has a different relationship with each of you?"

Jason nods. "It's taken a little time, but whenever she favours one of us over the others, we know they are providing what she needs. I wouldn't be surprised if Verity is like that with you three. There are a lot of similarities between her and Jazzy. I think you'll find out of the three of you; you will be her safety net."

I listen to everything he's saying and know there are signs that Verity comes to me when she feels vulnerable. Not just because she will message me or call me more. Last night, after she was sick, she leaned into me to hold her whilst she recovered. My brothers and I don't have a great relationship with Verity, and in truth, we know very little about her. But that's something we could change, and it wouldn't be that hard to do. We need to prove to her that we are sticking around and will be there for her. That's something I can certainly do anyway.

I look back to Jason and find him smirking at me.

"You are thinking about it a little more now, aren't you?"

"I guess I am."

Jason claps me on the back as he stands up and straightens his jacket.

"Well, if you go for it, I wish you luck. All I can suggest is you talk and act like adults. Let Verity be who she really is with you; don't try to force her to be anything else. From the times she has been around us, I could tell she couldn't truly relax, like she was worried about being herself. I know that's how Jazzy was when she moved in with us, and they are more similar than any of us realised."

I stand and offer him my hand, which he takes.

"Thanks, Jas."

Jason nods as I shove my hand in my trouser pockets. A laugh sounds across the foyer, and I turn to see Verity and Jasmine walking towards us. When Verity's eyes land on me, a big smile spreads across her face, causing my heart to swell. But when she realises I'm standing next to Jason, her smile drops, and she looks worried.

"I hope you're not starting on him as well because he's less likely to hold me back," Jasmine glares at me as she approaches.

"Calm down, Angel. We were talking, that's all," Jason says as she kisses him quickly before leaning against him. He puts an arm around her shoulders.

"Jasmine, I would like to apologise for how I spoke to you last night. I was concerned about Verity and not thinking rationally. However, that's no excuse for the way I treated you. So please accept my sincere apology."

I can see Verity smiling beside her and realise that even if Jasmine doesn't accept my apology, Verity will know I am genuinely sorry for my actions.

"Fine, apology accepted. But, if you ever speak to my fiancé, any of them, like that again, you will regret it quickly," she warns as Jason kisses the top of her head, chuckling.

"If you think we are protective of her, that's nothing compared to what she is like with us," he smirks. I nod to them both before turning my attention to Verity.

"You danced beautifully tonight, Sweetheart."

"So that was you I saw in the audience?" she asks excitedly. I smile, nodding at her.

"I thought I would surprise you and watch. The guys also wanted to, but I could only get one ticket."

Verity surprises me by excitedly dropping her bag and throwing her arms around my neck.

"If I had known how happy it would make you, I would have done it earlier," I laugh into her hair.

"You have no idea how happy I am that someone watched," she whispers before letting me go. When she looks at me again, I can see her eyes are full of tears. When was the last time anyone watched her dance? Has it really been that long?

"Come on, Jazzy, we need to get back. Sean and Maximus should be back by the time we get home."

Jasmine's face lights up; she turns to Verity and hugs her. I don't miss that she whispers something in her ear before kissing her cheek and stepping back to Jason's side.

"See you tomorrow, Verity," she calls before looking at me. Her smile drops, but she doesn't look like she wants to kill me, so I'll take that as a win. "See you later," she says with less emphasis before Jason leads her towards the door, her bag now in his hand.

"Later, Donavon. Think about what I said," Jason calls before disappearing out of view. I only manage to hold my hand up before he's gone.

"What did he say to you?" Verity asks as I take the bag from her.

"Nothing for you to worry about, Sweetheart," I reply before offering her my arm. "Let's get you home so you can rest," I add, leading her to the front door and out into the cold night.

Verity starts to shiver as soon as we are outside, and I remove my arm from hers and wrap it around her shoulder, pulling her against me, hoping to shield her from the cold winter breeze. As we reach the car, I ensure she is inside safely before placing her bag on the back seat and moving to the driver's side.

"Let's get you warmed up." I turn on the heated seats and the heaters and let the car de-mist as we wait.

"How you feeling now? Are you still cold?" I ask, looking to my left to find her smiling at me.

"Has anyone told you you're very caring and thoughtful?" she asks as her smile brightens further.

"I've been called many things, Sweetheart, but nothing like that," I laugh before turning away. She places her hand over mine, which rests on the dashboard, causing me to turn back to her. She is so beautiful, I don't know if she realises how perfect she is, not just in her looks but everything about her.

A strand of her blonde hair hangs down the side of her face, and I reach up to tuck it behind her ear. As my knuckles brush against her cheek, I don't miss how her eyes close and she leans into my touch. I act before I think and lean in, softly pressing my lips to hers. I expect her to move away from me, but she doesn't. Instead, she looks me in the eye for a moment before kissing me back.

There are a million things I should be thinking about right now, but all that matters is that her lips are finally against mine, and they feel so right. It takes everything in me not to drag her to the back seat and make love to her the way I want to, but this isn't how I pictured our first time—rushed in a car on a cold night. I want to take her home and make love to her all night in my bed or hers. Fuck, I wouldn't even care if one of the guys joined us. All I want is her. Jason's right; why shouldn't I tell her how I feel? How we all feel.

I pull away slightly and smile when I see the soft smile on her just kissed lips.

"I've wanted to do that for so long," I whisper, running my knuckles down her cheek.

"Travis?"

"Yes, Sweetheart?"

She looks up at me with the most amazing fuck me eyes that. I feel myself getting hard.

"Take me home."

Chapter Seventeen

VERITY

My heart is fluttering. I'm so happy.

Travis, watching the performance tonight means so much to me. I often pretend in my head that someone is secretly watching from the crowd. It's a little thing that gets me through challenging performances. I feel lonely after a show, especially now Jaz knows she has someone there every night. Everyone will talk about different friends and family coming to watch, but I never have anyone. I haven't for a long time.

I was sure I'd heard him whistle when I took my bow during the curtain call. I immediately looked in the direction it came from and, for the briefest moment, thought I saw him in the shadows. It's nearly impossible to see anyone in the audience when you are on the stage, but something told me I was looking straight at him. But I didn't want to get my hopes up in case I was wrong. He is the first person to watch me in years and it's given me the boost I needed to take that step forward to get over the last twenty-four hours.

Travis can tell how happy I am as he keeps glancing

over and smiling. He took my hand about ten minutes ago and hasn't let go since. A part of me is paranoid; he's just being like this because I slept with his brothers this afternoon. But then Travis has been there for me several times in the last six months. He's called to check I'm okay. Or if I need anything. Sometimes, he messages to say he is thinking about me. I've found myself thinking about him increasingly and even wondering if something was starting between us. But I never wanted to get my hopes up. At the end of the day, I'm ten years younger than him; would he really be interested in someone like me?

Then there is the fact that I slept with his two brothers only this afternoon. I still can't wrap my head around what happened.

I think I've been hanging around with Jasmine too much because I won't lie and say I haven't thought about being with all three of my stepbrothers, whether separately or together. It's so appealing that I can't say no if Travis wants to take me to bed. I know I probably should, as I have no idea what that was about with the guys earlier, and both said they wanted to do it again. But I don't even know if Travis is aware of what happened. Should I mention it to be sure? I wouldn't want something to happen between us and then for him to find out. Do I expect anything to come from it? No, not at all. I have every intention of just having some fun; that's what I will tell myself anyway.

"So, other than what I saw, did everything go okay tonight? No issues out back?" Travis asks, dragging me back to reality.

"No, it was all good. The girls cornered me and asked if I was okay, but other than that, everything was the same as any other night." I decided not to tell him about all the messages I had on my phone from Marshall asking where I was and why I wasn't answering my phone. He also sent one after he left mine, which didn't start off too pleasant, but I forced myself not to read it, and I'm glad I didn't. I don't think I saw the real him until today, and I have no idea how many times he has cheated on me in the past, and I let him because I was blind to it all. He was right about one thing: I throw myself into dancing. My dad has always said how proud he is of what I have achieved at the school, and he works so hard to ensure I get to stay there. So, I've never missed a lesson, practice or show for fear of disappointing him.

"I bet they had a few things to say about me after my outburst." Travis glances over at me nervously. "I hope you know that's not who I am. It was very out of character for me, and I will never treat you that way, ever."

"Jaz was just looking out for me. She thought you were Marshall, so she didn't want me to go with you. I guess that's my fault for never introducing him to any of my friends." I know he was worried about me, and Jasmine confirmed there is a lot of bad blood between him and Christian, but she wouldn't tell me what she knows. I'm not even sure if she knows the whole story. I have considered asking him what happened, but it's not my business, and unlike Jasmine and Christian, Travis has no reason to tell me the truth.

"I think they were shocked by how you and Christian were together. It's not often they see people stand up to him and get away with it."

"How much do you know about the O'Reilly's?" he asks, glancing at me quickly. I shrug as I look out of my window at the night sky as it flies past us.

"Nothing, really. I know they are the type of men you need to stay on their good side. They used to scare me, especially Christian, as he always comes across as bossy and controlling when speaking to others. Danielle says there are a lot of people who fear the O'Reillys. But whenever he's with Jaz, he's a different person." I turn to look at Travis and smile. "He loves her; they all do. There isn't anything they aren't willing to do for her."

That's what I want. Someone to love and look after me like the O'Reilly's look after Jaz. She's told me what happened when she was taken and how the guys got her back. She also admitted to more than she probably should have, like how she killed her mother. But she needed to talk to someone who wasn't the guys, and I'm here for her no matter what. I may disagree with her killing Carol, but at the end of the day, she was protecting her man, and there is something special about that.

She has also told me how hot the sex is and how they dominate her, which I need! But when she admitted that she doesn't need to worry about anything anymore and that they take care of everything, from her needs to what she wants, I realised I also want that. Okay, I don't think I could handle four daddies. However, I want someone who accepts who I am, takes care of me, and protects me when I need it. Someone who wouldn't want me to be anything but my true self, not the father-pleasing, well-presented, pristine woman I pretend to be. Because that's what it feels like sometimes, that I'm playing a role everyone expects to see. Sometimes I want just to be me. I want someone to let me curl up and mess around with them. I want to know that if I'm feeling vulnerable, they will hold me and show me everything will be fine.

"Christian was in the car when my father crashed."

My attention snaps back to Travis, amazed. He never talks about his dad. I know his death hit the brothers hard as they chose him over their mother when they separated. But no one mentions him.

"Is that why you hate him?"

Travis sighs, not taking his eyes from the road.

"I don't hate him. Not really. I did for a long time, but not anymore." Travis comes to a stop at a stop sign, and I squeeze his hand, which is resting on my lap.

"I knew Christian was with Dad when he crashed, but when the ambulance service and police got there, he was alone in the car. Christian had run, leaving behind a large batch of drugs. The police believed that my father was a drug dealer and had just picked up his supply when he lost control of his car." Travis glances at me as he starts driving again. "They weren't his drugs, they weren't even Christians, they had been to acquaintances, and they had confiscated them trying to help him. But someone told me Christian had been arguing with my dad, who wanted to sell the drugs on at a profit. The last time anyone saw him alive, he was arguing with Christian. So, I believed people when they said Christian had caused the accident. I hated him for leaving Dad to die alone and for the crash."

"Did you ever find out what caused it? Was it Christian?" I ask. Travis shakes his head.

"No, but I think I've known for a while that he wasn't to blame. What Jason just told me confirms it. Christian ran so he wouldn't be caught. Their father was a jackass, and Christian brought the others up from the age of fourteen when their mother died. That's why they all look up to him so much." Travis sighs and rubs his face as he turns onto the road that leads home.

"I know I need to speak to him, and I will for you." Travis surprises me by lifting our hands and kissing my knuckles. "I don't want ever to be a reason you feel you can't spend time with your friend or her guys."

"Yeah, it would make being Jasmine's bridesmaid difficult," I chuckle as a smile appears in the corner of Travis's mouth.

"Yeah, it probably would."

He pulls off the road and onto the driveway, parking in the large garage. When the engine stops, Travis turns in his seat to look at me whilst resting an elbow on the steering wheel.

"I would never hurt you in any way; I hope you know that?"

"I do," I whisper, realising there is some truth in that. I do know he would never upset me on purpose.

I smile as I look deep into his eyes. For a second, I think he's about to lean in to kiss me, and I want him to. But the garage light flicks on, and I blink while looking at the door that leads into the entrance hall.

"Dad!" I scramble from the car and rush to my father.

"Hey, pumpkin," he laughs as I throw myself into his arms. "Surprise."

Chapter Eighteen

TRAVIS

I walk up to Henry as he hugs his daughter.

"Travis." He holds his hand out, and I shake it, trying to be polite.

"Henry," I reply. Neither of us is putting any feeling into it. Do I dislike the guy? Not really. There again, I don't particularly like him either. The state I have seen his daughter in because of his absence does not help that fact. But I keep the peace to ensure she is safe and out of the world he has found himself a part of in the States.

"I can't believe you're back!" Verity clings to her father like she is scared to let him go. If I were her, I would be too because no one knows how long he will stay for this time.

"Well, I had to return at some point, Pumpkin."

So, not actually because you have a daughter you needed to check on. I bite my tongue as I walk into the house to see my mum in the kitchen.

"Travis, you are here," she walks towards me with her arms flung open, like I'm meant to rush to her. Those days have long gone.

"Mother," I reply dryly as I hug her. I look at my two brothers, who both roll their eyes at me.

"You finally decided to come back for a bit," I point out as I step away from her and head towards the alcohol cabinet, suddenly feeling the need for a strong drink.

"Oh, you know how things are. But we are here now," she announces, picking up her wine glass, which is almost empty. "Be a dear and give me a top-up, please?" I'm not sure she really needs another drink, but that's Mother dearest. I swear she spends more time drunk than sober. I rarely see her without a drink of some sort in her hand.

I take a deep breath and go about filling up her glass.

"How was the performance?" Ethan asks as he picks up his whiskey glass. I should have known he would already have one. Ethan has always struggled when around Mum. The two of them have a tense relationship that has worsened with time.

"It was great; you should watch it before it ends," I answer before turning to Mum. "Will you and Henry be going to watch?" I ask, not missing my mother's slight look of disgust before that fake smile spreads across her face.

"Oh, I doubt we will have time for that. Verity will send a recording of it, I'm sure."

"Send? Mother, how long are you staying for?" I ask, putting my glass down on the counter. "You are here for Christmas, aren't you?" I demand.

"Don't worry about that. We will discuss all our plans tomorrow. I want to get some rest tonight and see my boys. Is that too much to ask?" She flashes her signature smile, which is also a sign that we won't get any truth out of her tonight. It's best to play along and try again tomorrow when she is a little more sober.

"No," I reply through gritted teeth. "I guess it's not."

We all sit together in the lounge as Verity speaks to her father at a hundred miles an hour, telling him everything she's been doing. Leaving out the cheating boyfriend, fucking two of her stepbrothers, and getting so drunk she passed out.

Henry sits and watches his daughter, but I don't miss the occasional look he shares with my mother. He isn't listening to her and doesn't care about what she is telling him. I have to bite my tongue to stop myself from saying something to him because I don't think Verity notices. If she does, she is hiding it well. There again, if she has shown anything the last couple of days, she is fantastic at hiding her true feelings. We rarely see how Henry and Verity are together as we don't tend to be around when he's home. If we are, he tends to golf or work from his office. He always seems to be looking for a reason to be anywhere but with his child.

When Verity excuses herself to the toilet, Henry sits back on the sofa and sighs.

"I almost forgot how much that girl can talk."

"Maybe if you spoke to her more, she wouldn't have so much to say on the rare occasions you are home," Ethan mutters from his chair. Loud enough for all in the room to hear.

"You know I can't help being away as much as I am. That doesn't mean I don't talk to my daughter," Henry snaps on the defensive. Ethan is about to say more when I cough and stand up, distracting him. When he frowns at me, I give him a warning look as Verity skips back into the room.

"I'm going to my room to reply to a few emails. I'll see you all in the morning," I announce, walking to my mother and kissing her cheek as she would expect me to. Would she care if there weren't others around? No, she really wouldn't. She probably wouldn't bother with us at all if I didn't do their accounts for free. I know I'm a fool, but it helps me watch over Verity and ensure she has everything she needs.

"Oh, whilst I remember, I need you and Ethan to run an errand in the morning. I already asked Ryan, and he says he is busy with a client online." She rolls her eyes, and I find myself once again biting my tongue. This woman always expects us to drop whatever we're doing to run around after her. She should be our priority; she gave us life, after all. Or so she has told me time and time again over the years.

"Actually, you asked for all three of us to do it, and I said to send them as I'm busy here."

"Why would you need all three of us?" I ask, frowning.

"I need some bits picked up from the storage unit. I figured the three of you would manage it better with it being heavy."

Mum has a lot of stuff in storage, slowly making its way to the States or into this house. She also likes to order things and get them sent there to keep them safe until she can come back and place them in the "right spot" when she is home.

"Fine, give me a list, and we will head off early," I reply as she smiles happily and pulls a piece of paper from her handbag.

"Everything is listed here," she announces as she stands up and forces me to bend slightly so she can place a kiss on my cheek. "You are so good to your Mummy," she grins. I don't even bother to hide my eye roll as she is too drunk to see it anyway. I turn to look at Ethan.

"Be ready for six. I have to be back and getting stuff done by midday."

Ethan doesn't answer. He nods and climbs to his feet.

"Night, Mum," he says, forcing himself to kiss her on the cheek as I did.

"Good night, sweetie. Be careful tomorrow, both of you," she calls as we leave the room. I'm halfway up the stairs, wanting a word with my brother before we part ways, when I hear Verity calling my name. I turn around to see her rushing up the stairs towards me.

"Everything okay, Sweetheart?" I ask quietly. Verity nods at me, smiling.

"I just wanted to say thank you for the last twenty-four hours. You have done a lot for me; you all have," she adds quickly, smiling playfully at Ethan before turning back to me. "Plus, it meant a lot to me you coming to watch tonight. Thank you." She stands on the step above me and kisses my cheek. As I turn my head to look into her beautiful blue eyes, I find myself smiling back.

"I'll always help you any way I can, Sweetheart."

She smiles back before turning around to Ethan and kissing him on the cheek.

"Goodnight," she whispers before rushing down the stairs back into the lounge where her father and our mother are.

"I don't know about you, but I have a funny feeling they are trying to get us out of the way for a reason," Ethan whispers as we turn around and continue the walk to our bedrooms.

"That's exactly what I'm thinking. Which is why I want to be out of here by five so we can get back earlier than they expect us to."

Ethan nods, and we make a plan to be by my car at five AM at the latest. Ethan heads to his room, saying he will message Ryan the plan, and I head into mine and try to work out what the hell they are up to.

Chapter Nineteen

VERITY

I wake up and jump from bed, excited for the first time in weeks, maybe months. All I can think about is getting showered, dressed, and downstairs to see my dad.

I stayed up until midnight, telling him everything he'd missed while away. Sure, some of it was stuff I'd already told him on the phone or in an email, but it's different getting to tell him face-to-face.

I'm guessing that Linda has sent the guys to get Christmas decorations from storage. We have some here, the same ones Mum used to put up yearly, but Linda likes to use her own. Dad says we have to respect that as she may not want to use Mum's things; they don't have the same meaning to her as they do us. So, to make her feel at home and ensure we all have the best Christmas, I will do whatever she wants with the decorations. At least we will all be together, and that's the main thing.

Half an hour later, I rush down the stairs, excited to find Dad and see what he has planned for the day. I also have some great news to share with him.

Last night, when I went to bed, I messaged Jaz and told her he was back. She said that he could use the O'Reilly box any night he wanted to watch our performance. That way, I won't need to send him the usual video; he can watch it himself. I can't wait to tell him; he will be so excited and happy. He said all the tickets were sold out last night, but now he can still come.

I rush out of my room and down the stairs, heading to where I can hear Linda laughing. I can only hear one person's voice, so I'm guessing she's on the phone. I check my watch and see its half past six. Why is she up so early? She isn't usually. Maybe it's the jet lag? Is that a thing when coming from the States? I wouldn't know because they never let me travel.

I skip into the kitchen to find her not only awake but dressed and with her make-up on as well.

"Oh, I know. I can't wait either. It's been so long since we had a big family Christmas," she grins, her phone pressed to her ear, as she turns around and sees me. "I have to go; I'll see you later." She quickly ends the call and smiles at me.

"Sorry, Verity, dear. I didn't see you there. You're up awfully early," she points out, looking up at the clock on the wall.

"I always get up early. Dad says it's important to make the most out of the day. Is he still sleeping?" I ask, looking around.

"No, he's up in our room, dear. Per-"

I don't hear what she says past dear as I'm rushing back up the stairs towards his room.

As I get to the top, I see Ryan stepping onto the landing.

"I need to talk to you."

"Not, now I need to speak to my dad," I call, side-stepping around him and rushing for my dad's room.

"But that's why I need to speak to you, Kitten. I-"

"Not now, Ryan," I call, opening Dad's door and rushing inside. "Dad, you in here?"

"In the wardrobe, Pumpkin."

I almost skip to his large walk-in wardrobe, eager to see him. He is inside, with the suitcase open on the floor, and he places a hanger on one of the rails.

"I'm sure I'm meant to have a bigger wardrobe than you," I laugh as I hug him. I feel his arms wrap around me and, for a moment, savour the feeling. My dad has always given the best cuddles; I miss them when he's not here.

"You know most of this is stuff that Linda insists I have. I don't need half these suits, but she is adamant I don't wear the same one twice to an event."

He chuckles as he rummages through his shirts.

"So, I thought we could do something fun today. We could go to the Christmas market or out for breakfast and then for a walk. What do you say, Dad? Let's spend some time just the two of us."

"That sounds lovely, but I have plans; sorry, Pumpkin. Maybe another time," Dad replies, keeping his back to me as he looks through his shirts.

"Oh, okay, sure. Maybe tomorrow?" I offer, feeling deflated but trying desperately to hide it.

"I was thinking more like the new year if we're back."

My stomach drops as I realise what he means.

"You aren't unpacking, are you?" I ask as he finally turns around, smiling with a shirt in his hand.

"No. We're leaving any minute. We were offered a last-minute chance to spend the holidays with Linda's family in

Hawaii. We wouldn't have flown back a few days ago if we had known."

"A few days? You've been back and not even bothered to come and see me?" I demand. My dad looks at me with his disappointed look, and I instantly feel my stomach drop.

"You know I have to work hard, Pumpkin. Your school costs so much, and this house isn't cheap to run. But you deserve the best, and I work extremely hard to give it to you. Because of that, I've had all kinds of meetings; yesterday was my first chance to come back."

"I've told you I would give up the dancing and the house. That way, you wouldn't have to work away so much. You only just got home, and I haven't seen you in months." My eyes and throat start to burn as I feel the tears starting, which I know will disappoint him further.

He walks up to me and cups my cheek.

"Now, don't cry. I have missed you too. I know it's not ideal, but it's just how things have worked out. I'll make it up to you, I promise." He reaches into his pocket and hands me his handkerchief. "Now dry those eyes. No one wants to see that sad face."

I take the fabric from him and pat it under my eyes, forcing back the tears. He tips my chin up and smiles.

"That's better. Now, why don't we get this suitcase packed and have no more tantrums, okay?"

I nod, not trusting myself to speak, as I force a smile onto my face. "There's my sweet girl."

———

"Darling, have you put everything in the car?" Linda calls as I stand outside of the house, watching my father slam the trunk closed.

"Yes, honey. Everything is just the way you like it," he calls before walking to the front steps where Ryan and I are standing. Ryan has tried to speak to me a few times, but I've ignored him. I can't risk speaking for fear of crying.

"Come here and give your old man a hug, Pumpkin."

I walk to my father and hug him. He squeezes me like he always does, but it doesn't feel the same. I don't think they ever will again, not after this.

"We will be back soon, okay. Then we will take that walk."

"When?" Ryan asks behind me.

"I don't know yet, but we will sort something soon," my father replies sternly. I know that tone; it means don't push it. Dad looks at me and smiles. "Remember, no tears; no one likes it when you cry," he says before kissing my forehead. "See you later, Pumpkin. Have a good Christmas."

"Bye, Dad. You too," I reply as he walks back towards the car, and I wrap my arms around myself. I start to slowly count in my head as I watch him reach the car and wave before jumping behind the wheel. Linda waves happily as they pull away and head out of view.

Ten.

I force my feet to move as I turn around and walk back into the house.

Nine.

"Kitten, listen, okay. I know you are upset and have every right to be."

Eight.

Ryan grabs my arm to stop me from heading to the stairs, but I pull away from him.

Seven.

"Speak to me, little Kitten. Tell me what you need."

Six.

123

"A shower," I reply, not recognising my own voice.

Five.

I walk up the stairs and almost reach my room before he is there beside me.

Four.

"Stop and speak to me. I'm still here. *We* are still here." When I turn my attention to him, I watch him flinch, proving that my father has been right all along.

Three.

"I'm fine," I say as I walk into my room, closing the door in his face.

Two.

"No one likes it when you cry". He has told me that again and again over the years. So, I do everything in my power to stop. Even if that means I have to distract myself with something else.

I strip out of my clothes and turn on the shower, making sure the water is almost too hot to bear.

One.

I lean against the cold tiles as my legs go from underneath me, and my body shudders as the first sob leaves my chest.

"No one likes it when you cry," so I never cry in front of anyone. I keep it all locked inside until something like this happens. Then, I do whatever I can to distract myself from the internal pain.

I crumble to the floor and bring my knees up to my chest as the first silent scream bursts from my chest. I see my wash bag in the corner beside me. My razor is right there on the top. I run a finger over my hip and feel the bumps of the scars. I look at the razor again through the tears I can't let fall and grab it. I just want this pain to go away; if something else hurts, then it gives me something different to focus on, something that isn't the abandonment of the father I love more than anyone else in this world.

Chapter Twenty

RYAN

Shit.

I'm pacing outside her room and trying to decide if I should barge in and check on her or leave her alone. I wish Travis were here; he would know what to do.

I pull my phone out of my pocket and ring him, but it goes straight to voicemail. When I try Ethans, it's the same.

Fuck.

Mum knew what she was doing when she sent them there this morning. There's never any signal in that bloody storage unit or the surrounding area. I check the time and realise they left a little over three hours ago. Thankfully, they managed to sneak out at four, as none of us could sleep. We knew Mum and Henry were hiding something; I just never guessed it would be Henry abandoning his daughter again.

Poor Verity has been so happy to have her dad home. The change in her last night was unmissable; it's just a shame Henry has no respect for his daughter or even truly cares about her. Well, if that's the case, I have no issue with looking out for her from now on. I'm going to come clean to the guys and tell them I'm starting a relationship with her. If they want to share her, I'm happy to do that, but it's us and no one else.

I'm not a fool; I know they care for her just as much as I do. Until yesterday with Ethan, I would have never even considered sharing her with anyone. But there was something about the way the three of us came together. It felt so natural and so right. I couldn't help but wonder how it would be if Travis were to join in, too, not just as a four-way but in a relationship overall.

I stop in my tracks and hear a sound coming from her room. Is she crying in there?

Fuck this.

I charge in, not even bothering to knock.

"Little Kitten," I call out, but all I can hear is the sound of the shower in the bathroom. I know I shouldn't go in there, but when I hear a noise, and I'm unsure if she's crying, I throw caution to the wind and rush into the closed room.

At first, I can't see through the thick steam. It's fogging up the mirrors and filling the space. I turn to where I know the shower is, and that's when I see her leaning against the wall, with her head resting on her knees.

I walk into the shower, not caring about my clothes getting wet, as I can't leave her alone any longer. I sit next to her and pull her into my arms. At first, she fights me but then just stays stiff, as if she's too scared to accept any comfort.

"I'm here, little Kitten. I'm right here. If you want to cry, you cry. I'm staying right here until you are ready to talk."

Verity looks up at me with the saddest eyes, which breaks my heart in two.

"Why am I not enough for him?" She goes back to looking down at the floor as if unable to let anyone see the pain she's in.

My jaw clenches with anger at the man who has the nerve to call himself her father. No man should ever make their child feel this way. They should bend over backwards to prove that they are worth everything in the world and that there is nothing they wouldn't do for them. Not chastise them for showing any form of emotions. I heard what he said about no one wants to see her cry. Well, fuck him! I will watch her cry for as long as she needs if it means she can start to heal.

I don't know how long I hold her or how long she leans against me silently, but as we sit in that shower, I know her heart is breaking silently. I hear my phone ringing from the bedroom, where I threw it to the side when I rushed in. It will be my brothers, and they will be furious at me for not answering. But tough shit. Verity needs me more than anyone else right now.

She moves slightly in my arms, and I hear something hitting the shower floor. I look down, expecting to see a ring or bracelet that's come loose. But instead, I see a blade from a razor. I jump back from her and grab her hands, frantically searching her wrists, but there is nothing on them.

"What were you going to do with that?" I ask as she stares at the blade on the floor and doesn't say a word. "I don't care how bad things get; you never, *ever*, do something like that. Do you hear me, Verity?" I demand, grabbing her face and making sure she can see how serious I am. "I know you are hurting, and it feels like nothing will ever get better, but it will. I'm going to make sure of it. Things are going to change around here. But you have to promise me you will never consider a way out again. Promise me, Verity."

"I wasn't going to kill myself," she whispers as her whole body starts to shake, and I see her placing a hand on her thigh. I pull her hand away to see blood on it. I had been so worried about her and holding her I hadn't even noticed she was bleeding. I place one arm under her legs and another around her back.

"Put your arms around my neck."

She does as she's told, and I lift her from the floor before placing her on the closed toilet. Grabbing a towel from the side where they are kept, I place it on her right thigh and see there is only a small amount of blood on it. When I look at the cut, it's only tiny, but there are a few of them. They look like scratches, but I have a feeling it's not the first time she has done this. Now I'm paying attention; I can see lots of small scars all over her hip and thigh. They are easy to miss if you don't know they are there. But once you see one, you see them all.

"How long have you been doing this?" I ask softly as I look into her sad eyes. She doesn't say anything; instead, she looks away as her face loses all emotion. It's like she's switched off, and nothing will get through to her. I stand back up and press a kiss to her head as I do. Wrapping the towel around her, I lift her back in my arms. I will give her short, quick instructions and plan on getting her into bed where I can keep an eye on her.

Back in her room, I help her into a clean pair of pyjamas and brush her long blonde hair before helping her into bed. She instantly rolls to the side, facing away from me. Running a hand over her head, I sit on the edge of the bed to watch over her and ensure she doesn't do anything else to cause herself harm.

"Whenever you are ready to talk, I am here. I'm not going anywhere, I promise."

Verity doesn't show any sign of hearing me, but I keep one hand on her side as I unlock my phone with the other and message my brothers.

Ryan: You need to get back here now! They left, and Verity's broken. I found her self-harming.

Chapter Twenty-One

TRAVIS

"Why the fuck isn't he answering?" Ethan yells beside me as I zig-zag through the traffic.

My fucking phone has been out of signal most of the morning, so we are only now receiving Ryan's messages.

"He's probably focusing on Verity." I find a gap in the traffic and put my foot down.

"I can't believe they've left already!" Ethan growls as my jaw clenches further. They call themselves parents. Well, I'm fucking done with them both. I'm taking Verity away from there and ensuring no one ever hurts her again. My sweet girl does not deserve this. I've been on the fencepost about whether I should act on my feelings or not; well, now I am. This has been the final straw, and I'll do all I can to ensure my girl is safe and knows she is loved.

What Jason said last night about me being her protector keeps going through my mind. I'm not there protecting her now, and I've failed her before we've even begun. Well, I'm never failing her again.

"I can," I snap through gritted teeth. "They knew we

would try to stop them or give them a hard time, which is why we were sent on this stupid errand.

"Verity is a pushover when it comes to her father, and he knows it. He has moulded her that way. He has brought her up to be the perfect little girl who never says no and wants to please him. She'll do anything he says to get his praise and attention." I glance at my brother, whose face is red with rage. "Why do you think they never told us they were back last week?" I ask, looking back at the road.

"They've been back a week!"

I nod as I take the turning that leads us back to the house.

"Yep, I did some digging last night and noticed Mum's been making payments on her card in the UK. I was going to confront her this afternoon for confirmation before telling you all." I turn onto the last road to the house before continuing. "I want to know why they think it acceptable to be in the country and not even tell their children. I don't give a shit, but Verity would have wanted to see Henry, and they know it."

"Fucking arsehole," he hisses through his teeth. I nod as the house finally comes into view, and my heart races to get there. I'm terrified of what I'm going to find. But whatever it is, we will all face it together and give Verity all the love and support she needs.

Screeching to a stop in front of the house. Ethan jumps out before I've even turned the engine off. By the time I'm out, he has the front door open.

We rush for the stairs, taking them three at a time, knowing they will be in her room.

"No matter what, keep your cool," I warn quietly as we reach her door.

Ethan nods once as we enter the room.

Sitting on the bed, Ryan is next to Verity, who's curled up in the fetal position with her back to him. Ryan places a finger over his lips and stands. When he approaches, I expect him to say she is sleeping.

"Ethan, can you sit with her? She won't talk or move; she's shut right down," he whispers.

"What the fuck happened?" Ethan demands in a harsh whisper.

"I'll tell you everything; just sit with her while I talk to Trav. I've promised we won't leave her for a moment, so I can only talk to one of you at a time."

Ethan looks between the two of us, and for a moment, I think he's going to argue, but then he looks back to Verity, and his face softens as he nods. He walks over and sits on the bed, placing a hand on Verity's leg. She doesn't so much as flinch.

"Hey, Baby girl, how you doing?" he whispers, looking around her, but she doesn't move or reply. I can't see her face, but imagine she's just staring at a wall.

Ryan looks at me and nods towards the hallway. I follow him out and quietly close the door behind us.

"Let's go to your room," he whispers, but I shake my head when I point at his clothes.

"You need to change."

Ryan looks down as if realising his clothes are soaked for the first time. I hear him curse under his breath before nodding and heading to his room.

As soon as we enter, he closes the door behind us and rubs his face.

"Fuck Trav, I have no idea how the hell we're going to pull her out of this one. She's beyond broken," he sighs quietly, rubbing at his face.

"Tell me what happened whilst you get changed, and we will work something out."

Ryan looks up, nods once and pulls his wet t-shirt off.

"As soon as you left, I went for a run, wanting to get it over with before anyone else got up. But when I returned just over an hour later, I could hear Mum and Henry talking in their room as the door was open.

"They were whispering about whether they could get away before Verity was awake. I didn't know what to do. I tried to call you, but your phone was off. Mum caught me on the landing, and I tried to speak to her, but she kept saying she wasn't talking to me until I had showered as I was sweaty. You know what she's like, so I rushed and had the quickest shower." Ryan walks over to his wardrobe, pulls out some clean jeans and a fresh t-shirt, and proceeds to get changed.

"By the time I came out of my room, it was half six, and I found Verity rushing up the stairs towards her father's room. I tried to warn her, but she wouldn't listen; she was so excited about seeing him, nothing else mattered." Ryan stops talking while he pulls his new dry t-shirt over his head. When he turns his attention back to me, he looks like he doesn't know whether to be angry or sad.

"Travis, the change in her when she came out of that room was unreal. She walked in there with a spring in her step and more energy than I have seen from her in months. But when she walked out behind her father, her head was down as she followed him like a well-trained lapdog. There wasn't any sign of the Verity who went in there." Ryan rubs his face briefly, and I see he's fighting his anger.

"From them coming out of the room to Mum and him leaving, it must have been five minutes tops. They really couldn't get away quick enough. I tried to speak to her to see how she was, but Henry kept her attention purely on him. Every time she looked like she was close to tears, he would whisper something to her, and she would blink them back and show that fake as fuck smile. I wanted to kill him there and then, but I also wanted to stay focused on Verity, as I knew she would need me when they finally left."

"Do you have any idea what he was saying to her?" I ask as Ryan nods.

"He wasn't so quiet the last time as he was near his car. He told her not to cry because no one wanted to see that. I think once I heard him say something like, "Stop with the tantrum." Ryan looks up at me with his jaw clenched. "She couldn't have been further from a tantrum if she tried. She should have been throwing one. I wanted to throw one for her, but she just nodded and kept her head bowed and hands clasped in front of her."

"So, what happened when they left?"

Ryan proceeded to tell me how Verity had shut down and wouldn't even look at him. When he tells me about pacing outside the door, I try to put his mind at ease by confirming I would have done the same thing. There was no win in that situation; Verity had every right to privacy as she cried; she probably did need the space, as any normal person would. When your heart is broken, the last thing you want is people fussing around you.

"When I heard that sound from her room, I couldn't hold back anymore, and I went in." Ryan sits on the edge of his bed and places his head in his hands.

"She was beyond broken, Trav. She was sitting on the shower floor, the water pouring down on her; it was so hot that the steam was making it hard to see. The water must have been burning her. I sat out of the initial spray and still felt the heat in the steam. She didn't want to be held at first, but she quickly seemed to change her mind as she melted in my arms and shut herself down." Ryan sits in silence for a moment, and I let him. As much as I want to get back to Verity and hold her, he needs a moment to compose himself, and I need to know more to help her.

When Ryan looks up at me, there is no hiding his pain.

"I was so busy holding her that I missed the signs of the cutting. I failed her so badly. I should have noticed something." He places his head back in his hands, and a groan leaves him.

I walk over and place a hand on his shoulder as they shake. I've only ever seen him like this once before; he's struggling with the anger he feels not only for Verity's father and our own Mother. But he's also struggling with the anger he feels at missing how much she was hurting. He's blaming himself for her pain.

"You didn't fail her. You were there and occupied by ensuring she knew she wasn't alone. You were doing the right thing," I point out, hoping to reassure him.

"It doesn't feel like it," he replies before looking back at me. "I didn't notice anything was amiss until I heard the blade hit the tile floor. I thought she had been about to kill herself, Trav. I thought she had been pushed to the point of no return. It never even dawned on me that she was self-harming, not until she told me and I saw the blood on her hip."

She knew what she was doing. She's a dancer; her legs and arms are on display for people to see all the time. But her hips are usually covered by her leotard or skirt. No one would know unless they were looking for signs.

"How bad was it?" I ask.

"Not as bad as it could have been. That's when I carried her out of the shower and checked her over. It wasn't the first time. Once I knew what to look for, I saw all the tiny little scars. They are all small cuts, easy to miss. She has cut open a few more than once, so they stand out slightly more than the others, but not enough to catch your attention." Ryan runs his hand through his hair and sighs. "I asked her how long it had been going on, but that was when she shut down. She hasn't spoken since in the shower and won't respond to touch. She let me get her dried and changed, but as soon as she was on that bed, she turned away from me and hasn't moved, spoken or anything. It's like she has entered a state of shock."

"That's exactly what she's done. It's all become too much, and she's shut down to protect herself." I rub my face and try to work out what to do next. I know what I want to do, but I'm not sure if it's the right thing to do or not. I need advice, and the only person I can think to give it to me is the one person I swore I would never look to again.

"Compose yourself, then return to the room and sit with her and Ethan. I need to make a call." I turn around and walk out of the room, pulling my phone out of my pocket, praying I haven't deleted their number. When I find it in my contacts, I let out a sigh of relief.

Walking into my room and closing the door for some privacy, I realise this may be the hardest call I've ever had to make.

I stare at the screen for a few seconds, reminding myself I'm doing this for her before connecting the call. He answers in three rings.

"O'Reilly."

"It's me."

From the harsh laugh I hear, the smug bastard knows who I am.

"What have I done to deserve the displeasure of you calling?"

"I need your help," I answer, pacing around the room. Christian laughs again.

"Give me one reason why I should help you?"

"Because I'm trying to save Verity."

Christian instantly stops laughing and is silent for a moment.

"What's happened?" his tone's changed, and I know deep down I made the right decision calling him. I quickly fill him in, leaving out the self-harming as I know she wouldn't want Jasmine to know, and I don't particularly trust him enough to tell him anyway. When I finish, there is a silence before he speaks.

"What do you want me to do for her?"

I don't miss how he says, *for her*; he isn't doing it for me, and that's fine. She is the reason I'm even speaking to him right now.

"I know Jason will have told you we spoke last night, and what about. Verity needs a daddy, and I'm worried I'll fuck it up. Jason said you're Jasmine's protector, her provider, which is the role I think I am to Verity, too. But I don't want to make things any worse than they already are."

"What does your gut tell you to do?" Christian asks. I rub my face as I look to the door, knowing hers is on the other side of the hallway mine. I visualise her lying there on the bed, her back to me as she shuts down all emotions.

"I want to walk in there, pull her onto my lap and hold her, even if she fights me. All to prove to her I'm not going anywhere, no matter how hard she tries to push me away. I want to swear to her I will help her put herself back together and find out who she really is. No matter what, I'm here for the rest of my life." I look at the chair and see a gift I picked up for her yesterday. "All while giving her a fucking ballerina doll I planned to give her for Christmas," I almost laugh at the idea.

"Sounds to me like you are already thinking like her daddy."

"I think you're right." I have always been protective of her, even before she was spiked. All I ever wanted was to keep her safe, even if that meant stepping back and hiding how I felt. She has always been my main priority.

"At least we can agree on something. That is exactly what she needs. But you need to ask yourself, are you in it for the long run? Are you going to stick by her forever? What about your brothers? Are they in it for the long run? Or is it just appealing to them at the moment? Verity has been through enough and needs nothing major to change for a while."

"I know; I will speak to them. But I'm in this forever. I'm done pretending I don't care."

"Then you know what you need to do, and it sounds like you didn't need me at all."

I guess he's right; I didn't.

"How do I contact the school to let them know she won't be there tonight?"

"I'll sort that for her. Jasmine will back up that she is ill and will call when she's recovered. We will say she has a migraine for now."

"Thank you, Christian."

"I hope Verity starts to feel a little more like herself soon."

"So do I," I reply as I take a deep breath and end the call.

I look at the door momentarily before grabbing the rag doll and charging to her room.

When I walk in, I find Ethan still sitting on the bed, his hand on her hip as she looks at the wall. Ryan is sitting on a chair, leaning forward and just watching her. Both look so lost and obviously have no idea what to do. I look at Ethan and signal for him to move. He stands up and heads beside Ryan as I sit on the bed.

"Sweetheart, I need you to talk to me and tell me what's going on in that head of yours," I whisper as I place a hand on her hip. I look over her to see if she's asleep. She isn't. All she's doing is staring at the wall, and I know if I don't do what my gut tells me to do, she will never recover. I place the doll on the other side of her and, in one move, pull her onto my lap so she rests against my chest. As expected, she instantly tries to move away and fights against me, but I tighten my hold.

"You have been told you can't cry, you can't show emotion, and you can't throw a tantrum. They were wrong," I tell her as she fights to escape me.

"Let me go!" she begs as she tries to push me away.

"You can scream, cry, punch me and do whatever you need, but I'm not letting you go. Not now, not ever."

"Let. Me. Go!" she shouts louder, but I tighten my hold.

"Travis, let her go!" I hear Ethan shout, followed by Ryan telling him to shut up.

"Trust him," I hear him telling Ethan, who steps back a little.

"I'm never letting you go. You can scream, cry and shout, which will never change what you mean to me."

"Liar!" Verity yells, still fighting to get out of my arms. "You will leave. Everyone leaves."

"Well, not me, not anymore. I'm here and if I leave, you are coming with me. Understand?" I declare over her, thrashing in my arms. She punches my chest, and for a moment, I see a flicker of shock on her face. "Throw the tantrum you want to throw. Scream, cry and use me as your punch bag. I will take it all to prove to you I'm staying." She starts lashing out, but this time screaming. But I take it all. It hurts like a bitch, but not once do I even consider letting her go. I will take it all for her. I will be her punch bag when she can't punch who really deserves it. I will be her sounding board when she can't shout at the person who's upset her. I will be all that and more because she is everything to me.

"I hate you!"

Those three words would kill me if I thought for a moment she meant them, but I know she doesn't.

"Who do you hate, Sweetheart?" I ask, trying to provoke what she needs to shout.

"You!" she yells in my face as she stares at me with a hatred I never thought would be possible from her sweet blue eyes. "I hate you!" she punches my chest again, but this time, there's a small sob that escapes her.

"You don't hate me," I tell her softly.

"I do!" she cries as she punches my chest again. "I hate you! I hate you! I hate you!"

"You can scream it louder than that," I tell her, noticing that each time she tells me she is getting closer to that break in her defences that she needs.

"I hate you!" She screams louder right in my face.

"Louder," I tell her.

"I hate you!" she screams louder again.

"Louder!" I yell this time.

"I. Hate. You!" she screams at the top of her lungs. Her whole body goes ridged as she starts screaming and can't seem to stop. All those years of hiding her feelings and bottling them up because of her arsehole of a father come pouring out of her, and I barely manage to hold on to her as she continues to scream.

My eyes fill with tears as I see how much I have let her down. This woman has been in our lives for five years, but I never saw how much pain she was in. I never realised how unloved she felt. Well, never again, that I can swear on her life as I will never let her feel pain like this again.

"Let it all out, Sweetheart. I've got you," I whisper as she gasps for breath.

"I hate you," she whispers, her throat harsh from screaming.

"It's not me you hate, Sweetheart."

"I hate you," she whispers and as her voice finally breaks and I see that first tear fall, I know we are finally getting through to the pain.

"Who do you hate?" I ask quietly, looking into her red, tear-filled eyes.

"Him." That's all she manages to gasp before her whole body starts to shake, and she breaks down in my arms.

"I know, Sweetheart. Let it all out. Cry as much as you need to. I've got you; I'm right here. I promise I have you," I whisper into her hair as she grips my shirt, burying her face into my chest as she screams, cries and shakes. I hold her as tight as I dare, whispering words of encouragement, telling her that it's okay to cry, to have feelings and throw tantrums. I'm here no matter what. I turn my head to see Ethan and Ryan standing beside me, looking heartbroken as they watch the girl we care so much about falling apart.

"Go fill him in. He needs to understand," I whisper over

Verity's sobs. Ryan nods and tells Ethan to follow him. I know what I just did will seem extreme to him, and I hope that he will understand after hearing what Henry said to her.

As the door closes, I feel Verity stiffen in my arms.

"They aren't leaving; they're just going to give us some space," I whisper into her hair. She is no longer screaming; it's just a continuous quiet sob.

"I'm sorry I wasn't here. If I had known, I wouldn't have gone. I'm here now, and I am never leaving you again. Do you understand that, Sweetheart? I'm never leaving."

"You all leave eventually," she whispers into my shirt as she continues to cling to it.

"Not anymore. Now I know what you need; I'm going to make sure you have it." I reposition her slightly so I can look into her bloodshot, swollen eyes.

"You want and need someone to look after you, to be here for you on your good and bad days. You want to feel loved and protected, and I'm here for all of that."

Verity goes to look away, and I know she doesn't believe me, so I gently cup her face with my hands, forcing her head in my direction.

"Look at me. You want all of that, and I am here for it. If you want a Daddy to love you, then you have me. I will give you all those things because I love you. I have for a while and thought I was doing the right thing by hiding that. Well, I'm done with that bullshit. I am yours as much as you are mine. If you want the guys as well, that's fine, but you will only have us, no one else. Do you understand what I'm saying?"

Verity nods slowly, and I pull her into my chest.

"Good. Now, this is what's going to happen. You are going to take all the time you need. If you want to scream, cry, or continue to punch me, you do whatever you need to. I never want to hear or see you hiding your feelings again. You need to let off some steam; see me, and I will take it all. Don't listen to the bullshit that no one wants to see you cry. If you want to cry, then cry, understand?"

Verity nods against my chest as I kiss the top of her head.

"Glad we are on the same page. After you have taken all the time you need, the four of us are going to sit down and have a long chat. Things are going to change around here, and we all need to be in agreement." I run a hand up and down her back as I continue to shower her in affection when she needs it the most. "You aren't dancing tonight. I've already organised for the school to know, and they know you may not be there tomorrow night either. If things change, we will call them then, okay?"

Again, she nods into my chest. I press a kiss on her hair again before reaching over and picking up the doll. It's a blonde-haired rag doll in a pink tutu with pink ballet shoes. As soon as I saw it in the shop window, I had to get it for her. It was just a small present I hoped would make her smile.

"Lastly, this is for you. I saw it yesterday and wanted to give it to you for Christmas. But I think you need her now rather than later. So, from now on, if I see you with this doll, I'll know you need me, and I will drop everything to be there for whatever you need." I place a hooked finger under her chin and force her to look at me. "I know you have been told to hide your feelings, and it will take time to admit you need something. So, we'll use this doll as an unspoken signal for the time being. I don't want to ever see you hiding your feelings around me; I don't care what you need, you tell me. Okay?"

Verity nods as she takes the doll and hugs it against her chest.

"Thank you," she whispers into it as her eyes find mine. I kiss her forehead and hold her as she holds the doll.

"I really would do anything for you, Sweetheart. I don't care how long it takes for you to see that, as I'm never leaving your side again."

Chapter Twenty-Two

VERITY

I wake up alone on the bed, still clinging to the doll Travis gave me.

I don't remember much of what happened, from Dad leaving to Travis pulling me into his arms. I don't think I want to remember, either. My dad broke my heart in a way I never thought he would, and I don't think anything will repair it this time. Not when it comes to our relationship, anyway.

I roll onto my other side and look around, expecting to see someone sitting in the chair or standing close by, but the room's empty. Panic starts to build as I realise I'm completely alone. He promised he wouldn't leave, but he's left.

I cling to the doll and try to take a calming breath, but I can't. I've been torn open today, and I'm emotionally and physically drained. All the barriers I've built around myself over the years came crashing down all at once today, and I don't know how to put them back up.

"You can't tell me what to do when it comes to her. You're not the only one who gives a shit!"

I sit up and hear Ethan's raised voice outside my room.

"That's not what Travis is saying," Ryan sighs. "Think about it. If you have any doubts about whether you want a relationship with Verity, now is not the time to start it. Trav and I know what we want, and he's checking you do, too."

"This isn't me taking charge or anything like that before you start. But when she wakes, I want to be sure we are all on the same page. She has been abandoned enough. I don't want her to ever feel like this again," Travis adds.

"You think I don't know that? Do you think this is just a game for me? Well, it's not. She's my girl as much as she's yours," Ethan snaps. I sit back on the bed and rest against the headboard, holding the doll tightly against my chest with my knees up. Do all three really want to be there for me? I know that's what they are implying, but is it what they want? Or is this all because they feel sorry for me?

"That's all I needed to hear," Travis sighs before mumbling something I can't make out.

"Go sort yourself out; I'll sit with her for a bit. She'll wake up soon anyway; it's been over an hour since she fell asleep," Ethan says as I hear the door opening and Travis mumbles he'll be right back.

"Go get yourself a coffee, and me one whilst you're there," Ethan says a little louder as he's now in the room. I hear the door closing before he walks into view.

"Oh, look who's awake," he smiles, walking over to the bed and sitting on the edge. "How you doing?" he asks, gently squeezing my knee.

"I don't know," I admit. I feel so confused, hurt, tired, angry, and completely numb at the same time.

147

"That's to be expected, Baby girl. You've been through a lot today."

I nod, resting my chin on my doll. It feels right to cling to it. I might be twenty-one, but a part of me feels like the six-year-old who their father abandoned for the first time. It's never gotten easier, but this time hurts the most.

Ethan moves until he is sitting beside me at the top of the bed. I scoot over to give him some room and lean into him as he places an arm around my shoulders.

"I know you have been through hell and probably don't believe me. But It's not only Travis who's here for you. We all are, and we aren't going anywhere."

I let out a deep sigh as I smell the top of the doll. I want to believe him, but it's hard to believe anything anyone says right now. I don't know if I even trust my own mind right now. I haven't been able to trust anyone fully for a very long time, and I know that isn't going to change any time soon.

I hear the door open, followed by Travis and Ryan's hushed voices. Ethan and I look up as they both come into view.

"Hey, sleeping beauty, how you feeling?" Ryan asks, walking over and handing Ethan a mug. Travis approaches and holds out my favourite mug.

"I made you one for when you woke up. Do you want it now or in a bit?" he asks gently. I hold out my hands as I leave the doll resting against my chest. Travis hands the mug over, and I take a small sip, instantly regretting it as it feels like I'm swallowing a million tiny shards of glass. I start to cough, and Ethan quickly takes it from me.

"Here, let it cool a bit," he says, placing it on the small cabinet beside the bed. Ryan sits by my feet as I bury my face into my doll. I can feel all three of them watching me, waiting for me to break again.

"I'm sorry," I start, but Ethan and Ryan instantly start talking simultaneously, telling me to stop.

"Guys, chill it," Travis says quietly. Looking up, I see both look from him to me and apologise, precisely what they told me off for doing.

"Sweetheart, you have nothing to apologise for. Like I said to you at the time, never hide your feelings from us. We can't help you if you do."

"There's a lot we need to talk about, and I think there is even more we don't know when it comes to what's been going on around here. But we don't need to do that immediately; everything moves at your pace," Ethan says next to me as Ryan and Travis nod.

"I don't even know where to begin," I croak. My throat's so sore after screaming at Travis.

"How about we start with, are you hungry? Thirsty? Tired?" Ryan asks as he places a hand on my knee.

"Thirsty," I admit.

"Then let me go and get you some water. Then you can decide if you want all of us with you or just one."

"I want all of you," I say quickly, scared that if I pick one, the others will think I don't care about them and leave.

"Then how about I make you a sandwich whilst you get comfortable with this pair? We can put on a film or a TV show, and you can have a bite to eat and relax. We don't have to rush the chat or anything else," Travis offers. I nod as even though I'm not hungry, I am thirsty, and I like the sound of relaxing a little. "Good girl," Travis whispers as he leans over and kisses my hair. "I'll be right back," he adds before placing his mug on the side and heading out of the room.

"I could eat a sandwich if you are making one!" Ryan calls after him.

"Me too!" Ethan adds, both grinning at each other.

"I'm her daddy, not yours. Get your own fucking sandwich!" I hear Travis call as the others groan dramatically, and I feel one side of my lips lift slightly.

"Well, that's just rude," Ryan sighs as he moves to the other side of me and reaches into the cabinet for the remote. "What do you fancy watching, little Kitten? What's that vampire show you like so much?"

I shake my head as that's the last thing I want to watch right now. Ryan hums deep in his throat as he opens Netflix and flicks through my recently watched.

"Oh, *Gilmore Girls*, that's always fun!" Ethan calls out. Ryan and I both turn to look at him, frowning. "What? Lorelai is a hoot!"

"Idiot," Ryan mutters as he goes back to flicking through the programmes. "Oh *Friends*! That never fails to cheer anyone up!" he announces, looking at us. I nod, still holding my doll as I lean against Ethan, who tightens his arm around my shoulders and kisses my head.

"*Friends*, it is then," Ryan exclaims happily before starting the episode it's currently on and sitting back next to me. He holds my hand as the programme begins, and I try to concentrate on the screen, not all the dark thoughts racing around in my mind.

Chapter Twenty-Three

VERITY

I don't know how long I sit sandwiched between Ethan and Ryan, watching episode after episode of *Friends*.

Travis brought me a ham salad sandwich, but I only managed a quarter of it. My stomach was still too knotted up to digest food, and I found myself choking on it after two bites. Travis removed the plate and covered it, telling me to try again later. I've never been very good at eating when I'm in a low mood. Let's face it: my mood couldn't get any lower right now.

I try to watch the programme and laugh at the jokes that have Ethan and Ryan laughing out loud, but I can't. So many questions are running through my mind that nothing else is getting through.

The guys take turns showing affection and trying to distract me from sinking into another breakdown. I know they are trying their best, but I'm struggling to find the words to express my feelings because I don't understand them myself.

"Sweetheart?"

I realise I'd been burying my face into the doll Travis gave me, and I look up to see him sitting in the chair, his feet up on the bed. I can see the concern on his face and that he knows how much I'm struggling.

I don't stop to think. I climb off the bed and curl up on his lap. He instantly wraps his arms around me, caging me against him as I rest my head on his chest.

"Tell me what you need," he whispers into my hair as the smell of his aftershave invades my senses and calms me. It's not much, but it's enough to help me focus on the bigger question.

"What did I do wrong?"

Travis's arms tighten further as he holds me together.

"I can't even begin to understand what's going on in his head, Sweetheart. But I do know that you've done nothing wrong. Sometimes people lose sight of what they have in front of them because they are chasing bigger things." Travis runs a hand over my head as he sighs deeply. "All I can promise you is that we aren't going anywhere. We are all here for you, for whatever you need." Travis moves slightly so he can look me in the eye. "I know being your daddy isn't the same as your real father, but I will always put you first; nothing is more important to me than you."

"You say that now. But that will change," I whisper as I go to climb off his lap, but he stops me.

"Then, as your daddy, it's my job to prove you wrong. I'm here for you, and I'm not leaving. I will gain your trust, Sweetheart, as will Ryan and Ethan. We will make this work together and give you everything you need."

I lean into him and feel a tiny part of me take comfort from how he holds me.

"I don't know how to process everything; it's all so confusing," I admit.

"I can imagine. You have been dealt a lot of blows the last few days. Some have caused more upset than others, which is understandable. If you had to pick one emotion you are feeling right now, what would it be?" Travis asks. I take a deep breath and find it easier to answer than I thought.

"Angry." I look up at him before looking at the others. "Did you know they had been in the country for nearly a week?" Ethan and Ryan shake their heads, but I don't miss how they look at Travis.

"I found out this morning." I hear Travis say. I turn my attention to him as my anger builds. "I do their accounts, and I did a little digging before we left as something she said was playing on my mind. I saw they had made a few trans-actions in London. I didn't know anything for sure, as there could have been a simple explanation like they went to get Christmas presents or something. I planned to speak to them about it when we got back." He looks deep into my eyes as I feel the anger towards him subside. "Until this morning, I had no idea; otherwise, I would have called them out on it sooner. I promise I wouldn't hide that from you."

I lean back into him, believing him. He had no reason to hide the truth from me. Why wouldn't Dad tell me he was back? Even if he weren't here, I would know that he was in the country at least. Then something Danielle said the other day comes to mind, and I feel my eyes burning with tears again.

"Do you know where they spent last Christmas?"

"They were here with you," Ethan answers. I shake my head and look at the bed.

"They said they were stuck in the states."

"Sweetheart, we offered to come last Christmas, and they said no. That they were spending it with you, and then they would come and see us before flying back. They turned up the day after boxing day for a few hours before flying to the States."

I shake my head as the tears start again; there's no denying it anymore. He never wanted to spend time with me, not even during the holidays. I can feel myself shaking and know Travis realises as his arms tighten around me again.

"Let it out, Sweetheart. I've got you."

"He went to a friend's Christmas Eve party but didn't even come to see his daughter! They came to see you all but not me! Why?" I cry into his chest.

"Baby, I wish we had the answers, but we don't. Only Henry knows why he does what he does. I'm so sorry." I feel a hand touch my back as Ethan's scent gets closer, and he kisses my head.

"If we had known the truth, we would have been here," Ryan says. I want to believe them, but how can I?

"How am I meant to believe anything anyone says when my own father has lied time and time again?"

"You can't, which is why we are going to show you all the reasons you can trust us. We promise never to lie to you," Ethan whispers beside us. I turn my head away from Travis's chest and see Ethan sitting on the edge of the bed, looking at me.

"We will do all we can to give you whatever you need. You have to learn to trust us and always be honest about how you're feeling."

"Why?" I ask, looking around at all three of them. "Why do you suddenly care so much about how I'm feeling and what's going on? You never cared before."

I see Ryan sigh at the same time as I feel Travis doing the same whilst holding me.

"Travis and I have known about each other's feelings for you for a long time. We had no idea that Ethan felt anything until recently. We all thought you were happy and had everything you needed. You've been putting on such a great show, masking your pain. If any of us had known the truth, we would have gotten to this point quicker and hopefully prevented a lot of what you have been through." Ryan moves to sit closer to Ethan and takes my hand between his.

"None of us would have ever let you suffer to the point you felt self-harming was the only way to survive."

I look away, ashamed that they know about that. No one has ever even suspected. I've always been so careful with concealing the cuts and scars.

"When did it start?" he asks, reassuringly squeezing my hand.

"A couple of years ago." I look up to see all three guys watching me. "I was having a hard time with some things, and nothing I did helped. I cut myself shaving, and the pain took away everything else for the shortest time, but it was enough to make me think. It soon became a coping mechanism." There's no point lying; Ryan caught me and has seen for himself.

"I need to ask, Sweetheart. Have you ever thought about doing something more than just self-harming?" Travis asks. The lie is on the tip of my tongue, but when I look up into his eyes, the truth spills from my lips instead.

"Yes."

All three guys gasp as I bury my face into Travis's chest, pulling my hand from Ryan's, ashamed of my confession. My father believes showing emotions or admitting to having them was a sign of weakness. If it were up to me, Ryan wouldn't have witnessed what he did before, and I would still be hiding all of this from them and everyone else in my life. But he did catch me, and he saw what I had done. There is no hiding it anymore if I could have ever truly hidden it all from them anyway.

Yes, I have had suicidal thoughts a few times. I have held that razor in my hand and thought about who would miss me if I was no longer here. But each time, I managed to talk myself out of it, even if for a little while.

"Please speak to us if you ever feel that way again. Please don't ever think you won't be missed or that we wouldn't want to know because we do. We would never cope with losing you, Sweetheart," Travis whispers into my hair.

"Is it all related to things happening with Henry?" Ethan asks. I shake my head and go back to leaning against Travis rather than using him to hide.

"Then, is there something we can change to help?"

"That depends on what kind of thing this is between us," I admit. Telling them about everything seems like the right thing to do. At least that way, if they decide I'm too much, they can leave before I get attached or used to having them around.

"What do you want it to be?" Travis asks.

"I thought you were going to be my daddy?" I ask. "I thought you cared about me?"

"Sweetheart, I love you, don't ever doubt that. But if you don't have those kinds of feelings towards me, you have to say, and I will still be your daddy in a non-sexual way. I will be anything you want me to be for as long as you need me," Travis whispers, running his knuckles down my cheek.

"We all want to be in a relationship with you but understand that you might not want that. We don't want you to feel like you have to be with us. We are here for you no matter what," Ryan adds.

"Do you all want to be my daddy?" I ask, looking around at them all.

"Travis is and always will be your daddy, and if you want us all to be, then we can. But I think I'm more of the type to help you get into trouble with your daddy than actually being one," Ethan winks as Ryan chuckles and Travis groans.

"I'm not sure I'm daddy material either, but I can be if that's what you need," Ryan adds.

"That doesn't mean I value our relationship, if that's what you want, over the others. We are three different people who can fulfil your different needs. That's all. It doesn't need to be complicated," Travis says as I look up.

"I like the sound of that," I whisper, leaning into him. "I've had feelings for you all for a long time; I just never thought you reciprocated them."

"I think we all need to start talking more, not just you," Ryan says as he smiles at me. "So, what can we help with to remove some of your pain?"

I suddenly feel very self-conscious about what I was going to say. Can I really admit to them that I have a high sex drive? How do I explain that I'm addicted to the feeling of an orgasm to the point I have to cum nearly daily?

"You will laugh at me."

"No, we won't. Whatever it is, we can face it together, the four of us and come up with the best solution," Ethan says, taking my hand. I look down at it momentarily, trying to find the best way to say it.

"Sweetheart, for us to help you, we need to know everything you are feeling," Travis says softly as he runs a hand up and down my back.

"I have a high sex drive. As in *really* high! There I said it," I blurt out looking around at them. I'm amazed when none of them laugh, but I don't miss the smile on Ethan's face. "See, you think it's funny!" I exclaim, leaning back into Travis, who kicks Ethan as Ryan punches his arm.

"I don't think it's funny. I think it's cute you think that's going to be a problem for us," he laughs as he leans forward and cups my cheek. "Baby girl, you have three of us all here, eager to give you anything you need, that includes sex whenever you want it. You need an orgasm? What's the likelihood that no one is around to help with that? I know I will have no problem dropping whatever I'm doing to give you an orgasm or three. I'm sure the others feel the same way."

I look to Ryan, who shrugs whilst grinning.

"I'm happy to help whenever you need or want me."

But it's the smile on Travis's face that stops me in my tracks.

"Sweetheart, say the word, and I will drop to my knees and pleasure you in any way and as many times as you need."

God, that's hot.

"But I don't think that's what you need right now, is it?" Travis asks as I lean into him again. "You need to rest and come to terms with a few things. So why don't you lie on the bed with these two whilst I try to cook up something for dinner? Then afterwards, we can sit down and talk through anything else that's on your mind." He tips my head back before pressing a soft kiss on my lips. "Does that sound okay? Is there anything you fancy for dinner?"

"I don't know if I can eat much," I admit. Travis smiles slightly as he brushes away a little hair from my face.

"That's fine, just eat what you can. But you need to try and eat something."

I nod as he stands, placing me back on the bed before kissing my forehead.

"Rest with these, and I'll shout when dinner's ready."

I watch him leave the room as the other two sit so they are on either side of me again. Ryan pulls me against him as Ethan takes my hand.

"Come on, Baby girl, let's watch a little more TV before your daddy poisons us with his cooking," Ethan chuckles as Ryan groans.

I sit back and watch the TV, wondering if this will ever feel real. Or if I will ever get to enjoy the time with the guys without the constant voice in my head telling me they will leave eventually because everyone always does.

Chapter Twenty-Four

TRAVIS

Lying on my bed, arms behind my head, I stare at the ceiling and try to make sense of everything. There's so much to consider: ideas and plans I need to stop and think about, as well as trying to find the best way to help Verity recover from what seems to be years of abandonment issues. But I can't seem to pick just one to make sense of.

Considering how I thought this evening would go, Verity seemed to come out of herself quicker than I imagined. Which isn't a good thing. Considering she realised her father is a lying two face son of a bitch, I think the initial breakdown was caused by everything she has been through becoming too much.

Deep down, I think she's always known her father lied to her about where he was and what he was doing. She realised she wasn't his priority and hadn't been for a long time. But he's the only parent she has left, and she's a typical daddy's girl with serious daddy issues. Which is why I think she needs a daddy the way she does.

After dinner of chicken pasta, which wasn't as bad as it could have been, we all moved into the lounge, where we found a small bag of gifts. Verity's eyes instantly filled with tears when she realised they were from her father. The bastard hadn't even bothered to give them to her himself; he just left them in a cheap gift bag for her to find on her own. There isn't even a tree up that he could have put them under. I don't know why he bothered at all. I'd quickly moved them up to his room and told her if she wanted them, then she could have them at Christmas. Currently, she isn't sure what she wants to do with them.

A few times this evening, as we watched TV in the lounge, I noticed that now and again, she would look around the room and then curl up further against whoever she was sitting with. This house is a constant reminder of her parents and what her father did today and many other days. I'm considering a few options to make things easier for her, but I'm worried about how she will take it. At the end of the day, there are three other houses she could live in; I don't know how any of us would feel if she lived with one and not all of us.

There is still so much to consider and decide, and my controlling mind thinks we need to sort it all out now. But Verity needs time to consider all her options and decide what she wants to do. All I know right now is that I want to be wherever she is. I'm done hiding my feelings in the fear of Henry taking her from me. After what we learnt today, I am seriously considering never letting him near her again.

Verity dozed off on the sofa earlier, and the three of us chatted quickly in the kitchen, although a much deeper conversation is needed. The others told me to put all my focus on her, to help her come to terms with everything and give her the support she needs. There was no questioning why I took on the daddy role. Ethan pointed out that I've been a father to them since Dad died; it's a natural role to me and what Verity needs more than anything right now. I know he's right, but I worry they will think I'm trying to control their relationships with her.

When she went to bed this evening, Verity seemed a little more settled. We all walked her to her room, and she asked for some space tonight. We reluctantly gave it to her, but only after we made her promise not to hurt herself. She promised if she was struggling, she would come and find us. Do I believe her? I don't know, which is probably why I can't sleep. The thought of her ever doing something like hurting herself terrifies me. I hope she trusts us enough to ask for help when needed. I honestly don't know how I would cope if I were ever to lose her.

It will take some time, but I think she might realise quicker than I thought that she doesn't need to hide things from us. As I told her, for me to be her daddy, she needs to be honest with me because I will find things out, and it will be better for her if I find them out from her rather than others. I will still keep an eye out for any issues as she has problems trusting people, which is only understandable considering how she has been treated all her life.

I let out a deep sigh and close my eyes. I need to sleep because I want to get up early in the morning, as I know Verity will be up from six. I don't want her to be alone for any length of time. It's killing me her being in her room, but all I can do is hope she is getting some rest.

Rolling onto my side, I let sleep slowly take hold as I drift off to a restless sleep filled with cries of pain from my sweet girl and heartache I have never witnessed, all while reminding myself she is safe and I will do anything to keep it that way.

———————

I wake up with a jump as I feel the bed dip beside me.

"Sweetheart?" I reach up and turn on the overhead lamp. Turning to my left, I find Verity looking up at me with her doll in her arms as tears roll down her pale cheeks.

"Come here, Sweetheart," I whisper, pulling her into my arms against my bare chest as she cries. I run my hand over her head, peppering it with kisses, and shower her with encouragement.

"I'm sorry," she whispers when the tears have slowed.

"What for?" I ask, running my hand up and down her back.

"I hit you earlier, and I told you I hate you, and I don't. I don't hate you." I can hear the tears threatening again as I kiss the top of her head.

"I know you don't. That's why I pushed you to admit the truth like I did," I explain. It had been so hard holding her as she screamed and fought against me, but I would do it again in a heartbeat if it were what she needed.

"Thank you for the doll. It makes it all a little easier," she whispers, holding the stuffed toy to her chest.

"I hoped it would." When I picked it up a few days ago, I had planned on it being a fun little gift she would probably leave on a chair in her room and forget about. I never dreamt it would become so important to either of us.

"Does it make me childish to cling to it like I am?"

I move back a little to ensure I am able to look her in the eye while answering.

"No, it doesn't. There's a little girl inside you who is still waiting for their father to notice them and love them unconditionally," I explain quietly, brushing my knuckles down her cheek. "That little girl will always be there, but I will ensure she no longer feels lonely. That you both know you are loved and protected."

Verity watches me momentarily, her eyes not leaving mine as I tuck a stray hair behind her ears.

"If you don't love me, you don't have to say it; I will understand," she whispers, looking away.

"Look at me, Sweetheart." When she does, I see the tears in her eyes again. It hurts that she doubts me, but I know it's not her fault. Who was the last person to tell her they loved her and prove it? Her mother? She's been dead for thirteen years. I know she had an aunt she was close to who's also dead. Who has my girl had to show her what love truly is?

"I love you; I have for a long time, and I thought you would be better off without me. Now I know I should have told you, then maybe you wouldn't feel the way you do now. But I promise to make it up to you. To support you in whatever you want to do and love you unconditionally." I lift her hand to my lips and kiss it.

"Thank you," she whispers, placing a hand under her head and lying on the pillow facing me. I watch her eyes slowly close before she forces them to open again. She is exhausted and close to falling asleep.

"Do you want to sleep in here tonight?" I ask, guessing she would prefer not to be alone. She nods, and I lie back on my back, holding out one arm.

"Come here then, Sweetheart." She slides next to me and rests her head on my chest as I wrap my arms around her shoulders. "Get some sleep; it's been a long day," I whisper into her hair as I feel her relaxing into me.

"Night, Daddy," she whispers, catching me off guard. I find myself smiling as I close my eyes and listen to the soft sound of her breathing as it gradually slows, and I pray that my girl will be able to come out of this stronger and happier.

Chapter Twenty-Five

VERITY

I wake up, still wrapped in Travis's arm. I feel safe and protected as I remember how he comforted me last night.

I'd laid in bed for so long, trying to make sense of everything. From my dad's betrayal to the guys all saying they want to love and support me. So much had happened in such a short space of time, and I started to break all over again.

The one thing that stuck out from the pain wasn't what I thought it would be. Deep down, I've been waiting for the day my dad would stop wanting to be with me and choose his new wife and life. It's been coming for a long while, and I think, in a way, I was prepared for it. That doesn't mean it didn't hurt because I've never felt pain like I did yesterday, not even when my Mum passed away.

But when I was at my most broken, the guys were there in a heartbeat, and they held me together. It wasn't just Ryan for getting me out of the shower or Travis for making me accept and acknowledge the pain. But Ethan, as well, simply by being him, teasing his brothers and making stupid comments when watching TV. All the small gestures, as well as the big ones, got me to the point where I felt I could go to bed on my own and sleep.

I was wrong.

As I lay there going over the day, on repeat like a scratched record, the one thing that upset me the most was how I treated Travis. That man held me as I punched him, screamed in his face, and said unimaginable things. He should have thrown me on the bed and left me for being a brat. It's what my father would have done. But not Travis. He held me and showered me with affection and support. He told me to hit him and scream louder and that no matter what I said or did, he wasn't leaving. I vaguely remember thinking I would push as hard as I could until he left. But he didn't budge once.

It was when I realised how I treated him that I started to cry. When the realisation hit that he been truly there for me, nothing I did would have changed that.

Do I believe this will be long-term? I want to, with all my heart. But history has a way of repeating itself, and I know there is a real chance that Travis and the others will leave. But last night, I knew I would be safe with him, so here I am, lying in his arms as he sleeps soundly.

It's still dark in the room, but I know it will be six o'clock. No matter when I go to bed, I never sleep past six. For a moment, I think about getting up, showered and dressed as I do every morning, but I'm warm and comfortable, and I don't want to be the good girl my father wants me to be. It goes against everything within me to do something I know will disappoint him. But it also leaves me feeling slightly excited to do something wrong. It helps that I'm curled up against Travis's warm, firm chest.

Looking up to see if he's still asleep, I notice his necklaces hanging around his neck. He is wearing the usual thick silver chain his father gave him a year before his death. He also has a few leather cords, each with a different charm. It's then I notice the one I gave him on his last birthday. I have no idea what the charm means; it's a tribal mask surrounded by a border that made me think of the sun. I'm surprised to see him wearing it. I reach up and run my finger lightly over the charm, noticing how worn the cord looks as if he wears it daily.

I had been shopping with the girls when I saw it on a stand outside a hippy-style shop. It caught my eye, and I immediately thought of him. The design reminded me of his tattoos, and I knew I had to get it for him. I never expected him to wear it, but there it is around his neck.

I admire and trace the tribal design tattoos on his pecs, which are mainly black with a little colour. His chest is firm to the touch, showing how hard he works out. Have I ever been with men as well built as the guys? I don't think I have.

Travis moans slightly, and I look up nervously, expecting to see him awake, but his eyes remain closed as he sleeps. I retrace the same area, and he moans as he rolls, tucking me against his chest, holding me flush against his front, his morning glory pressing in almost the right spot. I can't help grinding against it slightly.

"Sweetheart, do you need something?"

Looking up, I find Travis watching me. I shake my head, suddenly very embarrassed.

"What did I say about asking for something you need?" he asks firmly. I look into his eyes and open my mouth to admit it, but once again, I'm too nervous to say it out loud. "Verity." The way he says my name in that warning tone makes my whole body freeze and obey him.

"I'm horny," I whisper. Travis's hand comes up and cups my cheek.

"Do you want me to help with that?" he asks, staring deep into my eyes. I nod, unable to look away.

Slowly, Travis rolls us so I'm on my back, and he is lying over the top of me. His lips brush against mine as if testing what I want. I want him, not just because I'm horny but because I need him. He kisses me again gently before moving his lips down to my jaw, which he kisses before moving to my throat.

I tip my head back to give him better access, and he rewards me by taking my breast in his hand. I have tiny breasts; I'm almost flat-chested. It's all the years of dance, I've been told. But the way Travis touches me makes me feel more of a woman than I ever have.

"Sit up for me, Sweetheart." I do as he asks, and he helps me out of the loose t-shirt I wore to bed, leaving me in nothing but my cotton knickers. "If that's an ex-boyfriend's t-shirt, I never want to see it on your body again. Understood?" His eyes darken, and he has that strict tone that turns me on and warns me not to test him at the same time.

Nodding in agreement, Travis watches me for a moment, checking that I'm not lying before encouraging me to lie back down.

"Good girl," he whispers into my ear as his teeth find the lobe at the same time as his fingers find my nipple. I gasp as he applies just the right amount of pressure, not too much that it's painful, but enough that it's not gentle either.

Travis continues to kiss his way down my neck to my chest, where he takes my nipple between his teeth.

"Oh god," I gasp, pushing my chest out further to give him as much access as possible. I know I'm soaking wet and so ready for him. It can be embarrassing how wet I can get, and I have even had men complain. I'm self-conscious about it, but I try to force it to the back of my mind as I always do. But when I feel Travis's hand on my leg as he forces it to bend before running his hand up my inner thigh towards the apex of my thighs, I feel myself stiffen.

"What's the matter?" Travis asks, looking up from between my breasts. I quickly shake my head, knowing he won't drop it.

"Sweetheart, if you want me to stop."

I shake my head vigorously; that's the last thing I want him to do.

"Then tell me what the matter is so I can help you."

"I'm wet," I whisper. Travis looks at me with one arched brow.

"I should hope so; otherwise, I suck at this."

I can't stop the short giggle, which earns me a smile from Travis.

"I mean, I'm *really* wet," I whisper.

Tavis lets go of my leg and moves so he is lying over me, his lips close to mine.

"Sweetheart, has anyone told you that's a bad thing?" When I don't immediately answer, Travis curses before rubbing his face. "What kind of morons have you been dating?" he sighs before looking deep into my eyes again. "You will never hear me complaining about how wet you are. I want to know you are satisfied to the point I have to change my sheets because they are covered in your sweet juices. Do you understand what I'm saying?"

I nod slowly as he watches me, determining whether I'm telling the truth.

"That's my good girl," he whispers in a deep voice and

my sex clenches just from those four words. A smirk appears on his face before resuming from where he was.

With his hand back on my leg and his lips moving down towards my stomach, I close my eyes and savour the feeling of him everywhere. As his hand gets closer to my pussy I find myself wiggling, trying to get them there quicker. Travis doesn't hurry his pace, though. Instead, I swear he slows down. By the time his fingers brush over the fabric of my underwear, and his lips find my lower stomach, I am on fire and desperate to be touched.

Travis sits up a little and looks down at the apex of my thighs. Before running a finger over the material, I know is soaking wet.

"I think we could get these wetter, don't you?" he smirks, before applying a little pressure in just the right spot.

I moan loudly and grind against his finger, causing him to chuckle.

"How badly do you want this, Sweetheart?" he asks, circling my clit through the material.

"So bad!" I moan as I move my hips again.

"How many times is the most you've ever cum in one sitting?" I hear him ask as he continues to rub me, bringing me closer to that sweet release. "Before my brothers," he adds quickly. "Two against one is a little unfair,"

"Twice," I moan as I realise he has stopped moving his fingers, and now it's me grinding against him, taking what I need to cum.

"That's it, Sweetheart. They're getting good and soaked now. Are you going to cum in these knickers like a good girl for your Daddy?"

"Yes," I cry as I do exactly what he asks. I can feel everything twitching and contracting inside the soaking wet material. I'm still lying with my eyes closed, enjoying the sense of relief when Travis grips the material on my hips.

"Lift for me, Sweetheart." I do as he asks, allowing him room to remove my underwear, leaving my pussy bare in front of him. Slowly his finger runs from my clenching entrance to my sensitive clit.

"So wet, so fucking beautiful," he whispers before looking up at me. "Do you want more?" he asks. I nod, desperate for him to touch me again. "Good because I have dreamt about this pussy so many times, but it's more perfect than I ever imagined."

Travis kisses my stomach before slowly moving downwards, kissing over my plump lips. I'm almost bare down there; it's easier because of the leotards. Nothing looks worse than a hair sticking out of the side when dancing.

All coherent thoughts vanish the first time I feel Travis's tongue slip between my lips to my clit.

"Oh God," I moan as he does it again.

"It's not God you need to moan for, Sweetheart. What's my name?" Travis asks before sliding his tongue up the slit again.

"Daddy!" I cry out as he circles my clit with his tongue. I feel his moan more than I hear it, and it feels better than any vibrator as he continues to lick my clit. I cry out his name when he slides one finger into me, followed by another. Which earns me another deep moan that vibrates against my clit.

"Don't stop," I cry out as another orgasm rushes through me. The guys the other day made me feel amazing, but the way Travis plays my body is out of this world. With the others, it was the sensation in two places simultaneously, but Travis is bringing me up all on his own, and I never want it to end.

By now, I'm thrashing against him, bucking my hips up to his face as I push his fingers in deeper. It's not soft and gentle, but hard and rough, just what I've always wanted. I'm using him for my pleasure, and it feels incredible.

"Daddy, I-" I don't get any more out before falling apart and screaming his name as he pushes me right to the limit before letting me rest.

I can't breathe or think. All I can do is melt against the mattress and pray I come out of the other end. That was the most extreme orgasm I have ever had. From the way Travis still has his fingers in me, I don't think he's done.

He kisses his way up my body before I grab his face and kiss him hard. I force my tongue into his mouth and love the taste of myself on his lips. For a moment, we attack each other's mouths as he kisses me in a way I've never been kissed. This is beyond passion; this is a pure primal need.

"Shall we try to beat your record?" he asks, positioning himself between my legs. "Or have you had enough?"

I wrap my legs around his waist and pull him against me.

"Are you sure that's what you want, Sweetheart? Because there's no going back from this," he whispers against my lips. I look into his eyes as he waits for my reply.

"I don't want to go back. I want you to stay with me," I plead. Deep down, I never want him to leave me or take back the words he has comforted me with. I want him with me forever, even if it's just a fantasy. Right now, it's all I want to focus on.

The colour of his eyes darkens before I hear his reply.

"What's my name, Sweetheart?"

"Daddy," I answer.

"And who does Daddy love more than anyone in this world?"

"Me?" I ask before Travis's lips find mine.

"Yes, you. Never doubt that, ever."

In one swift move, he removes his fingers and plunges into me with his hard large cock.

"Fuck," he curses as I cry out. He's enormous, but thankfully not too big. He holds still, his hips pressing against mine, taking him as deep as he will go. I try to move, but he pins my hip to the mattress with one hand.

"Don't. Give me a minute," he gasps. I love that I can turn this strong man into putty in my hand. If I wanted to, I could make him cum, deep inside me. He's balancing on the edge, and I consider teasing him, and from the look he's giving me, he knows it.

"Now is not the time to be a brat," he warns as I laugh out loud and see the way it vibrates through him. His teeth clench before he starts to move within me slowly.

"Fuck I can't wait to do all kinds of naughty things to you," he growls through gritted teeth as he starts getting harder and faster. His cock is the perfect size to hit every single one of my spots at the same time, and I feel like my body is going to explode. Travis lifts my leg as he leans up and gets rougher. No one has ever been this rough with me before, and it's everything I thought it would be.

"Daddy, yes!" I cry out as I meet him thrust for thrust. We are both a sweaty mess in no time, but we don't care. He is fucking me hard, and I never want it to end.

"That's it, Sweetheart, you feel so good, so fucking perfect." Travis drops my leg and rolls us so he's on his back, and I'm on top. I instantly start grinding into him whilst he holds my hips.

"Take what you need to cum on Daddy's dick," he growls as he reaches down with his thumb and starts to rub my sensitive clit.

"Oh god," I cry out. Travis slaps my ass, shocking me to the point I stop and look down at him.

"Who did I say to call for?"

"You, Daddy," I reply as a smile spread across his face.

"That's right," he replies as he starts lifting his hips to meet mine, and things start going wild. Things start moving faster as we both get louder, and I bounce on his cock until I cry out as I orgasm around it. As I cum, Travis grips my hips and takes control thrusting into me a few more times before filling me as he roars through his release.

I collapse onto his chest, and he wraps me in his arms as we lie together, gasping for breath.

"You are too perfect. I don't know how I thought I could carry on loving you from afar," he whispers into my hair. I rest my cheek on his chest as I look to the side of the bed where I slept half the night.

"Why do you think you love me?" I ask, scared to look at him.

"I don't think, I know. I knew you were special from the moment I met you. But I realised I loved you six months ago when you were drugged."

Travis helps me move so I'm lying beside him rather than on top. He pulls the blankets over us to stop me from getting cold. I place my hands together under my face as he lies beside me, propping his head up on a fist.

"I don't know if you remember, but one of your friend's parents called your dad that night. I called him the following morning to check something, and he told me." He reaches over and brushes some hair from my face. "I jumped in the car and was here within two hours. Your friend was here, but you were still out of it. You had no idea who I was and were unable to stay awake. All I knew was you had been out with the O'Reilly girl and had your drink spiked. I lost my shit and called Christian."

"Jasmine had been taken! It wasn't his fault," I start, but Travis places a hand on my cheek to calm me.

"I know that now, but we didn't know about Jasmine then. I don't know if you would have known the truth if Christian hadn't shouted it at me when I called him. I felt bad afterwards; had I known what they were going through, I would have never called. But all I could think about was what could have happened to you, and it killed me. That's why I started keeping more of an eye on you. I don't know if you noticed, but I have been back more often and messaged you almost daily. All of it was to know you were safe, and I still managed to miss so much."

"It's not your fault," I start, but Travis shakes his head as he tucks the blankets further around me, protecting me from the chill in the air.

"It doesn't matter whose fault it is; it still stands that you have been suffering, and none of us noticed or did anything to help you." He leans in and kisses my forehead. "But that is going to change, Sweetheart. If you are up for it today, I would like the four of us to sit down and talk about every-thing. I think you've been told many lies, and I want to understand them before I try to help you."

I nod as I know he's right.

"Good girl. I know it won't be easy, but we need to understand a few things to take care of you and help you understand who you are and not what you believe is expected of you. But first." Travis grabs me and rolls onto his back, taking me with him. I squeal, laughing as he pins me to his side. "Let me hold you for five more minutes before I get up and make you breakfast."

176

"I think I'm going to like you being my Daddy," I giggle against his chest.

"I haven't had to discipline you yet. You might change your mind then," he warns in that deep voice he gets when he goes into daddy mode.

From the way my body reacts, I don't think I will mind at all.

Chapter Twenty-Six

RYAN

This run is what I needed after the last twenty-four hours. It's giving me time to clear my head and think things through properly.

From the moment Mum and Henry arrived the other evening, I knew they would cause all kinds of trouble. They had come in all happy and cheery and seemed a little too relieved when I pointed out Verity was at the performance. They appeared less pleased when I said Travis was watching her.

"That's nice of him," Mum had said, putting no real feeling into it. Henry hadn't looked overly impressed, but what right has he got to have any say over his daughter's life? After yesterday, none.

I will never forgive him for the pain he caused Verity yesterday or any other day. I don't know what he said to her in that room, but he destroyed her. It was written all over her face, as well as the way her whole body language changed. She was broken beyond repair. Between me helping her onto the bed and the guys getting back, I tried so many times to get her to speak to me, but it was as if she couldn't hear me, yet Travis somehow got through to her.

That man did something I don't think I could. He held her tight and took the abuse and still gave her all of him. Afterwards, whenever she would curl up small on his lap like a young child would their father, I knew he had made the right decision in becoming her daddy. He knew it was what she needed and took on the role, which comes with a hell of a lot of responsibility, which he will be amazing at.

I waited for the jealousy to kick in whenever she curled up with him or clung to that doll like she was clinging to her sanity. But there was none. As I told her, if she wanted me to be her daddy, I would be, but I don't know if I'm daddy material, not like Travis. Yesterday, she needed him more than us, and it made sense. There will be times when she needs one of us more than the others, and we all have to accept that. Otherwise, this will never work, and I want this relationship to work for all of us. Verity deserves to be surrounded by love, and we plan to ensure she is.

I see the house approaching and slow down to a light jog to cool down a little. I have no idea how Verity is going to be today. I hope she managed to get some sleep, as she refused for anyone to stay with her last night. I thought I heard movement in the night, and it wouldn't surprise me if she went to Travis for comfort or even Ethan, as he has a way of making her giggle no matter how low her mood is.

We all have much talking to do, and I hope we can get things into place now. The biggest question will be where we will live in the long run. I don't know if Verity will stay in the house or if she would be up to moving to one of ours. We don't live together, but we aren't far apart either. But then, where would Verity live? We need to speak to someone with this kind of relationship and see how they do it. Maybe

Verity can talk to the O'Reilly girl as they are close. Perhaps she has already told her a few of their routines.

Everything is different from what I thought a relationship with Verity would be like. I always imagined it just being me and her. Why wouldn't I? That's a normal relationship, after all. But seeing how she is with my brothers, I know that would have never worked out. She needs more than one of us; she needs us all.

I come to the back door and start to stretch, already planning to shower quickly before seeing how Verity is doing today.

A loud scream comes from within the house, and I rush inside, expecting to find Verity crying again or having another breakdown. I don't expect to see Ethan straddling her on the floor as she laughs so hard she can't get anything out except the odd scream.

"Do I even want to ask?"

Ethan and Verity look to me as Travis looks over from the oven.

"Ryan, save me!" she calls out as Ethan returns to tickling her. "Ethan! Don't!" she cries out as he laughs. "Daddy!"

"Well, that's not going to get old fast," I chuckle, walking past Travis and heading to the coffee machine. "She seems a little better," I add quietly.

"She had a rough night, but she's getting there," Travis replies, looking over his shoulder as Ethan helps Verity off the floor. She pushes him away, but she's smiling, and that's the main thing.

So, it was her going to Travis that I heard in the night. I'm glad she didn't struggle on her own, at least.

"So, what's everyone's plans today?" I ask, leaning

against the counter as Verity takes a plate of food from Travis. I notice the rag doll beside her on the breakfast bar and smile as I sip my water. Who would have thought one doll could help someone so much?

"I want us all to chat about what will happen around here. We need to consider a few things as a family," Travis answers, pushing a plate towards Ethan.

"I was thinking the same thing, so that sounds good to me," I point out as I look to Verity, who is chewing on her bottom lip and suddenly looks less happy than she was a moment ago.

"What's up, little Kitten?"

Verity looks at me and shakes her head before returning to her food.

"Why don't I believe you?" I sigh before walking over to her. "If there's something you would like to do, just say, and we will fit our plans around you," I add, running a hand up and down her back.

"It's just … It doesn't matter. This is more important," she mumbles before forcing that smile.

"I thought we agreed you would be honest with us and say what you need and want. That fake ass smile doesn't work on us, Baby girl," Ethan says beside her. I catch her looking behind me and turn to find Travis giving her his serious look. That man had no problem slipping into the daddy role.

"What were you about to say?" he asks.

"It." Verity stops, and I can see she's struggling with whatever is playing on her mind. "It involves something I'm not meant to tell you about," she answers as she starts picking at the jumper she's wearing.

"Sweetheart, has Henry asked you to keep stuff from

us?" Travis asks, leaning on the other side of the breakfast bar. Verity nods, still unable to look any of us in the eye.

"What kind of things?" I ask as I run a hand up and down her back again.

"Mainly small things that aren't even important. But then there is this one which is kind of big, and I don't know what to do." Her voice wobbles slightly as she struggles to decide what to do for the best. She looks at Travis, and I know it's her way of asking him to decide for her.

"If you think it's important, then you can tell us, and I will deal with any repercussions from Henry." Travis reaches over and cups her cheek. "No matter what you tell us, even if he tries to cause you any upset for it, we will always stand up for you. Do you understand, Sweetheart? You are who we will protect, no matter what your father says and does."

She looks into his eyes momentarily and nods once to show that she understands.

"You remember me telling you about my Auntie Trisha?" she asks quietly.

"Your mum's sister?" Ethan asks. Verity nods as she goes back to picking at her jumper nervously.

"It's her birthday today, and I wanted to take her some flowers."

I frown as I look at the others. Trisha was killed in an accident just before Mum met Henry. We only know about her because Verity let it slip once that she once had an Auntie who loved to watch her dance.

"Why couldn't you tell us that, Kitten? We will happily drive you to the cemetery or wherever you go to pay your respects." I look to Travis, who is watching Verity intensely.

"She's not dead, is she?" he asks. Verity shakes her head, and I stare at Ethan over her.

"But I thought she was killed in an accident?" Ethan asks, but Verity shakes her head.

"She wasn't killed, but she was left with brain damage. Dad put her into a nursing home and told me I was never to see her again as she gets confused, and it would upset me."

"But you've been going anyway and not telling him," I realise as it all starts to make sense. Of course, she would be worried about telling us. Not only has Henry lied to us about her. Verity has lied to her father and visited even when told not to.

"She can get cross, which is upsetting, especially as she hates my dad so much. She blames him for everything, even though they were good friends before the accident. I do get upset, especially if she is having a bad day. But I can't leave her alone in there. No one goes to visit her but me, and I know she's sad." Verity leans into me as I place an arm around her shoulders. "Are you mad at me for lying?" she asks quietly.

"Of course not," Ethan protests as he runs a hand over her head. "You were doing as you were told; it wasn't your decision."

I kiss the top of her head, and Travis nods at her with a small smile.

"Do you mind if I go and see her?" she replies quietly.

"Why on earth would we stop you from seeing your Auntie? We are not here to control your life; we want *you* to take control of it. You have acted how others expected you to for so long, you don't even know who you really are!" Ethan exclaims next to her.

"What Ethan is trying to say is that none of us would ever tell you where you can go or who you can see. Is that what you thought this was going to be like?" Travis asks as he stands beside me.

"Well, no, but you all want to have this big chat, and I know it's important, but my Auntie is more coherent in the morning, so I wanted to see her first," she answers, and I realise another reason she is so worried about asking us.

"Would anyone else make you change your plans to fit around theirs?" I ask. Verity chews on her lip and shrugs. I can imagine her father telling her not to argue or throw a tantrum if she asked to do something when he already had plans.

"How does this sound? I will get showered and dressed whilst you eat breakfast, and then I'll drive you to the home while Travis and Ethan do whatever they want. Then, once we return, we can all sit and have lunch and decide on a few things together," I suggest.

"That sounds like a good idea to me. Do you feel up to dancing tonight? Or would you rather have another night off?" Travis asks.

"I don't know. Can I think about it and let you know?" she asks, looking around.

"Of course you can, Sweetheart, take all the time you need. Just tell us what you want to do, and we are here for it, okay?"

Verity looks to Travis and smiles, thankfully not with a fake one like earlier.

"Good girl. Now, eat your breakfast. By the time you finish that and get your coat and scarf, Ryan will be ready too," Travis announces, pointing to her plate of bacon medallions, eggs and plum tomatoes.

As Verity starts cutting up her food, I walk past her and kiss her cheek.

"I'll be ready when you are," I tell her, rushing up the stairs with a coffee cup in my hand, heading for the world's quickest shower so I can be washed and dressed by the time she finishes her food and is ready to leave.

Chapter Twenty-Seven

VERITY

I chew on my thumb nervously as Ryan drives. I have the small gift I picked out for my Auntie on my lap and a box of her favourite chocolates.

"What exactly is wrong with your Auntie?"

I glance over at him and shrug.

"I don't know the exact diagnosis. She suffers from memory loss as well as gets confused easily. She has also developed a type of paranoia. If you had met her before the accident, you would have seen that she was the nicest, calmest person you ever met. But now she has angry outbursts and swears and shouts. She has good days and bad days. The last time I went, she didn't recognise me; she thought I was my mum. They said she had become para-noid during the night, and they had sedated her, which caused the confusion. She kept telling me to watch as they were after my money. Or something like that."

"That can't be easy to witness. How often do you go to see her?" Ryan reaches over and takes my hand, lifts it to his mouth to kiss my knuckles.

"I try to go a few times a month. Sometimes, I'm only there for a couple of minutes and have to leave. Sometimes, they wouldn't let me see her because she was having an episode. But occasionally, she will be in a lovely mood, and I stay there for an hour or two talking to her." I look out the window and try to focus on the memories of days she was more lucid.

"It's lovely that you try so hard to keep her in your life. She must have meant a lot to you." Ryan says, squeezing my hand slightly.

"She was the only friend I had for a long time. I spent weekends at her place, playing in the garden with her and her dog. She was the one who encouraged me to keep dancing after Mum died.

"My Auntie got along with Dad but never forgave him for always leaving me and Mum behind. My mum would say he had asked her, but she didn't want to disturb my life by moving back and forth to the States. So, instead, we stayed home. When she got sick, he still travelled as much and wasn't even here when she died."

I take a deep breath to try and control my emotions as I look out of the car window as the world flies by.

"I made so many excuses for his behaviour in the past, and they all seemed liable. But I can't find an excuse this time, which makes it worse."

Ryan squeezes my hand, letting me know he's there.

"I know the three of us aren't the same, but we will never leave you like he has. Even though Travis wants to be your daddy, that doesn't mean Ethan and I don't want to care for you and offer any support you need. We aren't here for the sex; we are here for you and to make you feel safe and happy again." He lets out a deep chuckle and shakes his head. "I've never been very good at expressing my feelings, and I know I'm probably making a pig's ear of this. But what I'm trying to say is, I care for you so much, and I want to help you to realise how loved you are and to see you don't need him because you have us three." Ryan turns to look at me as he parks up outside the home. "Am I making sense? Like, even a little bit?" he asks nervously. I smile slightly, nodding.

Ryan's lips lift on one side as he reaches over and threads his fingers into the hair at the back of my head. He applies pressure, and our lips meet in the middle. It's a slow, loving kiss, just like that first one the other day.

He pulls away just as I start to want more before remembering why we are here. These men are going to break my heart if I'm not careful. They are making it very hard to keep them at arm's length, as I know I should.

"Do you want me to come in with you? Or stay here."

"You can come in if you want, but I understand if you can't stay. She can be a bit much," I offer with a smile. I like the idea of having some support in there. It can be hard sometimes, and the thought of Ryan holding my hand through it gives me a little more strength.

"Come on then, let's go and see the birthday girl," Ryan chirps as he climbs out of the car. I take a deep breath before exiting the vehicle and heading to where he awaits me. He takes my hand, and we walk to the entrance, as I hope she will at least remember me today.

We walk into the communal lounge a few minutes later after briefly chatting with a carer I recognised and signing in. As usual, I use a false name. They all think I'm her friend's daughter, so her Doctor doesn't realise I have been here. He told my dad the first few times I came, which caused a huge argument. Since then, I have lied to the staff about who I am. I know a few suspects, but they never say anything.

When asked who he was, Ryan introduced himself as my boyfriend, which was a bit of a shock, but I liked how it sounded. He's never really felt like a stepbrother anyway. The carer tells us that my auntie is in a lovely mood and has even come down to the lounge, which is uncommon for her. He offers to take us all to her room for privacy, but I can't move her if she's so happy.

We enter the lounge and see Auntie Trish surrounded by balloons and banners I had forgotten I'd dropped off the last time I visited. One look at her, and tears fill my eyes. She looks so happy as she laughs with the carer sitting beside her. She looks up and sees us entering, and her smile gets even more prominent.

"Jellybean, you came!" She jumps to her feet and rushes to me with her arms open. Ryan lets go of my hand and steps to the side as she engulfs me in one of her special hugs. I can't remember the last time she recognised me immediately, let alone called me by the nickname she and my mother gave me before I was born.

"Happy birthday, Auntie Trish," I whisper as I close my eyes to fight back the tears. This is just what I needed. A hug from my auntie is like having a hug from my mum.

"Hey! What's with the tears?" she asks, holding me at arm's length.

"They are happy tears, I promise," I smile at her. "I've missed you."

"Well, I've missed you too." She threads her arm through mine and turns her attention to Ryan. "Do I know you?"

Ryan smiles, shaking his head.

"No, ma'am, I'm Ryan," he says, holding out his hand.

"Oh, don't come that formal rubbish with me. I might be crazy, but I'm not old," she announces as she lets go of my arm and pulls Ryan in for a hug. He laughs before hugging her back.

"It's good to see someone has snatched up my favourite niece," she winks as she turns around and walks back to her chair. The carer has vacated the one next to her for us, and Ryan signals for me to take it. Auntie Trish turns her full attention to me and smirks. "Why does he look so familiar?" Trish asks as she turns and frowns at Ryan. Suddenly, she clicks her fingers and jumps a little in her chair. "You are Ryan Donavan, no? Verity's stepbrother! You have two brothers!"

Ryan bursts out laughing.

"How do you know that?" he asks, looking between me and Auntie Trish.

"Well, Jellybean told me all about you and showed me some pictures on her phone, of course. She talks about the three of you all the time. I knew she liked you all," Auntie smirks as she looks at me. "So, you finally snatched one of them up? Or are you copying your little friend and doing all three?"

"Auntie Trish!" I exclaim, looking around, checking who would have heard her as Ryan bursts out laughing.

"Something like that," he laughs.

"Ryan!"

I bury my face in my hands, so embarrassed. I haven't come to terms with the fact that I have two boyfriends and a daddy. I certainly had no intention of my auntie ever knowing!

"Oh, my sweet Jellybean, there is nothing wrong if you are. Who cares what society thinks?" my auntie laughs beside me as she takes my hands and lowers them. She takes my face in her hands and looks at me lovingly. She looks just like my mum but is a little older.

"You, sweet girl, have the biggest heart and so much love to give. It makes sense you would love all three."

From her soft, warm face, I look at Ryan, who is smiling at us from where he stands. He gives me a small wink, and I realise I feel a little less embarrassed by it all.

Auntie Trish chuckles as she kisses my cheek and sits back, looking happy and content.

"Now, as it's my birthday, I insist we have some tea and cake. I know the girls said there was some waiting for us, so let's see if we can get it now."

Chapter Twenty-Eight

ETHAN

Lying back on my bed, I flick through my emails, not reading more than the subject line. I'm bored and killing time before Ryan and Verity come back.

I took advantage of the time they were out and picked up a couple of Christmas gifts for my girl before heading to the gym for a short, intense workout. I feel so much better for it and know I made the right choice in going this morning because I have no idea what will happen this afternoon.

I haven't had a chance to speak to Verity since everything that happened between Ryan, her, and me. But so much has occurred in that short time I don't know how she feels about it all. She says she doesn't just want one of us, but does she really want all three? Will Travis be more important to her than the rest of us? There's no mistaking he's the perfect one to be her daddy. He knew exactly what to do yesterday, and she obviously feels she can go to him. But I don't like the idea of her choosing him over me. Am I being selfish? Probably, but I just don't know how to feel about it all.

There's a knock at the door, and I call out for them to enter without looking up from the phone. I hear the door close and feel the bed move before I even register that it's Verity, not Travis.

"Hey, you're back?" I smile as she curls up beside me. "You look happy," I add, seeing the broad smile on her face.

"Auntie Trish was in a great mood."

I lean in and risk pressing a kiss to her lips. When she deepens the kiss further, I hold her close against me, pulling her on top so I'm able to run my hands up and down her body. I squeeze her ass, causing her to moan straight into my mouth.

"Do you want some attention?" I ask, lifting my hips a little to grind against her.

"Yes," she gasps as I do it again, and she moans into my neck. "I want you."

I roll us so I'm on top and look down into her sweet fuck me eyes as I make short work of helping her out of her t-shirt and bra.

"Good, 'cause I want you too. Take hold of the head-board, Baby girl." She does as I ask with a smile on her face.

"Now, don't let go until I say," I whisper before kissing her. "One day soon, I'm going to tie you up so I can do naughty things to you, and you won't be able to do anything about it."

I don't miss how she gasps and takes her bottom lip between her teeth.

I unfasten her jeans and start to pull them down, leaving her beautiful and bare in front of me.

"Would you like that? Giving yourself over to me completely? I could do anything to you, and you wouldn't be able to stop me," I whisper as I run a finger through her slit. "What do you think, Baby? Would you like that?" I ask again as she nods. "Say it," I demand as I push one finger into her already wet entrance.

"Yes," she cries out as she tightens around my digit. I bend it and do a come here signal inside of her, causing her to cry out again as I rub her G-spot. She starts grinding against my hand, making me harden. She is so horny, even though I know Travis pleased her more than once this morning. I know because I heard her crying out as he made her cum again and again.

"That's it, beautiful; I want them to hear you downstairs as you come in my hand," I add a second finger before leaning in and kissing her vulva.

"Ethan," hearing my name on her lips as she cries out makes me want to hear it again and again. I gently lick the tip of her clit, causing her to cry out again.

"That's it, Baby, call my name as I make you feel good." I start a slow and deliberate assault on her clit with my tongue whilst fucking her with my fingers.

She wiggles and moans loudly as I feel her getting close to coming. Every time she cries my name, I nearly cum in my pants. This woman is bringing all kinds of emotions out of me; I've never been so horny in my life, and to think she wants to be dominated, just as much as I would love to dominate her.

I watch her moan and wiggle as I lick her, fuck she's beautiful. I wonder if I can make it even better for her.

Well, she did say she was open to anything.

I remove my fingers from inside her. They're wet and slick with her juices. Without warning, I push one finger back into that beautiful pussy, and the other into her back passage.

"Yes!" she screams as she orgasms so hard I think she's about to break my fingers. Fuck, well, that just confirms she meant it when she said she is up for anything.

I continue to fuck both her holes with my fingers as I give her swollen clit a moment's break. Watching my fingers disappear into her as she moans through her orgasm may be one of my new favourite ways to spend my time. I can't wait to fuck her in the ass as she screams my name.

Reaching forward, I take her nipple between my thumb and finger before rolling it.

"Play with your clit, Baby. Show me how you do it whilst I fuck you."

Verity looks at me momentarily before a grin spreads across her face, and she moves her hand down to her nearly hairless mould. Watching her spread herself wide as I climb off the bed makes me get undressed in record time. In seconds, I'm kneeling between her legs again as I rub my shaft, covering it in her juices.

"Last time, Ryan took you from behind. How did Travis take you this morning?" I ask as she watches me pleasuring myself as she rubs her clit slowly.

"I was on top for most of it," she answers.

"Have either of my brothers had this?" I ask as I push a finger back into her ass.

"No," she moans as her eyes roll to the back of her head.

"Has any man?" I ask, and she shakes her head. "But you were willing?" This time, she nods. "Fucking idiots," I groan as I scoop some of her juices and massage them around her puckered hole. "Has anything been in here before?" I ask. Verity nods, and I know exactly what's been where my finger is now.

"I think you have more than one toy in your room, don't you?"

She nods again, and I know I'm going to have a lot of fun with her over the next few days as I explore her toy collection with her and possibly my brothers.

"Get on all fours and hold on to the headboard," I order as I remove my fingers from her tight ass. As she re-positions herself, I don't hold back and slap her on the ass. She cries out and moans at the same time, causing my cock to twitch with the need to enter her.

I climb off the bed, grab some lube from my drawer, and throw it beside her. I don't think I'll need it as she gets so wet her juices should be enough. I plan on fucking that beautiful pussy before taking her arsehole, which will get everything nice and wet for me.

As I climb back on the bed, I can't resist the urge to slap her ass again. There is something about the way she moans and cries out at the same time that makes me almost feral.

"I love the look of your ass when it's red from my hand," I hiss through gritted teeth. "If your daddy ever thinks you deserve a punishment, I will gladly administer it."

I don't miss the gasp that leaves my sweet blonde girl as she looks over her shoulder, letting go of the headboard with one hand, giving me the perfect excuse. I spank her again and watch her eyes roll this time.

"Did I say let go?" I ask before massaging her sweet pink behind. She quickly grabs hold of the headboard and looks over her shoulder.

"Sorry," she whispers. I press a kiss to her pink, warm skin and hear her moan again.

"That's better, Baby girl," I praise her as I position my fingers at her pussy entrance. "Now, do you have a safe word?" I ask. She shakes her head, which excites me more. I bet none of the fuckers she has been with before us would know how to handle this little minx properly.

"How about we use the word 'black' if it becomes too much, and if you need me to ease off, you say 'orange'?"

"Yes," she replies.

I lean over and press a kiss to her temple.

"You never have to do anything you don't want to with me, you know that, don't you?" I ask, making sure. Verity turns to me, smiling, and nods.

"I want you to dominate me."

Fuck how could any man say no to that?

"Do you want to know what I'm going to do to you? Or should I just do it?" I ask as I push two fingers back into her soaking wet pussy.

"Tell me this time," she answers before moaning.

"I'm going to fuck this sweet pussy," I whisper into her ear. I slowly remove my fingers and start rubbing them around her arsehole. "Whilst I get this nice and warmed up." Slowly, I push one finger in before adding a second. Verity moans loudly as she clenches around my digits. "Before fucking it, until you scream my name as I fill it with my cum." I lick her neck as I finger her sweet ass hole. "How does that sound?"

"Yes," she moans as I bite onto her shoulder slightly. This woman is perfect for me.

I kneel behind her before slowly sliding my cock into her soaking wet pussy.

"Fuck, you are perfect."

We moan together as I start slow, moving in and out of her whilst keeping my fingers in her ass.

Ryan was right. She is fucking heaven; there is no better feeling than being buried deep within her. I want to stay in her forever. But I have somewhere else I want to be before I blow my load. First, I want her to cum on my cock before I take her ass.

It's not easy, but eventually, I get into a rhythm so I can fuck both holes at the same time. Verity is moaning loudly, and I know she is close to her first orgasm. The closer she gets, the looser her back passage becomes, and I know I will be able to take her in just a moment.

"Ethan, yes!" she cries as she falls apart around my cock and screams out as she orgasms. And that prick said she was a quiet lover? You do it right, and she can't stay quiet.

I slip out of her as she comes down from her orgasm but don't give her time to recover before slowly working my way into her back passage.

"Remember your safe words," I hiss through my teeth as I force myself to slow down. I may have prepared her, but she's still tight as fuck. Verity moans out loud, and I can't tell if it's too much for her or not.

"You okay, Baby?" I ask, checking in with her.

"Don't stop," she gasps, which makes me smile. She's so good, so perfect and all ours.

"You are doing so good, Baby. I'm so proud of you," I growl as I slip the last of me inside her. "Fuck," I growl as I stay still a moment, letting her adjust to me. "Are you okay, Baby girl?" I ask, checking in again. She nods her head as she breathes heavily. The great thing about how wet her pussy gets is that I haven't needed the lube as expected.

Slowly, I start moving within her, taking my time and letting her adjust as I do. But it doesn't take long until my kinky little girl is begging for more, and I get to fuck her ass whilst holding on to her hips.

"Let go with one hand and rub your clit, Baby," I order

as I feel myself losing control. I won't be able to hold off for much longer, but I refuse to leave her hanging.

Verity starts rubbing her clit just how she likes it, and before long, we are both crying out as we reach that sweet release. I fill her with my cum, and for a moment, I'm disappointed that it's not her pussy. I want to impregnate her and make sure she can never leave me. I want her pregnant with my child as soon as possible.

Shit, where did that come from?

I slide my now soft dick from her battered ass before falling next to her and holding out my arms.

"Come here, Baby."

She lets go of the headboard and lies in my arms as I hold her close. Both of us sweating and breathing heavily. Sex is a full workout with this woman, and I can't wait to do it all over again.

"Are you okay?" I ask, kissing her forehead as she rests her head on my shoulder.

"Yes," she answers, smiling up at me as she tips her head back.

"You did so well. You took all of me your first time," I praise, knowing how much she loves it. The joy on her face is evident, filling my heart with happiness after the way she was this time yesterday. I look deep into her eyes, and everything feels so right with the world.

"I love you." I have never said those three words before. But they flow easily from my mouth. For a moment, I see a glimpse of her panic, and I quickly remind myself she is still so vulnerable from all she has been through. I don't let her panic hurt my feelings. Instead, I use that tiny fleeting look to remind myself how much she needs me and my brothers to show her she *is* loveable.

"You don't have to say it back any time soon. But I want

you to know how much I love you, and I'm not going anywhere," I whisper as I run my knuckles down her face. "Whatever happens from now on, you have us, okay? We will look after you and all your needs."

Verity nods before cuddling up to me. I rest my head on hers and relax with her in my arms for a few minutes.

"I was only meant to come up and get you for this family meeting," she giggles. "You really are going to get me in trouble with Daddy," she adds playfully. I grin as I roll forward and hover above her so I can press a kiss to her lips.

"Well, we better make sure we make it worthwhile," I tease before jumping off the bed and picking her up.

"Ethan!" she laughs a loud as I carry her towards my bathroom.

"What? I don't know about you, but I need to freshen up before I face my brothers," I tease her lips with mine as she grins up at me.

"A shower does sound nice."

Chapter Twenty-Nine

TRAVIS

"Well, I don't think they will be down any time soon," Ryan laughs as he walks into the lounge and falls into his usual chair. "From the sounds coming from Ethan's room, they will be busy for a little while at least."

"Unless he blows his load in about two minutes and leaves her needing more," I smirk, picking up my glass and taking a sip of whiskey. "She seemed happy when you got back. Take it the visit went well."

Ryan nods as he sips his drink.

"There were moments Trish would repeat herself or call Verity by her mother's name, but the majority of the time, she was pretty coherent. She was definitely observant, that's for sure," he chuckles before looking around and leaning forward a little. "It turns out our girl has been talking about us to her auntie for a while, and she not only realised I was dating Verity in seconds, but she guessed we all were."

"Fuck off." There's no way she would have just come to that conclusion.

"I thought it was weird as well, especially as she was so

cool about it. She told Verity that it made sense she would love the three of us as she has too big a heart for one man.

"Anyway, Trish asked Verity to go and get her a fresh jug of water, which left me alone with her, and she let something slip. She told me to watch and protect Verity as she's in danger. She hinted that Henry is the one we need to protect her from. That he can't control her forever and has no legal rights to her anyway."

"What?" I nearly spill my drink as I sit forward so fast.

"That's what I said. I was sure she was having an episode or whatever she has due to the brain damage, but she seemed so sure and when Verity returned, she changed the subject and carried on as normal."

"So what? Is he not her biological father? Or not on the birth certificate? Could you not get more out of her?" I hiss before looking up at the stairs and checking for Verity again.

"I swear to God, that's all she said. It may be worth looking into if he gives her a hard time when he finds out we are all in a relationship with his daughter."

Ryan has a point; I've been wondering what to do about him finding out, as I have no doubt he will make her life difficult to the point she may rethink this whole thing. I finally have her; there's no way I'm letting her go, especially because of him.

"Leave it with me; I'll see what I can dig up. You're right, though. It may be worth checking out."

I excuse myself and walk up to my bedroom. Ryan was right; from the noise up here, I don't think they will be out of that room any time soon. It surprises me, though, how much it doesn't bother me. Sure, I wish it was me making her cry out like that. At the same time, this morning, that *was* me, so it's not as if she's choosing one of us over the others.

I walk into my room and see my laptop on the bed. Why am I working here when there is a perfectly good office downstairs? I hadn't been using it out of respect for Henry, but fuck that. I have absolutely no respect left for that man after the way he has treated his daughter.

I grab my laptop and briefcase with my paperwork and stationery before heading to the office.

As I walk through the house, I realise there are hardly any photos on the walls. There are a few photos here and there of Verity, but nothing from the age of six. That was the age at which her mother started to fall ill. I'm guessing that was when there was no one to take the photos. The only pictures of Verity's mum are in her room. I know that would be my mother's doing as she wouldn't want to look at her husband's first wife. She is selfish like that.

I have always had a rough relationship with my mother and would prefer my father's company over hers. Maybe it's because she is so self-centred. I swear she wouldn't have even had kids if my father hadn't begged her for us. By the time Ethan arrived, she was done trying to parent, and he was brought up by me and the constant strings of nannies she hired. Not that any stuck around for long; she wanted them to be her personal slave, and they wouldn't do it.

I was always surprised that she had married someone with a child, especially a widower who couldn't palm the child off to the mother, but it turns out he didn't need anyone to watch over her whenever he disappeared. He was happy to leave her alone, with no one but the cleaner and gardener to keep her company.

I walk up to the office door and find it locked. Why would Henry lock the door when only his daughter was in the house? Unless it's locked from us using it. Unluckily for him, I have an expert lockpicker in the family. I'll get Ethan on the case as soon as he graces us with his presence.

I head into the dining room and set up at the table.

I've only been working for twenty minutes when the door opens, and Verity bounces in. Her hair's wet from what I'm guessing was a shower. I take a second to admire her, as she has a genuine smile on her face.

"Why are you working here?" she asks as she stops beside me.

"The office is locked. Any idea why?" I ask, looking back at the spreadsheet in front of me.

"Dad always keeps it locked. There must be a key some-where, as the cleaner used to clean it once a week."

It suddenly dawns on me that I haven't seen the cleaner here in the three days since I arrived.

"When does the cleaner come?" I ask. Verity shrugs and goes to walk away, but I reach out and take her hand, stop-ping her. "Sweetheart, how can you not know when the cleaner comes? They haven't been here in a few days. Are they on holiday?" I ask, frowning at the way she looks down at the floor and shakes her head. "What aren't you telling me?" I ask, tugging her towards me as I turn in my chair so she can sit on my lap. "Does a cleaner still come?" I tip her head back with a hooked finger under her chin to ensure she's looking at me. When she shakes her head, little things start clicking into place.

"When did he fire them?"

"When I turned eighteen," she answers quietly.

"Why don't I know that?" I ask.

I remember seeing a cleaner when we first visited for the day or the odd overnight trip. I even asked Mum where they were on one visit a couple of years ago, and she said she asked them not to come when we were here as there were too many people in the house for her liking. It made sense, and I just accepted it. From the look on Verity's face, I know exactly why I don't know about the cleaner not coming around anymore.

"Was this one of the things you were told to lie to us about, Sweetheart?"

Verity nods, and I see those tears back in her eyes. I hate that I've taken her smile away. I wrap my arms around her, giving her a big hug.

"I'm sorry I upset you; I didn't mean to. Do you think you could tell us what's been going on?" I ask, pressing a kiss to the top of her head.

"They will be angry at me," she whispers, causing my jaw to clench. What the fuck have they been doing to this girl to make her so damn obedient and scared.

"Even if they are, we won't be and will stand up for you. I promise they will never control any part of your life again." I softly encourage her to look at me and give her a small smile. "Who am I?"

"My ... Daddy."

"And who will always protect you from this moment on?"

Verity doesn't answer straight away, which I expected. She is still to come to terms with our relationship and what it means for her. I lean in and press a soft kiss to her lips. "You, Sweetheart. I will protect you until my last breath because you are everything to me, do you understand? No matter what hold he thinks he has over you, it's nothing like the love I have for you. Your father has been controlling you, and we are here to help you become free and the person you want to be, not what he has tried to shape you into."

Verity looks at me for a moment before taking a deep

breath and pushing her shoulders back. She gives me a slow nod, and I know she is going to try to accept it.

"Good girl," I whisper, giving her a wink. "Shall we sit with the others, and we can all have this discussion? We have been waiting on you and Ethan," I grin at her as her cheeks turn bright red. Considering what a kinky little thing she is, she looks so innocent with her blonde hair and blue eyes. Her skin is so pale and flawless that it seems almost unreal.

"Sorry, we got a little distracted," she smiles at me sheepishly. I laugh as I stand, placing her on her feet simultaneously.

"A little? Sweetheart, you two could be heard from a mile away." Wrapping an arm around her waist, I pull her roughly against me as she hides in her hands, as she does every time she's embarrassed. "I love hearing you having fun almost as much as I love having fun with you," I growl in her ear as she squirms in my arm.

"Guys, I have to be online in two hours! Can we have this discussion today or not?" I hear Ryan call out as Ethan laughs.

"To be continued," I whisper in her ear before taking her hand and pulling her into the lounge where I know my brothers are waiting.

Chapter Thirty

VERITY

I walk into the lounge with Travis, hand in hand, to find the other two laughing together.

"Sorry we were talking, unlike some," Travis says, giving a side eye to Ethan, who just winks at me.

Travis sits on his usual spot on the sofa and pulls me down to sit next to him. My heart starts racing as I realise a lot of home truths are about to be revealed, and I don't know how I feel about it.

"Verity has just told me some things our parents didn't want us to know."

Ethan and Ryan frown in my direction, and I find myself leaning into Travis for protection. They are going to be so mad at me. I don't know right now who I'm more worried about upsetting: Dad, Linda, or the guys. Once they know the truth and how much I was told to hide, they're going to be furious at me for not telling them sooner. Travis wraps an arm around me and whispers in my ear.

"Breath, Sweetheart."

I try to do as he says, but it's hard when so much atten-

207

tion is on me. Travis pulls me onto his lap and wraps his arms around me, holding me together like he did when I fell apart yesterday.

"No matter what you tell us, you are not in trouble. You were only doing what your father said, and it's not your fault he told you to hide things. But for us all to move forward and help you, we need to know the truth." He presses a kiss to my forehead, and I close my eyes in an attempt to centre myself. "Do you remember what I said to you a minute ago?" he asks, and I nod. "Good. No matter what, we will never be mad at you for doing as they told you to do. We are here for you, no one else."

I take a deep breath and open my eyes to look at him. I nod, letting me know I'm okay.

"That's it, Sweetheart. We are right here with you, okay?"

"Okay," I whisper, forcing a small smile.

"Why don't you tell the others what you just told me, and we will start from there."

I nod before turning back to look at the other two, who are still watching me.

"Dad and Linda fired the housekeeper the day I turned eighteen. Since then, there hasn't been one."

"What? But Mum said-" Ethan starts.

"Mum lied, and I have a good idea why," Travis interrupts before looking back at me. "Who does all the cleaning and cooking now?"

"I do. But I don't mind!" I answer, emphasising the point. "At the end of the day, I live on my own most of the time, so I don't make much mess," I add.

"But it's a big house, Kitten," Ryan points out.

"Dad pays me an allowance each month. That's to cover the costs of food and anything I need for the house.

Most people don't have that at my age or parents willing to pay for their dance school."

"But what did they say would happen when you graduate?" Ryan asks. I shrug as I lean back into Travis's chest.

"Then I need to find my own place. It's no big deal. In many ways, it's saving me money as I don't have to worry about rent and bills yet."

"Okay, so what about when they are back? Do you still have to clean up after them?" I see the moment the realisation hits Ethan. "Have you been cleaning up after us?" he demands. I nod slowly.

"I hadn't even thought about that. I've been leaving dishes in the dishwasher and washing in the laundry room. Why didn't you say anything?" Ryan asks.

"Because she was told not to," Travis reminds them. He looks down at me and offers a small smile. "Was there anything else they told you not to tell us?"

I nod slowly and look at the front door.

"Dawn pops in twice a month to ensure I'm keeping up with the housework and that things are presentable."

"Mum's friend Dawn?" Ethan asks.

"Yeah, one time she came, and there was a load of washing waiting to go in and plates in the dishwasher. They weren't happy," I sigh. I will get in trouble with them for telling the guys anyway; I might as well admit it all.

"What did they do?" Travis demands as the others watch me.

"They stopped my allowance until she came back and checked everything was as they wanted. She usually comes fortnightly, but that time, she left it four weeks."

"How the fuck are you meant to survive on the tiny amount of money you get from the shows? They would have known you were at risk of going hungry!"

"I was fine; I make enough to survive; I'm not that skint. I was more peeved that they wouldn't listen to me about why the stuff was there."

"Why was it?" Ryan asks.

"Because it was when I was when my drink was spiked."

"But they knew you were unwell and why. How could he stop your allowance when it wasn't your fault?" Travis points out. I shrug as I realise how much my father has put me through over the last year.

"None of this explains why she was told not to tell us. Why did they want us to continue thinking a cleaner was doing all our clothes and so on for us? Why not just say, do it yourselves?" Ethan points out.

"Three reasons," Travis answers. "The first is that they didn't want us to know that they do not have the perfect house, with expensive cleaners and cooks and housekeeping. Mum has always liked to feel superior to others, and she does that through the money she has.

"The second reason is simply they think they are better than everyone else. I can guarantee you that it's Mum behind most of it, but Henry is too blind to see it. He is easily manipulated, and she knows how to play him. Plus, you are forgetting who does their accounts," Travis shrugs.

"Have you noticed anything different on them?" Ryan asks.

"I've noticed a few things, like the other morning when I saw they had been in the UK even though they claimed they were in the States. I plan to review them and see how often they have done that. But there is still a monthly payment going out for housekeeping as well as Verity's allowance. Would be interesting to see where that money's been going."

I lean back against Travis as they start talking among

themselves. If Dad and Linda have lied to the guys about stuff, what have they lied to me about? How often have I made excuses for something they said or did when I shouldn't have? Has everything they have put me through been about punishing me? But for what? I have always done everything they asked of me. Even if it went against everything I believed in, I love my dad and want him to be proud of me.

"The third reason is they wouldn't expect us to be here still. They would have figured we'd leave as soon as they did. They have no idea we are even still here, as I certainly haven't contacted them. Have any of you?"

The three of us shake our heads as I'm hit with another realisation. They think I am alone, even though it's almost Christmas. Travis is right; they wouldn't have expected them to be here still. My dad left smiling and excited about spending his Christmas in Hawaii while thinking his daughter will be sitting at home alone in a big house. What kind of father does that?

"Little Kitten?" Ryan's voice brings me back to the room, and I look at him, confused.

"Pardon?"

He gives me a look that tells me he knows my mind has wandered.

"I asked if you are okay," he repeats with a small smile. "You looked like you had zoned out there for a moment."

"I did," I reply as Travis kisses my head.

"Is there anything else you were told not to tell us?" Ethan asks.

"Only that if asked, I don't tell you how much time I'm actually alone here, and if there are any issues, I contact them, not you."

"Well, they can fuck off with that one. I want to know

everything from now on. Plus, you will never be alone again, not now you have the three of us. One of us can always be home with you," Travis says as I curl up into a ball on his lap.

"That's one thing we need to work out," Ryan says from across the room. "Where will home be?"

"Can we not stay here?" I ask, looking around at the guys.

"For the time being, yes, but in the long run, probably not," Travis sighs. "When your dad finds out about us, I don't think he will take it well, and I think he'll try and get between us."

"Can't we just hide it from them? It's not like they are ever here. Plus, I will need to find my own place in six months anyway," I point out.

"And what happens when Dawn tells them we are constantly here? Or they notice themselves?" Ryan points out. "I, for one, am not hiding anything from them. The last thing I want is for them to return and try to upset you again. They knew what they were doing yesterday; they wanted to leave before you woke up. I tried to warn you, but you were too excited to listen and understandably. But I will never forget how you looked when you came out of that room with your dad."

I sigh and force myself to ignore the despair that washes over me whenever I think of yesterday.

"How long do you want to hide it from them, Baby? Cause I know they will start asking questions when you change your name or fall pregnant." Ethan laughs.

"What?" I yell, sitting up straight. "It's been like a day!" I protest as I stand up. The smile on Ethan's face drops.

"Baby, I was joking; bad timing. I'm sorry."

"So, you don't want to marry me or for me to have your

212

kids?" I demand, realising they are already looking for a way out. Ethan stands from the sofa and blocks my escape.

"Baby, I want all of that, but I know it's not something that will happen immediately. I didn't mean to freak you out, and I'm sorry." He reaches up and cups my cheek. "I told you upstairs I love you, and I'm not going anywhere. One day soon, we will have to decide where we will all live and how this will work with us all. But one thing is for sure: you will become a Donavon because, for me, this is it."

I look around at the others and realise they are on their feet, too, standing close.

"Sweetheart, none of us are going anywhere; we know it's still early days. But things need to be worked out to ensure you are safe and protected."

"No one is going to hurt me," I point out.

"Not physically, because I would kill them. But your dad has been abusive and toxic for so long I don't think you realise the damage he has caused," Travis says from behind me. I look at him, and he steps forward and takes my hand. "That man has taught you not to cry, voice your opinions, or ask for anything. If he walked through that door right now and told you it was him or us, which would you choose."

I open my mouth to say him, it's instinct, but after yesterday, I don't know.

"He's my dad; he's meant to love me, to teach me right from wrong," I point out as I blink back the tears.

"He's meant to, but not the way he has. No one should ever tell you that you can't cry or show any kind of emotion. You are human, after all; why wouldn't you show emotion? You were in pain yesterday, and he told you to stop having a tantrum," Ryan says as he steps up beside me. "You were in so much pain you shut down for over an hour. No one, parent or not, should make you feel like that."

I look around them as my head starts to spin. It's all becoming too much; the pain from my father abandoning me is still so fresh, and I know deep down what they are saying is true, but I can't just cut off the only parent I have, even if they've done just that to me.

"Sweetheart, look at me."

I turn and look at Travis, the words "help me" on my tongue, but all I can hear is my dad's voice.

"You can't demand my attention. There are more important things for me to deal with than one of your tantrums."

"I need a minute," I whisper as I walk past them all, but Travis places a hand on my arm.

"Where are you going?" he asks. I look down at his hand on my arm, and he removes it.

"I'm fine; I'll be right back."

I don't give any of them a chance to try and stop me again. I force myself to calmly walk out of the lounge, up the stairs and into my room before I lean back against the closed door.

I close my eyes and force the tears back.

"No one wants to see you cry."

Chapter Thirty-One

TRAVIS

I stand at the bottom of the stairs and look up towards the direction of her room. Yesterday, when she shut down, everything told me to go into her room and show her I was there. This time, it's the opposite; I feel like I should give her space and let her take some control. Let's face it: She's had people telling her what to do and how to behave for so long that she doesn't know what to do for herself anymore.

Forcing myself to move away from the stairs, I head towards the office.

"Ethan?" I call, knowing he will hear me from the kitchen where he and Ryan are making coffees for us all.

"Yo!" he appears, drinking from his mug.

"I have a job for you; follow me." I lead him down to the office and point to the door. "You can either look for the key or pick it. But I want access to that office A.S.A.P. That fucker is hiding something in there, and I want to know what."

Ethan squats down in front of the door and looks at the lock.

215

"I should be able to pick that. Do you want Verity to know or not?"

I think about it for a moment and shake my head.

"Not yet. I want to know if there is anything worth her knowing first. She has already had too much to deal with the last few days."

Ethan nods, stands, and looks up to the stairs.

"I didn't mean to freak her out. But I want everyone to know she is ours. I don't want to hide our relationship like it's some dirty secret." He rubs his face, letting out a deep breath. "I'm also worried what Mum and Henry will do when they decide to show their faces again. What they have been doing to her is evil, but Henry has her so conditioned."

"He's her father, and she doesn't know any different. I wouldn't be surprised if they have more control over her than we are aware of. It will take a long time for her to truly trust us enough to tell us everything and really open up. I don't think we will see the true Verity for a while." I place a hand on his shoulder and give it a reassuring squeeze. "I understand why you said what you did. Fuck, I feel the same way. I can't wait for all of those things with her. But at the moment, she is waiting for us to disappear, and we need to prove to her we aren't. When you said what you did and then backtracked to our girl, that was you changing your mind, even though that wasn't what you were saying at all." I'm hoping he will understand why we can't rush her. She will put on her brave face and hide her true feelings from us. This is one of the reasons I took on the daddy role so easily, as she seems to open up the most to me.

"For now, let's just concentrate on getting her through Christmas. We can try to make it as magical as possible for her. After we know Mum and Henry are back from Hawaii, we can start dealing with the rest."

"What are we going to do about them?" Ethan asks. I turn around and look up the stairs, feeling like it's time to go up there and see her.

"I don't know. All I do know is I don't want anyone treating her the way she has been treated her whole life ever again. For now, we need to concentrate on getting her stronger so she can deal with whatever is thrown her way when the time comes."

Ethan lets out a sigh as he looks towards the stairs. I can see him thinking about it all, and I know he will follow my lead as we start this new way of life.

"Hey, I'm going to take her up a coffee and see how she is," Ryan says as he walks into the hallway.

"Good idea. If you need either of us, shout," I reply as he disappears. I look back to the office door and know I need to get in there. "Let's see if we can find this key; if not, you can pick it and get us in."

In ten minutes, we managed to rule out the keys in the dining room and lounge. We are just starting the search of the kitchen when Verity walks into the room with her dancing bag over her shoulder.

"Hey, Baby girl, you going to dance tonight?" Ethan asks, leaning back against the counter.

"Yeah, I spoke to Mrs Florence, and she's happy for me to dance if I feel up to it. I might as well as after tomorrow. I have the weekend off before the couple of weeks of performances before we have three weeks off for Christmas."

"Why don't we all come to watch you together tomorrow night? Then we could go out for a drink for a change of scenery," I suggest, wondering why I hadn't thought of it before. Verity's whole face lights up as her eyes widen, and she looks at us all. From the look on my brother's faces, they like that idea too.

"You will all come? Really?" she asks excitedly.

"Of course, sounds like a brilliant idea. I haven't seen you dance for nearly two years," Ethan grins as he places his arm over her shoulder and kisses her head.

"That's it then, we are coming. I'll sort out the tickets. Even if we have to sit apart, we will all be there tomorrow."

The look on Verity's face is enough to melt any cold heart. If something as simple as watching her dance can make her smile like that, then I'll ensure one of us is at every performance.

"Do you want one of us to take you tonight? Or would you rather drive yourself?" Ethan asks.

"I'm taking her as I already said I will watch her tonight," Ryan answers.

"You don't have to now you are coming tomorrow," Verity says, looking up at him. Ryan smiles as he looks into her eyes.

"I'm more than happy to watch both. I love watching you dance," he answers as her smile grows. He leans in and presses a soft kiss on her lips. "Get what you need and say goodbye to the others. I know you are looking forward to seeing Jaz and Danielle."

Verity rushes towards the fridge and pulls out a water bottle before heading to Ethan.

Whilst she's distracted, I stand next to Ryan.

"How was she when you went up?" I ask quietly.

"Okay. She was on the phone with Jaz, who's meeting her to chat. It might be what she needs. From what I hear, they have a lot in common, and Jaz may put her mind at ease when it comes to us."

"I hope so; it will do her good getting out of the house anyway." I quickly turn to face her, smiling as she approaches.

"What are you two whispering about?" she asks nervously. I place an arm over her shoulders and smile.

"Christmas secrets, ones you don't need to worry about," I tease, winking. Verity rolls her eyes at me before lifting onto her tiptoes and kissing my cheek.

"Have a good performance, Sweetheart. I'll see you when you get back." I cup her cheek as I press a kiss to her lips.

"Okay," she replies as her cheeks warm under my touch. She is so beautiful; it's hard to tear myself away from her. But she needs this time with her friends to help make sense of everything that must be running around in that gorgeous head of hers.

I press one last kiss to her soft lips before letting her go and forcing myself to step back.

"Come on, little Kitten, let's get you to the girls before they send out a search party," Ryan laughs as Verity waves to us and heads out of the house, following him.

I watch as they leave and wait until I hear the car pull away from the house before turning back to Ethan.

"Right, let's get into this office."

Chapter Thirty-Two

VERITY

The door to the dressing room slams as it flies open, making me jump and nearly poke my eye out with my eyeliner. Two arms wrap around my neck from behind as Jasmine appears in the reflection of the mirror I'm sitting in front of.

"Are you okay? I've been worried sick!"

"I'm getting there," I whisper, placing a hand over her arm before she lets me go.

"What the fuck happened? She only got a small explanation from Christian," Danielle says as she leans against the vanity table in front of me.

"How would Christian know anything?" I demand, turning to frown at Jasmine.

"How do you think? Travis called him. He wouldn't tell me what they talked about, just that you wouldn't be dancing last night or maybe tonight as you were unwell. I know he knows more, but when I tried to get him to tell me, he gave me the full name treatment and warned me not to push my luck," Jasmine pouts whilst standing on the other side of me with her arms crossed.

"Why did Travis call him? I thought they hated each other?"

"As far as I'm concerned, they do, but Travis needed help with something to do with you, and Christian wouldn't say no to that; he knows how much you mean to me. So, spill bitch, what the fuck happened that your stepbrother had to call my daddy?"

Something clicks as a warm feeling in my chest. Travis must have called Christian for advice on how to be my daddy!

"My father was home the other night when we got back to the house."

Jaz nods, as she already knows after I messaged her. But from the look on Danielle's face, she knows what happened.

"He didn't stay, did he." It's not a question, she knows. I shake my head as the smile drops from Jasmine's face. I look down at my lap, where my fingers are now busy pulling apart the cotton wool pad I'd been holding.

"He was gone in less than twelve hours. Apparently, spending family time with Linda's family in Hawaii is more important than spending time with me."

"Then why the hell did he bother coming back at all?" Jasmine yells. "Isn't Hawaii closer to the States than here?"

I nod, unable to look at my friends.

"He said he wouldn't have come back if he had known they would be heading there before coming home," I admit as my eyes fill with tears. "They had been back nearly a week and not even bothered to let me know."

"That son of a bitch!" Danielle curses as I look up at her.

"You were right. You did see him at the Christmas Eve party last year." I fill them in on how I spent Christmas home alone, all because of my dad and his wife, how they told the guys not to come, that they wanted me to be alone.

"Oh, Verity, I'm so sorry," Jasmine says as she hugs me. I try not to cry, but my barriers are weakened after the last twenty-four hours, and I'm too tired to put on the front anymore.

As I cry into Jasmine's shoulder, I feel Danielle's hand on my back, offering me support when I need it the most. My two friends hold me as I cry for the first time in front of them. I'm tired of being the strong one who has everything right in their life. That has been a lie for so long, and I don't think I can keep it up anymore.

Eventually, I pull away from Jasmine, and Danielle hands me a tissue. I thank her and start drying my face.

"I hope you know you are welcome to spend Christmas with us, so you're not alone," Jasmine says as she hands me another tissue.

"The guys are staying with me. Things have kind of changed in that department," I reply, looking up at Jasmine sheepishly as she starts laughing.

"So Christian was right? Travis does have feelings for you?"

"He says he does, and he kind of said he wants to be my daddy and look after me," I admit as I watch the smile drop from her face. This time, it's Danielle who starts laughing.

"Please don't tell me you now have three daddies!" she laughs. I shake my head, smiling slightly.

"Three boyfriends, but only one is my daddy."

Jasmine starts squealing as she hops from one foot to the other.

"I love this so much! Please say you have done the group thing already because that is so much fun!"

"I am not getting into this discussion with you!" I yell as

my cheeks heat up, and she laughs at me. I climb to my feet and head over to where my costumes are hung up to check them over as Jasmine giggles at me.

"I don't need to hear about either of your sex lives, thank you very much," Danielle sighs from where she is standing. I turn in time to see her pushing herself away from the vanity table and approach me. "But if you ever need to talk about anything else, you know I'm here for you, right? I know I've been a bitch in the past, but…" I can see she's struggling to finish her sentence, so I give her a hug and step back, smiling.

"I know, thanks."

She nods once before heading for the exit, calling that she needs a coffee, closing the door behind her, leaving me with a grinning Jasmine.

"What?" I ask as I pull out a fresh pair of tights to put on.

"How are you *really* feeling about the whole three guys thing?" she asks. Jaz knows me better than anyone, and now she is the only one I can speak to about this.

"I'm scared," I admit, taking a deep breath. "No one ever stays around for long. My own father doesn't even want to be around me. So why would three guys? Travis says he wants to be my daddy, but what if he's doing it just to be nice?"

Jasmine walks forward and takes my hand whilst smiling.

"If you need any sign that he isn't just doing this to be nice, look at the fact that as soon as you needed help, he called the guy he has hated for ten years." I go to argue, but one look from Jaz tells me she hasn't finished. "Do you know why Christian and Travis aren't talking?" she asks. I nod, and she gives my hand a small squeeze. "Then you must know how hard it would have been for Travis to call him and admit he needed his help. Christian's whole attitude towards him changed after that phone call, so whatever was said made Christian see him in a different light."

"And you have no idea what they talked about?"

Jaz shakes her head and lets go of my hand.

"I really don't. When I asked Christian, he just said it was between them, and that's it. He tried saying he only spoke to him because it concerned you, but I think there was more to it. I think the two of them are more alike than they were willing to accept. It would make sense, as they are both daddies. How did the whole daddy thing come about?"

I let out a short breath as I take a seat in the chair I had been sitting in. Jasmine takes another, and I tell her most of the details regarding my breakdown. I don't tell her everything, and I hope Travis didn't tell Christian about the self-harming. That's something I know I need to stop, and I know that won't happen overnight. But the fact that someone knows about it makes the whole thing feel different.

By the time I finish telling her how he held me and got me to open up, Jaz has tears in her eyes. When I tell her about the doll and why he gave it to me, she wraps her arms around me, and we both shed a few tears.

It feels so good to open up, especially to someone I have been hiding so much from. There have been hundreds of times she has asked if I'm okay, and I wanted to tell her, "No, I'm not". But instead, I would force a smile and act like everything was fine. But now it's out there, and once I start telling her stuff, I can't stop. The whole while, she sits there holding my hand and giving me the occasional hug.

She lets me cry on her shoulder and promises to be there for anything I need in the future.

By the time I finish, and we have talked, cried and laughed together, I feel like the weight of the world has been lifted from my shoulders. I know it's only the start of the healing process, but it's better than I have been feeling and a step in the right direction.

"From now on, you don't hide anything from me because if I find out you have, I will phone your daddy and tell him," Jasmine teases a giggle out of me as I wipe my eyes. I know she isn't joking; she would have no problem calling Travis if she thought it was in my best interests. "Promise me, Verity. I don't care what it's about or what time of the day or night it is; you call me if you need me. I will never not listen."

"I know, I'm sorry," I reply, smiling sheepishly at her.

"You will be if you do it again. You can't hide anything from me; that's not the kind of friends we are."

I smile at my friend and nod before looking in the mirror and letting out a deep sigh.

"How am I meant to hide these swollen eyes?" I ask, noticing how much the crying has made my eyes puff out.

"I have just the thing." Jasmine jumps to her feet and holds the door open. "Come on, I left my bag in the communal area; let's go and grab it before the other dancers all turn up and see us looking like this."

I follow my friend out of the room, knowing I should have confided in her long ago. She has my back in a way no one has before, and I couldn't love her more for it.

Chapter Thirty-Three

RYAN

I walk away from my seat, buzzing after watching the performance.

Verity was breathtaking, and there was no mistaking the pure joy she felt when dancing. Everything is different about her when she's on the stage. The first time I ever saw her dance was about three years ago.

I never had much to do with my mum; none of us did. We didn't even meet Henry until the day of the wedding. We attended her wedding and met our new stepfather and his daughter. I didn't pay much attention to them on the day. If I'm honest, I thought she was just some spoilt little daddy's girl. I was busy setting up my new business, having just left university, and rarely came to see Mum afterwards. If I ever saw her, it was at my place whenever they would turn up on the way to the airport. But about three years ago, they asked us to come back for a family event, and Verity was there. I remember seeing her properly for the first time; she was the most beautiful woman I had ever seen.

That night, I had a bit too much to drink and admitted to Travis that I thought she was beautiful. He had told me under no uncertain terms to forget it. She was our stepsister, and nothing could ever happen. The following month, I watched her dance in Midsummer Night's Dream and fell head over heels in love with her. But Travis's voice in the back of my head stopped me from doing anything about it. At the end of the day, he was right. She was our stepsister and out of bounds. That didn't stop me from calling her Little Kitten because she looked so innocent with her big blue eyes. I knew then I would never find anyone like her, and although I tried to get over my feelings for her, nothing and no one even came close in comparison.

I had been on away the night Travis let slip that Verity's drink had been spiked while out with the O'Reilly girl. He told me how he'd rushed to be by her side and had been worried sick about her. He was so furious with whoever had spiked her drink, and when I heard about him calling Christian, I knew it wasn't just a man looking out for his kid stepsister.

A few days later, he told me I had to pop back to check up on her myself. I heard he had been there for nearly a week and started making regular contact with her. I tried to call him out on it, but he denied everything. He kept saying he didn't like the idea of any harm coming to her, but I knew deep down it was more than that. Especially when I heard him on the phone one day calling her 'Sweetheart', I knew then my suspicions were right, but there was no way he would admit them to me.

I guess now everything has come to light, and it's hard to believe that he has gone from denying all feelings for her to telling her he loves her and becoming her daddy. But I know it is the perfect relationship for them as he will look after her in a way Ethan and I would struggle with. Does that mean I won't become her daddy in the future? I don't know, but for now, I'm happy to be one of the guys who get to call her theirs.

"Hey! Donavan!"

I turn around to see the O'Reilly twins walking towards me.

"Hey!" I reply, smiling at them as they approach.

Even though there has been a lot of bad blood between Christian and Travis, the rest of us have tried to keep out of it. Sure, we aren't as close as we used to be, but we don't argue like the two of them whenever we see each other.

"You here watching your sister?" Maximus asks as I shake his hand.

"Stepsister, and well, guess you could call her my girl-friend, actually," I laugh.

"So it's true then? The three of you are with Verity?" Sean asks as we shake.

"Yeah. How did you find out?"

"Jaz," they answer in unison. I should have known Verity would tell her everything, and she would tell her guys. Let's face it: if there were anyone for Verity to talk to about all of this, it would be Jasmine.

"So, you joined the world of daddies?" Maximus asks, nudging me with his shoulders.

"No, that would be Travis. Ethan and I aren't up for the whole daddy thing," I admit as we all move to the side of the foyer as everyone else leaves.

"Yeah, I thought that too. But the moment I saw how much Jasmine needed all of us, I didn't have to think; I knew it was a role I wanted to take; we all did," Sean says as he leans against the wall.

"Is it bad I want to do all that but not complicate it with

the whole daddy thing? Travis is perfect for the role, and I know Ethan has a different kind of dom-sub thing going on with her. But it feels different for what she and I have, you know?" I ask, looking between the two of them. I'm surprised when it's Maximus that answers me.

"I get that completely. I guess out of all of us, I was always the one who struggled with the sharing and daddy thing. When we first started discussing it as an option, I wanted to refuse and take my Shorty away from them all," he admits.

"What changed?" I ask as Maximus rubs his face whilst shrugging.

"As Sean said, when I stopped overthinking it, I realised it was just right, and the role of Daddy was something that happened without any of us really realising."

"It was literally the night before that it was decided it wouldn't just be Christian and Jason being her daddies. We saw how she'd been living and wanted to protect and shower her in love. Even at that point, we hadn't realised how bad it had got for her," Sean adds.

"Do you ever regret it now?" I ask.

"No," both answer together.

"I can honestly say I never regret the decision to share our woman or for us all to be her Daddies. Yes, it can get confusing as she does call us all Daddy, but it's worked for us. She has every one of us wrapped around her little finger, and she knows it," Maximus laughs.

"She acts differently with each of us, and we all have our own relationship with her. But we formed partnerships with her before we started the romantic relationship. I guess that's harder for you guys as you weren't that close before," Sean adds. I realise he's right.

Travis had a relationship with her before all of this; it

had started after she was spiked. That's probably why the daddy thing came so naturally to him. But Ethan and I had kept our distance, and neither of us ever really noticed that the other felt anything for her. Other than that one chat outside of her room when she cried herself to sleep, we never really discussed this as brothers to see where we stood with it all.

I realise now that's something that we shouldn't be putting off. We need to discuss this properly before things go too far and someone ends up getting hurt.

"You look deep in thought there. I hope we haven't put you off the whole thing," Maximus laughs. I shake my head.

"No, nothing to do with that. I have waited too long to call her mine, and I don't plan on losing that privilege any time soon. But you have made me realise my brothers, and I have a lot to discuss."

"Yeah, talking is a major factor in this kind of relationship. I lost count of how many hours we spent putting everything together and coming to agreements about it all," Sean answers.

"Which all went out the window once we realised Shorty was living the way she was, and we needed to step in and protect her," Maximus laughs.

"Look, whatever happens, if you need to talk to anyone, give us a shout or catch us at the gym. You still boxing?" Sean asks.

"Kinda. I don't have anyone but Ethan to go against. I could do with a challenge. Why you offering?" I chuckle.

"You know what? Yeah, I am. Fancy going a few rounds tomorrow afternoon?"

"Yeah, sounds good. The usual gym?" I ask, knowing Sean trains at the gym closest to home more than anywhere else.

"Yeah. I'll meet you there at two. We have our last fitting for the wedding suits in the morning. But I can meet you after I've had a bite to eat." He pulls a card from his wallet and holds it out to me.

"If there are any issues, give me a call, and we can rearrange. Or if you want to talk about any of the other stuff."

"Yeah, cheers, mate, will do. I'll keep it quiet from Travis, though," I laugh.

"Nah, can't see it being a problem anymore. Not after he called Christian for help the other day. Think they have finally started putting the past behind them, in a way at least," Maximus shrugs from where he is standing.

"Travis called Christian? When?"

Sean and Maximus fill me in on the phone call Travis made to Christian and the chat he had with Jason, and soon, everything starts to make a little more sense. I make a note of speaking to him about it and seeing how he is doing with it all.

I'm just about to ask if they know anymore when the girls arrive, both smiling and looking happy.

"Ryan, have you met Jaz?" Verity asks as she reaches us. I shake my head and hold out my hand.

"No, but I've heard all about her. It's nice to finally put a face to the name," I say, shaking her hand.

"If it's anything these two have said about me, it's all lies, I promise," Jasmine laughs before looking at the twins. "I'm an angel," she adds, fluttering her eyelashes at them.

"Shorty, we all know that is an absolute lie, and you know what happens when you lie," Maximus growls, grabbing her ass and pulling her roughly towards him as she giggles loudly. I place an arm around Verity's shoulders as she leans into me, laughing at her friend.

"Oh, behave, Daddy. We're in public." Jasmine walks out of Maximus's arms and straight to Sean, who kisses her.

"You know that never stops him, Princess," Sean laughs. "You were wonderful tonight, by the way," he adds, kissing her again.

"You say that every night," she laughs, but I can see how much his praise means to her. I turn my back to the three and focus on my own girl.

"Did you enjoy the show?" Verity asks, smiling up at me nervously.

"I loved it; you were amazing, little Kitten. I felt so proud sitting there watching you. You took my breath away," I whisper against her lips as she smiles up at me. I can see tears in her eyes and realise how much a little thing like us watching her performances means to her.

"Come on, let's get home and see the others before they go to bed," I smile as I take the bag from her and hold out my hand for hers.

"See you tomorrow, Jaz," Verity calls as she takes my hand, and we turn back to the twins and Jasmine.

"See you tomorrow," I nod at Sean, who salutes me playfully.

"What's happening tomorrow?" Verity asks. I look down at her and wink.

"I'll fill you in when we are in the car."

Chapter Thirty-Four

VERITY

I'm walking from the car to the house when Ryan stops me by grabbing my hand. He spins me around and presses a kiss to my lips.

"I know you want to see the guys, but after, can I have you to myself tonight? I want to hold you close as you fall asleep if that's okay with you?" he asks.

"That sounds perfect, but I need to speak to Travis about something first. Is that okay?" I reply, hoping he doesn't think I'm putting Travis over him. But the smile on Ryan's face puts me at ease.

"Absolutely, I'll meet you upstairs in your room," he says, kissing me once before letting us into the house.

"I'll be right there. I need a shower before bed, though," I smile as we reach the bottom of the stairs. Ryan wraps an arm around my waist and pulls me against him as he leans over me, looking sexy as hell.

"Can I wash your back for you?" he asks, his lips brushing against mine as his voice deepens.

"Just my back?"

233

Ryan slowly shakes his head as his grin widens further.

"I can think of a few more places if you want me to."

I can't quite find the words to answer, so I nod whilst giggling happily.

"I'll be waiting for you then." He presses one long, hard kiss to my lips before winking and heading up the stairs, taking them two at a time.

I rush towards the lounge where I can hear the TV, eager to see Travis quickly so I can get upstairs where Ryan will be waiting for me.

"Hey, Sweetheart, how did tonight go?" Travis asks from where he is sitting on the sofa. I rush to him and throw my arms around his neck, holding him tight.

"Hey? What's the matter?" he asks, pulling me onto his lap.

"Thank you," I whisper into his neck before sitting up.

"What for?" He reaches up and runs his knuckles over my cheek.

"I know you called Christian. I don't know what you said, but I know you did it to help me, and it couldn't have been an easy call to make. So, thank you."

Travis watches me for a moment before he looks deep into my eyes.

"It wasn't a question of it being a hard call to make, not when I knew it would benefit you. There isn't anything I wouldn't do for you, Sweetheart."

"I'm starting to believe that," I whisper honestly. If he was willing to call Christian to help me, then that just goes to show that I must mean more to him than I was willing to believe.

"Good, and I will keep showing you how much you mean to me until you never doubt it again." He leans in and kisses my lips.

"What did you call him about?" I ask, wondering if he will tell me the truth. I can see he's thinking about whether to or not, but when he sighs and runs his knuckles down my cheek again, I know he will.

"Jason had told me the night before about Christian's relationship with Jasmine and how he is her main daddy. That he's the one she turns to when she is scared and needs protection. That's what I want to be for you, but when I saw you lying on that bed, not moving or talking, and Ryan told me how broken you were, I was scared I was going to make you worse, so I called Christian for advice." Travis looks at me for a moment before continuing. "It was a short conversation; he asked me what my gut instinct was, and when I told him, he agreed it was the right thing to do. He said that I was already thinking like a daddy for you and that I should follow my gut, so I did."

"I'm glad you did because it was what I needed," I admit as I lean my cheek against his chest. "You got through to me in a way I don't think anyone else could have."

"I'm glad I could help you when you needed me the most. Whatever the future brings, Sweetheart, I am and always will be here for you. Like I said, if you want me as your daddy, I am completely here for that, as it feels so natural to be in that role for you." He kisses the top of my head as his arms tighten around me. "I love you, sweetheart; never forget that. I will always love you."

Those three words are there on the tip of my tongue, but I can't quite bring myself to say them. Whenever I tell people I love them, they leave, and I never want the guys to leave me. I know Travis notices the silence, but I also know he won't expect me to say it, not yet.

"Why don't you go and get into bed? I'm sure Ryan is

up there waiting for you," Travis whispers into my hair. I lean out of his arms, smiling.

"Were you listening to us?"

Travis smiles as he shrugs.

"You weren't exactly being quiet," he winks as he helps me off his lap. "Go to bed. I have a meeting in the morning, but I will see you when I get back."

"We have our last dress fitting in the morning for our bridesmaid dresses. But I will be home for about one," I answer. Travis smiles up at me and nods.

"Then I will see you when you get back. Good night, Sweetheart. If you need me, you know where I am."

I lean over and press one last kiss to his lips.

"Good night, Daddy. Thank you for everything," I whisper before rushing up the stairs to where I know Ryan is waiting for me.

Chapter Thirty-Five

VERITY

I pull up outside the house and notice that Travis's car is the only one here. After a lovely morning with Jasmine and Danielle, I'm in a great mood. We all had our last fitting for our dresses for the wedding. The next time we see our dresses will be the week of the wedding when we collect them from the shop.

Jasmine is going to be the most beautiful bride ever. I'm so happy for her, getting the happily ever after she deserves. No matter how bad I think I've had it, it has never been as bad as what she dealt with from her mother. I'm so happy she now has her four guys to show her just how special she is.

I move the rear-view mirror to check my make-up before heading inside. Even though Ryan gave me three of the most amazing orgasms last night, I've had to listen to Jasmine going on about how she spent the night. Apparently, she decided to go on full brat mode with Maximus and had the most amazing sex. So, of course, after hearing all about it, I am now horny as sin and hoping Travis will help ease some of the tension between my legs.

I climb out of the car and head towards the house, swinging my handbag in my hand, trying to think of a way I can get Travis to give me what I need.

Since speaking to Jasmine and Travis last night, I feel less worried about my relationship with the guys. I hope I'm not letting my old insecurities take over by falling hard for anyone who shows me a bit of affection. I'm sure I'm past that now. But the worry that they will eventually leave is still there. I'm just trying to stop it from holding me back.

Entering the house, I'm met with silence. I'm about to call out when I hear Travis's raised voice from my dad's office.

"Don't give me that bullshit!"

Pushing open the door a little, I see Travis sitting at my father's desk with his mobile to his ear and pinching the bridge of his nose with the other. He lifts his head and looks in my direction. He beckons me in further with his finger before pushing the chair back and holding out an arm, signalling for me to go to him. I rush forward nervously; standing by his side, he wraps an arm around my waist and pulls me onto his lap.

"You pay me to keep track of your money; if you don't like it when I point out you are spending more than you are bringing in, then go find another accountant. You need me a lot more than I need you," he snaps as his hand lands on my thigh and starts moving up my skirt.

"I'll tell you what then. Go find yourself another fucker who will bend over backwards for you 'cause I'm done with your shit." He ends the call and slams the phone onto the desk. He doesn't give me any warning before he stands, lifting me with him and placing me on my feet.

"Lose the knickers, Sweetheart. Daddy needs that sweet pussy to take the stress away," he demands as he starts unbuckling his belt. I quickly pull my underwear down, leaving my skirt in place.

The moment I kick them to the side, Travis grabs my hips and lifts me onto the edge of the desk.

"Open those legs; let me see you."

I do as instructed as he drops to his knees and opens them further. "So, fucking perfect," he moans through gritted teeth as he parts my lips with his fingers and runs one from my entrance up to my clit. Without any warning, he grabs my legs and pulls me further to the edge of the desk as his head lands between my legs.

"Oh God," I moan as his tongue finds that magic spot instantly. There is no warmup from him today. He continues to lick my clit as one, then two fingers slip into my pussy. In less than sixty seconds, he has me on the edge of the desk, crying out for him as I cum. No one has ever made me cum that quickly, not even me. But there is something about the way he works which makes my body respond to him instantly.

Not giving me time to recover, Travis pulls me off the desk and kisses me hard on the lips.

"You are so irresistible; I need more," he moans as I wrap my arms around his neck.

"I'm all yours. Use me any way you need, Daddy. I trust you."

Travis looks deep into my eyes for a moment before cupping my cheek.

"How much can you take?"

"Give me all of it; I'll safe word if it's too much." I lean in so my lips are by his ear before whispering my safe words. Travis stills for a moment before grabbing my hand and spinning me around so I'm facing the desk. He bends me over and knocks my legs further apart as I sprawled across the desk.

"Only naughty girls have safe words," he growls behind me as he lifts my skirt. "Place your hands behind your back." I quickly do as I'm told and jump when I feel the leather of his belt being tied around them. "Do you know what happens to naughty girls?" he asks as he starts massaging my ass. When I don't reply, I feel the sting of his hand against my ass cheek as he spanks me.

"Answer me, Sweetheart," he growls as I feel myself getting wetter. "Do you know what happens to naughty girls who have a kinky side?" he asks again.

"No," I reply quickly, but he spanks me again. This time, I moan out loud as I feel it right through to my aching, dripping sex.

"No, what?" he asks firmly.

"No, Daddy," I reply quickly as he starts massaging my ass cheek again.

"They get taught a lesson by their Daddy," he declares as I feel him grabbing my cheeks and pulling them apart, revealing all of me to him. he starts rubbing my asshole with a finger, and I can't hold back the moan.

"Has anyone had this yet?" he asks as he continues to torment me with his finger.

"Yes, Daddy," I answer quickly.

"Who?"

"Ethan, Daddy," I answer as I hear the zipper being opened.

"Well, I will have to take it soon as well. But not yet."

With no warning, Travis grabs my hips and plunges into my soaking-wet pussy, making me cry out. He fills and stretches me, and it feels incredible.

"Fuck, you are so perfect." Travis wraps my ponytail around his hand and tugs my head back a little as he leans forward, pushing into me deeper as his lips brush against my ear. "Are you going to be Daddy's good girl and take everything he gives you?" he asks.

"Yes, Daddy. Let me make you feel better," I cry out as he starts to move within me. Travis starts to pick up speed as his thrusts get harder. His hand releases my hair and moves around to my throat. It's where I always dreamt of a hand being, but he doesn't apply any pressure like I desperately want him to. I lean into his hand, hoping he gets the message.

"Yes, Daddy," I cry as his hand tightens.

"Fuck," I hear him growl louder as his hand tightens further, but not enough to cut off air supply completely.

Travis gets rough as he thrusts into me, the pressure of the desk on my stomach adding to the pleasure.

"Are you going to be my good girl and cum on Daddy's cock?" Travis calls as he lets go of my throat, grabs my hips and fucks me harder.

"Yes, Daddy! I'm cuming!" I cry out as the most fantastic orgasm rips through me, and I know I squirt a little.

"Fuck!" Travis roars as he fills me with his release. Pressing himself so deep, I swear I feel him against my cervix. The feel of him cuming, pulsating deep within me, causes my orgasm to be dragged out and leaves me panting face-first on the desk.

I find myself giggling as Travis loosens the belt from around my wrists and pulls me back until I'm sitting on his lap as he holds me against his chest.

"What's so funny, Sweetheart?" he asks, holding me

tight. I snuggle against his tight-fitted t-shirt and smile happily.

"My Daddy just fucked me against my father's desk," I point out as Travis bursts out laughing.

"That thought crossed my mind as well." He lifts one of my hands and runs a thumb over my wrist before pressing a kiss to it. "Did I hurt you?"

I shake my head and look at him, smiling.

"No, I would have told you if you had," I inform him. He looks at me for a moment before nodding once and checking my other wrist. "Do you feel better now?" I ask, going back to leaning against his chest.

"I always feel better when you're around, Sweetheart. You have no idea how happy you make me," he whispers into my hair as he kisses my head.

"Because of the sex or me?" I mean it as a joke, but Travis repositions me on his lap so I can see him. His eyes seem darker and more serious than they were a moment ago.

"You, Sweetheart, always you. Never think I'm with you for the sex because I would happily go without it for as long as it took you to realise I'm with you for who you are." Travis leans in and kisses me whilst wrapping my hair around his hand. He gives it a tug, which forces my head back so he can look into my eyes. "If you believe one thing I tell you, ensure it's that. Understand?"

I nod slightly as he watches me carefully to see if I'm lying to him. When he seems content, he kisses me as he stands, lifting me into his arms and walking from the office.

"Where are you taking me?" I giggle as he carries me through the house, towards the stairs.

"There is a huge bath in our parent's room. I'm dying to try it out with you."

Chapter Thirty-Six

TRAVIS

I don't think I will ever tire of watching our girl dance. She is breathtakingly beautiful and stands out from all the other dancers. I may be biased, but I believe she is the most talented on that stage.

"I swear her head was held higher tonight than last night," Ryan says next to me as we make our way to the foyer.

"She knew we were watching and pulled out all the stops," I reply.

"She was the most beautiful on that stage, that's for sure," Ethan adds behind me as we walk past the stairs that lead to the top boxes.

"Not as beautiful as our Jasmine."

We all turn around to find the four O'Reillys standing on the stairs. Of course, Christian is in the front in his pristine suit and perfect hair.

"O'Reilly," I say with a nod.

"Donavon."

We stare at each other momentarily, and a deadly silence surrounds us.

"Guys, not here. Think of the girls," Ethan warns next to me. I don't say anything as I take a step forward and hold out my hand. Christian looks at it for a moment before shaking it.

"Thank fuck for that," Jason sighs as Christian smirks at me. I don't forgive him, not completely, but I do believe he isn't to blame for my father's death. I think I've known that for a while now.

"Is everything okay after our chat the other day?" Christian asks as he walks beside me. I shove my hands into my suit pockets and nod.

"As good as they can be after all she has endured."

"I'm sure you all will have her back to the old Verity soon."

We stop at the far end of the foyer as we wait for the girls together.

"I'm hoping she will become the real Verity rather than the one who has been conditioned by a toxic parent." When I turn to face Christian, I find him looking into the distance, nodding his head slowly.

"Jasmine was the same. She had spent so long on the defensive or being who her friends wanted her to be that she didn't know herself. But she got there with our help, and I know Verity will manage just fine with the right guidance from you all."

I look around at my brothers, chatting and laughing with the twins and Jason.

"How much do you know about Verity's dad?" I ask whilst the others are distracted.

"Not much. You?" I look at him and shake my head. "I thought you did his accounts?"

244

"I do," I admit. "But I have recently found out the money isn't going where he says it is. For example, he pays three thousand pounds a month for housekeeping. It turns out he's had Verity doing it all to 'earn her keep'." I watch as Christian looks deep in thought whilst rubbing his face.

"Anything other than that which stands out?" he asks. I nod as I move closer to ensure no one else hears.

"There used to be money going to Taylor."

"Well, that says it all. Nothing good came from that man. He seems to make as much trouble from his shallow fucking grave as he did when he was alive."

"Yeah, I heard about Geralt. I'm sorry. I know your families were close."

Christian thanks me and lets out a deep sigh. It's obvious Geralt Young's death is still raw for him, and I know not to push that. Geralt was a decent man and didn't deserve to die the way he did. Not for something he had no knowledge of.

"As far as I'm aware, Verity's father has no dealings with anyone I'm associated with, and I don't remember him being one of Taylor's guys. But I will do some digging and let you know."

I thank him as we turn to join our brothers, who all seem glad to see the arguing is finally over between us.

By the time the girls join us, we are all laughing and chatting.

"Verity, why is your daddy laughing with mine?" Jasmine teases as she loops her arm around Verity's, who starts laughing.

"We can go back to arguing if you'd prefer?" Christian sighs as Jasmine stops in front of him. She lets go of Verity, who walks straight into my arms so I can kiss her like I've longed to all evening.

"I swear you get more beautiful every time I see you on the stage," I smile as I look into her bright eyes.

"You were something else, Baby girl," Ethan adds, pulling her from my arms and spinning her around before kissing her. The laugh that escapes her sounds like it comes from deep within, making me think we may finally be getting her to a better place.

"Let's get a drink, and then we can head home to enjoy a full day and night with you," Ryan grins, pulling her from Ethan's arms and taking her into his own.

"Before you go, I wanted to speak to you about something."

We all turn to look at Christian as he nods to Jason, who has his arm around Jasmine, smiling.

"I think Jasmine's Maid of Honour would enjoy the day even more if her three men were with her. Would you all like to escort her to our wedding next month?"

I stare at Christian as Jasmine squeals excitedly and throws her arms around his neck. I turn to see a smiling Verity.

"Would you like us to come with you?" I ask, smiling at how happy she looks. Verity nods, unable to hide her excitement. I glance at my brothers, who both nod once—turning back to Christian, who has an excited Jasmine in his arms.

"We would love to come. Thank you for inviting us."

Jasmine squeals again and rushes for Verity, who throws her arms around her friend. We both turn to look at the girls, who are laughing and smiling together, and I realise just how special Jasmine is to Verity and how much it will mean to our girl that we will be there also.

"Come on, Shorty, there is a large ice cream sundae with my name on it," Maximus calls as he and Sean say something to Ryan, who nods and turns to face us all, smiling. I make a mental note to ask him about that later, but right now, I want to get our happy girl home and make her smile a whole other way.

Chapter Thirty-Seven

ETHAN

"Are you sure you don't want anything?" Verity asks, looping her arm through Travis's as they stand from the table.

Verity admitted she hadn't eaten much today when we arrived at the bar. Travis had her finish her drink and is now taking her to order a takeaway whilst we finish our drinks before heading home.

"We're fine; we ate before coming out. We'll meet you by the car in ten minutes," I reply, leaning in and kissing her.

"Don't be long. I won't be waiting around," Travis calls as they head off through the crowd and towards the door. Verity turns around and waves before they disappear from view.

"You know it's probably a good thing we have him to take care of her. Otherwise, we would have her necking shots rather than going for food." I'm all up for taking control in the bedroom. Fuck, she called me Sir the other night, and I nearly lost control. But outside, I'm all about having fun and doing stuff Travis would probably frown upon.

"Have you thought any more about the whole daddy thing?" Ryan asks as he picks up his pint.

"Yeah, and it's not for me. What about you?" Watching him, I notice he's deep in thought.

"I'm reconsidering it."

"Really?" I ask, amazed. "You seemed so sure the other day that it wasn't for you."

"I know, but I want to look after her and give her every-thing that she may need, which includes a daddy if she needs one." Ryan looks into his glass and shrugs absent-mindedly. "I don't know. I was lying there last night, watching her sleep, and I knew that there was nothing I wouldn't do to keep her safe and happy. I mean, I'm sharing her with you guys, after all. But it was more than just being in love with her." He starts swirling his drink around his glass absentmindedly.

"Have you spoken to her about it?"

Ryan shakes his head before looking around the bar.

"No, but I spoke to the twins, and Sean thinks I should ask her what she wants from me. At the end of the day, we never asked her if she wanted this relationship; we forced it on her when she was at her most vulnerable. What if once she has begun to heal, she realises this isn't what she wants?"

"I think you're looking too into it," I sigh, picking up my glass. "Verity is stronger than we give her credit for, and she knows what she wants. She wants us; she has made that obvious in her own way. She just doesn't trust us not to hurt her, which is understandable after everything she has been through with her prick of an ex and sad excuse of a father."

"You mean that excuse of an ex there?" Ryan asks,

nodding behind me. I turn around just in time to see the very prick take a seat at the table two down from us. A brunet sits on his knee.

"Is that the woman he was cheating with?" Ryan asks as he grabs his glass and necks it.

"Yep, looks like it. Wonder if she knows how much of a dick he is?" I down the rest of my pint, and we stand together before heading towards the table, purposely not looking directly at it until we are beside it.

"Oh look, if it isn't numb nuts, Marshall. Is this the woman you cheated on Verity with? Or is it a different one this week?" I ask as he glares at me.

"Don't worry about him; Verity's better off now anyway. At least she doesn't have to resort to toys, as you don't leave her sexually frustrated," Ryan laughs beside me.

"No, she no longer needs the toys unless we feel like a bit of fun." I turn my attention back to Marshall. "I hear she needed them after most nights with you, as you could never find the magic button."

"You're fucking your sister?" Marshall asks, amazed as his friends laugh.

"Stepsister, not blood-related. So perfectly legal and hot as fuck." I lean on the table to get closer to the chick on his lap. "So, is this the one who wouldn't sleep with you? I hope you are still holding out, love. Otherwise, you might be left disappointed." I look over my shoulder at Ryan and see him smirking. "What was his excuse for cheating?"

"He had to prove to himself he wasn't a failure because he could never make Verity cum."

"That was it!" I look back to Marshall, who's bright red and glaring at us. "Has he managed to make you cum yet? Or do you have to fake it for him like his ex did?" The girl looks away, embarrassed, and his mates roar, laughing. "I'd take that as she fakes it," I wink, standing up and turning to my brother.

"Come on, I've had enough of the crowd in here tonight; they seem like a waste of space and limp dicked. See you later, numb nuts!" I pat him on the shoulder as we walk past, and I hear his friends start laying into him.

"Do you feel better now?" Ryan asks as we walk out of the bar, thanking the security guys as we pass.

"Yep. It would have been better if he gave me a reason to punch him again, but we can't win them all."

We head to the car park, where I can see Verity and Travis almost reaching the car. I wink at Ryan before sneaking behind them and grabbing her around the waist. As Verity screams, Travis spins around, ready to punch whoever was manhandling his woman. But rolls his eyes instead when he realises it's only me.

"Dickhead," he mutters under his breath as I spin Verity around in my arms and pick her up so her legs are wrapped around my waist.

"Talking of dickheads, we just bumped into one," I announce, grinning as Verity places her arms over my shoulder and grins down at me.

"That's not a nice thing to call, Daddy."

"Hey!" Travis protests as he opens the car door and drops a bag of take out of the footwell on the passenger's side. He strides up to me, and I pass over a wiggling Verity who starts protesting loudly.

"I was only joking; I would never really call you a dickhead!"

Travis grabs her ass whilst holding her tightly against him, not giving her room to move away. Trapping her between him and the car, he looks her in the eye. I can see her biting her bottom lip as she smiles sheepishly at him.

She is full of life tonight, and I know she's going to try and be a brat.

"I haven't had to discipline you properly yet, have I?" Travis asks as Verity shakes her head. "Maybe the three of us need to start setting some ground rules and the punishments for breaking them. Starting with *I shall not call my daddy a dickhead*."

Verity flutters her eyelids as she grins down at him, trying to look as innocent as possible.

"Can I pick the punishment? I'm sure I can think of a way the three of you could punish me together."

Travis stares at her for a moment before a deep moan escapes him, and he kisses her hard, and he grinds against her. Verity leans her head back and moans loudly as Travis nips at her collarbone.

"You are getting naughty, little girl," Travis warns.

"Just the way you like me, Daddy," she answers.

"I think the three of us need to teach you a lesson, brat," he warns through gritted teeth.

"I'll happily take anything the three of you give me," she replies, testing him. Travis opens his mouth to respond but gets interrupted.

"I always knew you were an easy lay, but never put you down as a whore!"

I spin around to see Marshall strutting towards us. Ryan is beside me in an instant as Travis lowers Verity to her feet.

"There was me thinking you were fucking your brother, but instead, you are fucking him and the moron here," he calls out, coming to a stop a short distance from us all.

"Who the fuck do you think you're talking to?" Travis warns as he stands in front of Verity. He's gone into protective mode, and I know Marshall is treading on thin ice now.

"I'm talking to that slut behind you. Are you as thick as

you are wide?" Marshall laughs. "Have all the steroids made you dumb?"

"Apologise to her. Now!" Travis hisses through gritted teeth.

"What's the matter? Can't satisfy the bitch on your own, so it takes two of you?" he laughs as he turns his attention to Ryan. "Or are you taking part as well?"

"Shut up, Marshall, just leave!" Verity yells from behind Travis. I hear in her voice she's on the verge of tears and see the moment Travis does, too.

"Shit," Ryan curses as Travis launches forward, grabbing Marshall around the throat before slamming him to the ground.

"Get the fuck off me!" he shouts as he swings at Travis but misses.

"You think you deserve to live after you upset our woman?" Travis grins down at him, and I see the moment Marshall realises he fucked up. I will never understand why people underestimate the damage Travis can do. If he wants you dead, you might as well start saying your good-byes because you won't survive.

"Sweetheart, say the word, and I will fucking end the prick."

I look to Verity, who has tears running down her face.

"No," she whispers, shaking her head. Travis nods once and punches Marshall hard.

"Here's what's going to happen," Travis explains to the kid who's now looking less cocky and more like a deer in the headlights. "You are going to get up, apologise to Verity and fuck off with your limp dick between your legs. If you try any funny business or say one thing other than sorry, I am going to make sure your body is never found. Do you understand?"

Marshall nods, and Travis slaps his cheek much harder than necessary. "Good. You might want to throw in a thank you while you are at it, as she just saved your life."

Travis stands and pulls Marshall to his feet. He stupidly tries to make a run for it, but he heads straight towards me, and I take great pleasure in taking his legs out from underneath him so he lands face-first on the tarmac.

"Oops, let me help you up there," I say as I grab his floppy hair and pull him to his feet. I push him towards Travis, who grabs him by the shoulder, purposely pushing his thumb into his collarbone.

"Well, that was stupid, wasn't it? Let's try this one last time, shall we?" Travis turns so he and Marshall face a crying Verity, leaning into Ryan. I watch as Travis's thumb digs further into his shoulder as he cries out in pain.

"What do you have to say to Verity?"

"I'm sorry, okay! I didn't mean it!" Marshall cries out as Travis squeezes his shoulder to the point his legs buckle underneath him.

"What part are you forgetting?" Travis asks calmly.

"Thank you for saving my life!" he yells before he starts to cry like the little shit he is.

"There, see, that wasn't too bad, was it?" Travis sighs as he pulls him to his feet and walks him away from Verity but towards me, as he whispers in his ear.

"Now, you are going to fuck off home with your little dick between your legs and never so much as look in her direction again. If any of us discover you have even walked down the same street as her, I will make sure you are never seen again. Say what you like about me and my brothers; we don't give a shit. But upset our woman, and you will forfeit your life. Now fuck off!" Travis pushes him forward so hard that he trips over his feet and lands face-first against the ground. Marshall scrambles to his feet and runs out of view.

"Ryan, make the call," Travis orders as he sees Ryan already has his phone to his ear. He kisses Verity's cheek once before letting Travis take her from him. He walks away as our guy answers the call.

"It's me. We need CCTV wiping."

I don't listen to the rest of the call. I look over to where Verity is crying against Travis's chest.

"That's what everyone is going to think of me. They are all going to say I'm a slut," she sobs as Travis holds her.

"Do you care what others think? Does Jasmine care? Because I don't. Let them think what they want. They will just be jealous that you have three men all willing to kill to protect you. Say the word Sweetheart, and I will take him out. No one, and I mean *no one*, speaks to you like that!"

Verity looks up at him with tears in her eyes, and my heart breaks. She had been so confident and happy five minutes ago, but now she is crying again, and it's all my fault.

"I want to go home," she whispers. Travis holds her against his chest as he kisses her head.

"Then let's get you home." He throws the keys to Ryan as he opens the back door. "I'm riding in the back with her."

Chapter Thirty-Eight

VERITY

Why is it that whenever something starts feeling right, someone is around the corner, ready to ruin everything for me?

I never thought I would see that guy again. Why would I? We don't hang around in the same crowd and only met through a dating app. To be honest, I hadn't even thought about him; there have been more important things to occupy my mind. But when I least expected it, there he was, calling me every name under the sun.

Why did I think people's reactions would be any different from his? I'm one woman sleeping with three different men. I've seen first-hand how people treated Jasmine when she went public with the guys. I know she hid it from the O'Reilly's, but a few girls we dance with have been so mean, and they have caused all kinds of trouble that Danielle and I have witnessed. But Jasmine is so much stronger than me, and she has risen above it all, coming out the other side like a new woman. I'm so proud of her.

I know that's what I need to do. But it's hard when you

have spent your whole life doing what others expect of you. I don't want to be that person anymore. Yet, I don't know how to change.

"I'm so sorry, Baby girl, that was all my fault."

I look up to Ethan, who is sitting in the passenger seat. He's turned around to look at me as I sit beside Travis, leaning against him, not wanting to be alone.

"What do you mean?" Travis asks. Ethan lets out a sigh and rubs his face.

"He was the dickhead I was referring to when I said I had bumped into one. He came into the bar with the woman he cheated on you with and some mates. I didn't think and humiliated him in front of them all."

I hear Travis groan beside me.

"How?" he demands through gritted teeth.

"By repeating his excuse for cheating on her and asking the girl if she ever had to fake it. I also pointed out that I have no issues making Verity scream." Ethan stares at me for a moment, obviously waiting for me to cry again, but instead, I find myself giggling. I know how much Marshall loves to brag to his friends and would have made out that I was the problem when he switched to a new woman.

"You aren't mad?" Ethan asks from his seat. I shake my head as I smile at him.

"No, that would have been the worst thing you could have done to him. Take it the woman didn't argue when you asked if she faked it?"

Ethan shakes his head, but Ryan answers as he glances at me through the rearview mirror.

"She looked embarrassed as hell. Which just confirmed Ethan was right."

"No wonder he was so pissed off," Travis says beside me. "What were you thinking?"

"I wasn't really. I just wanted to hurt him like he had hurt her." Ethan reaches round for me to take his hand. "I'm sorry, Baby; I was so angry with him I didn't think about the consequences it would have on you. I don't ever want to be the reason you cry."

I squeeze his hand once before letting go to sit back in my seat.

"I know you didn't mean for all that to happen. I wouldn't have expected that kind of reaction from him," I admit. It was out of character for Marshall. Yeah, he could be a nasty piece of work; look how he reacted when I ended it. But to square up to Travis like he could have beaten him. That's not the Marshall I know or dated.

I turn to look at Travis, who's watching me carefully.

"If I had said yes, would you have killed him?"

Travis nods before he answers.

"No one speaks to you like that and gets away with it."

I stare into his eyes for a moment and realise there is no doubt in my heart that he means every word, and I finally start to see that everything he has been saying to me is true.

I don't stop to think. I unfasten my seatbelt and climb onto his lap, straddling him. Grabbing the back of his head, I kiss him like I wanted to when he had me trapped between the car and him.

Travis kisses me back with such passion I feel my sex clenching with a need, not only for him but for the others, too.

Ethan may have gone the wrong way about it, but he stood up for me when I couldn't do it myself. Not only today but also when Marshall and I broke up. Ryan had been by my side as Travis took care of Marshall, holding me and ready to protect me if I needed him.

"Guys, I hate to break up the party back there, but

police are out in force tonight. Can we not get caught with you two fucking in the back," Ryan laughs from behind the wheel.

"To be continued," I wink at Travis before climbing off his lap. He wraps an arm around my waist, pulling me as close as possible to him.

"Or just repositioned. Open those legs, Sweetheart, and show the guys what's waiting for them when they get home."

As always, being around these three gives me the strength to fulfil all my sexual desires. I open my legs as Travis's hand reaches around and pulls my underwear to one side. I knew wearing a skirt tonight would be a good idea. Ethan looks around at me, and I see the desire in his eyes, especially when Travis runs a finger up and down my slit, which is soaking wet and waiting for them to take it.

"How wet is she?" Ryan asks as he glances in the rearview mirror.

"Wet enough to fuck," Travis replies as he circles my clit with his fingers. "Think we can make you wetter, Sweetheart?" Travis growls in my ear as he pushes a finger inside of me.

"Yes," I whimper. Travis nibbles on my ear as he starts rubbing my clit again. I moan loudly as I begin to feel myself heading quickly to that sweet release. I don't know if it's because Travis is touching me the way he is. Or whether the fact two of the guys are watching, but I am hornier than I have ever been before, and I know exactly what I want.

"Tell me what you need tonight, little Kitten. What can we do to make you purr?" Ryan asks.

"I want all of you together. I want each of you to take me until I lose track of whose cock is where and where one orgasm finishes and another starts."

"Then let us witness that first orgasm, Baby; let us hear and see you cuming before we get you home and to bed," Ethan says from his spot as he watches Travis pleasure me.

Travis removes his fingers and starts focusing on my clit.

"Faster, Daddy. I'm so close," I call out as he does exactly as I ask. Before long, I'm crying out as I come apart in the back seat of Travis's car.

Travis gives me no warning. He pulls me away, forcing me to lie on my back, and his head disappears between my legs.

"Oh my god," I cry out as he licks me clean. His tongue not touching the places he knows will give me the right stimulation to cum again.

The car speeds up, and I know we are nearly home, and the guys are as eager to get there as I am.

Chapter Thirty-Nine

ETHAN

Ryan screeches to a stop outside of the house as we all throw open our doors. Travis grabs Verity and throws her over his shoulder before carrying her to the front door as I go ahead and open it.

By the time Ryan joins us inside, Verity is wiggling and laughing as Travis marches up the stairs.

"Put me down!"

Travis's hand lands on her bare ass, where her skirt has risen, revealing her white cotton thong. Verity lets out a combination of a moan and cry. Fuck, I will never get bored of that noise.

"Not until I get you on a bed," Travis growls.

"Take her to my room; I have cuffs," I wink at her as she lifts her head to look at me.

"Since when?" she demands as I laugh.

"I had a delivery today."

Travis carries her to my room and drops her on the bed before straddling her to ensure she doesn't move.

Whilst I unpack the cuffs, I see him kissing her.

"You got anything else in that package?" Ryan laughs next to me.

"Not for tonight; they are Christmas presents," I wink before looking to Verity, who grins as Travis takes her hands and holds them over her head.

"Fancy showing these two how a good girl behaves?" I ask as she turns her head, frowning at me. I watch the penny drop as a grin spreads across her face.

"Yes, Sir."

Travis and Ryan both look at me with an arched brow.

"Travis, can you release our girl, please?" I can't bring myself to look anywhere but the beautiful blue eyes staring back at me.

Travis climbs off Verity, who stands from the bed, our eyes still locked.

"Get into position like a good girl," I order as Verity slowly starts to strip from her clothes. Her cheeks are flushed, and I know she is a little self-conscious and turned on. We've never gotten the chance to do this before. We only discussed it after our sex yesterday. I had hoped to get some training done before we invited the others to join in, but seeing her tonight and how open she was in the car had my whole body aching to dominate her.

Once naked, Verity looks up at me sweetly as she kneels between me and the bed, her hands behind her back and chest pushed out, holding her head high.

"You forgot something," I point out, approaching the bed. I can see Travis and Ryan watching her intently as she stays in the position. Reaching forward, I pick up a strand of her long blonde hair hanging loose over her shoulder.

"I don't have a hair tie, Sir."

"Lucky I'm prepared then." I don't look away from her as I

address my brothers. "Could one of you go into the top drawer and pass me a hair tie, please?" I hold out my hand whilst still keeping my eyes on Verity and wait for someone to place a band in my hand. As soon as they do, I hold it out for her.

"Thank you, Sir." Taking the elastic from me, she makes short work of gathering her hair and tying it into a high ponytail. I step back and take in the beautiful sight before me.

This woman is the very definition of a Goddess, from her pale, flawless skin to her blonde hair and big blue eyes. But I know deep inside is a kinky little vixen waiting to come to the surface.

Forcing myself to look away, I turn to see my brothers watching our girl intently. Like me, they are mesmerised by her beauty.

"Shall we tell the others what we discussed?" I ask, looking back at our girl, who nods.

"Verity admitted she had always wanted to be dominated. So, as you can see, we came to the agreement that when we are in this room or in a sexual mood, I am Sir, and she is my Sub."

Travis walks over to Verity and squats down. Taking her chin between his thumb and forefinger, he tips her head back to ensure she is looking into his eyes.

"Is this why you have the safe words?"

"Yes, Daddy."

"And this is what you want? From all of us, or just Ethan?"

She looks into his eyes and smiles. "You all dominate me in your own way, and it's everything I've ever wanted, even if I didn't realise it."

"You know you don't have to do anything just to please

us, right?" he asks. I knew Travis would be the one to question this the most.

"I know, Daddy," she smiles up at him before cupping his cheek. "I promise always to use my safe words."

Travis kisses her palm before standing back.

"What's your safe words, Sweetheart."

"Black for stop. Orange, if I need you to ease off a little." She makes a point of looking at all of us with an excited spark in her eyes. "I won't agree to anything I don't want to do." Travis watches her, and for a moment, I think he's going to put a stop to it. He has that look he gets when he thinks something is a bad idea. But before I can explain why this is perfectly fine, he nods and steps back.

"Then tonight, we will take Ethan's lead."

The excitement on Verity's face is unmissable, as is the smile on Travis's when he sees how happy he has just made her.

Clearing my throat to bring her attention back to me, I walk up to her and make a motion with my finger for her to turn around. She does as she's told and places her hands back behind her.

"These cuffs are made so they don't hurt your wrists, but if they become uncomfortable, you just have to say, and we can loosen or remove them completely." Opening one of the buckles, I place the thick leather cuff around her right wrist. I picked these as I didn't want to leave any marks on her that others may see. I know how important her appearance is to her when she dances. The cuffs are a wide piece of leather which wraps around the wrist. A small buckle on the top of the leather is similar to one found on a belt. The two cuffs are connected by a short chain that can be switched for a longer one if needed. But for tonight, I think the shorter one will suffice.

Once I have both cuffs in place, I tug on the chain slightly to check they are secure.

"How do they feel, Baby?"

"Good, Sir." She looks up at me with a smile. I can't help wrapping her hair around my fist before tugging it back to kiss her lips.

"I think we should keep you right there for the time being; you look so perfect on your knees, like a good little girl." Kissing her hard once more, I let go of her hair and step back.

"I know Ryan and I have had the pleasure of feeling that naughty mouth around our cocks, but has Daddy?"

"No, Sir," Verity blushes as she looks behind me to where Travis is standing.

"Then I think he should go first," I turn to Travis and smirk. "She's all yours."

Travis walks forward again as he undoes his trousers to free himself. Watching Verity's face as he stops in front of her, his cock in his hand, she licks her lips and looks up at him with a smile.

"I've been dreaming of this mouth," Travis growls as he wraps her ponytail around his hand and tugs her up so she lifts onto her knees, making her the perfect height to suck his cock.

"I've been dreaming of sucking it, Daddy."

Travis curses under his breath as he runs the tip of his cock over her lips.

"Then open wide, Sweetheart and show me how good it is." Verity takes him into her mouth, and Travis's head instantly tips back as he moans. "Fuck, that mouth."

I watch momentarily as Travis and Verity get lost in each other. He starts fucking her mouth as she moans around him. Tears streaming from her eyes as he gets deeper. I step back so I'm next to Ryan as we watch the show before us.

"How did we get here?" He asks, readjusting his cock in his trousers.

"We all fell for the same sex-mad woman. I don't think one was ever going to be enough for her," I answer honestly. Ryan nods in agreement as we watch the scene in front of us.

"As much as I fucking love that mouth, I think your other men need some attention." Travis steps back, his cock in his hand. "If I don't stop, I won't last much longer," he adds, looking at us.

I look behind him to see Verity wiggling slightly on the spot where she is still kneeling. Walking up to her, Ryan smiles and takes her face in his hand.

"Do you need some attention, Kitten?"

"Yes, please," she answers, wiggling on the spot again.

"Then I have the perfect plan." He grins at me and nods towards a small stool in the corner. "I reckon you could sit on that as she rode you and sucked my dick at the same time."

Grabbing the stool, I walk over to where Ryan is helping Verity to her feet. We both make short work of stripping before I sit on the stool, take hold of the chain between Verity's cuffs and pull her onto my lap so her back is against my chest.

"You ever done reverse cowgirl before, Baby?"

"No, Sir."

"You are going to love it," I whisper as my hand slides over her thigh and to her perfect mound. I slip a finger between her lips and tease her entrance. "But first, I need to ensure you are ready," I whisper, slipping one finger into her. "Are you ready for me?" I ask, slipping in a second as she moans.

"Yes," she gasps as I remove my hand and slap her pussy, making her squeal.

"Yes, what?"

"Sir. Yes, Sir!" she corrects herself quickly. Kissing her neck, I slide two fingers back into her. She instantly relaxes against me as I rub that spot inside of her.

"That's better." I continue to tease her, bringing her closer to that release she is craving. "What do naughty girls get?" I ask, teasing her further.

"Punished, Sir." She is gasping for breath now, and I know she is nearly there.

"And good girls?" I ask, picking up speed.

"Orgasms, Sir." There's a pleading in her voice that causes my cock to twitch with the need to fill her.

"You'd better cum then," I groan as I remove my fingers, lift her hips and guide her hard and fast onto my waiting cock. I thrust into her twice hard before she clamps around me and cries out as she finds her release.

I hear my brothers both cursing as they watch us, but I'm concentrating on not blowing my load before the fun has even started. Every time I enter this woman, I turn into a teenage boy with no self-control. There is nowhere as perfect as buried deep within her. She brings out a primal need in me to make her mine.

Verity leans her head back, resting it against my shoulder as she comes down from her high. Pressing a kiss to her cheek, I grind up against her, coaxing a moan from her.

"I hope you can take more, Baby girl. The fun has just begun," I tease as I grind into her again. She lifts her head and smiles before facing Ryan, who is now standing right in front of her. Verity leans forward to where he holds his cock in his hand. She swirls her tongue around the tip of it before he steps forward, pushing it deeper. Her lips wrap around it as I start thrusting into her.

Before long, she is bouncing on my lap as she alternates between sucking Travis and Ryan's cocks. I not only have my cock in her, but I'm finger fucking her ass at the same time. I don't think the three of us can last much longer as we are all cursing and sweating from holding back. Plus, I'm cramping up from the way I'm sitting on this stool. It isn't the comfiest way to have sex.

"Step back," I demand as I grab Verity's legs and stand up whilst holding her in place, but as I move, I feel myself slip from her and take the time to place her on the bed.

"Tell us what you need, Baby," I demand as I lean around her and remove the chain from her cuffs, allowing her to bring her arms forward.

"All of you, I want you all to fill me."

A grin spreads across my face. This is precisely what I hoped she would say. I've fantasised about the three of us taking her at the same time. Filling each of her holes before bringing her to heights she never knew existed.

"Who do you want where?" I watch as she thinks about it for a moment before a cheeky smile appears on her face.

"You in my mouth, Ryan in my pussy and Daddy my ass."

"Little Kitten, that can certainly be arranged," Ryan leans around me and kisses Verity as I climb onto the bed by the headboard. We all get into position as Verity is on all fours over Ryan.

Travis slaps her ass, causing her to moan and cry out a little at the same time.

"Ethan wasn't only fucking your sweet pussy, was he?"

He is spreading her cheeks and looking at her back passage, which I know is open and ready for him. Verity looks over her shoulder and smiles.

"No, Daddy. He likes to be everywhere when he takes me."

I really do. I love knowing I'm in her pussy and her ass at the same time.

Travis spits on his fingers, and I know the moment he penetrates her by the way her eyes roll back.

One by one, we slowly fill our girl. I love that she is so open to us and willing to try everything. She orgasms within a minute of the three of us filling her with our cocks. I know this will be short-lived, but I really don't care. It's a night I don't think I will ever forget.

Watching my girl get fucked by my brothers is something I never thought I would see, let alone enjoy. The four of us get into the perfect rhythm together, and soon, we're all moaning and cursing as things speed up. Verity is the perfect woman for us, and I plan on showing her that as often as possible. I never knew sex could be this amazing.

"Fuck, I'm so close," I hear Ryan growl as Travis roars, plunging into her hard as he finds his release, quickly followed by Ryan and I as we feel our woman's orgasm rather than hear it. Her whole body comes alive and takes us with it. I empty my full balls so deep down her throat I'm worried she may choke on it.

The four of us stay there, frozen in our positions as we try to catch our breath and see straight again. Verity has released my now soft dock from her mouth and is lying on top of Ryan, who has wrapped her in his arms, holding her against his body.

"Are you okay, little Kitten?" he asks, kissing her cheek.

She nods before moving her head to the side to look at us all.

"More than okay," she giggles as Travis moves off the bed, smiles at her and heads into my shower room.

"Hold on to me, Kitten," Ryan instructs as he tightens his hold on her and sits up before climbing off the bed. "Pull back the covers."

I jump from the bed and do as he asks so he can place her down gently. Travis walks in moments later with two towels.

Following his instructions, Verity lifts her hips so he can put one towel underneath her and cleans her with the wet corner of the other. I leave them alone for a moment as they speak to each other quietly. I pull on some boxers as Ryan does the same, and Travis dumps the towels into my wash basket before gathering his clothes.

"Do you think we could all fit in here?"

We all turn our attention to Verity, who is looking gorgeous, lying in the middle of the bed.

"Is that what you want, Kitten?" Ryan asks. Verity nods sheepishly. The three of us share a look and shrug before climbing into bed with her. Ryan to her left, me to her right, and Travis lying on his side next to Ryan as Verity faces him, leaning on Ryan's chest.

"I love you, little Kitten."

She looks at Ryan and smiles. Looking at my brother, I know he is no longer on the bench about what we discussed in the bar.

"I want to talk to you about something," he says, brushing some hair from her face. "I know I said I didn't want to be a daddy to you, but I've changed my mind." He looks deep into her eyes before continuing. "For the last few days, I've been thinking about it more and more and have realised I want to give you everything. I want to protect you and guide you to become your best version.

"I know you have different relationships with each of us, and I don't want to come between you and Travis. He is the perfect daddy for you, but I want to try and be one too."

"You really want to be my Daddy?" she asks, smiling; Ryan nods and presses a kiss to her lips.

"I do, more than anything. But I don't want you to call me Daddy, as that is Travis. I think you should choose a different name for me."

Verity is beaming as she looks from Ryan to Travis, who's smiling. I knew he would support any role we took in her life. At the end of the day, we each love her equally, and there is nothing we aren't willing to do to show her how loved she is.

"Sounds good to me, Sweetheart."

Verity looks to me over her shoulder.

"Don't worry, I don't want to be a daddy. I've told you I'm more than happy being the one to help get you into trouble with them," I wink as she giggles. I love dominating her in the bedroom, but that is as far as it goes for me, and I am more than happy to keep it that way.

Verity turns her attention back to Ryan and smiles.

"I like the idea of you being my daddy, too, but I don't know what to call you."

"What does Jasmine call the O'Reilly's?" I ask.

"They are all Daddy to her. She adds their name at the end if she is with more than one of them. Except Christian, he is always just Daddy."

I know that would be confusing for two, but for four, I have no idea how they keep track of who she is referring to.

"I know!" she bounces excitedly, nearly head-butting my chin. "Papa Bear, but Bear for short!"

Ryan laughs next to her, frowning.

"Okay, why?" he asks as Travis laughs behind him.

"Because you give the best bear hugs!" she snuggles into him to prove her point. Ryan laughs into her hair as he tightens his hold on her.

"Papa Bear it is then," he smiles before kissing her. Verity smiles at him before turning to me.

"But you don't have a nickname. I don't want you to think I care less for you than the others."

Placing my arm over her bare stomach, I kiss her soft lips and give what I hope is a reassuring smile.

"I know you don't care any less for me. They may be your Daddy and Papa Bear, but I get the fun job of being your partner in crime. How does that sound?"

She nods before turning so she can hug me properly.

"I like that a lot."

"Good," I reply, squeezing her before she rolls on her back so she can see us all again.

"Is there anything you want to do between now and Christmas, Sweetheart?"

For a moment, Verity looks conflicted, like she isn't sure how to answer, but Ryan comes to her rescue.

"What are your favourite memories of Christmas? Ones you wish you could do again." for a moment, I can see her thinking about it, and I'm worried she can't remember a good Christmas. We have no idea how many Henry's missed, and she has been on her own. But then a small smile appears on her face, and I feel a little more at ease.

"I used to love decorating the house in all my mum's Christmas decorations. I haven't got to do that in years. They are probably in the back of the loft by now, behind all of Linda's things." She smiles up at the ceiling as she remembers her childhood Christmases.

"We used to decorate the house, bake cookies and drink hot chocolate whilst watching Christmas films. We played the music loud and danced around the house whilst decorating. My Auntie usually joined in, too."

"It sounds like you used to have a lot of fun," Ryan says, smiling at her as he takes her hand. I watch as sleep starts to take over, and her eyes drift closed as she smiles.

"I always had the best Christmases with Mum." She leans more into Ryan as she drifts off to sleep.

"I think we can make sure you have that again," he whispers into her hair before the three of us share a look. Travis looks down at the now-sleeping Verity and smiles.

"And I know just how to make sure of It."

Chapter Forty

VERITY

I wake up in Ethan's bed alone. I look around the room and see no sign of the guys, not even a sock on the floor. It's as if they were never here.

For a fleeting moment, my heart breaks as I envision them leaving in the night. But deep down, I know they would never do that, so I force myself to focus on the fact that they may already have gotten up and didn't want to wake me. That's a more rational reason, so I force myself to focus on that.

As I climb out of bed, I look at the clock on Ethan's wall. I'm shocked to see it's five past seven; I can't remember the last time I slept this late. I look to the shower as I know I should rush to it and get washed and dressed as soon as possible. It's what I've always done. But then I remember I don't have to. Just because my father wanted me to be an early riser doesn't mean I have to be. I wanted him to be a present father, and look how that turned out.

I spot my dressing gown on the bottom of the bed and realise one of the guys must have put it there for me. I hardly ever use it as I was taught to wake up, stretch, shower and dress. The guys told me I could do whatever I wanted, and they would still love me. Feeling brave, I grab the dressing gown and wrap it around myself before opening the door, walking out of the room, and rushing towards the stairs. I'm not even halfway down when I hear the hushed voices of the guys below coming from the dining room.

I throw open the door and stop in my tracks. There are my three guys, all surrounded by boxes. When I look closer, I realise they all contain Christmas decorations; many still have my mum's handwriting on the boxes.

"Surprise!" Travis and Ryan shout together as Ethan spins around to face me. I'm frozen with shock as I take in the view around me. I never thought I would see these boxes again. There are decorations on the table that I haven't seen since I was eight. Tears fill my eyes as I try and take it all in. Travis comes to stand beside me as the others smile.

"What did you do?" I whisper, looking from the decorations to him.

"We wanted to surprise you. So, we woke up early and got all the decorations we could find. The tree is old and needs replacing, but everything else seems okay," he announces, putting an arm over my shoulder.

"I can't believe you did this!" I exclaim, lifting my hand to my mouth as my eyes well up further. "It must have taken ages to find them all up there!"

"It wasn't easy, but you are worth it." Ethan steps forward and presses a kiss to my lips. "We have the full day planned," he announces, stepping back to reveal Ryan beside him.

"You and Travis are going to get a new tree whilst Ethan and I run an errand. By the time you are back, we will be too, and we can spend the rest of the day decorating."

"While we get the tree, we will also get some logs for the fire, which I checked out this morning and is good to go. So, we can have the fire lit tonight and drink hot chocolate whilst watching Christmas movies." Travis kisses my head as I look around at the three of them. They listened to everything I said last night and are ensuring I experience it all again.

"I don't know what to say," I whisper as my voice cracks. "You guys are amazing."

"No, Sweetheart, you are amazing and deserve the Christmas of your dreams. Not just this year but every year, and we want to start on the right track before adding traditions for our new little family."

Ryan hooks a finger under my chin, forcing me to look at him.

"You haven't celebrated Christmas as you should have the last few years, but that's all changing. You have us now, and we'll make sure you never celebrate another Christmas surrounded by anything but love and support. Because you, little Kitten, are more loved than you could ever imagine." Ryan kisses me as I throw my arms around his neck and pull him in close.

"Yeah, okay, let's stop that there before you get carried away. You know what you're like, and we are on a tight schedule," Travis declares. I reluctantly turn in Ryan's arms and lean against his front as he holds me from behind.

"What are you trying to say, exactly?" I ask as sweetly as possible. The way Travis crosses his arms over his chest tells me I'm not fooling anyone. The laughter coming from Ethan and Ryan confirms it.

"I'm saying you are as addicted to sex as we are to you.

Which means I know exactly where that will end up if it continues."

I turn around to look at Ryan through my lashes and place my hands on his firm chest.

"Where would that have ended up, Bear?" I ask sweetly. Ryan grabs my ass and throws me onto the top of the table as I squeal before he slides between my legs, grabbing behind one of my knees and lifting it so he can get in closer.

"Right here where I can bury my cock so deep into your waiting pussy that they won't know where I start and you end," he growls, leaning in and kissing me. He slides his hand up my thigh until it reaches my ass, and I hear the moment he realises I'm naked underneath my robe.

"I want that," I moan as his finger brushes over my entrance. "I really want that!"

"Tough, we have things to do, and you need to be dressed for us to do them." He kisses me hard before pulling me from the table as I giggle.

"I think Daddy may have been right; I'm addicted to sex," I point out as Ryan's deep chuckle fills the dining room, making my heart beat harder. I love it when I make the guys laugh. I don't think I could describe how happy it makes me. The little signs like that tell me they are here because they want to be, not because they feel they should be.

"If he tries to discipline you for it, let me know, and I will administer the punishment," he winks at me.

"I don't think that's how it works!" I exclaim. "It would probably be your fault anyway!" I point out. Ryan wraps an arm around my waist and tugs me against him.

"My sweet little Kitten, it will always be your fault as you are too irresistible and adorable. How are we meant to say no to you?"

"By trying harder!" Travis calls as he walks out of the dining room. Ryan bursts out laughing as I hide against his chest. He whispers something about facing the music and leads me out the door into the lounge, where Travis and Ethan are watching us. Ethan has a huge grin on his face, but Travis's eyebrows have disappeared into his hairline.

"Sorry, Daddy, I'm being good," I say quietly, giving him my best puppy eyes. Ethan and Ryan laugh as Travis beckons me over with one finger.

I sheepishly make my way over to him and come to a stop, so I have to look up through my eyelashes to see his face. I bite my bottom lips to stop myself from smiling. I know he would never really be mad at me for trying to get some action from them.

"Go, get washed and dressed; we leave in fifteen minutes. I will have your coffee and breakfast waiting for you, so hurry up," he orders, pointing towards the stairs. I can see the smile threatening to ruin the firm look he is trying his hardest to uphold. Lifting onto my tiptoes, I kiss his cheek.

"Yes, Daddy," I whisper before turning around and rushing towards the stairs.

"Make sure you wrap up warm," he calls after me. "We are getting a real tree!"

I scream happily as I rush up the stairs even quicker, desperate to get ready in record time and spend the day doing all kinds of Christmas things with all three of my amazing men.

Chapter Forty-One

TRAVIS

I sit back in my usual spot on the sofa, watching Verity laugh as she dances with my brothers. Christmas music is blaring, the mulled cider has been drunk, and we are now on our own drinks of choice. The tree is up in the spot she chose, and she's been in charge of decorating the whole house.

I don't think there's a room that doesn't have some kind of decoration in it. She even insisted that we hang them in each of our rooms, and we, of course, let her. She has gotten whatever she wanted today, and I know she will always get what she wants as we are all wrapped around her little finger, and she knows it.

I sip my whiskey as Verity's laughter rings out over the music, and I know we have managed to achieve precisely as we planned. Our girl is laughing, carefree and, most importantly, happy.

In the short time since we arrived, Verity has been through so much, but she has started to come out of the other side, and I know she will be happier for it. Of course,

I know she isn't magically healed just by us putting up some decorations and getting a little drunk with her. But it is a start, and that is all we can ask for at the moment.

I look up in time to see Verity frowning at the window as car lights shine through it.

"You expecting anyone?" Ethan asks as Verity shakes her head and looks out of the window.

"It's Dawn. Oh my god, I haven't cleaned up since we made cookies! I'm going to be in so much trouble." Verity starts to rush towards the kitchen, but I jump to my feet and stop her.

"You are not going to get into any trouble because I won't let you," I whisper as I cup her cheek. "Now, this is what you're going to do. You are going to take a deep breath, relax and let her in. The guys and I will stay here, and when she asks if you are alone, you will say no. I will come out if she starts to give you a hard time, okay? You will not get into any trouble because you have done nothing wrong. You are entitled to have a life."

Verity takes a deep breath and nods as she pushes her shoulder back. I press a kiss on her forehead and smile.

"Good girl, we will be right here. Remember, this is your home, not hers."

Verity walks into the hallway as the guys come and stand by me so we are out of sight.

"I will go out first; you two come out if you hear me say you are here. I want to see how she reacts as I'm calling her out on this bullshit," I explain as I hear the front door open.

"Dawn. What are you doing here?" I hear Verity ask, her voice wobbles as her anxiety flares. I hate that she feels like this in her own home. Nowhere is safe for her; well, that's changing now. I've never liked Dawn; she is Mum's best friend and is always looking for the next rich man. She even tried to come onto me once, and I quickly shot her down. I have avoided her at all costs since.

"I was passing and heard the music from the road. Are you having a party?" I hear Dawn ask.

"The music isn't loud enough to be heard from the road," Ryan whispers next to me.

"I know," I answer, trying to hear how Verity answers.

"No, I have a few people over, but it's not a party," she replies nervously.

"Well, she's not lying," Ethan mutters as Ryan laughs a little too loud. Ethan punches his arm as I shake my head. These two are a little drunk, and it's showing.

"Oh, Verity. Look at this mess."

Ethan and Ryan both stop their quiet bickering as Dawn starts trying to upset Verity.

"I was just about to clean it up," Verity starts, but Dawn cuts her off.

"I don't want to hear excuses, Verity. You know your parents want this place to be clean and tidy at all times. This is unacceptable. And what's with all these tacky decorations? Linda will hate what you have done with the place."

"Fuck this, wait here," I mutter, storming out of the lounge and heading straight into the kitchen. Dawn is looking down her nose at Verity, whose shoulders have slumped and her head bowed. Verity put her heart and soul into decorating this place, and I, for one, will not stand for Dawn ruining this for her.

"Is there a problem?"

Dawn looks around at me and stares for a moment.

"Travis, what are you doing here? Linda said you would have gone home," Dawn stutters as I stand beside Verity and place a hand on her back. Letting her know that I'm there. I will see to it that this is taken care of once and for all. No one should be made to feel bad for living in their own home.

"We decided to stay. So, I will ask again, is there a problem?"

Dawn looks flustered for a moment, but it's Verity who answers.

"She said the kitchen was too messy and my father wouldn't be happy."

I look to Dawn with a raised brow.

"All I see is a lived-in home. We were going to get around to tidying up eventually. I don't see the problem with that." I frown at Dawn hoping to make her feel as uncomfortable as she was making Verity. "And did I hear something about the decorations? I will have you know I personally love them, and I know Verity put a lot of work into making this place more like a home than my mother ever has.

"What are you even doing here?" I ask as I place my glass on the counter and cross my arms, mimicking how she stood over Verity.

"I was passing and heard the music," she starts, but I shake my head.

"Passing from where? There is nothing around here, and I know you live on the other side of town, so try again." I turn to look at Verity before asking the next question. "I didn't hear anyone knock at the door. You must have good ears to hear it over the music."

"She didn't knock; she never does", Verity answers. I turn back to Dawn, who's looking nervous.

"Do you have a key to this house?"

"Of course, your Mum asks me to check in on Verity occasionally. They worry about her being here alone so often," Dawn smiles sweetly like she has been doing the honourable thing. I know she would have taken great pleasure in lording it over Verity that she could leave her with nothing simply by making a phone call. Dawn thinks she is better than everyone else when she is just a gold digger living off her dead husband's money.

"And to do that, you have to just walk into her personal space? If they were that worried about her, they could spend some time in the country for a change rather than leaving her alone for Christmas," I point out as I feel my temper getting the better of me. "How often does she come in here like this?" I ask Verity, who starts chewing on her lip and looking at Dawn nervously.

"Not very often. You are making a big deal out-," Dawn starts but stops as I turn my attention to her.

"I don't remember asking you," I snap as I turn back to Verity, who looks ready to cry. Fucking Dawn has put me in the worst mood.

"Not often," she says quietly.

"Do you want to try that again without lying to me?" I ask. Dawn tries to interrupt again, but I hold up a finger to shut her up.

"Every couple of weeks," Verity answers, looking down at the floor. I turn my attention to Dawn, who looks like she wants to be anywhere but here. "She checks to make sure the house is how Dad and Linda like it and that it's clean and tidy."

"Is that why it's more like a show home rather than one that's lived in?" I ask her. Verity shrugs and looks at Dawn. "Give me the key," I demand, holding my hand to Dawn.

"What? No. This is not your house. If you don't like the agreement, take it up with your parents."

"That man is not my parent," I snap, as my patience is

running thin now. "I will not have Verity living on edge in her own home, worrying about when you will next be round to poke your nose into her business."

"I am not giving you my key," Dawn argues.

"Then I will take great pleasure in ordering a locksmith to come around tomorrow to change all the locks."

"Henry will never agree to pay for that," Dawn laughs.

"Then it's a good job. I'm his accountant," I smirk back as she stops laughing.

"I'm leaving," Dawn snaps as she turns on her stiletto heels and marches towards the door.

"Just so you know, Dawn, I will be here a lot more, and if you think I'm going to live in a show home, you have another thing coming." I step forward as my brothers come out of the lounge so she sees they are there too.

"If Verity ever tells us that you have been around, making her feel uncomfortable in her own home again, I will get a restraining order out against you to ensure you can never come into this house uninvited by her again. Is that understood?"

"Perfectly," Dawn snaps as she storms to the front door.

"Don't let the door hit your arse on the way out, Dawn," Ethan grins as Ryan gives her a little finger wave.

"Your mother will be ashamed when I tell her how you have treated me!" she snaps.

"She should be ashamed of how she and that husband of hers have treated his daughter," Ryan snaps, stepping forward.

Dawn slams the front door shut behind her, and we all listen in silence to the sound of her car starting and revving down the drive and onto the road.

"She will be straight on the phone to your mum," Verity

sighs beside me. I turn around and pull her towards me so I can cup her face.

"What are they actually going to do? They aren't here, we are."

"They will stop my allowance; I need that money," she starts, but I shake my head.

"You don't need a thing; you have us now."

"But if they kick me out." I can see the panic building in her, and I hate it. I hate Dawn for coming into the house and ruining her evening. I hate my mother for treating Verity this way; I know this will be her doing. Why have I never seen how badly she treats her stepdaughter before? Mum has always been a shit parent, but this is abuse. But out of everything, I hate Henry for allowing his daughter to feel like this. To be treated like a nuisance rather than a human being. If they didn't have Verity, who would look after this house for them for free? They owe her far more than she owes them.

"Sweetheart, you have us. No one will ever make you feel uncomfortable again; I won't allow it. That includes your father. If he wants to cause trouble, let him. You have two daddies and a man-child who will look after you."

"Hey!" Ethan protests, punching me in the arm, which makes Verity giggle as intended.

I reach out, take Verity's hand, and pull her towards me, spinning her.

"Now that's sorted; I think a dance and another couple of drinks are in order," I hold her tightly against me, making her smile.

"Okay, but first, I need to go and grab my phone. I have the perfect playlist for tonight." Verity rushes from my arms, heading for the stairs. As she passes Ethan, he slaps her ass, causing her to cry out, smiling.

"Hurry up, I'm making my famous cocktail!" he calls as she disappears from view.

"You know Mum's going to be furious you called Dawn out like that," Ryan sighs, leaning against the counter as Ethan walks around to the makeshift bar we have created.

"What the fuck is she going to do about it? She's in Hawaii after all," Ethan points out as he examines the bottles.

"What about Verity, though? She could make her life hell from now on. You know what Mum can be like."

"We will just take her away from the situation. They don't deserve her, and I don't plan on living in separate houses for long anyway. Do you?"

My brothers both shake their heads as I rub my face.

"In the next few days, we will sit down, the four of us, and discuss the future. We will work out living arrangements and so on. But for now, I want to concentrate on giving our girl the Christmas she deserves."

Both of them nod as we hear Verity running back down the stairs. Looking out of the kitchen, I see her messing with the laptop we are playing music through. The music cuts off, and I smile as she starts muttering to herself. I know what's coming before she shouts.

"Daddy! Fix it!" She drags out the pleading as I walk up behind her, smirking.

"Out the way."

Chapter Forty-Two

RYAN

"Time!"

I step back from Maximus and lean on my thighs whilst trying to catch my breath. Training hard with someone as physically fit as me feels so good. I might be a personal trainer, but it isn't easy to find people to train with when you are the one coaching them.

"You've improved in the last week," Sean laughs as he leans on the ropes. I spit out my gum shield and head over to stand in front of him next to Maximus.

"It's so good to be training with someone in my weight category. It makes such a difference when they also know how to fight."

"I think that may be the nicest thing you've ever said to me, Donavon," Maximus laughs beside me as he pulls off his gloves.

"I was talking about Sean." I jump out of his reach as he swings his fist at me; Sean laughs from the ringside as Maximus starts cursing me under his breath.

"You thought any more about my offer?" Sean asks as I start removing my own gloves.

"I have; there are a few things I need to work out first. I'll need to talk to my brothers as well. There is a lot up in the air with Verity and stuff at the moment."

"What's going on?" Maximus asks, handing me my water bottle.

"We just need to work out living arrangements and stuff. I don't want to agree to anything until I know where I will be living first." I take a deep drink of cold water from my bottle as I finally catch my breath.

"If I can give you a piece of advice, it's this. It's so much easier if you are all in one house. That way, there is no schedule or pressure on anyone. Let Verity choose who she is with and when; you will all find it's the easiest option." Sean holds open the ropes for us as we climb through and head for the showers.

"Seans right; I don't think we could have the life we do if it were determined by where and when we had Jaz with each of us. She is almost in complete control unless she has done something to piss Christian off. Then he tells her she is sleeping in his bedroom after she has been punished," Maximus laughs as Sean shakes his head.

"You are just as bad. How many times have you carried her off like a caveman? Shouting you are going to teach her a lesson."

"She's more of a brat for me than any of you. It's not my fault I have to discipline her more," he replies, winking at me as I laugh aloud.

"She's a brat because your punishments are fun. She's your brat, and you love her for it," Sean points out.

"Yeah, I do. She's perfect for me, and I wouldn't have her any other way," Maximus agrees, as his mind obviously drifts to Jasmine, and I can see how much he really does love her.

Verity is yet to be a real brat for us. She has started playing up a few times, and I know she has that side to her, and I can't wait to explore it. But at the moment, things are so up in the air that whenever she starts to relax and we see the true version of herself that's been repressed over the years, something happens to remind her that she isn't free of those who have controlled her for so long.

Last night was a prime example of that. She had such a good day and had a perfect evening with us. But then Dawn turned up and ruined it for her. Since then, she has been waiting for her father to be in touch, as I've been waiting for our mother to contact one or all of us. It's bound to happen sooner than later, and I dread to think what damage it will do to all the progress we are making with Verity when it does.

"What are you guys going to do regarding your parents?"

I look at Maximus as we reach the lockers in the VIP changing rooms.

"What do you mean?"

"Well, how do you think they will take it when they find out about you all? It'll be hard for Verity as she is close to her dad, isn't she?" he asks, looking surprised when I shake my head.

"Not as close as you may think. He is a manipulative arsehole. I don't give a shit what he thinks, and I think Verity is starting to see how toxic he has been as well."

I quickly fill them in on the stuff that Christian hadn't. I know Travis told him a lot, except for the self-harming and stuff, which I also leave out. By the time I finish, I can see how shocked and appalled they are by Henry's behaviour.

"Fuck what he thinks, take her away and never let him near her again! I wish we'd done it with Jaz and her mother long before we did. Then maybe she wouldn't have suffered the way she did, thanks to Carol." I stare at Sean for a moment. He is the calm one of the twins. Maximus is more likely to fly off the handle and start swinging his fists, whereas Sean tends to talk him down and deal with the situations in a nonviolent and calm manner. But from the venom in his voice, I can only begin to imagine how Jaz was treated by her mother.

"What is it with sweet girls being mistreated by their parents? Neither of them deserved what they have been through," I sigh as I retrieve my bag and pull out my phone to check for any messages.

My heart freezes when I see two missed calls from my mother, two from Verity and one from both Travis and Ethan.

"Shit," I mutter as I open the voicemail which Ethan has left. It's short and straight to the point. "Fuck." I grab my bag and throw my stuff into it, not bothering to shower or change.

"Everything okay?" I hear Sean ask.

"Funny you should ask how our parents will take it. The shit has just well and truly hit the fan. I have to go." I throw my bag over my shoulder as Maximus tells me to call if there is anything they can do to help. I shout thanks as I run for my car and rush towards the house.

Thankfully, the gym is only a ten-minute drive from home, giving me time to calm down and think rationally. I have no doubt Travis has gone into protective mode, especially if Verity is upset. But one of us needs to be the voice of reason, and I have no doubt that responsibility will land on my shoulders. Fucking great.

From what I could gather from the angry voicemail, Henry had called Verity to demand to know why we were still here and why Dawn was so upset. Knowing him, the arsehole probably wanted her to spend Christmas alone; it wouldn't have even crossed his mind that we might have decided to stay to spend time with her. But why wouldn't we? Even if things weren't progressing the way they were with us, we would still want to be there for her if she was sad or alone. No one should spend Christmas alone in a big house like that.

My phone rings through the dashboard, and I connect the call.

"I got your message as soon as I was out of the ring. I'll be there in two minutes," I call out as I make the turning that leads to the tiny village where Verity's family home is.

"Good, because it's all going to hell here. Have you heard from Mother dearest?" Ethan asks.

"She called but didn't leave a message. Fill me in when I get there. Is Verity okay?"

"No, not at all. Travis is with her." I can hear the frustration in Ethan's voice. He will hate not being able to do anything. Ethans is the type who deals with everything head-on, face-to-face.

"I'm less than a minute away. See you in a sec." I end the call and put my foot down as I speed towards the house. Of all the times to not have my phone on me, it's when she needs me the most. I only started being her daddy two days ago, and I've let her down already.

Pulling in front of the house, I find Ethan waiting for me. If I didn't think it was bad before, I do now.

"What the fuck happened?" I snap, jumping from the car and striding towards the front porch.

"I'll tell you before you go in," Ethan says quietly as we move away from the front door.

"Everything was fine; Verity was a little hung over but laughing and joking with us. Her mobile rang, and she went off to answer it. Before she had a chance to come back, Travis got a call from Mum demanding that he apologise for upsetting Dawn and wanting to know why we were still here. When he said it was none of her business, she started shouting, 'If I find out any of you are fucking Henry's daughter, I will disown you. You will ruin everything.' Travis lost his shit and demanded to know what she meant by that, and there was nothing she could do about it if he were. Mum lost her shit, screaming so loud that I could hear her even though the phone wasn't on loudspeaker."

"Where was Verity when all this was going on?" I ask, looking towards the house, wondering where she is and how she's doing.

"Turns out she was on the phone to Henry and heard Mum screaming; when Henry heard what was going on, he started screaming at Verity, which Travis heard and lost his shit further."

"So, they know everything then?" I ask, but to my surprise, Ethan shakes his head.

"They only know about Verity and Travis. He managed to stay calm enough to realise that throwing the fact we were all with her was bad timing for Verity. He didn't give a shit about upsetting the parents, just her. He ended the call and found her standing on the stairs holding her doll in floods of tears. She's been a mess since."

"Fuck," I curse as I rub my face. There was never going to be a good time for them to find out, as they were never going to take it well. But why now? After we had been working so hard to pick Verity up from the damage they did in the twelve hours, they were here.

"I'm going in. Whatever happens, we face it together, and don't let her think for one moment that we give a shit about what they think."

Ethan nods as I take a deep breath and walk into the house, gearing myself up for whatever is happening inside.

From the moment I open the door, I can feel the tension in the air. The warm, happy feeling that enveloped this house when I left two hours ago has gone, and all I can hear is the soft whispering coming from the lounge.

I find Verity curled up on Travis's lap, her doll in her arms, as he holds her and whispers into her hair.

"Hey, little Kitten. I hear you've had a rough afternoon."

Verity looks at me as I sit beside her and Travis on the sofa. Her eyes are bloodshot again, and she looks as if she's about to cry. I hold out my arms, and she leaves Travis to come and sit on my lap. She curls up so small as if protecting herself from everything out to hurt her.

"Is there anything I can do?"

Verity shakes her head as she leans it against my chest.

"Dad said that if any of you are still here when he gets back in the new year, he will kick you out and stop me from seeing any of you again," she says quietly as I run a hand over her head.

"Well, good luck with that. We won't be going anywhere without you," I reassure her.

"We won't be here when he comes back anyway. There's no way I plan on seeing either of them, especially when they are going out of their way to make you miserable, Sweetheart." Travis stands from the sofa and walks from the room to try and calm down.

"He's angry about the way they both called me a slut and a whore," Verity says, looking up at me.

"They did what?" I yell, quickly reminding myself to keep my cool. The last thing my girl needs is for me to lose my shit. "You know they are out of order, don't you, Kitten? You are far from either of those things."

"That's what the others keep telling me, too. But it's hard to ignore when your own father calls you one."

What I wouldn't give to have five minutes with that man so I could tell him a few home truths. But it just feels like we are constantly going over old ground when it comes to him.

"Baby girl, how do you fancy getting out for a few hours? We could go for a walk while Ryan gets washed up, and then all go out for dinner somewhere." I turn to Ethan and nod.

"A change of scenery might do you a world of good," I agree, smiling at Verity, who looks a little brighter at the idea of getting out of the house.

"I would like that," she answers, sitting up. "And you do need a shower. You stink," she smirks at me.

"What do you expect when I spent the morning beating up Maximus," I laugh as I start to tickle her, glad to see a smile on her face.

"Bear, stop!" she squeals as I continue. "Help!" she screams as Ethan pulls her away from me.

"Go and get sorted; we will leave as soon as you are ready," he laughs, pinching her ass as she passes him.

"I'm going, jeez, keep your hat on," she sighs, grabbing his baseball cap from his head and rushing towards the stairs, laughing at the top of her lungs.

"Oh, little girl, you better run because me and you are about to fall out," he yells, chasing after her. He throws a wink my way as he takes the stairs three at a time. I know he may be the best one for her at the moment. Travis is in protective mode and unable to look past her upset; I need to know more about what was said so I can help come up with a plan. But Ethan is there with his humour and ability to make her smile when she needs it the most.

I laugh, watching them disappear from view. Heading towards the kitchen, I hear rustling coming from the office. I head in there wondering what Travis could be up to.

"She sounds happier," he says as I walk into the room.

"Ethan is taking her out for a couple of hours. We figured a change of scenery would help, and it seems we were right."

Travis nods, not looking up from the papers he is flicking through.

"You looking for anything in particular? Or just being a nosey bastard?" I ask as I look at the papers lying all over the desk.

"Did you know that Henry pays out over ten thousand pounds a month to companies and people that don't even exist?"

"No. But you're his accountant, not me. Surely you would know if he was doing something illegal," I point out.

"I do, but he has always denied it. I didn't bother pushing it as I didn't see it affecting Verity. Her school is paid for each month, as is her allowance. I didn't see the point in pushing anything."

"But now?" I ask as he leans back in the chair and rubs his face.

"Now, I know he is going to try and make her life a living hell, and I refuse to let him. I think he is hiding money so that she isn't entitled to it, and I plan on finding it all to ensure she gets a decent cut."

"Will she need money? We all make more than enough

to keep her dancing and living the life she deserves. If we all move into one large house, we can split the bills and save money that way," I point out. But the more I look at Travis, the more I think he's hiding something. "What aren't you telling me?" I ask as we hear Verity scream. We both turn to the door, ready to bolt, when her laughter fills the air, and we visibly relax.

"What the fuck is he doing to her now?" Travis growls.

"Whatever it is, he's cheering her up; that's all that matters," I point out. It's been a while since I saw him this worked up.

"I know, you're right," Travis sighs but quickly smiles when Verity rushes into the room and heads in his direction.

"Save me!" she laughs, jumping onto his lap.

"What did you do?" Travis asks as he rolls his eyes at her. Ethan walks in, putting his cap back on backwards.

"If you think he's going to save your ass, you are greatly mistaken. You need to leave the safety of his arms at some point, and I'm more than happy to wait," Ethan smirks as Verity grins at him.

"What if I say I'm sorry and will never touch your hat again?" she asks, grinning. We all know she's lying; she's never been able to resist annoying Ethan by stealing his hat. But we also know she could be in a worse mood than she is right now.

"Fine, now come on. We need to go to the shop and get some milk before they close," he says, holding out his arm, signalling for her to leave the office. Verity kisses Travis` before rushing up to me and doing the same.

"See you when we get back," she calls, rushing towards the door.

"Just quickly, Sweetheart. Do you have your passport?" Travis calls.

"No, why?" she asks, frowning.

"Nothing, I was just thinking of maybe booking a holiday for when you graduate in a few months," he shrugs, but I know he's lying.

"I've never needed one, as Dad doesn't let me travel with him."

"You've never been abroad?" Ethan asks, amazed. Verity shakes her head. We should have realised this, especially with Henry being so against her going to the States with him.

"What about your birth certificate? Do you know where that is?" I ask.

"I don't know. Dad deals with things like that. He sorted my driving licence and stuff for the school."

"Okay, Sweetheart, I'll see if I can find everything. Have a good afternoon."

Verity waves as she joins Ethan. I listen as they leave the house with her talking at a million miles per hour as she does whenever she gets one of us to herself.

"Okay, what you up to?" I ask as soon as the front door closes.

"I'm going to get her stuff together so when they get back, she isn't here, and there is nothing they can hold over her head." He pushes himself away from the desk and stands, heading to the large filing cabinet. "We are taking her home. She can live in whichever house she wants as long as it's not here."

I quickly tell him what Sean said about the living arrangements, and he agrees it's the best plan.

"My place has three rooms, but I would prefer it if she had her own space. When we discussed it over breakfast, Verity said that Jasmine likes having her own room, even if she hardly ever sleeps there alone. It's somewhere she can go if she needs to breathe or to relax without any of them bothering her. I want Verity to have that, too."

"We can all discuss it later, but I think looking for a new house would be best. One that's not too far from the school, as Verity will still be dancing for the company when she graduates."

He nods in agreement before rubbing his face and sighing deeply.

"Mum got to you?" I ask, taking a seat on one of the other chairs.

"More than she should have. She kept saying I would ruin everything and that Verity was not for me. She meant something by that, and I plan on finding out. I also don't like that she and Henry made Verity feel so guilty about following her heart. They know nothing about her. Yet they called her a slut and whore, simply for falling for someone."

I can tell there is more, and I don't like that he's hiding it from me.

"There's something else. Spill it."

Travis looks around him for a moment and starts pacing.

"I can't find anything of Verity's. No birth certificate, anything that may have her parentage on it."

"And since Trish said what she did the other day, it's playing on your mind." I finish for him.

"Yes. I have a bad feeling and don't like it." He turns to look at me, and I realise I won't like it either. "Do you think Henry would force his daughter into an arranged marriage?"

"What?" I snap, sitting upright. Travis starts rubbing his face as he paces.

"I don't know anything for sure; it's just a feeling I get. But the way they kept saying I would ruin everything and that Verity was to make sure she kept us away, it all feels very suspicious, and I don't like it."

"But to say they might be looking to arrange a marriage." It seems very far-fetched. I didn't think people did that anymore. But from the look on Travis's face, he knows otherwise.

"I've seen it so many times, Ryan. People want more money and a higher social status, so they arrange for their kids to marry into bigger families. I can't shake the feeling that's what's going to happen here if we don't get her out."

The thought of anyone marrying our girl other than us fills me with rage. Over my dead body, will anyone other than a Donavon make that woman their wife. I jump to my feet, unable to sit still any longer.

"So, we pack her bags now and get her out today."

"That's what I'm trying to do. But I don't want to scare her by telling her what I suspect." Travis has always acted on certainty, not suspicions.

"Especially as you could just be being paranoid," I point out.

"Exactly. I don't know what to do!"

Travis admitting he is worried and confused proves how bad this could be.

"Say you are right, and we run off with her; what is the worst that could happen?" I ask, not sure I actually want to know the answer.

"The family she has been promised to could try to take her for themselves, and if Henry is in debt with them, which I think he is, then he won't do anything to protect her, and we could lose her forever." Travis slumps into the chair again, and I see how much shit we are really in if he is right.

"Fuck."

Chapter Forty-Three

ETHAN

If there is one thing I hate, it's being kept in the dark.

Verity and I were enjoying our walk when Jasmine called to invite her for a sleepover. At the same time as she received a call, I received a message from Ryan.

Ryan: KEEP THIS FROM VERITY. You need to bring her back so we can get her to the O'Reilly's. She is staying there tonight, and we will discuss a few things with them. If she asks any questions, we will be discussing the past and putting it all behind us for her and Jaz.

Ethan: What's really going on?

Ryan: I can't say right now. We will explain everything when Verity is with Jasmine. If she tries to put off going, encourage her to go. Don't let her suspect anything.

Ethan: What the fuck is going on?

Ryan: We will tell you everything, just not yet. Don't blow this. Get her back so we can get her there ASAP!

I tried to get more out of Travis when we got back to the house, but he snapped at me to wait as he rushed around with his phone to his ear. I get they don't want Verity knowing whatever's going on, but I'm livid they won't take the time to tell me.

The ride to the O'Reilly's is tense. As light as Ryan and Travis try to keep things, I know Verity was also picking up on their apprehension.

When we arrive at the house, Travis helps Verity out of the car and holds her hand as we walk to the front door.

"Daddy, is everything okay?" she asks, looking up at him. He smiles whilst looking down at her nodding, but even I know it's fake as fuck.

"Everything's fine, Sweetheart. I guess we are a little on edge about discussing the past. But I want to put it all behind us for you."

I can tell Verity doesn't buy it, and neither would I. Especially when I see Ryan and Travis sharing a look as we reach the door.

"Afternoon Verity, I'm glad you could come. Jasmine has been driving us all mad, preparing everything for you both." Christian holds open the door, and we all walk through.

"Thank you, Christian. Is she in her room?" Verity asks, turning to take her overnight bag from Travis.

"The TV room. I think the twins are helping her set up a film. Why don't you leave Travis to take your bag upstairs, and you can go and join her."

"Okay, thank you," she replies, polite and quiet as she is with anyone outside our little family. When she turns to

Travis, I notice how nervous she looks. Does he not realise she isn't falling for all this crap?

"Go on, I'll get this to the right room, I promise," he says with a smile. Verity kisses him on the cheek before rushing off. I don't miss how he watches her until she is out of view.

"She is perfectly safe here. There's no way anyone can get to her," Christian says, closing the door behind us. "I have put security on high alert, and there are more people here than usual just to be on the safe side."

This doesn't seem to settle Travis's nerves, though.

"Now we are here. Is anyone going to tell me what the fuck is going on?" I demand, looking around. Christian looks from me to Travis, and I don't miss the way he cocks a brow.

"He was out with Verity as things were coming to light. I said I would fill him in here once I knew she wouldn't hear anything," Travis explains before turning his attention to me. "And I will let me just get her stuff upstairs."

Christian tells Travis that he will show him to the room as Jason comes into view.

"Jason, take Ethan and Ryan down to the office. I will be there in a moment."

Jason nods once at us to follow him before leading the way through their large house.

There are pictures of Jasmine dancing throughout the areas we see as we follow behind Jason, and I know there probably will be more elsewhere. Jason leads us into a room and signals for us to take a seat in one of the leather sofas.

"Drink?" he asks, heading over to a table with a selection of glasses and bottles on it.

"Thanks, I think we will need one," Ryan sighs as he looks around the room. As I thought there are several other pictures of Jasmine dancing. I notice one and smile when I realise Verity is next to her. They both look so happy and carefree as they do what they love the most.

"That was taken last year. Jasmine loves that print, and because we spend a lot of time in here, she asked for it to be put on the wall." Jason looks at it for a moment and smiles. "Those two have become closer in the last year, especially since Jazzy went through everything. Verity has been a huge support to her as she healed. Which is why we will happily do anything to help keep her safe." He turns to look at us, and I feel my anger rising.

"Why does everyone seem to know what's happening but me?" I turn my attention to Ryan, who sighs as he rubs his face. "What the fuck is going on? Why is Verity not safe?" I demand.

"Because I think her father is going to force her into an arranged marriage."

I look to the door where Travis and Christian enter the room with the twins behind them.

"You what?" I stare at Travis, who looks exhausted and stressed. This man has been taking on so much the last week or so. He needs a break as much as Verity does.

"You heard what Mum kept saying earlier. 'You will ruin everything; she is not for you'. The more I thought about it, the more I realised she wasn't just talking about ruining her marriage to Henry," Travis explains as he walks into the room and sits on the sofa opposite me.

"But Verity would never agree to marry someone because her father said to," I point out, but Travis shakes his head—the doubt showing in his eyes.

"Think about it. He's been training her for this all her life. She's been brought up being told not to question him and do as he says. That showing any emotion is having a tantrum, and he will always do what is best for her."

"But marrying her off, and to who?" I demand.

"We don't know. I don't know if I'm right, but I'm unwilling to take the chance."

"Henry and Mum are making their way back from Hawaii. They will be here tomorrow evening. By then, we will have taken Verity and gone into hiding," Ryan says beside me.

"So, what? We are going to leave the country with her?" I ask, looking between the two of them before it clicks. "That's why you were asking about her passport. So, we can run."

Travis nods before letting out a deep sigh.

"Like you heard, she hasn't got one. We can't find any of her documentation, and I wouldn't be surprised if it weren't to ensure that she didn't run away. Henry has covered all possible scenarios except one."

"Which is?" I ask.

"Verity falling in love with one or all of you," Christian answers as he passes Travis a glass of what I'm guessing is bourbon. "When he realised what was happening, he realised that he needed to speed things up and make sure that you didn't ruin all his best-laid plans," he adds.

"If we can't leave the country, what's the plan?" I ask.

"You go into hiding. We make sure there is no way for him to track you," Jason says, passing me a drink. "It will be tough, especially as I have no doubt he will get the police involved, but it's the only way to do it for now."

"So what? We hide in one of our houses until he decides he won't marry his daughter off?"

"No, our are the first places they will check. The last thing anyone would expect is the O'Reilly's to help us. As far as everyone is concerned, we still hate each other. So, Christian has offered us a car and one of their safe houses." Travis looks at me as he leans on his thighs, his hands wrapped around his glass.

"We need to go completely underground. We send messages to clients saying we are unavailable until further notice; we leave our laptops, phones, cars, and anything that could be traced at our houses. Verity won't be taking part in the last of the performances. I emailed the school saying a family emergency has come up, and she isn't available until the new year. We are going completely off the grid. There is no phone line, internet connection, or anything at this address. We stay there until we can find out who Henry's trying to sell our girl to and what we can do to prevent it from happening."

I stare at Travis momentarily, realising how much we are all willing to give up without a second thought for our girl. If there was ever any doubt about how dedicated we are to her, this will put her mind at ease.

"So why are we here now?" I ask before looking up at Christian. "No offence."

"None taken," he shrugs before sitting forward in his own seat. "To ensure you are properly protected and hidden, some work is being done to the safe house. I'm having one of the companies I use to install CCTV and signal blockers. No one will be able to use any mobile devices in the area. They are also sorting out CCTV and sensor traps surrounding the premises to ensure no one can get near the place without you knowing in advance."

"You trust this company?" Travis asks. Christian turns and nods.

"If I were in your shoes, I wouldn't trust anyone else with Jasmine's life."

"One of the owners used to be my personal guard and has saved my life more than a few times. He and his mates are all ex-US SEALs and know their shit better than anyone," Jason adds as Christian nods in agreement.

Travis looks at him for a moment before nodding.

"If you trust him, then I will."

"So, what now?" I ask as Ryan sighs next to me.

"Travis has asked me to see if any of my contacts know of anyone getting married soon. When I hear something, I will contact my guy, who will let Travis know. Then we start working out how to get Verity out of it safely," Christian explains.

"For now, Ryan is going to stay here. You and I return to the house and pack up all our stuff as quickly as possible before running a few errands. There, we will stay until we come to get Verity in the middle of the night," Travis answers, downing his drink.

"We let Verity have one more night of peace before we rip her world apart tomorrow and take her to the safe house. Then we can do nothing but wait until we work out who is trying to marry our girl."

I don't like the sound of any of this. We are relying too much on other people to do things that we should be doing. But is there any other way? I guess only with time will we see who we can trust and who we can't.

"Excuse me," Christian announces as his office phone starts ringing. He walks over to it and picks it up before it can stop.

"O'Reilly." His head snaps up to look at Travis, whose back straightens. "I'm putting you on loudspeaker; others in the room need to hear this." He presses a button and places the receiver back on the stand. "Are you still there, McIntire?" he asks.

"I am and have the information you were looking for." A strong, deep voice fills the room, and I close my eyes, realising one of the most powerful men in the country is speaking to us.

"You know who is looking to marry?"

"I can do one better and tell you who will marry the Stevenson girl."

"Who?" Travis demands as he jumps to his feet. Christian shakes his head at him in a warning to stay calm.

"Is that who you said was dating the girl?" McIntire asks.

"Yes, it's Travis Donavan. His brothers are here as well," Christian answers, giving us all a warning look.

"I knew their father, good man. I thought you had fallen out?"

"That's what we would like people to continue to think so that we can assist in keeping Verity safe. Jasmine and her are very close, and she is like family," Christian says, not taking his eyes off Travis. "Who did you find out was looking to marry her?"

"Nicholson's eldest son. It has been on the card for about two, maybe even three years; she was promised to him on his twenty-eighth birthday next month."

A silence fills the room. Nicholson is a piece of work, and his son is no better.

"Do I even want to know why Verity has been promised to him?" Travis asks.

"All I know is that a large sum of money was owed, and this is one of the ways Stevenson could clear the debt. He accepted, and his debt would be cleared once the marriage is official."

"Son of a fucking bitch," Travis curses as Maximus, Jason and I all jump to our feet, ready to control him if we have to. He starts pacing around the room with his head in his hands. Every muscle on his body is rippling, and I know he's losing control.

"Thank you, McIntire. That helps a lot," Christian says, not taking his eyes from the pacing Travis.

"I wish I could give you more information, but at the moment, I have none. If I hear any more, I will be in touch."

Christian lifts the receiver and thanks him again before hanging up.

We all stare at one another briefly, knowing that we are about to take on the biggest, most dangerous man in the UK, and we can't even guarantee we will win.

But one thing's for sure. The three of us will have to be dead before he gets his hands on our woman.

Chapter Forty-Four

VERITY

Even though I'm sitting in an oversized chair I have fallen asleep in so many times, I can't seem to get comfortable or relax. I pull the blanket around me as yet another ice-cold sensation flows over me. Something's wrong; I can feel it, but I have no idea what.

When we arrived back at the house, Travis had been tense, and I knew something wasn't right. Ryan hugged me a little harder and longer than usual, and Travis hardly let me out of his sight.

There were also the constant questions of 'Where is your birth certificate?' 'Do you know where any of your documentation is?' he's up to something, and I don't like that he's hiding it from me because I sure as heck don't buy the 'I'm planning a holiday for after graduation' rubbish.

"What made you think of doing this at such short notice?" I ask, turning to look at Jasmine.

"It was just an idea," she replies, not taking her eyes off the screen where *Twilight* is playing. We always end up having a Twilight marathon whenever I stay around.

I look to the door, hoping to see one of the guys coming in to say bye. But no one is there besides Layton, sitting in a chair with a bag of popcorn playing on his phone. His feet up as he relaxes, obviously not on duty.

"I thought he could leave you alone when you're home?" I ask, frowning.

"Maybe I'm here for the movie," Layton replies, not looking up from his phone. "Go, team Edward," he adds, holding up a fist. Jasmine laughs next to me as I roll my eyes. I'm not buying it. Not once has he looked at the screen. I turn back in my seat and try to relax and enjoy the movie, but it isn't working.

"What do you think the guys are talking about?"

"I don't really care as long as they don't start fighting again." She looks at me with a massive grin on her face. "I would hate for my daddy to kill yours."

"Maybe mine will be the one doing the killing?" I suggest shrugging casually.

"One's an accountant, the other the equivalent of a mafia boss. My money's on Christian," Layton pipes in from his seat. I turn round and throw a piece of popcorn at him as Jasmine roars laughing.

"You can shut up as well," I mutter under my breath as she nudges me with her shoulder.

"I'm sure no one will die today. They will talk, have a drink, then another until they are all drunk, and your guys end up having to stay the night as well," she laughs. "That's probably why Christian suggested this sleepover in the first place." Jasmine's smile slips for the briefest moment as I turn to look at her.

"I thought you said the sleepover was your idea?"

"It was, I meant."

"No, you said Christian suggested the sleepover. That

means it wasn't your idea at all. What aren't you telling me?" I demand.

"Nothing. Yes, Christian suggested it, but only because Travis wanted to speak to him about stuff, and he thought-"

"This isn't just about their past, is it? I know Travis is hiding something from me. I could tell the moment I got home to pack for tonight. What's going on, Jaz?" I demand as Jasmine starts looking uncomfortable.

"I don't know, and that's the truth!" Jasmine turns her whole body to look at me, and when I see her face, I know something's wrong.

"Christian suggested you spend the night. I was in his office earlier when he got a call from Travis. Christian asked me to leave, which he hardly ever does. It doesn't matter what he's talking about; he only asks me to leave if it is personal to the person calling and they don't want me or the others knowing."

What the hell would Travis be talking to Christian about that would result in him suggesting a sleepover and telling Jasmine to make out it was her idea? I don't know, but I plan to find out.

I throw the blanket off my lap and jump to my feet, not bothering to put my shoes back on.

"Where are you going?" Jasmine demands, scrambling to her feet as well.

"I'm going to find out what's going on." I storm towards the door, but Layton steps in front of me.

"That's not a good idea right now, Hun. The guys are all discussing something important," he says, placing a hand on my shoulder. I shrug him off and push past him.

"Which somehow involves me," I snap. I see from the glimpse that I caught of his and Jasmine's faces that I'm right. I storm through the door and rush away from them before they can try to stop me again.

"Fuck," Layton scrambles behind me as he tries to keep up.

I head for the office, knowing that's where they were going. Thankful that I know my way around this house so well. I doubt the others would give me directions if I asked.

I turn down the corridor, where I can see the door to the office. But as I start heading towards it, Layton and Jasmine get in my way. Layton holds up his hands to stop me from going any further.

"Verity, I get you are upset, but give me a moment to go ahead."

"No!" I snap loudly, cutting him off. "I'm getting sick and tired of people lying to me."

"No one is lying to you," Jasmine starts, but I stop her with one look.

"But you're all hiding something from me, and I'm sick of being the last to know!" I shout, looking back to Layton. "Get out of my way, now!"

"Verity!"

I look behind Layton to see Travis standing at the door with Ethan and Christian behind him.

"What's going on?" I demand, staring at him.

"Nothing for you to-"

"Stop fucking lying to me!" I cry out. My head's pounding in time with my heart, and my stomach is so tight, I'm sure I'm going to throw up. "You promised you would always be honest with me," I point out as I storm forward and stop right in front of him. "You said you would never hide anything."

I watch as Travis lets out a deep sigh and rubs at his face.

"You're right, I'm sorry, Sweetheart." He steps forward, closing the gap between us. "I was trying to let you have a little more time before things had to change, and I should have just been honest with you from the start."

"Are you leaving me?" I ask as my voice wobbles. Travis's eyes go wide before he pulls me into his arms.

"Fuck no! I told you I'm never leaving, not now, not ever."

"Then what are you hiding?" I ask as my eyes burn, and it starts getting harder to breathe.

"She deserves to know the truth," I hear Ethan say from the doorway.

"I know," Travis sighs into my hair.

He turns us around and leads me into the room, where I realise all four O'Reillys have been sitting with my guys. Ryan walks over to me and wraps me in his arms.

"Come here, Little Kitten." He pulls me onto his lap as Ethan sits on one side of us and Travis on the table in front of us. I'm aware of Jasmine and the O'Reilly's in the room with us, as one of them whispers to Jasmine, but my sight is fully set on my three guys.

"It's bad, isn't it?" I ask. Travis nods as he takes my hands.

"I don't know how to begin; it's so bad. I wanted you to have one last night without worrying about everything. But, as usual, you are too clever for your own good." He tries to make a joke of it, but I can tell none of us are in a teasing mood.

"After I got off the phone with Mum this morning and heard what Henry had been saying to you, something started playing on my mind. I realised that you might be in danger, and since then, I have been doing everything I could to discover if I was right, hoping I wasn't." Travis looks stressed, and I expect him to say more, but instead, it's Christian who speaks.

"Have you ever heard of a man called Thomas Nicholason?"

"Yes, Dad took me to his house once for dinner," I answer, frowning at him.

"Was there anything that stood out to you about that meeting?" Ryan asks. I look at him and shrug.

"Not really. I was left on my own with his son for most of it. Something about Dad needing to talk business with Thomas."

"How was his son to you?" Travis asks.

"Fine, we didn't really talk. Dad told me to remember my manners and only speak when spoken to. He asked me a few questions about my background and what I liked doing. But he soon left me alone in the library. Why do you ask?" I don't miss the look Travis gives his brothers before lifting my hand to his mouth and kissing my knuckles.

"Today, after you went out with Ethan, I called Christian. So many things were playing on my mind, and like I said, I had a bad feeling about something Mum kept saying."

"What did she say?" I ask cautiously.

"That I was going to ruin everything, and you were not for me," he answers, closing his eyes and taking a deep breath. "I thought she meant that you were promised to someone else. That they had already picked you out a husband."

I burst out laughing but quickly stop when I see everyone else is straight-faced.

"Are you serious? This isn't the fifteen hundreds. People don't arrange marriages like that in this country anymore." I look to Ethan and Ryan, but when there is no sign of them joking with me, I look to Jasmine, but she is leaning against Sean with her hand over her mouth.

"Do they?" I ask, looking back to Travis. He takes a deep breath and nods.

"Sometimes, yes."

I feel like the ground has opened up underneath me. There is no way.

"He wouldn't do that. I know my dad is far from perfect, but he wouldn't arrange for me to marry someone without my consent."

"I wasn't sure either, so I asked Christian to see if he could get any information."

My head snaps to Christian, who looks at me with the softest face.

"I'm sorry, Verity, it's true. Your dad has promised you to a Mitchell Nicholson. You are to be married next month."

I can't breathe; it feels like something is pressing against my chest and back. I shake Travis's hands from mine as I pull out of Ryan's arms. I need space; I need to breathe.

"Sweetheart, look at me," Travis stands at the same time as I do. He cups my face between his hands, forcing me to look into his eyes. "Breathe, I've got you."

I shake my head as I gasp for breath, but Travis continues to look into my eyes whilst holding my face.

"No one but my brothers and I are going to marry you. They will have to kill us first, and we are tough fuckers. No one is taking you from us." He says it in the softest voice, but his eyes tell me he is ready to fight. The first tears start to fall from my eyes as Travis pulls me into his arms and holds me as I fall apart.

"I won't. I can't," I gasp, becoming hysterical. Every time I start feeling good about something. Whenever I feel like my life is finally heading on the right track, something has to come and take it from me.

"Why?" I ask, clinging to Travis's t-shirt as I soak it with my tears. "What did I do?" I ask.

"Nothing, you did absolutely nothing, Kitten." Ryan takes one of my hands and presses a kiss to my knuckles.

"No one is getting you, Baby. Do you hear me? No one is getting within a mile of you," Ethan adds from behind me as I feel a hand on my head.

"How can we stop this?" I ask, looking up at Travis.

"We have a plan. We will keep you safe until I can sort this whole shit show out, and you will be free from it all." He leans in and kisses my forehead. "I won't let anything happen to you, Sweetheart. I will die before anyone gets near you."

Chapter Forty-Five

TRAVIS

I walk into Verity's room, a bag in hand and look around it. Everything is pristine and in its place, like everything in this house. Part of me wants to grab a baseball bat and go to town, smashing the place up. It's what the bastard deserves after everything he has put her through.

My phone vibrates in my pocket, and I open it to find a message.

Ryan: We are settled in our room here. Jaz has taken Verity to continue watching the film, but I don't think it will distract her. Let me know when you will collect us tonight, and I'll make sure we are ready for you. Be safe, and don't do anything reckless.

I smirk as I type out a reply telling him to be ready for two AM. He knows me too well. I shove my phone back in my pocket and throw the bag on the bed.

Walking over to the chest of drawers, I pull out her underwear and anything else in there. We have no idea how long we'll be in hiding; we have to plan for this to take months to get sorted. However, I want it over and done with as soon as possible. My girl has been through enough, and I don't want her to suffer longer than she has to.

I couldn't bring myself to tell her there was a chance she would never be able to return to the only home she had ever known. Even if we get her out of the arranged marriage, I know the relationship between her and Henry will be ruined. He'll probably stop her from returning to get her personal effects. That's if he makes it through the hell we have found ourselves in. Will Nicholson kill him when he discovers Verity has gone? What will happen to our mum? How deep into this is she? A part of me wants to grab her and make sure she is safe as well, but that could all be for nothing. At the end of the day, Mum is aware of Henry's plan for his daughter, and she is obviously fine with it. In my eyes, that makes her as bad as her husband.

I'm just packing Verity's pyjamas when my phone starts ringing. I pull it out without checking who it is.

"Donavan."

"I've just received an email about Verity not attending the rest of the shows. Where the fuck is she?"

A rage like I have never known fills me as I realise who's on the phone. I told the fucking school not to contact anyone about the matter, as it was private, and Verity wished to keep it that way.

"Somewhere you can't get to her," I growl through gritted teeth.

"Bring her back now. Otherwise, I will call the police and say you have kidnapped her!" he screams. I can hear the fear in his voice; he knows if he loses his daughter, he will have to face Nicholson, which would never end well for him.

"Go ahead. Verity has made a lovely little video we can send them. It's detailing exactly why she has fled her father, who's trying to force her into an arranged marriage." I really wish I was there to see the look on his face as he starts screaming all kinds of shit down the phone at me.

"How the fuck did you find out?"

"You do know who I work for, right? That I'm not your advantage accountant. I rub shoulders with some of the most dangerous people in the country, and it's amazing what I can find out by just making a couple of phone calls."

"You son of a fucking bitch, they will kill me!"

"Good, saves me a job!" I yell back. "Don't think I haven't noticed the damage you have done to Verity over the years. You act like a loving father, but you are never here, and you treat her like a child. You hide from her when you are in the UK and break her heart over and over again. Well, no fucking more. You will never see her again or come within a hundred feet of her. We are already getting a restraining order placed against you and my bitch of a mother."

Henry starts screaming shit again, but I'm past caring. I'm not listening to a word of it. I pull Verity's phone from my pocket and place it on her bed. It isn't coming with us. We can't risk it being tracked. She has already transferred everything off it onto a hard drive I purchased for her that will stay in my car, which I am leaving in a safe place.

"If you want to live through this, call off the marriage. If you do that, I may help you raise the funds to pay off Nicholson."

"Do you know who he is? The interest on the payments is enough to bankrupt me!" Henry roars down the phone.

"So, in other words, getting out of debt is more important to you than marrying your daughter to a thug who is known for beating women?" I ask through gritted teeth.

"They will kill me!" he yells again.

"Good. I hope they make you suffer."

I end the call and stop myself from throwing my phone against the wall. Fuck I have never been as angry as I am right now. How can he call himself a father when he's willing to sell his daughter to clear his debts?

"Take it that was the prick?" Ethan asks as he walks into the room with a big bag in each hand.

"Yeah, fucking bastard has no intention of protecting his daughter. It's purely down to us."

Ethan walks over to the wardrobe, grabs a load of clothes, and tells me to get the stuff from the bathroom.

I look at my watch and realise we only have eight hours to pack up Verity's stuff and take my car to a barn near the safe house, so we have a spare vehicle in case we need to make a run for it. As well as buy supplies for my brothers and me as we only have a few things with us and no time to go back to our houses to gather stuff. All of this and return at the O'Reilly's by two AM to get Verity and Ryan.

I take a moment to lean against the sink and take a breath. Everything has been running a million miles an hour, and I don't think I have had time to process everything. After telling Verity everything, I kissed her and left to come here and get everything she needed. Taking one last deep breath to try and clear my head, I focus on packing her things up.

I quickly grab the bottles of soaps and shampoos from the bathroom. Making a note of them so I can get her some spare. As I place a bottle in a wash bag, I catch my finger on something sharp.

"Son of a bitch," I hiss through gritted teeth looking at

my bleeding finger. I open the bag to see a razor blade sitting on the bottom. My heart breaks for the girl who has sat; God only knows how many times she has cut her skin and drawn blood. The little girl who just wanted the love of their father, who thought they had it, but was only being trained to make him money.

I look at the blade in my hand and vow that she will never question if she is loved again. She will never crave the love she deserves because the three of us are going to love her until our last breath and long into the afterlife.

Verity always wanted a dad, but now she has a Daddy, Bear and partner in crime to shower her in love every single day. She will never be alone again, and I will die before we have to see her in the hands of someone else. She is ours, and we will fight to keep our family together.

Chapter Forty-Six

VERITY

"We're nearly there. Is she asleep?" Travis whispers over the sound of the car engine. It's still pitch-black outside, and we must have been driving for a few hours. I have no idea where we are or what time it is.

"I'm awake," I whisper, rolling onto my other side. I'm lying in the back seat of a borrowed car, resting my head on Ryan's lap. Travis and Ethan are in the front, Travis driving as usual.

"Did you manage to get any sleep, Sweetheart?"

"No." I catch him watching me in the rearview mirror. Ryan runs a hand over my head before placing it on my shoulder. I look at the dashboard and see it's just gone five in the morning. No wonder it's still dark.

"We'll be there in less than ten minutes; you can go to bed for a few hours then. I think we could all do with a nap," Ryan says, squeezing my shoulder slightly. I don't reply; I just nod against his thigh and look ahead to find Ethan watching me.

"I wish this wasn't happening to you, Baby."

"You and me both," I sigh, sitting up.

We are running out of things to say on the matter, so the rest of the journey is in silence. I don't miss the way all three guys keep checking on me or the looks they share. But I have a feeling that's not going to change any time soon.

We pull off the main roads and start travelling down dirt ones. There are no streetlights or even many houses on the way. The further we drive, the less there is around us. I guess it is the ideal place for a safe house.

Travis mutters to himself as he looks out for the property. He still misses the turning and has to back up and take the sharp turning Christian warned him about. I almost find myself smiling at how he sits behind the wheel, calling Christian every name under the sun as he navigates down the thinnest road I have ever seen.

"It's a path, not a fucking road."

I look to Ryan, who rolls his eyes. "Someone needs to feed the daddy; he's getting hangry," he jokes. I giggle as Travis manages to tell him to fuck off and nearly crash the car at the same time.

When the cabin comes into view, I notice a car parked outside. I lie down quickly out of view, having already been warned about not being seen.

"The licence plate is the same as the guy who's meeting us. But I'm not taking any risks." I watch Travis lean over and open the glove compartment. He pulls out a gun and checks it's loaded.

"There is another one in there. Anything happens, get her out of here," he says before climbing out of the car and leaving the engine running. Ethan unfastens his seatbelt and climbs behind the wheel, ready in case we have to make a quick getaway.

I hold my breath and count in my head. I don't even

323

get to thirty before Travis comes back into view with his thumb up. Ethan turns off the car as Ryan opens the door. I hear Travis calling that all is fine as Ryan helps me out of the car and hurries me into the house. It all seems so unreal.

We walk into the cabin's lounge, and my mood lifts significantly when a familiar face stands before me.

"Calvin!" I rush to him and wrap my arms around his neck.

"Good to see you too, Verity," he chuckles as he hugs me back.

"I see you know him then," Travis laughs. I turn around and nod.

"He watched over Jasmine a few times whenever Layton wasn't available," I answer as I turn back to Calvin.

"How is Luna and Chelsea? Are they okay?" I've only met his girlfriend and her daughter once, just over a month ago, when Calvin and his two business partners, Logan and Drew, brought them to watch our performance. Jasmine, Danielle, and I went out front in our costumes to meet Luna, as she loves ballet.

"They are good thanks. The five of us have all moved into a new house, and Luna can't wait to be a big sister."

"Chelsea's pregnant?" I squeal as I throw my arms around him again.

"Has he managed to get it into the conversation already?"

I turn to see Logan walking in with Ryan, each carrying bags.

"Hey, Logan! I'm so happy for you all," I laugh as I throw my arms around his neck, taking him by surprise, but he soon hugs me back.

"Thanks, Verity. We are very happy, too."

I step back to see Travis, Ryan and Ethan, all watching me with smiles on their faces.

"What?" I ask, looking around.

"Absolutely nothing, Baby," Ethan chuckles as he places an arm around my shoulders.

"Come on, let me give you the grand tour of the place and all its new features before we leave you in peace," Calvin says as he holds out his hand, signalling for us to follow him further into the cabin.

"You know what? I can think of much worse places to hide out," Ethan says as he falls onto the sofa next to where I'm curled up with a blanket and book.

"Wait until you've gone a full twenty-four hours without your phone and see if you feel as positive," Ryan chuckles from his seat.

"I'll just do as our girl and pick up a book. What you reading, Baby?"

"Just some book I found in my room." I place the book on the side and stand from the sofa.

"You, okay?"

I turn to look at Ryan to find him watching me. They have all been watching my every move, and it's getting annoying fast. I nod as I head out of the room.

"Where are you going?" Ethan yells after me.

"I'm obviously not going far, am I!" I call back, not meaning for there to be so much venom in my voice. For a moment, I consider going back into the lounge to apologise, but I keep walking, needing to clear my head.

As I head towards my room, I see the bathroom door is open and notice the large bath. A deep bubble bath sounds perfect. I spot my wash bag on the side and look in it to find all my favourite toiletries. For a moment, I look inside and feel my chest tighten when I notice my blade is missing. I hadn't planned on using it, but I can't explain the feeling I get when I realise it's gone. It's like a child missing their comfort blanket. They may not use it, but they like knowing where it is.

"I picked up extra bottles for you. They are all under the sink."

I turn around to see Travis leaning against the doorframe with his arms crossed.

"Thank you," I whisper, placing the bag on the side.

"I took the blade."

"That wasn't-" I start protesting, but he cuts me off.

"Don't lie, Sweetheart. I know that's what you were looking for," he sighs as he pushes himself away from the doorframe and walks further into the room. "I get it, I really do. You have been trapped your whole life, and now you are trapped in a tiny cabin with the three of us. But it won't be forever, I promise." He reaches up and tucks some hair behind my ear.

"I know, I'll get used to it," I reply, placing my bag back on the side before wrapping my arms around his waist.

Travis holds me tight as he buries his face into the hair at the top of my head and lets out a deep sigh as he whispers.

"I don't plan on you being here long enough to get used to it."

Chapter Forty-Seven

RYAN

"Okay, I'm starting to really miss the outside world."

I spin around and shush Ethan while checking for Verity or Travis.

"Don't let Verity hear you saying things like that; it won't help the situation," I warn before returning to the book I was reading, but I'm not taking any of it in.

It's been two and a half weeks since we arrived here, and it feels like time has dragged and flown all at the same time. The cabin luckily has four bedrooms, so we all have our own space, somewhere we can stop and unwind without the others bothering us. We agreed that if one of our doors is closed, we leave them in peace. The only person who can walk around freely into any room, whether the door is closed or not, is Verity.

We are getting increasingly worried about her. She's hardly sleeping. She eats when we put food in front of her, but never the whole plate, and is clinging to Travis more than the rest of us. I now understand how the twins could say they never get jealous of each other. Sure, I wouldn't turn down any time with Verity. But we always knew that Travis was her protector and her safety net; it's only natural that she would rather be with him at the moment. On the few occasions Travis hasn't been available, she has come to me as her second daddy. She knows there is nothing we wouldn't do for her, and we will protect her no matter what.

"Have you noticed Travis is spending longer out each morning with that Logan?"

I put my book down and look around, checking for Travis before nodding.

"I think he may be on to something but won't share it until he knows for definite."

Travis goes out before dawn every morning to meet with Logan and uses his laptop to check for any information. I don't know what he might have found that is causing the trips out to last longer each morning, but he is getting increasingly more stressed and angrier. It could be the isolation or the situation itself that's stressing him out. It could be the lack of progress, too. As far as I know, Henry has made no attempts to find us. The police aren't involved, but that's thanks to Verity's little video. How she thought to make a video telling the police everything, I don't know. She watches far too many true crime programmes. But the threat of her exposing Henry was enough for him not to report her as missing.

That doesn't mean we can come out of hiding. Verity is still in danger of being married to that man. Consent would mean nothing to them. They would have a way of making the marriage legal without all the business of a ceremony. We have already heard how Nicholson apparently eloped with his wife. They could easily use the same story with Verity and his son.

"Did Verity sleep in with you last night?"

Ethan nods as he yawns.

"We didn't get much sleep, and not just because of sex. She tossed and turned all night. I don't think she has had a sound sleep since we got here," he sighs.

"I don't think any of us have. Let's face it, the three of us aren't used to relying on others to sort shit out; we have always done it together."

"RYAN!"

We both jump to our feet and run upstairs to where Travis's voice came from. My heart starts racing, terrified of what could have happened.

"Where are you?" I shout as we take the stairs three at a time.

"Bathroom!"

We skid to a stop at the door to find Travis sitting on the floor with Verity. She is wrapped in a towel, her hair still soaking wet as he holds her.

"What's happened?"

"Get me the first aid box," he snaps as I realise Verity's crying. I grab the box from the cabinet before rushing back to him. It's then I notice the blood on the floor and in the shower.

"There is a cut under my hand. I need you to check if it needs stitches." Travis lifts his left hand from her hip to reveal two deep cuts.

"Oh, little Kitten," I sigh as my heart breaks. Where the hell did she get a blade from? We have all hidden ours to ensure there wasn't anything she could use. If she needs a blade to shave, she asks for one, and we sit in with her just to be safe.

I check them out and breathe a deep with relief when I realise none need more than butterfly strips. Luckily, Travis had thought ahead and picked some up to be on the safe side. Keeping them covered for a day or two should be enough to help them heal. I hear Travis asking Ethan to get her some dry clothes as I place a dressing on her leg.

"I'm sorry," Verity sobs against Travis's now wet chest.

"I know you are, Sweetheart. Why didn't you come and get one of us?" he asks, running a hand over her head, trying to remove the wet hair from her face.

"I didn't want to be a nuisance."

Travis and I share a look, and I can see the anger on his face. He's not mad at her; we could never be mad at her for this. She has been told her whole life to suppress her feelings. It's no wonder she turned to self-harming as a coping mechanism. We wish she would realise we are here now, and she'll never have to hide her emotions again.

"You are never a nuisance, not to us. Even if you walked in during a meeting with a client, I would put you first every single time." I know he's trying to reassure her, but with everything going on, I don't know if it will get through to her. She is in survival mode, and let's face it, who can blame her?

"All done," I whisper as I sit back on my heels and look at her hip. I know one of them will scar; it will be a new addition to the rest of the tiny ones that pepper her soft, pale skin.

I'm just climbing to my feet when Ethan walks in with some pyjamas and her dressing gown.

"Come on, Kitten. Let's get you dressed while Travis gets changed." I help her to stand from Travis's lap as he climbs to his feet.

"I'll come and see you in a minute, okay, Sweetheart?"

Verity nods as I watch my brother walk from the bathroom, rubbing his face. I can see in his body he is struggling with everything. I'm just worried this may be the icing on the cake that pushes him into doing something stupid.

Chapter Forty-Eight

TRAVIS

I pull on my t-shirt and lean against the chest of drawers, Gripping the edges so tight that my knuckles turn white.

I'm failing her.

We have been here for eleven days. It's only three days until Christmas, and I wanted to be home for it. Instead, we are still here, and she is cutting herself to deal with everything.

I'm failing her.

I've always been able to take control of any situation, but this is a whole new ball game, and I'm at a loss. How the hell do I save her whilst keeping her safe from not only the outside world but from herself?

I didn't even know she was there when I walked into that bathroom. I didn't hear the shower as I was so caught up in my head, trying to piece together the puzzle that will save the woman I love from being forced to marry someone else. But when I opened the door and saw her sitting on the shower floor, my heart broke. My heart stopped completely when I noticed the blood running in the water as it flowed down the plughole.

I grabbed her from the shower and held her to me while screaming for Ryan. I don't think she even registered I was there until I pulled her from the hot water. She was so trapped by her pain and heartache that the outside world ceased to exist.

I'm failing her.

I take a deep breath and try to push my burning rage down. I don't want her to see it, to see the version of me that I'm saving purely for her father and the bastard who thinks he can marry her. She is ours, and no fucker will change that.

With one last deep breath, I stand and turn to the door to find Verity standing there with her doll tightly in her arms as she hugs it to her chest. She looks so lost and scared, and I fucking hate it.

"Come here, Sweetheart," I whisper as I hold out my arms. She runs to me and starts to cry. Jason was right; there is a little inside of her that is desperate to be loved and protected, and I'm so glad she feels safe enough with me to show that side.

I pick her up and carry her to the bed so we can lie together. She always seems to relax more when lying in my arms, and I'm more than happy to hold her for as long as she needs.

We lay on the bed in silence as she cries quietly. I run a hand over her head and hold her tight, wishing she wasn't going through this.

"I'm sorry, Daddy."

I lean back a little so I can see her tear-soaked face. Placing a hand on her cheek, I press a kiss on her forehead.

"I know, Sweetheart. You have been so strong and brave. I'm so proud of how well you have been doing."

"I've not been any of those things," she whispers, looking away. I apply pressure under her chin to make her look at me again.

"Was today the first time you cut yourself whilst we've been here?" When she nods, I feel a little pressure lift from my chest. At least she hasn't been doing it without us realising again. "Then you *have* been brave and strong. Because otherwise, you would have done it before now." I pull her against my chest and bury my nose in her still-wet hair.

"Just please, don't do it again. None of us will ever see you as a nuisance, never. We're not him; we want you to open up and explain how you feel. We want to know everything about your day, and nothing you ever tell us will make us wish you would leave. We love you so much, Sweetheart."

"But you have given up so much to be here because of me." I hear her voice wobbling as she starts to cry again.

"Sweetheart, we would have left the country if you had a passport. We would have left and never returned." I roll so I am lying over her, trapping her head between my arms so she has no choice but to look at me. "Do you understand that, Sweetheart? We would give up everything because losing you is not an option."

She nods slowly as a tear rolls down the side of her face. I lean in and brush my lips against hers, needing to show her that I love her, as the words don't seem to get through the concrete barrier she has built around herself.

"There is absolutely nothing I wouldn't do to keep you safe and happy with us. Please remember that no matter what you think we are doing, you are always our priority."

For a moment, Verity and I stare into each other's eyes. Neither of us blinking or looking away. Just as I'm about to give her some space, she grabs me around the neck before her lips crash into mine.

Things could escalate quickly from here, but I don't plan on fucking her. I want to shower her with so much love and affection that she feels suffocated. I want her to know that she is the very air I need to breathe to survive, and there is nothing that will stop me from making sure she has the perfect life she deserves.

I purposely slow down the kisses and softly run my fingers over her skin to signal there will be no rushing tonight. I want to tease her and kiss every inch of her body. I want to eat that sweet pussy for so long that I can still taste her on my lips in the morning.

"Daddy," she gasps as I start kissing her neck just the way she likes it.

"Daddy's going to take it all away tonight," I whisper against her soft, silky skin. "I'm going to make you feel safe and loved, just as you deserve," I add as I help her out of her clothes whilst removing my own.

I look down at her lying on the bed sheets; she is so beautiful and perfect. The only flaw on her precious skin is the dressing Ryan applied. I run my fingers over it gently, testing how much it hurts.

"I don't feel it," Verity whispers. My eyes find hers again, and I don't stop myself from leaning down and kissing her lips again.

"One day, you are going to realise how loved you are," I whisper against her lips. "There is no part of you that isn't perfect in my eyes.

"I love the way your eyes sparkle when you are pushing your luck with Ethan or when we pay you the attention you crave," I whisper, gently kissing her closed eyelids.

"And the two little dimples that appear on your cheeks

when something makes you laugh so hard you hold your stomach." Kissing the spot of her dimples, I can taste the salt from the tears that she has cried tonight, and I vow to make Henry pay for each little drop of water that has ever left her body because of him.

"I love the way you smile when you hear a piece of music you love and how your hands move ever so slightly as if you are choreographing your own dance to it."

Verity lets out a soft sob, and I know she is starting to listen and realise how much I have noticed about her, how much I can see.

"There is nothing you can hide from me because I am so in tune with you that my heart would cease to beat if yours did."

I kiss my way across her collarbone and towards her breasts. Telling her how I love the way her nipples harden when she is aroused, how I can tell what she needs just by the way she's breathing. That I ache to hold her all day and all night, and there is nothing in this world that feels as right as when she's in my arms.

I make my way down her body, kissing every part of her whilst avoiding touching anything between her legs, wanting to tease her for as long as possible. When I reach her hips, I press a kiss to the top of the dressing.

"One day, you will realise you don't even think about doing this anymore because you will finally believe you are worthy of our love."

"Daddy." The quietest sound comes from her, and I only just make out my name. I know she's crying, and that's okay; she needs to cry, and I'm here to help with it.

"Daddy's got you, Sweetheart. I know what you need." My lips press to her plump pussy lips, and I feel her whole body tense. Forcing my tongue between her folds, I lick her in one long stroke from her entrance to her clit. Verity cries out as I start flicking her clit with the very tip of my tongue. I drink her up, desperate to taste as much of her as possible. I suck her clit in hard, and she cries out again, louder this time, as I push one then two fingers into her.

I continue to lick her and rub those spots inside just as she likes. It doesn't take long until she gives me her first orgasm, which quickly leads into a second until she becomes too sensitive and can't handle it anymore.

I make my way back up her body, leaving a trail of kisses in my wake before pressing a long, hard kiss to her lips.

"I love the way you taste before and after you cum. There is something sweeter about your juices after you have screamed my name." I'm so hard I don't have to hold myself to find her entrance. I slowly ease my hips forward until I feel the tip of my rock-hard cock at her wet and ready pussy. Her lips wrap about me as if trying to guide me home.

"Daddy," she gasps as I push into her as slowly as possible. Feeling every inch of myself being sucked into heaven.

"I love the way you were made for me, how I fit in you perfectly," I growl through gritted teeth as my balls rest against her. "What's our record, Sweetheart?" I ask, my lips brushing against hers.

"Four, Daddy," she moans as I grind my hips against her.

"Then let's see if we can hit five."

I thrust into her once more before letting myself accept the overwhelming feeling of her. My name's on her lips as she joins me, and we cum together. Both gasping for breath and sweating after we made love for longer than I ever have before.

There was something special about tonight; from the moment her lips first found mine to us both finding our last release together, it has been perfect. I have been in love with this woman for at least six months, but tonight, I could have wept with the overpowering feeling of that love. I enjoy any time I spend with this amazing woman, but tonight, we came together in a whole new way, and it was perfect.

I roll onto my side and pull her against me as I hold her tight.

"That was more than four," Verity giggles against my side.

"I am more than happy to try and beat that record another time, maybe not just now, though," I laugh, kissing her head as she giggles again.

"Can I sleep here tonight?" she asks.

"You never need to ask to sleep with me. You know that, Sweetheart. What is mine is yours."

"I know," she whispers, and for the first time, I'm starting to think she believes me.

"Close your eyes, Sweetheart, and get some rest. I'll be back soon; I need to lock up." I press a kiss to her head and slide out from underneath her as she closes her eyes and quickly falls asleep.

I make my way around the cabin, checking the windows and doors, even though I know my brothers would have as well. It's gone eleven, and they are both in bed. Time doesn't exist for us here. I wake up at four every morning, sneak out to meet Logan, and use his laptop. I'm back before the sun's up, and here I stay until four the following day. No one else leaves except for the odd walk around the perimeter to get fresh air. But we haven't been able to get Verity past the back door. She's terrified, and I hate it.

As I re-lock the front door and turn to leave, I feel something cold underneath my bare foot. Looking down, I see an envelope with my name on it. I recognise the writing instantly as Logans and open it.

Something I thought you might be able to make more sense of than me.

I read through the information on the page twice before I truly understand what I'm seeing. By the time I return to the bedroom, it all makes sense, and I know I can use this to my advantage.

For the next half an hour, I sit in bed with Verity's head on my lap while scribbling on a writing pad I had brought with us. Her soft breathing keeps me focused, and I pour everything onto the page. When I'm finished, I slide out from underneath her and fold up the paper before placing a gift for her on top of it.

I watch her sleeping soundly for a moment, taking in every feature on her face. Tucking her doll into her arms, I kiss her head. Before walking to the door with a bag, I kept packed just in case.

I take one last look at my girl sleeping soundly in the bed before slowly closing the door behind me as I sneak through the cabin, praying that I showed her tonight how much I love her and that she forgives me for breaking the promise I swore I would never break.

Chapter Forty-Nine

RYAN

A high-pitched scream wakes me with a jump. I don't have time to register what time it is as I scramble out of the thick blankets and rush for the door. Skidding into the hallway, I catch a glimpse of Ethan as he runs into Travis's room.

"Baby, calm down," I hear him beg as I reach the door.

Verity is sitting in the middle of the bed, crying so hard she's hyperventilating.

"Where the fuck is Travis?" Ethan yells as he tries to pull her into his arms, but she is fighting against him. She curls up into the fetal position and screams into her doll. I rush to the bed and push Ethan out of the way.

"Little Kitten, look at me," I grab her face and look into her pained eyes as she cries. "I can't help you if you don't tell me what happened."

She tries to speak but is too hysterical; nothing is making any sense.

"I'm going to find Travis," I hear Ethan snap, which causes Verity to cry harder. I turn around and look at the clock. Next to it is a balled-up piece of paper. I grab it and read the first line.

"Fucking idiot," I snap as I pull her onto my lap, and the realisation hits.

"What?"

"He's left," I yell as Verity cries in my arms, her whole body shaking violently. No wonder she is in such a mess; he's done the one thing he promised over and over again he wouldn't.

"Go see if you can work out when. He might still be close," I snap as Ethan rushes for the door.

"It's okay, Kitten, we'll get him back. We'll find him before he can do anything stupid," I whisper into her hair as I rock her gently, trying to console her but knowing I'm fighting a losing battle. This is worse than when her dad left because part of her expected that. But this is ripping her apart at the seams because he was the one who, from day one, repeatedly promised her he would never leave her side. Yet he's done just that.

"I'm sorry, little Kitten."

"He left!" Her tears soak my bare chest. "He left me," she starts to heave as she hyperventilates again and throws up over the side of the bed.

I'm going to fucking kill him. He must have known what leaving was going to do to her. She is hanging on by a thread to the point she is cutting herself, and the prick just leaves. I'm sure in his head, he is doing the right thing, and he has a plan, as I know he loves her too much to put her through all of this on purpose. This woman is his whole world as much as ours, and he swore always to protect her.

I continue to rock and hold Verity as she cries in my arms until she calms down. Instead, she sits on my lap, holding her doll to her chest as tears silently roll down her cheeks.

"Did you read the whole letter?" I ask, running my hand over her head as she shakes it.

"He left, Bear." Her voice is so tiny, and I'm scared she'll never truly recover from this if we don't get him back.

"I know. Can I read the letter?" I ask, gently pressing a kiss to her head. She nods as a small sob escapes her, and she buries her face into her doll. I close my eyes for a moment to try and calm my anger before picking up the crumpled piece of paper and reading it.

Sweetheart,

I'm writing this whilst you sleep peacefully beside me. It is the hardest thing I have ever had to do, but please know I'm doing it for all the right reasons.

I have no choice but to break the one promise I made to you, the one I said I never would. I need to leave for a little while. I need to put this right for you.

I hate seeing you suffering like you are. I can't stand knowing that there is someone out there who thinks they have the right to take you from us. Henry believes he has the right to decide who you marry and spend the rest of your life with. I won't stand by and watch you hurt yourself or let him hurt you anymore, which is why I'm going away for a little bit.

Everything I said to you tonight as we made love was the truth. I never believed in love until you walked into my life and made me see everything in a new light. I tried to hide how I felt about you, but I couldn't do it anymore. I belong to you as much as you belong to me and my brothers. There is absolutely nothing I wouldn't do for you, which is why I'm leaving you now.

I have found the key to getting you out of the arranged marriage, and I have to take it. If you are ever going to walk down the aisle to marry someone, it will be a Donavon and no one else, which is why I'm leaving this ring box with you.

The ring inside was our grandmother's engagement ring, which she inherited from her mother, who was given it by her mother. It has been in our family for generations, and I want you to be the next Donavon to wear it.

If the worst happens and I don't return, marry my brothers and know I will always look over you. You are my whole world, and death itself couldn't keep me from you.

I will set you free, Sweetheart, and I will ensure you get to live the life you deserve more than anyone I know. I hope you will forgive me for leaving in the first place.

I love you with all my heart, body, and soul.
All my love always and forever.
Your Daddy Travis
xxxxxxxxxxxxxx

I close my eyes and try desperately to blink back the tears. He's an absolute fucking idiot. I'm going to kick his ass when I get hold of him. Even if he has found a way to get Verity out of this arranged marriage, to just sneak off like this, not taking one of us with him, I swear to God, if he doesn't get himself killed, I will do it for him.

"I think you need to read this, Kitten. It will help everything make more sense," I whisper as I hand her the paper. I hold her tight as she reads it, and I hear her crying quietly. That man really does love her with all his heart, and I know it must have killed him walking away like this, but he should have told us. He should have made sure someone was watching his back.

Verity sits up slightly from my lap and picks up the box from the side as Ethan walks into the room. I look up at him, and he shakes his head. As I expected, he hadn't found him. He would be long gone by now.

I watch as Verity opens the box and looks inside to see the ring.

"Is that Granny's?" Ethan asks, walking forward. I nod as Verity lifts it from the box.

"Travis left it for her," I whisper, holding out the note for him to read. I take the ring from her and place it on her left ring finger. It's a perfect fit as if it were made for her.

"We will get him back, little Kitten and then we will make you an official Donavon," I whisper as she leans back into me, holding her doll and looking at the ring.

Chapter Fifty

VERITY

I can hear Ryan and Ethan whispering outside of the bedroom door, but I'm too lost in my heartache to pay attention to what they're saying.

Waking up this morning, I knew something was wrong. Even though my mind told me Travis had just popped out to meet Layton like he always does, my heart was telling me he'd left. The bed was too cold, and I knew I didn't fall asleep holding my doll.

I'd turned on the light, saw the ring box and the letter, and knew what it would say. The pain that tore through me with those first few lines was like nothing I had ever experienced. When my dad left, it was partially expected, but this was so out of the blue I couldn't make sense of it.

Last night, when Travis made love to me, we had a connection I'd never experienced before. Everything felt deeper and perfect, and I know I wasn't the only one who felt it. Never in my wildest dreams did I think he was saying goodbye.

The pain rips through my chest raw, forcing the air from my lungs as I cling to my doll and cry into it.

He left me.

I know he has done it to save me, to make sure I don't have to marry someone I don't love, but I lost the man I do for that to happen. Because I love him, I love all three of them, and I never got to tell him. I was so busy trying to protect my heart that I hadn't even told him it was his, that I'm his. My heart, body, and soul are divided equally between the three Donavon brothers, and if I don't have all three, then a part of me will always be missing.

"How you doing, Baby?"

I don't move; I can't speak, and all I can feel is the pain in my chest where part of my heart is missing.

Ethan squats down in front of me and places a hand on my cheek. I'm still curled up in Travis's bed, needing his scent from the pillows to try and numb the pain. The thought of leaving this bed and losing that last part of him causes me to feel physically sick. So, I lay here and miss him and wish I could have told him not to go. Because I know there is a real chance he will never return.

"Baby, you need to eat or drink something. Travis will want you to look after yourself," Ethan whispers, running his hand over my head. I can't find my voice to tell him that I need to stay here and wait for my missing piece. I need them all here with me so I can be whole again.

Ethan sighs as he stands and places a kiss on the top of my head.

"Ryan will be back soon. He went to see if he could find out when he left. We will get him back for you, Baby. We will get him back for all of us."

I want to tell him we need to leave and find him now.

We must find him before it's too late, but I can't find the words.

Sometime later, I feel the bed move as Ryan puts his arm around my waist, hugging me from behind.

"I said I wanted to be a daddy to you too. I promised you that night that I would always put you first and love you no matter what. I plan on keeping that promise. I'm not implying that your daddy hasn't, but as much as I want to run off out there and find my brother to bring him back to you, I won't." Ryan removes his arm, and I hear a piece of paper rustling before he holds a folded piece in front of me.

"Travis left a note for us, too. I want you to read it, and then I want you to understand why I am choosing you over my brother. I want you to see that the three of us love you more than life itself and why we are all doing what we are right now."

I take the note from him and feel his arm fall over my stomach again, so he holds me as I read it.

Guys,
I know you will hate me; I know our girl will be heartbroken, but I need you to stay with her no matter what.
I found a way to end this so we can move on as a family of four and give our girl all the love she deserves. Doing this without you two having my back is fucking hard, but you need to do something more important than back me up; you need to protect Verity.
I will never say I love her more than you; we have all proven that we love her in a million different ways. But this is something only I can do. She is my whole world, as she is yours, and I know I can make life better for her again.

That being said, there is a chance I won't make it back. If that's the case, then pay attention.

Everything I own is in your name, but to go towards keeping her free. I have a huge savings account and the money in the bank. Sell the house and everything in it, sell my company, the full works and run. Take our girl and hide her wherever you have to; keep moving and keep her safe.

That is all I will ever ask of you. I know you can shower her with the love she deserves, so do it. Marry her, make her a Donavon and give her the world.

If you go to my house, there is a safe hidden under the floorboards in the bathroom. The code is Verity's mum's birthday. Inside are the contact details for a guy who will make up fake IDs and passports for you. He is already working on Verity's; there is also the five thousand each for your new IDs in the safe and an address to a garage where I have hidden a car.

I have provided everything for you to get her away from this shit show. Protect her with your life.

If I'm successful, I will be in touch in three days. If you don't hear from me, start running. I will find you.

I'm proud of both of you and honoured to be your brother. I know we don't ever say it, but I am now. I love you both and hope you know that.

Take care of each other and love our girl enough for all three of us.
Travis

"I know it may seem like we are doing nothing. Like, we are choosing to stay with you over going to find him. But for me to keep a promise to him as well as the one I made you, I need you to survive this, little Kitten. I need you to eat, drink, and live through this long enough for him to find us. Because he will return to us, I can feel it in my gut. I can't lose my brother and you; I love you both too much. So, I need you to live, Verity. If not for me and Ethan, then for your daddy. It's what he would want you to do."

Ryan kisses my temple as the tears roll over the bridge of my nose and onto Travis's pillow.

"I'm going to make us all some sandwiches, then we will sit down and devise a plan. Yours will be on the table in five minutes. I expect you to be there to eat and have a glass of water, if not for us, for him."

I feel the bed dip again as he climbs off the other side and listen as he walks out of the door, closing it quietly behind him.

I look at the letter in my hand and reread it, memorising every word like I have my own. I need to do as Ryan asked; I need to survive this for all of them; I just don't know how. The ring on my left hand catches my attention, and I look at it. As far as I'm concerned, I'm now engaged to the Donavon brothers; no one could tell me otherwise. But I don't plan on having only two husbands; I want all three.

I climb off the bed and walk over to Travis's wardrobe. I look at his clothes still hanging up and wonder what he's taken until I notice the missing backpack from the bottom. He always planned to leave in a hurry if he had to. I should have known he would be prepared for every situation.

I look through the clothes he's left and pick out a hoodie he wore a few days ago. It still smells of his deodorant and aftershave. Pulling it on over the pyjamas Ethan helped me put on earlier, I bring the fabric up to my nose to inhale his scent, closing my eyes to picture him. The way he looked into my eyes last night as we made love. How he laughed when I was bored, and he caught me attempting to draw a picture the other day, even though I can't draw more than a stickman. But most importantly, the way he looked the moment I realised I love him as much as he said he loves me.

We need to find him; our family isn't complete without him, and I need to tell him he is mine, and I refuse to give up on us. Not now, not ever.

Chapter Fifty-One

TRAVIS

Well, isn't this just fucking wonderful. Not that I was expecting anything different, mind you. What did I think was going to happen when I strolled up to the front gates of a notorious drug lord and demanded to speak to him? I wasn't going to be invited in and offered a tray of cake and sandwiches whilst we sipped tea. I had a feeling I would end up locked in a fucking room. I just wish there was more than a chair and barred window.

At least I'm not chained up or dead. I suppose that's a bonus. *'Look for the silver lining'*, my grandmother would always say. Well, right now, I'd just be happy to see anything other than these four fucking walls.

I look up at the clock on the wall and wonder if it's even moving. I've apparently been in here for two hours, but it feels more like six.

I have no idea if Nicholson is here or if he even knows who I am. To them, I'm probably some junkie looking for a hit.

I rub the back of my neck as I walk over to the window and look outside into the dull, wet day. My mind wanders straight to Verity as it has since I left. Is she okay? Does she understand why I'm doing this? Will she ever forgive me for leaving her, even if only temporarily? I might not plan on dying, but I do know it's a real possibility; that's why I left my grandmother's ring with her.

Granny always hated our mother, so she gave me the ring instead of her and told me to give it to the love of my life. I bet she never dreamt the love of my life would also be the love of my brothers as well. I smile as I picture the way our Granny would shake her head in dismay at that one.

She would have loved Verity, as would my father. If he had a daughter, there's no way he would have ever treated her how Henry has treated Verity. My father loved his kids more than life itself, and there was nothing he wouldn't do for us. That is how a parent should be and how I will be when we have kids. But first, I need to get Verity out of this fucking arranged marriage and leave here, ideally with all limbs still attached.

The door flies open, and I'm greeted by the arsehole who escorted me in here with a more presentable guy behind him. I could take them both easily. The new guy's not thin, but he's not as built as me. Plus, I'm taller and know how to fight. I bet this guy relies on his gun shoved in the back of his trousers.

"Is he in, or am I just to wait patiently until he arrives?" I ask, crossing my arms and leaning back against the window.

"Like I'm telling you shit. Apparently, you haven't even given us your name!"

"Actually, I did; your mate there just wasn't listening," I sigh, rolling my eyes. When he just stares at me, I shake my head and try not to lose my composer. "It's Donavon, Travis Donavon. I have something that the boss might be interested in."

"Oh yeah, and what's that?" the guy who brought me in here asks as he tries to appear relaxed and leans against the doorway behind the new guy. Instead, he looks like the class nerd trying to copy the cool kids and failing miserably.

"A deal, I get what I want, and he makes a lot of money. It's a win-win." One good thing about working with some of the people I do accounts for is that I've learnt how to handle the rich and dangerous. I know when to be cocky and when to suck up. There's no need to suck up to the guy they send to do the digging. The guy who brought me in here is nothing but a cheap security guard who probably gets paid in whores and drugs. There's no need for pleasantries. This new guy, however, seems to be higher up the chain and could even be Nicholson's second. He has the suit and the attitude of someone above the other guy's paycheck.

"Alright, Donavon. I'm Justin, the second in command. The guy behind me is Phil. Don't mind him. He doesn't get to throw his weight around much and is hoping he gets to fight someone soon. If you want to see the boss, it's my rules you need to play by."

Great, a second who is up his own arse, just what I need.

"Would I be right in thinking what you want to see the boss about is something to do with this one?" He turns his back to me as I push myself away from the wall. I know he's up to something, but I don't know what until I see who is being held behind him.

"You put him in here, and I will kill the fucker," I warn through gritted teeth.

"I wouldn't do that if I were you. The boss wants to

speak to him, and I have a feeling you will want to be in the conversation," Philip laughs as he pushes Henry into the room. My blood boils as I look at the guy who has sold his own daughter to these lowlifes.

"Have fun, and try not to spill any blood; it's a bastard to clean off the carpet." Justin slams the door, laughing before I hear the sound of the key turning in the lock.

"Where the fuck is she?" Henry hisses through his teeth.

"Somewhere you won't find her," I reply as I lean back against the wall, trying to put as much distance between me and this piece of shit. It is taking everything in me not to kill the fucker where he stands. It wouldn't be hard; this man has never fought in his life, and it shows. But if Nicholson wants him alive, then I have to keep him that way. For now, anyway.

He looks worse for wear than when I last saw him. He's taken a bit of a beating and looks like he hasn't showered or shaved in a few days. His usual tidy salt and pepper hair is ruffled, to say the least. No life-threatening injuries, unfortunately, but enough to scuff him up a little.

"Do you have any idea what you have done?" Henry storms towards me, his little fists clenched by his side. I doubt he has ever punched anyone, either.

"Yep, and it's only going to get worse for you unless you help me get Verity out of this arranged marriage."

"I can't. What part of they will kill me are you not understanding?"

"I understand that part perfectly well; I'm just trying to work out how that is Verity's problem," I snap back as I lean over him. When he doesn't have an answer, I shake my head and go back to leaning against the wall.

"You really are the lowest of the low. I'm just glad your *daughter* will be far away from here when you fall from the little pedestal you've placed yourself on." I start walking away from him, needing time to figure out the last few details to share with Nicholson. Cause if Henry is pissed now, he will be well and truly fucked off by the time I'm finished with him.

Chapter Fifty-Two

RYAN

I'm going to kill him.

If the son of a bitch doesn't get himself killed, I am going to do it.

What the fuck was he thinking running off like this leaving us to pick up the pieces of Verity's broken heart? He knew what he was doing, and it wouldn't surprise me if he had been planning it from day one.

Verity seems to have listened to me after reading Travis's letters. She came out of his room, ate and had something to drink. She also listened to Ethan and me discussing our options. She commented on a few little things, then said she was tired. Ethan is now lying with her in Travis's room while I wait for Calvin to go over a few things and find the best route to getting out of the country without being seen.

When Travis left, he didn't take the car he had driven us in. I know he had his vehicle hidden close by in case of emergencies, and it seems he walked or ran to that. Logan is trying to track it using their access to CCTV, but nothing has shown up so far, which doesn't surprise me. He might only be an accountant to most, but Travis has trained himself to be stealthy as fuck when he wants to be. I know he always has fake licence plates to hand and can change them quicker than any car thief.

When we arrived, Calvin told us he had hidden a burner phone with a few guns. One we can use to make calls if we need to, so we can plan ahead if we need to run. I need to put as much in place as possible, ready for the three-day deadline. But I can't seem to do what needs to be done.

The thought of running when my brother could need us is killing me. We have faced everything together our whole lives. We have always had each other's backs, no matter what. But Travis was right; we need to put Verity's safety first this time. If Travis survives this, he will find us. I will leave him a sign each time we move on to somewhere new.

I pick up the burner phone and look at the blank screen. It's a real piece of shit. When was the last time mobiles had buttons on them? It's as low-tech as they come, which is perfect for what we need it for. Things like apps and new mobiles with GPS are easy to track and to hack. This piece of shit probably doesn't even have predictive text. I bet Verity couldn't even use it. Thankfully, being older means I learned to text on phones with buttons.

I'm just trying to work up the courage to turn it on and start making calls when I hear the knock at the front door before someone enters. I hold out the gun and aim it at the door as I wait to see who it is.

"It's me, don't shoot."

I let out a sigh of relief as Maximus walks into view with his hands up.

"What the fuck are you doing here?" I snap, putting the gun down on the side.

"I heard about Trav. I've come to be an extra pair of eyes and ears until you have a plan or leave," he says, walking further into the room, shrugging off his jacket as he approaches.

"You actually have no idea how much of a relief that is to hear," I sigh, rubbing my face. I've been contemplating not sleeping at night, and now we are down a guard for our girl.

"I thought it might be. How's she doing?" he asks, looking around.

"She's sleeping at the moment, I think. She has hardly spoken since he left. She got herself so worked up that she vomited everywhere. I don't know what she will do if he doesn't return," I admit as I lean against the kitchen counter.

"Well, just keep an eye on her and make sure she doesn't do anything stupid," Maximus replies, not realising how accurate it is.

We haven't told anyone about the self-harming; that's her business, and we are happy to keep it that way for her. But if she starts getting worse, I will get others involved. I just don't know how to do that while on the run. Fuck, this isn't going to be easy.

I hear footsteps on the wooden stairs and look up in time to see Verity and Ethan walk into view.

"Maximus? I thought I heard your voice," Ethan says, greeting him with a handshake.

"Yeah, just come to help keep an eye on things." He turns to look at Verity, who is dressed in some yoga pants and Travis's hoodie. "How you doing, Verity?" he asks as he hugs her.

"I'm okay," she lies whilst stepping back. She knocks his coat from the back of the chair as she does and quickly apologises whilst picking it up and carrying it to the coat hooks on the other side of the room.

"You didn't have to do that; I would have hung it up," Maximus frowns as she shrugs, walking back.

"I want to keep busy," she replies before leaning against me. I wrap my arms around her and kiss her head.

"Do you want anything, little Kitten? Coffee? Toast? A large gin?" I offer, forcing a smile, but I don't get one in return. She just shakes her head and walks over to the kettle.

"I'll do it. Anyone want one?" she asks, looking around. We all shake our heads and watch as she makes herself a hot chocolate. She looks so small and vulnerable it's hard to watch. I want to stop her and make her sit down so I can do it, but she says she wants to keep busy, and I have to let her. I know the feeling, so I leave her to it and look to Maximus and Ethan, who are also watching her.

"Do you guys know what he may know to get her out of this?" Maximus asks quietly as Verity whisks some milk.

"Yeah, the three of us discussed it before," I reply, letting him know Verity can hear this. "Logan said he found evidence that Henry was hiding more money. He doesn't know everything but knew Travis would. He left some print-outs for Travis, as he said he would if anything came to light. He never expected him to run off alone to tackle it, though. That was a surprise to all of us."

"Logan is a good guy and wouldn't want to see Travis hurt, not only because he is under his care, but because Logan does this job for a reason. He would have gone with Travis as backup," Maximus explains. I have to agree. He couldn't apologise enough when he popped around earlier. He had no idea Travis would be stupid enough to rush off alone.

A commotion catches all our attention, and I see Verity standing with milk pouring onto the floor by her.

"I'm sorry; I will clean it up. I didn't mean to," she sobs as she bursts into tears.

I move her away from the mess, which looks like she has knocked over the milk she was whisking.

"I'm sorry, Bear," she sobs again.

"Stop apologising; it was just an accident. Did you burn yourself?" I ask, checking her hands. I can only see it down the front of Travis's hoodie, which will upset her more than anything. When I see she is unharmed, I pull her into my arms and hold her against my chest.

"Hey, there's no point crying over spilt milk, right?" I ask, offering her a small smile. "Why don't you go and change your top, and I'll finish making your drink for you? Ethan can help clean up the mess," I add a wink to try and lighten the mood, but she just nods and starts towards the door. As she goes to leave, she stops and looks at the two of us.

"I love you, both of you. You know that, right?"

I stare at her for a moment, my breath catching as she says the three words I wasn't sure she would say for a long time.

"We love you too, Baby girl," Ethans says as I nod and give her a more genuine smile.

"I never told Daddy, and I wish I had. I don't want any of you to think I don't love you because I do, more than anything," she whispers before turning around and hurrying out of sight.

"Shit," Ethan sighs as he turns to look at me. "I didn't expect that to hurt as much as it felt amazing to hear."

Maximus claps him on the shoulder and gives it a reassuring squeeze.

"I know what you mean," I reply, rubbing my face before taking a deep breath to settle my nerves before I start cleaning up the mess. We stay silent for a short while, both lost in our thoughts.

I always imagined Verity saying she loved me for the first time in a romantic way, not as a heartbroken woman who may have lost one of the guys she loves forever.

She looked so sad and lost standing there in the hoodie that swamps her, so it hangs almost down to her trainers.

I freeze the cloth in my hand.

Why was she wearing shoes?

Dropping the cloth, I spin on the spot and rush towards the stairs.

"What's going on?" I hear Maximus and Ethan call behind me. I don't have time to reply as I take the stairs three at a time and rush to her room, throwing open the door to find it empty.

"Kitten!" I yell out as I rush to the next room, which is mine, but it, too, is empty.

"What is it?" Ethan demands, stopping in front of me.

"She had shoes on!" I yell, pushing him out of the way as I barge into the bathroom; it's empty. I turn to see Ethan checking his room and cursing, telling me she's not there. We get to Travis's room together, and we throw open the door at the same time as I hear car tyres skid on the gravel outside. Travis's window is open wide, and she's used the emergency exit the O'Reillys had fitted in case their safe house was compromised.

"Fuck!" I yell as we rush down the stairs and out the door, but the car's long gone.

"I'll get my keys!" Maximus yells, rushing into the lounge and pulling the coat from where she hung it.

We all run to the car and try to open the doors, but nothing will open.

"Come on!" I scream as Maximus starts rummaging around in his pockets.

"Fuck!" he curses as he drops his coat and pats down his trousers. "She's taken my key!"

"What?" Ethan and I shout together as I grab the coat from the ground and start checking all the pockets.

"She must have taken it when she hung the coat up!" Maximus curses.

"Fuck!" I yell, throwing the coat onto the ground as I start to pace with my head in my hands.

"What the hell do we do?" Ethan yells at me.

"I don't fucking know!" I scream back as I look around. The car was here for us to use. We only had the one to ensure the extra vehicles didn't attract unwanted attention. We already know Travis has taken his car.

I rush back into the house and back up to the rooms to see if there is anything that tells us she knows where she is going. But all I find is a piece of paper with her handwriting on it.

I'm sorry, I have to save him. I love you both so much.
Yours always
Verity
xxxxxxxxxxxxx

Chapter Fifty-Three

TRAVIS

I look out the window into the night and try to see if there is anyone below. The viewpoint from up here is shit. Other than the prick who threw Henry in here earlier, we haven't seen or heard anyone.

"Hey! HEY!"

I turn around as Henry starts banging on the door.

"Will someone tell me what the hell is going on?" he yells, banging on the door again.

"Shut the fuck up. They won't tell you shit until it suits them," I snap, reminding myself for the hundredth time that I can't kill him. Yet.

"This is all your fucking fault! Why couldn't you just leave when we did? I told you to stay the hell away from her!" He turns and storms forward as I stand tall and look down at the short prick as he tries to glare at me. He's not as brave as he makes out.

"My fault? I don't remember agreeing for Verity to marry a drug lord's son! One who is known for beating women. Nor do I remember getting into so much debt with said drug lord that I had to sell my daughter to him as payment." I poke him in the chest, causing him to, thankfully, distance himself from me. "How the fuck did you end up owing him anyway?"

"That's none of your damn business!" he snaps, walking away from me.

"It's my business if it involves my girl!" I snap.

"She's not *your* girl! She was never going to be your girl! Let's face it, you will be dead by morning anyway, so who will she turn to then? Me. That's who! So, which of us will win this one?"

I look at him for a moment before laughing in his face.

"You think getting her to trust you will be easy? That you'll go up, pat her on the head, and she will come back like the little pet you have trained her to be?"

"She doesn't know anything else. Now you are out of the picture; she will do as she's been told like always."

"But you will need to find her first, and my brothers will make sure that never happens. You may have hidden all her IDs, but I have already ensured she can travel."

"Your brothers won't protect her forever; they will get bored."

"They will never get bored of protecting what's theirs." I take great pleasure in watching his smirk drop. "That's right, the three of us are with her. She finally knows what true love is and knows that the three of us will do anything to ensure she is protected from the abuse you have dealt her over the years."

"I never hit her!"

"No, you belittled her until she believed she wasn't good enough to be loved!" I roar, advancing forward. "You made her feel so small and insignificant that she doesn't even know who she truly is! So yes, you never hit her, what you did was a fucking worse!" I lift my fist, ready to punch him, when the door opens. I spin around as Phil strolls in with two guys behind him.

"Nice to see you two getting along so well." He looks smug, which makes me dislike him more. Snarling at Henry, letting him know I'm not finished with him, I turn to Phil.

"What do you want?"

"Now, now, no need to be so aggressive. I've only come to tell you the boss will see you both now." The guys behind him walk forward, and I see handcuffs hanging from their hands. I had expected it and sigh as I hold out my hands. I'm no threat; I don't plan on causing trouble; for Nicholson anyway. Henry, however, sees the cuffs and freaks out. He immediately starts to back away from them, cursing.

"What do you think you're doing? You're not putting them on me."

I could tell him to shut up, but instead, I take great pleasure in the way they take him down, cuffing his hands behind his back roughly. He tries to buck them off, and I roar, laughing when one grabs the hair on the back of his head and slams it into the floor, hopefully breaking his nose.

"Enjoying the show?" Phil asks. I shrug as I follow him to the door.

"If it causes that arsehole pain, I'm all for it. Just gutted it's not me making him bleed," I admit, grinning.

"No love lost between father and son then?" he smiles, quickly throwing his hands up as I snarl at him.

"That prick is not my father. Just because my bitch of a mother married him does not make him family, got it?" I warn, through gritted teeth.

"Loud and clear," Phil smirks as I follow him out of the room, not bothering to check if Henry is following us.

He leads us down a flight of stairs and along a corridor,

stopping in front of a door. He knocks twice before a deep voice calls for us to enter.

The door opens into a dark red office. There's a large desk to one side, and a short guy with a bald head sits behind it with his feet up on the desk as he puffs on a joint from the smell in the air.

"Ahh, Travis, is it? You got some balls, I'll give you that," he laughs, pushing himself away from the desk as I walk over to greet him.

"I'd shake your hand, but…" I hold up my cuffed wrists, and he laughs.

"Phil, uncuff the man. I don't think he's going to be any trouble, are you, son?" Thomas Nicholson says, smiling.

"No, sir. I just want to talk," I answer, flashing him my friendliest smile. Nicholson looks behind me and frowns.

"What happened to you, Stevenson? You look like you took quite a blow to the face."

I don't even try to hide the smirk that spreads across my face when I turn to see Henry with a nosebleed.

"These thugs did it when they put these cuffs on me." Henry turns around to show Nicholson like he wouldn't know about them. But he just shrugs and goes back to smoking his spliff. I have to stop myself from waving my hand in front of my face. I hate the smell of weed or any drug. I never understood the attraction myself. But the last thing I want to do right now is disrespect the guy in front of me. Not if I'm hoping to win him over and save Verity.

"Why are you here again, Stevenson?" Nicholason asks, looking at Henry, who clamps his mouth shut, not knowing whether to remind him. "Oh yes, I remember you lost my son's bride." He turns to me and smiles. "I think you know something about that, don't you?"

"I sure do; that's why I'm here now," I answer, looking

around. "Mind if I take a seat?" I ask, wanting to keep the mood as casual as possible. Nicholson waves towards a few comfortable-looking chairs on the other side of the room. The two of us sit whilst Henry is luckily kept out of the way. I make sure I can see him and Nicholson, wanting to see his face when I make my proposal.

"So, tell me, where is the lovely Miss Stevenson?" Nicholson asks, sitting back in his chair. Looking a little too relaxed, but I try not to show how uncomfortable that makes me.

"I swear I had nothing to do with this. He took her!" Henry starts shouting, but one look from the boss and he shuts up quickly.

"She is safe; that's all you need to know for the time being," I answer as I put on my business face. I know the more confident I seem, the higher my chances of being heard are.

Nicholson watches me for a moment.

"Let me guess why you are knocking on my door instead of booking an appointment like a normal person. You are in love with the sweet Miss Stevenson and want me to cancel the arranged marriage? Am I right?"

"Yes, sir," I answer. "I don't want to cause any trouble; I have no qualms with you. My anger is purely towards that bastard there," I answer, pointing to Henry.

"And what if I say no? My son is quite fond of Miss Stevenson and looks forward to taking her as his bride."

I force my toes to curl instead of my fists as I try to keep my calm.

"Does Verity have no say in the matter?" I ask, trying desperately to keep my tone relaxed.

"Of course she does. In fact, we could always ask her if only we knew where she was." He sounds cocky, and I don't like it one bit. Fuck I should have told my brothers to run instead of waiting for three days. Have they found them? With the length of time I've been here, they could have tracked them down, retrieved Verity and returned. Is that why I was kept in that room for so long?

I watch Nicholson as he stands from his seat and walks over to the office door, smirking at the guys standing by Henry.

"You might want to watch him."

Before I can even get to my feet, a hand lands on my shoulder, pushing me down as a warning to behave.

Nicholson watches me momentarily before opening the door, and my world comes to a crashing standstill.

Chapter Fifty-Four

VERITY

Thomas Nicholson holds out his hand for me to enter the office. I heard Travis before I even set eyes on him.

"No! Get away from her!"

I turn just in time to see two guys tackle him to the floor. Travis fights against them, sending one flying as he turns to punch the other. I've never seen him violent before, but as he fights to get to me, he's like a madman.

The two guys from before take him down again, and two others rush into the room and help them pin him to the floor. He continues to fight against them, but they handcuff him whilst digging their knees into his back.

"Stop, you said you wouldn't hurt him!" I cry out, looking at Mr Nicholson as he smirks at Travis.

"Please stop fighting them," I beg him as his eyes land on me. "Please, Daddy," I mouth as a tear rolls down my cheek.

Travis stops instantly, but his eyes never leave mine.

"What are you doing here?" he demands. "They were meant to look after you."

"I snuck away," I begin. "I'm sorry. I couldn't leave you to get hurt because of me." The tears continue to fall as I look deep into his eyes. I start playing with the ring on my left hand. When he sees it, his eyes close as he takes a deep breath. Hopefully, he will calm himself down.

"Pumpkin?"

I spin around to my father's voice. I hadn't even noticed he was in the room. He was the last person I expected to see here.

"Why are you here?" I ask, taking a step back as he walks towards me. There is blood on his face and top, and his hands are cuffed behind his back.

"Pumpkin, I've been so worried."

For a moment, I want to believe him. Why wouldn't he have been worried about me? He wouldn't have known where I was.

"Why aren't you in Hawaii?" I ask, as it dawns on me that he isn't meant to be in the country. There again, it's not the first time he has lied to me about his whereabouts.

"I was going to surprise you, but you weren't home," he starts.

"You lying, son of a bitch!" Travis roars. I turn my attention back to him as he snarls at my father. "Tell her the truth. You wanted to make sure she was delivered here!"

"Stay out of this," my father shouts back, causing me to flinch away from him. I remember how he spoke to me on the phone and screamed at me for ruining everything.

Looking at Travis, I remember the way he held me together when I thought I would never feel whole again.

"I think we all need to calm down and remember why we are here," Mr Nicholson says, placing a hand on my back and guiding me further into the room.

"Verity, I know you are aware of a little agreement that's

been made about you marrying my son. Your father believes it would be a good match. However, Travis thinks you disagree. What do you think about it all?" he asks. I know by his tone that he's being condescending, and I hate it.

"I don't want to marry your son. I want to leave here with Travis and never see anyone else again," I admit, looking up at him through my eyelashes. I told myself I was going to be strong, forceful and confident. But now I'm here, and I can see Travis being pinned to the floor; all strength has evaporated.

"She doesn't know what she's saying. It's him, he's got to her," My father yells before yelping in pain. I turn just in time to see someone give him a backhand across the face.

"Shut up," the guy warns him before looking back to his boss.

"Do you know why your father agreed for you to marry my son?" Nicholason asks. I nod, still not quite believing the whole thing.

"He owes you money," I answer, hating that my father would choose to give me up over any amount owed.

"He does, which is where we come to a standstill because if you don't marry my son and let me access your inheritance, then I will be out of pocket by a lot. And if there is anything I hate more in the world other than liars, it's losing money." Mr Nicholson moves to be next to me and places an arm around my shoulder, pulling me closer. Travis instantly starts fighting again, but I shake my head at him, and he stops.

"What inheritance?" I ask, frowning. "I don't have any inheritance to give you."

Mr Nicholson looks from me to my father and laughs.

"You weren't lying; she really doesn't have a clue." He looks back at me and smiles. "Your mother left you a hefty sum of money, Verity. When you marry, it will become available to you, and your father has promised it all to me."

I look at my father and see from his face that Mr Nicholson isn't lying. How much am I meant to get?

"Can't I just promise it to you, and we leave it at that?" I ask, hopeful he will accept the offer. But when he shakes his head, my heart sinks further.

"How can I trust you to do that when your father has done everything he can to get out of paying me what is owed? You must understand why I can't just let Mr Donavon here take you so you can have your happily ever after. I need you to marry my son and let me turn your inheritance into more than it is already worth." He nods to one of the guys who is holding Travis down. He moves so quickly it takes a second to register what's happening.

One second, Travis is pinned to the ground, staring at me; the next, he has a gun to his head, and his whole body freezes.

"No, please!" I beg as I start to panic. "Please don't hurt him!" I try to get to Travis as my heart races, but Mr Nicholson keeps hold of my shoulders, pinning me in place.

"I don't want to hurt him, Verity. I just can't have you leaving here with him and me losing out on all that money. It wouldn't be good business."

"Please," I cry as I stare at my Daddy lying there with the barrel of a gun at his head.

"It's okay, Sweetheart. Whatever happens, it's okay," Travis whispers calmly.

"It's not okay; I want you; I love you!" I scream, shrugging off Mr Nicholson's arm and rushing to Travis. I wrap my arms around his head to try and protect him.

Crying, I look up at Mr Nicholson and then at my father.

"Please, don't make me do this?" I beg him. "If you love me at all, you will stop this," I beg. Praying that he will show me some sign that he is still there, that he's still my dad.

"Now stop it. You are throwing a tantrum, and I won't have. This is not the girl I raised. You are acting like a spoilt child." I stare at him as I feel Travis stiffen in my arms. "You will do as you are told and act like you have been brought up to behave. Get up from that floor, and enough with this nonsense."

I stay there staring at the man I have spent my whole life looking up to. I have changed who I am to suit him, yet I beg him to save me from a forced marriage, to save the love of my life from being shot in the head, and he has the nerve to tell me I'm throwing a tantrum.

Before I can reply, I feel someone grab my arms and pull me to my feet away from Travis. I start screaming and fighting to get back to him, but all I can hear is my father screaming at me to behave and remember myself.

"Sweetheart, stop."

His voice gets through to me when nothing else does.

"Look at me, no one else, just me."

I turn my head to look at Travis lying on the floor, the gun back pointing to his head.

"I know you are hurting, Sweetheart. I know you are scared, but I need you to be brave for me, okay?"

I nod my head slowly as I look at Travis.

"I love you, Daddy," I whisper as I see a smile spread across his face.

"I love you too, Sweetheart."

"Did you just call him *Daddy*? What the fuck?" my father snarls as I spin around to face him. Whoever has hold of me lets go, and I charge forward before pulling my hand back and slapping him hard around the face.

"Fuck you," I scream at him. As I hear Travis roar, laughing.

"Oh, looks like you pissed off the wrong lady," Mr Nicholson laughs as he comes behind me. He pulls me backwards as my father charges forward, but the guy behind him keeps hold of the cuffs so he can't reach me.

"Now, now, Stevenson, I am going to say you deserved that one. You are technically selling her after all," Mr Nicholson chuckles as my body stiffens.

"How much?"

We all turn to Travis, who is still lying on the floor with a gun to his head.

"Pardon?" Mr Nicholson asks.

"How much to get her out of the agreement? How much does he owe?" Travis asks. Nicholason watches him for a moment before shrugging.

"A lot, more than you would ever be able to raise if that's what you are thinking."

"How much does he owe?" Travis asks again, slower this time.

"With interest? Let's round it up to a nice sixteen mill."

I swear someone moves the ground from underneath me. How does he owe so much money?

"I'll give you twenty, but I want Verity to be free. There will be no wedding, no chasing after her after a couple of months or years. She no longer exists to you."

Mr Nicholson stares at Travis for a moment.

"When? I've waited long enough already," he demands.

"Give me a laptop and half an hour; I will put it in your bank of choice. But you must first agree that the arranged marriage is off, and Verity and I go free, never to be bothered by you or anyone working on your behalf again."

I look from Travis to Mr Nicholson, who is staring at

him. Does he really have twenty million sitting around in a bank somewhere?

"When I see the money is in my account, you can both leave, but I will hunt you down if the money is taken back."

"It won't be because it's his money," Travis nods to my father, who stares at him, his eyes wide with shock.

"You fucking arsehole, that's my savings!" he yells as he tries to get to Travis, but it's Mr Nicholson who steps between them.

"You were willing to hide away that money and let your daughter be married against her will. Fuck even I'm not that evil. That's your own flesh and blood, man!"

"Tell them the truth, arsehole; she deserves to know why you keeping twenty million was more important than your daughter!" Travis yells.

"That slut is not my daughter!"

The room falls silent as I grab hold of the desk behind me to keep myself upright.

My father turns his attention to me as he turns his nose up in disgust.

"Your mother was pregnant when we met. I loved her and said I would bring you up as my own, but fuck, I hate kids. You moaned and threw tantrums over the littlest thing. I wanted to be as far away from you as possible. The only reason I kept you around was your mother's money. When she died, her Will said you were to inherit everything on your wedding day. So, I had to ensure you had nothing left to get. But now he somehow has access to it, and the money will be gone! I'm going to have nothing, and it's all your fucking fault."

The only warning I get is Mr Nicholson grabbing me as he shouts, "Let him up."

Travis barrels past us before taking my father down. He

punches him hard enough to break his jaw. One of Travis's handcuffs is still attached, where they only had time to release one.

"You never fucking deserved her, you piece of shit." Travis looks at one of the guys who had been holding my father. "Uncuff the fucker, I won't kill a chained man!"

"Stop!" I yell as the guy throws the keys to Travis, who catches them with one hand.

"Sweetheart, after everything he's done?" Travis yells, staring at me.

"Please, don't kill him."

Travis looks down at the man I thought was my father and punches him hard once more before climbing to his feet.

"If it were up to me, I would kill you and warm my feet beside your body as it burned," Travis growls before spitting on my father, who's curled up in a ball. "Give me the laptop. I'll transfer it to you now. Then, I want your word; Verity is finally free to live her life as she wants." Travis stares at Mr Nicholson, who nods slowly and holds out a hand.

"Deal. But first, I want to know how much of the twenty mill is meant to have been hers?"

"All of it. Any money that arsehole made was from the interest and his work for you," Travis answers as I try to wrap my head around it all.

"Then transfer sixteen to me. Let her keep the rest. I'm still making a profit, and she has some of what is rightfully hers."

I feel myself swaying for a moment, but Travis places a hand on my back and turns to look at me.

"Are you okay?" the worry evident on his face. I shake my head because I am far from it. Cupping my cheek, he looks into my eyes. "I'm here, and it's going to be okay. I've got you."

"This is the new deal I would like to make."

We both look to Mr Nicholson, who holds up his hands. "Hear me out. You transfer the sixteen and keep the rest, but only Verity leaves today. I require your help with something. I will ensure you are home in time for your Christmas dinner. Then, neither of you will hear from me or my family again."

"And Verity is free? All I have to do is stay for a couple of days?" Travis asks as I lean into him.

"Absolutely, I will even let you call your brothers to collect her so they see you are safe and well."

"Fine, but she doesn't leave my side until my brothers arrive. No one else is to come near her."

"Fine," Mr Nicholson answers as he holds out his hand; this time, Travis takes it, and they shake. "My laptop is on the desk; I'll leave you to do your thing." He turns around to the guys who have surrounded my father. "Take him back upstairs. I will deal with him later." Mr Nicholason turns to me and offers me a warm smile. "Unless there is anything you would like to say to him, as I can't imagine you will ever want to see him again."

I look to the man who has made me an emotional mess. He's the reason I pretended to be someone I'm not my whole life, because it earned me his praise. I shake my head; I don't know if there is anything left to say. I've had so much thrown at me in such a small space of time that I need to process it all, but that, him, is too much.

I turn my back as my father is pulled out of the room, screaming and shouting all kinds of evil at us. I lean against my daddy as he wraps his protective arms around me, showing me he is here for me, no matter what.

Chapter Fifty-Five

ETHAN

I feel sick to my stomach. How the hell didn't we see what she was planning? I stood there and watched her put on her shoes. I didn't even think it was odd once.

How the fuck did she know to take Maximus's keys? I need to have words with that little brat when we get her back. There is no IF about it. She will be back with us by the end of the night and over my knee, receiving her punishment before I fuck her until she begs me to stop.

We are currently in Logan's car; Maximus is driving whilst Ryan sits in the front. When we moved into the cabin, we had placed all our phones in a security box, which Calvin had taken with him. He brought them around with Logan when we called to say what had happened. We figured at least this way, if Travis or Verity try to call us, they can get through.

A mobile ringtone brings me from my thoughts as I look at Ryan, who is looking at the phone in his hand.

"I don't know the number," he admits before answering it cautiously.

"Hello?"

"It's me."

I swear my heart jumps out of my chest from the sound of my brother's voice.

"Please tell me Verity is with you. She ran away!" Ryan snaps.

"I'm here, Bear."

My whole body relaxes as I hear her voice, knowing she is safe with Travis.

"Little Kitten, me and you are going to have a long chat about you scaring the shit out of us after I have tanned your ass to the point you won't be able to sit down for a month." After watching my brother for the last five hours, I wouldn't want to be Verity when he has her alone.

"I'm sorry, Bear," she whispers down the phone.

"Brat, you are lucky I'm not your daddy because you'd never sit down again. Where are my keys?" Maximus curses.

"I have them," she replies, and I hear Travis whisper something on the other end of the line.

"We'll discuss it later," Ryan says, giving Maximus a warning look. "Are you both okay?"

"Yes, it's over," Travis says as I silently pray before asking the big question.

"The arranged marriage?" I ask, leaning forward from the back of the car.

"Off. Our girl is free."

"Thank fuck," Ryan and I exclaim together, both visibly relaxing in our seats.

"I need you to come and collect her. I'm staying for a couple of days to sort some shit out for Nicholson, but then I will join you wherever you are. How soon can you be here?"

We both look to Maximus, who grins.

"We are ten minutes away from his estate. I take it that's where you are?"

Travis confirms it's correct, and he'll meet us at the front of the house before hanging up. I let out a deep sigh of relief as I fall back into the seat.

"I swear to god I have aged twenty years in the last forty-eight hours," Ryan says.

"When I get that little brat home, I'm chaining her to the bed and going to sleep. Don't expect me to wake up before Christmas morning at the earliest."

"Shit, it's Christmas Eve tomorrow. I still need to sort out Shorty's gift!" Maximus curses from behind the wheel. Ryan and I both burst out laughing.

"Someone's going to be in the doghouse," I tease, opening one eye in time to see Maximus flip me off.

I go back to closing my eyes and focusing on the positives. Both Travis and Verity are safe; she is out of the arranged marriage, and we can all come out of hiding. If that isn't worth celebrating, I don't know what is.

———————

I must doze off for a few minutes. I wake with a jump when I feel the car stop, and Maximus announces we are here.

I open the door and climb out just in time to see Ryan rushing to Verity and lifting her so he can hold her as she wraps her legs around her waist.

"Do you have any idea what we went through when we realised you were gone? I was worried sick, little Kitten!"

"I'm sorry, Bear, I had to do something," she sobs into his neck.

"I hope Daddy gave you hell!" I snap, walking to my

brother and pulling him into a hug. "You ever run off like that again, and I will fucking kill you myself. Understood?"

"Whatever," he chuckles as he steps back from me. But when I look at his face, there is a look I don't see very often. He knows he scared the shit out of us, and I don't think he will do it again, or at least any time soon.

I turn around and see Verity looking at me sheepishly. Seeing her there safe and unharmed causes a sense of relief to overcome the anger. Closing the distance between us in two strides, I thread my fingers into the hair at the back of her head, wrap an arm around her and kiss her with everything I have. I never want to let this woman go.

"From now on, you are always being chained to one of us. You even think about running, and I will not be held responsible for my actions, Baby girl. Understood?"

"Yes, Sir," she replies like the perfect sub she is.

"I'll decide on your punishment later. But first, I want to know everything that's happened." I look between Verity and Travis, who is talking to Maximus and Ryan.

"I need to go. I shouldn't be here. But you good for a car?" Maximus asks.

"Yeah, we have two here," Travis answers, shaking his hand. Maximus turns his attention to Verity, who pulls a car fob from her pocket and walks up to him, holding it out.

"Sorry, Maximus."

He looks at her for a moment before letting out a sigh and pulling her into his arms.

"You are lucky I'm too relieved to see you unharmed to scold you. What you did was reckless and stupid." He holds her at arm's length and smiles. "Also, please don't tell Shorty how you did it. She would try and do it herself when being a brat, and I like my car in one piece."

Verity giggles, nodding at him as he hugs her again, kissing the top of her head.

"I'll see you all in a week or two; I need to go," he calls, hurrying to his car. We all wave as he drives towards the estate entrance and out of view.

"I need to know what's happened and where we go from here. Why are you staying?" I ask Travis as he wraps an arm around Verity's shoulders and lets out a sigh.

"Come inside, and I'll explain everything."

Travis and Verity share a look before taking the lead and guiding us into the house.

Chapter Fifty-Six

VERITY

We walk into a sitting room that Mr Nicholson said we could use to talk about everything before I'm forced to leave Travis here with him. Mr Nicholson has sworn to me that no harm will come to him, and I can call and message him as much as I like. But that doesn't stop the feeling of unease. I want him with me. I want all three men with me, the way it should be.

Travis sits on a sofa chair and pulls me onto his lap, where I curl up small. I'm exhausted, but my mind is on overdrive, and I know I won't be able to sleep any time soon. There has been so much to process.

Ryan closes the door behind us and sits in one of the other chairs as Ethan paces, as he usually does when on edge.

"Want to tell me what the fuck has been going on?" Ryan asks. I can hear the anger in his voice, but I know some of that would be from the fear he would have felt when I ran. He would have been at his wits' end with two of us being Awol.

The need to remind him that I'm okay and safe overwhelms me. I climb off Travis's lap and move to Ryan's. As soon as I'm leaning into him, I feel him relax a little as he wraps me in his big, protective arms.

"I'm sorry, Papa Bear," I whisper again as I lean against his chest.

"I know you are little Kitten. But that doesn't change the fact you scared the shit out of us. Do you have any idea what we would have felt if something had happened to you?"

I look up at him and nod.

"The same as I would have felt if anything happened to Daddy."

Ryan looks into my eyes for a moment before letting out a sigh and nodding. He knows I would have never recovered if we'd lost him. I wouldn't have recovered if I lost any of them.

"Did they hurt you at all?" Ethan asks from beside us as he sits on the sofa before taking my hand.

"No, I'm relatively unharmed," I reply, leaning into Ryan.

"Relatively?" Ethan asks, his eyebrows disappearing under his cap. I nod and look at Travis.

"I want you to tell them everything. I'm ready to hear it now."

Travis looks at me and nods before sitting forward in his chair. His elbows lean on his knees as he looks at the three of us.

"As you know, I've been suspecting that Henry has been hiding money. Especially after I learned that the staff he was paying for didn't exist. So, I've met Logan each morning and used his laptop to hack Henry's banks. What I found was a lot of money in different offshore accounts, which I knew nothing about. Logan managed to get me in on the ones I couldn't get access to. There is nothing that man can't hack.

"The night I left, Logan had posted through a copy of a document which showed that the money started being transferred into the accounts four months after Verity's mum's death. It was then everything started to make sense. Henry had been slowly moving her inheritance into different accounts and making it look like it was being used for her upbringing, which was all part of the clauses of the Will. Verity was to continue living the life she was accustomed to, being cared for by staff, and attending any school she wanted until she turned twenty-one or graduated from school, whichever came first."

"Which is why he said she would have to move out when she graduated," Ryan says as his arms tighten around me. I close my eyes for a moment and breathe in the smell of his deodorant, using it to anchor myself to him, needing his presence to help me process everything.

"Exactly. All the time I've been doing the accounts, I thought he still paid for cleaners, a laundry company to collect the washing twice a week, a gardener as well as extra lessons at the school and a one-to-one tutor for her dancing." Travis adds.

"I haven't had any of that since my eighteenth, some even longer," I point out. "I was told not to tell anyone as it was family business, and he didn't want anyone, you guys included, knowing the truth."

"Which is why I never picked up on it all. I never did any digging when I did his accounts, as it was all straightforward. In truth, I didn't care what state they were in as long as Verity had everything she needed. He did a good job of hiding the truth from me."

"So how much had he managed to hide away?" Ethan asks.

"Twenty million," I answer, still unable to comprehend how much money that is.

"What the fuck!" Ryan and Ethan curse together loudly. I nearly fall from Ryan's lap as he jumps. Luckily, he tightens his arms around me before I fall.

"I had already realised how much he had hidden and had started transferring it to an account I created under a fake name. Which is why I came here, to offer the money to Nicholson to get Verity out of the debt, but it got a little messy."

"How messy?" Ryan asks.

"Thanks to the dance school, they thought Henry was up to something. Even though I told them to keep it quiet, the school announced Verity would not perform in the rest of the shows. Nicholson thought Henry was trying to hide her away so she didn't have to go through with the marriage. They grabbed him and brought him here. I had the pleasure of his company for most of the day," Travis sighs, rubbing his face. He looks exhausted, physically and mentally. I want to go over to him and offer any comfort I can. But my body doesn't seem to want to cooperate. I'm frozen with shock as everything is explained.

"Is he still alive?" Ryan asks.

"The last we saw, yes. Things got heated in the meeting with Nicholson after Verity turned up; some truths came out, and I flipped. The only reason he is alive is because she asked me not to kill him." Travis's eyes land on me as I wipe a stray tear from my cheek.

Everything has happened so fast that I haven't been able to ask the most important thing.

"How long did you know?"

Travis stands from his chair, walks over, and squats down in front of Ryan and me. He takes my hand in his. I notice his knuckles are split from hitting ... what do I even call him? My father? Henry? It feels weird calling him anything but Dad.

"I've had an inkling for a few weeks but nothing concrete until yesterday. Even then, I wanted to be wrong; I didn't want to have to tell you the truth. But I should have done, and I'm sorry, Sweetheart."

I look into his eyes as he reaches up and wipes a tear away with his thumb whilst cupping my cheek.

"What did you find out?" Ryan asks. Travis doesn't take his eyes off me. I know he's asking my permission to tell them. I force the words from my mouth, which leaves a bitter aftertaste.

"Henry's not my real father." Will those words ever feel real?

"What?" Ethan demands, but I don't miss the silence from Ryan or the look Travis gives him. I turn in his lap to look at him.

"You knew?"

Slowly, Ryan shakes his head.

"Like Travis, I had an inkling. It was something your auntie said that day we went to see her." He reaches up and tucks some hair behind my ear. "When you went to get her a drink, she said something about you being in danger and that Henry had no legal rights to you. I told Travis, which made us look into it."

I lean against his chest and take a deep breath to centre myself as my heart threatens to break completely.

"I get why you didn't tell me, either of you," I add, looking at Travis. "I don't think I would have believed it if I hadn't heard it from his own mouth."

"He told you himself?" Ryan asks. I nod against his chest as I look at Travis.

"He really hates me," I clench my jaw as I swallow back the lump in my throat. I promised myself I wouldn't break here. I have to be as strong as possible. The last thing I want is for Mr Nicholson to see me as weak.

"He didn't take the time to know you. If he had, he would've realised how amazing, funny, smart, and beautiful you are inside and out. He didn't deserve you in his life, and you sure as hell didn't deserve what he put you through," Travis says as he lifts my hand and kisses my knuckles.

"So where is the prick now?" Ethan asks.

"As far as we are aware, he has been taken back to the room where he and I were held all day," Travis answers.

"Do we know how much he owed Nicholson and how he came to owe him money?" Ryan asks. Travis nods and looks at me. I asked him earlier not to tell me everything, to send the payment and call the guys, knowing they would be frantic. I had never expected them to be as close as they were, and we had only just gotten outside when they arrived. All of this is going to be news to me, too. I give him a nod to show I'm ready to hear it whilst leaning further into Ryan for comfort.

"Do you remember a couple of months ago, Geralt Young was killed in an attack on his building?" he asks, looking around. We all nod. I know about it from Jasmine, who is close to Mr Young's daughter Abigail. She was meant to be one of Jasmine's bridesmaids but pulled out after her father's death. I've only met her a couple of times prior to that.

"Well, they were searching for some drugs that Taylor had hidden in the basement before selling the building to Young. It turns out Taylor had stolen those drugs from

Nicholson years before. He had a feeling Taylor was involved, but they never found the drugs or had any proof."

"What's that got to do with Henry?" Ryan asks over my head.

"I'm getting to that bit," Travis says as he cups my hand between his. It's as if he knows I need all three of them at the moment. Or he just can't bring himself to let me go; I'm not sure which, but I'm not complaining as I need them all close.

"Taylor had help taking the drugs; he shouldn't have even known about the shipment; it was kept so quiet Nicholson figured he must have had a mole in his ranks."

"Henry was the mole," Ethan says, but Travis just shrugs. "Apparently not, but he was in charge of the shipment, and when it went missing, he was told he either paid for the lost drugs or Nicholson would kill him.

"But then Nicholson saw Verity and realised she would be the perfect arm candy for his son, and Henry told him about the inheritance, so the deal was made. Henry was still paying off the money, but it was nothing compared to what he would have to pay if he didn't get her to marry the son."

"So, how much was the debt?"

"Nicholason is known for adding his extreme interest rates. There were three million pounds worth of drugs stolen. He had been looking to make five times that in their sale and distribution. So, all together, he wanted sixteen, so I offered him Henry's savings of twenty."

"He had the money sitting there and was still going to sell his daughter?" Ethan shouts as I start feeling sick again. Travis kisses my knuckles as he nods.

"Even Nicholson called him out on that one," Travis says, still holding my hand to his lips. He looks down, sees his grandmother's ring on my finger, and smiles softly.

"It's as if it was made for you," he whispers, kissing it before looking me in the eye. "Whatever happens now, remember we are here for you. We will all help you deal with this together as a family. No one will ever make you do anything you don't want to do again. You are in charge of your own destiny."

"But you will still be my Daddy and Bear, right?" I ask, looking between Ryan and Travis, who both nod, smiling. I look to Ethan and give him a small, "And you, my partner in crime?"

"Always, Baby," he answers, winking at me.

"That's okay then because I never want to lose any of you," I reply as I lean back against Ryan, relieved to finally have my three guys back, even if only for a little while.

Chapter Fifty-Seven

TRAVIS

"Any idea what he wants you to do?" Ryan asks as we stand at the front of the manor house Nicholson lives in.

"Something to do with accounts, no doubt highly illegal. But as long as she's safe, I don't care." I watch Ethan and Verity together, sitting on a bench far enough away that they can't hear us, and we can't hear them. "Keep a close eye on her. The cracks are starting to show, and she will be a mess when it all sinks in."

"What? Like when she woke up and you were gone?" he replies. I can hear the anger in his voice and know I deserved it.

"How bad was it?"

"She screamed and cried until she was sick. She wouldn't let us near her and clung to that doll like it was the only thing keeping her afloat. You thought she was bad when her father left; it was worse."

I rub my face as the hate inside me grows.

"I hate myself for doing it, but I don't at the same time," I admit. I watch as she leans against Ethan's shoulder, and he kisses the top of her head. "I couldn't let her suffer anymore. I figured a few days of pain was better than a lifetime on the run." I turn to look at my brother, who is also watching our girl. "I had to do it alone. I couldn't risk two of us being killed and her only having one left to protect her."

"I know," he sighs. "I would have done the same myself. But I think after all of this, we need to get her into counselling. There's so much pain and abandonment issues buried after years of suppressing everything; she needs to come to terms with it and accept the truth."

"Like the guy she spent her whole life being emotionally abused by wasn't her real father? Yeah, I'd already thought of that; I'll contact someone I know in the new year. I want her to start opening up about it as soon as possible."

"And the ring?"

I shrug as I continue to watch Ethan and Verity sitting together.

"She can marry whichever one of us she wants. I don't care if we put our names in a hat to decide as long as she's a Donavon. I want to distance her from that bastard as quickly as possible."

I stop talking as I see Ethan and Verity standing and heading toward us. Verity has her arms wrapped around her waist as Ethan keeps her tucked against his side.

"You okay, Sweetheart?" I ask as they reach us. She looks ready to drop. She must be exhausted. It's gone three in the morning, and I know she has been up nearly twenty-four hours.

"I want to speak to him before we leave." She looks up at me, and I know this is something she needs to do. She needs the closure.

"Come on, let's see if they will let you speak to him."

Verity

I stand outside the room with my three guys and Mr Nicholson. The man I have known as my father is in there, still cuffed and bleeding. I look at the TV monitor to my right that shows inside the room.

Dad is sitting on the floor with his back against a wall.

"You know, you don't have to do this. You could just walk away and forget all about him," Mr Nicholson says behind me. I shake my head and look at the guys.

"Can you wait by the door? I want to face him alone."

They share a look before nodding.

"I will keep it open, but if we come in to get you, you leave, no questions asked," Travis says as he watches me. I nod and look at the screen.

"I'm ready."

Mr Nicholson walks past me and opens the door.

"Stevenson, you have a visitor," he says, stepping back so I can walk in. I look behind me to see the three Donavon brothers standing side by side, each watching over me. I take a deep breath and turn to look at my dad.

"What do you want? Come to gloat?" he snarls before hissing. His hands are now cuffed in front of him, allowing him to wipe some drawl and blood from his face.

"What's there to gloat about? The fact that the man I have loved and whose approval I have ached for my whole life hates me? Because I certainly don't feel like gloating about that."

My dad rolls his eyes whilst groaning.

"Me, me, me. That's all I've ever heard from you. You never shut up."

I hear a commotion outside and know one or more of the guys have tried to come in here; my dad hears it, too.

"Is your *Daddy* out there? Doesn't he like the way I speak to his, *Sweetheart*?"

"This has nothing to do with him. This is between you and me," I reply before taking a few steps closer to him, feeling stronger than I ever have as I look down at the man I thought was my father.

"I changed everything about me for you," I point out as I look at him. "Everything I ever did was for your approval, yet I never got it. I begged you to love me, to want me, and to be the dad I thought you could be, but it was all a lie. You never loved me for me; you loved what you could get from me. You left me alone, scared and vulnerable all because of the money?" I step closer, stare at the man I have loved my whole life, and see nothing but resentment in his eyes.

"I hate you."

I whisper it the first time, scared of his reaction, but then I realise I don't care anymore.

"I hate you and never want to see or hear from you again. You have broken me for the last time. So, fuck you and fuck being the perfect little pumpkin you tried to make me. I hope you burn in hell, you piece of shit."

I spin around and walk straight out of the door with my head held high. I don't stop until I reach Travis, my Daddy, who welcomes me with open arms. One of the three men who have held me together through some of the most challenging times I have ever experienced and shown me that I do deserve to be loved because they love me, each in their own way.

I look up at him as he cups my cheek and smiles down at me.

"I am so proud of you, Sweetheart. You are so brave,"

he leans in and kisses my lips before standing straight. "Although we may need to reel in the cursing a little, I don't think I like how it sounds coming out of that sweet mouth," he adds with a wink as I find myself laughing for the first time in days and finally feeling like we might all be okay.

Chapter Fifty-Eight

VERITY

"Baby! You're phones ringing!"

I rush down the stairs, nearly tripping over my own feet in my hurry to get to the lounge where I left my phone on charge.

"Answer it!" I call as I hear Ethan laughing.

I come to a skidding stop as I enter the room to see him talking into my phone.

"Yeah, she's fine, but you have lost your room, though. Her stuff has taken over the whole house," he laughs as I pull the phone away.

"He's lying; I didn't bring that much with me," I protest as Travis laughs down the line.

"Sweetheart, you can put your stuff wherever you want. It's only temporary anyway until we can find a bigger house. Have you managed to get any decorations up?" Travis asks as I look around the bare lounge.

"No, I didn't manage to actually go into the house. Bear and Ethan went in for me. All the decorations are still up there."

The guys had taken me to my childhood home today to collect everything I wanted to bring to Travis's house. For now, we will all live here as it's three bedrooms and the bigger of the guy's houses. I didn't want to spend Christmas in a house with so many bad memories. Sure, there were good ones, too, but after everything that had come to light regarding my father, I knew I needed the closure the guys were offering me. This way, we can start the new year together and move ahead as we look forward to life together.

"Well, I promise next year we will decorate the whole house and celebrate Christmas for the whole month of December," Travis says in an attempt to cheer me up.

"Do you know when you will be home yet?" I ask, falling onto the sofa beside Ethan, who puts his arm around my shoulders.

"No, Sweetheart, it will definitely be tomorrow, though. I just don't know what time, sorry."

"It's fine. I know you would rather be here with us."

"I really would, but I will make it up to you. We'll have a weekend away or something soon, whether all four of us or just me and you."

"I like the sound of that," I reply, smiling as Ethan starts running a hand up and down my arm.

"Me too." I hear someone calling Travis, who sighs and shouts he will be there now. "I have to go, Sweetheart. I'll call again later, okay?"

"Okay, Daddy, I love you."

"Love you too."

The phone line goes dead, and I sigh as I place it beside me.

"He will be home soon, and then you will be sick to death of him in no time." I know Ethan is trying to cheer me up, but it's not working. It's been two days without him, and I miss him like crazy.

It's mad to think how much has changed in the short time since we started this whole relationship. If you had told me a month ago that I would be in a reverse harem with my three stepbrothers, as well as Henry Stevenson was not my father, I wouldn't have believed you. But here I am, recovering after some of the most challenging days of my life, surrounded by the love I always craved, knowing I will never be alone again.

"I'm back!"

I look up to see Ryan walking into the lounge with a grin.

"I managed to get a chicken and pigs in blankets. I hope you like sprouts as they were the only veg left in any of the shops I went to, and I have four potatoes. Everything else was gone, sorry," he calls, holding up two shopping bags.

"I told you we were too late to get anything," I laugh as I stand, grab a bag from him, and kiss his cheek.

"I had to try. I did find plenty of snacks to eat whilst watching a film, though, if you are up for it."

I nod as he wraps his arms around my waist.

"That sounds good to me."

Ryan kisses my cheek before reaching round and extracting something from the bag I just placed on the counter.

"Come on then. I'll start dinner; you can help by chopping the onions."

Chapter Fifty-Nine

VERITY

I wake up and look around the empty room. Finding myself alone for the first time in days.

Taking a deep breath, I let my mind wander for the first time in what feels like forever since the guys never let me leave their sight. They are worried about everything I learnt and how I'm handling it all. If I'm being honest, I have no idea if it's even sunk in yet. Everything has been moving a hundred miles an hour since we left Travis.

There has been so much to organise and sort out that I haven't had time to stop and process that so much of my life has been a lie. I know I need to face it all, and I will. I'm just not ready yet.

Yesterday, the guys and I shared a feast of snacks Ryan had found for us. After a call from Travis, who still doesn't know when he will be home today, the three of us curled up in Ryan's bed and watched a Christmas film before falling asleep.

We were all exhausted after a busy couple of days.

Going to the guy's houses and getting their things took a whole day. They have already decided to put their houses on the market in the new year, so they can put the money towards getting us a bigger one for us all to share and have our own space. But I know it isn't going to happen overnight, and we will be here for a few months at least unless I buy us all a place.

No one has mentioned the money I now have. I still can't grasp my head around that. I'm a millionaire; my mum was a multi-millionaire, and I never knew. How did I not know that? I always assumed all money came from my father, and she was a stay-at-home mum. Why would I think any different? So many of the people I dance with have the same setup. One parent earns the money, and the other stays at home and handles family life. There were never any signs that I can think of that she was the one with all the money.

Trying not to fall down that rabbit hole of questions, I sit up and reach for my phone, hoping there will be a message from Travis. It's just gone six in the morning, and there is nothing waiting for me. I know it's early, and he said that Nicholson has him working through the night most of the time, but I was hoping he would know when he would be home.

Opening the message app I decide to message him first.

Verity: Merry Christmas, Daddy. I hope you can get home as quickly as possible, as I miss you and need a Daddy cuddle. Love you xxxx

I sigh as I click send and place the phone back on the side.

Ryan and Ethan have been amazing while Travis has been away. They have ensured I have everything I want from the house and helped me unpack my things. I couldn't bring myself to enter when we went to my father's house to get a few things. I had a panic attack on the steps into the house, so the guys took it in turns to sit with me whilst the other collected things. They have said they will go back whenever I want to get the rest of my belongings; all I have to do is ask.

I want to go back at some point and face the ghosts of my past. I want to get as much of my mother's things as possible before he can take it all from me. I just don't know when I will be up for it.

The bedroom door opens, and Ryan walks in wearing joggers and a t-shirt.

"Merry Christmas, little Kitten."

"Merry Christmas, Bear," I answer with a smile. "You weren't here when I woke up," I pout playfully, trying to hide the pain that was starting to form in my chest.

"We woke up early," he smiles, walking over and kissing me. "Ethan's downstairs putting the coffee on. It looks like Santa's been," he winks as I scramble from the bed excitedly. Forcing myself to leave all my worries behind, even if for a short while.

I can't remember the last time I was excited about Christmas. I've been on my own for so long now that nothing was ever a surprise. But this year, I feel the excitement I had as a young child.

Before coming to bed last night, Calvin had dropped off the stuff from the safe house, which he had packed for us. The presents I had for the guys before we had to go into hiding were all hidden in my suitcase, and I left them piled up by the fireplace before coming to bed. I'm not expecting anything from the guys; there's no way they would have had time to buy me anything. It's not the presents I'm excited for; it's the time spent with my guys, and every hour that passes is one closer to Travis coming home.

Ryan chuckles as he holds up my dressing gown for me.

"Put this on; you're not going downstairs naked; it's far too distracting," he laughs, helping me into the fleece gown and wrapping the soft belt around my waist. "We could have some fun with this," he points out, tying a knot.

"I'll keep that in mind," I smile, lifting onto my toes. I press a kiss to his lips as he pulls me against him. "But first, presents," I grin, grabbing his hand and pulling him out of the room as he laughs loudly.

"I only said he had been, not that he had left you anything," Ryan points out.

"But I left presents downstairs for you," I smile over my shoulder. "Now hurry up!" I continue to drag him as he laughs down the stairs before coming to a stop at the lounge door.

There, in one corner of the room, is a beautiful Christmas tree covered in lights and ornaments; I recognise Mum's angel on the top, as well as other family ornaments. Underneath are more presents than I can count. The whole room is decorated and looks amazing, making the room feel more like home than my house ever did.

"You went back for it all," I gasp as my eyes burn.

"It wasn't us," Ryan whispers. I'm about to ask him who when a voice sounds behind me.

"Merry Christmas, Sweetheart."

Travis is standing in the hallway, smiling with Ethan behind him.

"Daddy," I gasp as I rush forward, leaping into his arms

so I can wrap my arms and legs around him. He lifts me as I cry into his shoulder. "You're home." He is really here, and my heart finally feels whole again now the missing piece has returned to me.

"I'm home, Sweetheart, and I'm never leaving you again."

Chapter Sixty

TRAVIS

In all the years I have lived in this house, it has never felt more like home than it does now.

When I got off the phone with Verity yesterday, Nicholson called me to his office. He informed me that I had done all that he needed and asked if there was any way he could help give Verity the Christmas she deserved.

I have heard a lot about the bastard over the years and know people who have disappeared after wronging him. But there is one thing that he respects above all else, and that's his kids. So, seeing the truth behind Henry's intentions for his daughter was all he needed to develop a soft spot for Verity. Plus, his son wasn't too worried about the wedding being called off. It turns out he didn't want to marry her anyway; it was just something that needed to be done.

I explained to Nicholson about the lack of decorations and that the guys hadn't even been able to get together food for a Christmas dinner, and he went out of his way to make sure I had everything we could need for a full Christmas feast. It may have gone in my favour that I just saved him a few million in taxes and hidden even more from the authorities. Saving people that amount of money can put you high up on their good list. He let me leave just after five yesterday evening, and I headed straight to Verity's childhood home with a boot full of food and drink.

The place was dark and felt strange when I arrived. I could see damage in the lounge where Henry had obviously lost his temper and smashed a few things, mainly things that belonged to Verity. I'm unsure if the guys told her, especially when I saw the damage he had done to some of the Christmas decorations she had spent hours hanging around the place. I had packed up anything salvageable and piled them into the car, as well as things we could put to use, mainly alcohol and snacks, before getting my head down for a few hours. I set an alarm for two and set off just after, planning on surprising Verity in the best possible way, and I managed it with the help of my brother.

Spending the day with our girl and seeing her smiling was the best Christmas present any of us could have asked for. But as much as she has smiled and laughed, there are still signs of the cracks slowly developing in her well-built armour, and the fall isn't far away.

I spoke to my brothers as we decorated the room this morning, and they told me that she's been okay, considering everything she learned. We know that she hasn't had time to process everything, and me being away would have kept her mind occupied, but I plan on speaking to her tomorrow about a few things. But not today; I want her to have at least one happy memory from this Christmas.

Looking around, I see Ryan and Ethan playing a round of poker, but Verity isn't in the chair she sat in a moment ago. I had been so lost in my thoughts I hadn't noticed her leave.

"Where's she gone?"

"She said something about getting a drink," Ethan answers, not looking from his cards. I pick up my glass and head into the kitchen, where Verity stands over the sink, washing up. Her hands are moving in the water, but she isn't looking at what she is doing. It's almost like she's on autopilot, staring out the window.

I watch her for a moment, waiting to see if she notices me, but she doesn't. She stares out the window, no longer even washing up. It's not until I see her lift her arm and wipe what is probably a tear from her face that I let her know I'm there.

"There is a dishwasher, you know," I point out as I walk up behind her and wrap my arms around her waist from behind.

"I know. I just wanted to get them done quickly," she answers. I lean my chin on her shoulder, and she instantly leans her head against mine.

"You okay?" I ask quietly. Verity nods and shows me that fake smile I have learned to hate.

"Do you want to try that one again, Sweetheart?" I ask, knowing she's lying to me. She shakes her head and goes back to washing up by hand.

"Not today. Can we just focus on spending Christmas together and enjoying that you are home?" She turns and looks at me. "Please?" One look into her beautiful eyes, and I nod, smiling.

"If that's what you want, then that's what will happen." I kiss her lips before removing my arms from around her waist and retrieving a tea towel from the drawer.

"You wash, and I'll dry. Then we will go into the lounge and open the very expensive bottle of champagne I received yesterday," I wink as a more genuine smile spreads across her face, and she nods. "Good, now how about a little music?" I connect my phone to the Bluetooth speaker and play a random party mix.

Verity giggles when the Spice Girls come on, and we start laughing and singing along together. Before long, I take hold of her hand and spin her around, causing her to laugh and squeal loudly.

"You are ridiculous!" she laughs as I pull her into my arms and dance.

"Ridiculously in love with you, Sweetheart, and don't you forget it," I wink before kissing her and forcing away all the worry, even if for just one day.

Chapter Sixty-One

VERITY

Yesterday was by far the best Christmas I've had since my auntie had her accident, maybe even since my mum was alive.

The guys spoiled me rotten, not just with gifts but by spending time with me and making the whole day fun. Sometimes, my mind would wander to my father, wondering where he was or if he was still alive. But each time, I forced myself to think of other things and concentrate on what matters. My new family, my three guys and me.

"Baby girl, what do you want for lunch? We're having turkey and stuffing sandwiches. Do you want one?"

I look to Ethan and nod from where I'm sitting in the lounge, with a new Kindle Travis had got me for Christmas. I'm currently reading '*Broken Butterfly Dreams*' by Euryia Larson. Not that I'm taking much in, thanks to the hangover from a full day of drinking yesterday.

"You okay, Baby?" Ethan asks, tipping his head to the side slightly.

"I'm fine." The lie slips easily from my lips as it's one I've told for so long I don't know how to stop anymore. From how Ethan looks at me, I know he doesn't believe me.

"Why don't we all eat lunch in here and watch a film or something together? Your choice," he offers me with a smile. I nod and reach for the controller, which is on the coffee table.

"Sounds good," I reply.

"I swear to God Nicholson thought we were feeding the ten thousand. This food will last us a month," Travis walks in, laughing. He looks from Ethan to me, and his smile slips.

"What's up?"

"Nothing; Ethan was just offering to let me pick a movie for us all to watch," I answer, smiling. Ethan and Travis share a look, and I know they aren't going to let it drop. But before they can say anything, I hear a car pull up outside the house.

"Let me see who that is, then you can tell me what's really going on," Travis calls, giving me his Daddy look, and I know he isn't going to drop it.

"I'm fine, just hungover," I call back, hoping he will drop it, but judging from the deep hum I hear, I know he isn't.

"What the fuck do you want?"

Ethan and I both turn to see Travis holding the front door open, but we can't see who's outside.

"I need to speak to you," the female voice answers, and I know it's Linda.

"Well, I have nothing to say to you, so you can leave." Travis goes to close the door, but Linda must put her foot in the way or hold the door open as it stops.

"Please, Travis. I'm in trouble and don't know where else to go. Your brothers aren't home, so I guessed you are all here or still in hiding." I can hear the fear and upset in her voice, and I feel sorry for her.

"What the hell do you want, Mother? Travis close the door," Ryan snaps as he comes out of the kitchen.

"Ryan darling, please, I need your help."

"I won't be helping you with shit. I'm done with you and that waste of space of a husband." I have never seen Ryan look so angry or scary. He means every word, and from the look of the way Ethan is nodding, he feels the same.

"Goodbye, Linda." Travis closes the door and turns away from it. I look back at the door and know Linda is out there alone and scared, and it doesn't feel right.

"Let her in."

All three guys look at me frowning.

"What? After everything they did?" Ethan asks. I nod and start to head towards the stairs, knowing I am the last person she will want to see.

"Let her in and see what she needs. We don't know how much she knew. Let's face it: my father lied to everyone; she may not have known the full truth. Give her a chance; if you don't like what she says, then fine. But please, we don't all need to lose our parents this Christmas."

Travis steps forward and cups my cheek.

"You are too good and pure for this world, Sweetheart." He kisses me before nodding to Ryan. "Let her in." Travis looks back at me and points towards the lounge. "You stay in there; I don't want you upstairs alone. You know why, and I'm not going to be worried about you up there whilst dealing with her in there."

I know it's only fair, so I nod and head back into the lounge. As I close the door, Ethan puts his foot in the way.

"Leave it open a jar. You have as much right to hear what she has to say for herself as we do."

I nod before leaving the door open a bit and stepping back until I'm beside the sofa. I sit down and listen to the conversation outside.

"You have five minutes. If we don't like what you have to say, then you will be shown out," I hear Ryan snap.

"Thank you. I knew you wouldn't see your poor mum out on the streets," I hear Linda sniff.

"Don't push it, Mother." Travis sounds fed up already, and I know he wouldn't be giving her the time of day if I hadn't asked him to. "So, what have we done to be graced with your presence?"

"Can we sit in the lounge? I'm tired and cold," Linda starts, but Travis cuts her off.

"It's here or the kitchen."

"I guess the kitchen will do. Any chance of a glass of wine? Or maybe something a little stronger?"

"I'm pretty sure Travis told you not to push your luck," I hear Ethan sigh as the sound of their footsteps heads towards the kitchen. I creep closer to the door. Ethan is right. I have every right to know what is being said; it's about me and my father, after all.

"So why are you here, Mother?" Travis asks.

"Henry is missing. I have no idea where he is or if he's even alive. I went out the other day to get a few bits for Christmas and returned to find the house empty and unlocked. I think he has done something stupid." Linda bursts into tears, and for a moment, I feel bad for her. Maybe she doesn't know how deep my father is with someone like Mr Nicholson. I certainly had no idea he associated with people like that.

"And it's taken you three days to try and find out what

happened?" I hear Travis ask. "Where have you been all that time?" he adds.

"I've been at the house too scared to leave in case he returned. He was so upset about Verity leaving the way she did, and he was worried sick."

I'm surprised when Ethan bursts out laughing.

"Travis, didn't you stay at the house Christmas Eve?"

"I did, and I certainly didn't see you there," Travis answers. Why did he stay at the house? "And I know for a fact you knew exactly where he had gone and that Verity hadn't run away."

"How would I know any of that?" she argues.

"Because from what I can gather, it was your idea for Verity to marry that man, even though you knew she wouldn't want to, and I am sure you are well aware that Henry had twenty million in savings."

"You have no idea what you are talking about. You are just bitter because of Verity running off like she did. I know you tried to help her, but some people just aren't worth helping. Her mother spoilt her, and poor Henry has been left to deal with her ever since that dreadful woman died. You are better off without her in your life, son. She will bring you nothing but heartache like she did her poor father."

I feel my anger exploding in a way it never has before. I storm out of the lounge and head for the kitchen as I hear Ethan shouting at his mother. I stop and listen for a moment, knowing the guys have more right to kick her out than I do. This isn't even my house; she forced me out of mine!

"Get out right now, you evil bitch!"

"Not until you help me find out where Henry is!"

"Henry or the money?" Ryan asks. "Because knowing

you, Mother, you will want to know where the twenty million is!"

"Well, I am entitled to some of it. But mostly, I want to know where that girl is so I can give her to the relevant people and get my husband back."

I storm into the kitchen and stop behind her.

"I'm right here."

Linda spins around and stares at me. Her face goes from shocked to livid in the space of three seconds.

"What the hell are you doing here?" she demands, jumping to her feet. "Do you have any idea the trouble you have caused?"

"Me? What the hell did I do?" I demand, placing my hands on my hips. "I never asked to be treated like a cash machine. You and that man only kept me around so you could live off my inheritance!" I yell. "You are nothing but a desperate housewife who wants to spend her days drinking and getting everything handed to her on a plate."

"You can't speak to me like that!" Linda spins around and looks at the guys, who are all smiling at me. "Are you going to stand there and let her say such horrible things about me?"

Travis shrugs as he crosses his arms over his chest.

"I'd correct her if she were wrong, but she speaks nothing but the truth so far."

Linda looks to the other two, who shrugs in agreement. She spins back on her heels and looks at me.

"What are you even doing here?"

"She lives here," Travis answers as he walks over and places a hand on the bottom of my back.

"We all do," Ethan adds as he stands on my other side, and Ryan stands at my back. "We all live here together."

"You can't; she is promised to someone else. You are honestly willing to put yourself in danger for her!"

"Verity will marry whoever she wants to marry, and anyone who tries to tell her differently will have to answer to us," Ryan says behind me. I reach around and take his hand, needing to feel them all as they give me the strength to stand up for myself. Linda sees this, though and bursts out laughing.

"You think you can stand together with this little slut and stop someone like Nicholson? He will kill you all and take what's promised to him. You must see that this is a short-term thing, and you will lose eventually."

"And let me guess, when she marries him, you and Henry will skip off into the sunset with your stashed millions, not giving a shit what happens to her?" I can hear the anger in Travis's voice. Looking up at him, I can see the muscles around his jaw bulging each time he clenches them.

"It's not as much as you think?" Even I can see she is trying to downplay what she knows, Travis was right.

"Well, it's down from twenty to four now, and nowhere you can find it as it's all been transferred to its rightful owner." Travis places an arm around me as I watch Linda's face turn purple. "If you want any of the other sixteen, I hear Nicholson's son is back to looking for a bride after gaining the money that was promised to him. Maybe he wants an old, spent alcoholic who spends more time drunk than coherent," Travis laughs.

"You fucking bitch!" Linda launches towards me, but Ryan pulls me out of the way whilst Travis grabs their mother, holding her back. "Do you have any idea what you have done to your poor father?"

"Poor father? More like a poor excuse for one. There

again, he's not even my real dad, is he Linda? He only kept me around to use my money!" I growl at her, my eyes and throat burning as all the emotions I've been holding back since that evening come flooding in at once.

"I cleaned up after you, kept your house clean like you wanted. Made sure everything was pristine and all without complaint. You left me alone in that big house for months on end, and I said nothing. What did I do to deserve you both treating me like you did? What did I do that was so wrong that you couldn't even spend a few days with me over the holidays? Am I that horrible to be around?"

"Yes! You whine and talk nonstop. You act like you are little Miss Perfect, but look at you, sleeping with three guys at the same time; it's disgusting; you should all be ashamed of yourself."

"Enough!" Travis roars as he starts dragging his mum towards the front door. "I've heard enough. Get out of our house and our lives and never come back."

"Where is my husband?" she screams as Ethan opens the door so Travis can throw her out.

"Hopefully dead! If you do actually want to know, go and ask Nicholson; last I heard, he was still locked in a holding room with a broken jaw and nose! Now, stay the hell away from any of us. If I see you again or you try to approach Verity, I will make sure you are handed over to the authorities for stealing her inheritance. Now fuck off!"

Travis slams the door closed and looks around to where Ryan and I are standing. Ryan has his arms around my shoulders as I shake with rage.

"Do not let one thing that fucking woman said upset you. Do you hear me, Sweetheart? She is a special kind of evil and as toxic as they come. Why do you think we hardly have anything to do with her? That!" he points to the door for emphasis. "That is the evil bitch we grew up with, not the one who smiled and laughed around you. Ever wonder why we took Dad's side in the divorce? That is why."

I look up at Travis, and for the first time, I see that I'm not the only one who suffered due to a toxic parent. The three guys who have stood by my side have also had to deal with one.

Stepping out of Ryan's arms, I walk up to Travis and wrap my arms around his waist, holding him like he has me so many times. For a moment, he freezes before letting out a deep sigh and holding me whilst burying his face into my hair.

"I'm sorry," I whisper into his chest.

"What in the world have you got to be sorry for?" Ryan asks as he steps closer to us.

"For the fact you just had to throw your own mother out. For the pain she has caused you over the years. And for not slapping her when I had the chance."

All three of the guys laugh as I look up to Travis.

"Do you think my dad is dead?" I ask. The question has been on my lips since Ethan and Ryan brought me back that night.

"I honestly don't know. Nicholson asked if I wanted to know his fate, and I said no. You asked me not to kill him, and I accept that. I didn't want to know anything about what happened to him." Travis cups my face as I take a deep breath, desperate not to cry.

"Can you find out?" I ask. "I need to know."

Travis nods before pressing a kiss to my forehead.

"Go and sit in the lounge with Ryan; I'll get my phone. Do you want to hear the conversation?"

I think about it for a moment and nod.

"Okay, I'll be right back." Travis walks away from me as Ryan places an arm around me.

"Come on, Kitten, let's get you sat down."

Chapter Sixty-Two

TRAVIS

I have been dreading this moment. I knew that one day, she would want to know what happened to Henry. He might not be her father by blood, but he is the only one she knows. It will take a long time for her to stop referring to him as her dad; she may never stop, and that's something only she can decide to do and when.

I grab my phone from my bedroom and see Verity's doll on the bed. She slept in with me last night, the others giving us a little space and time, just the two of us. It was as perfect as the night I left. I made love to her for over an hour. After she lay in my arms, we talked about why I left the way I did, and I promised her I would never do it again. I know I chipped away at her trust in me that day, and I'm willing to do whatever it takes to put it right and prove to her I am here for as long as she wants me.

As she lay there, looking up at me, her blonde hair sprayed out on the pillow underneath her, I lifted her left hand and pressed a kiss to my grandmother's ring, which still sits on her left ring finger and promised, one day soon, one of us was going to propose properly, and she would become a Donavon as quickly as possible. Whether the wedding is big or small, she can decide. All I know is that as far as I am concerned, she will be my wife, whether legally or otherwise. I had to laugh when I realised the irony of the conversation. A few weeks ago, Christian told me he didn't need a piece of paper to know Jasmine was his. I understand what he meant now, and I guess we are more alike than we care to admit.

Picking up her doll, I head back downstairs, feeling sick to my stomach. No matter what, I know this call will break her heart and start the downward spiral that will come with accepting all that she has learnt. I have been mentally preparing myself for it, as my brothers have. All we can do now is support and give her whatever she needs.

"Are you sure you want to do this, Baby? There is no rush to know the truth," I hear Ethan say as I descend the stairs.

"I need to know. I hate living in limbo and constantly wondering. I think this may be the closure I need," she replies.

I walk into the lounge, and all three heads turn to look at me. Verity is sitting on the sofa next to Ryan. Her legs tucked up underneath her as she leans into his side. He has his arm around her, keeping her close. Ethan sits beside her, holding her hand. When she spots me holding her doll, she instantly reaches out for it.

"I thought you might want it," I explain, passing it to her.

"Thank you," she whispers as she buries her face into its hair, leaning more into Ryan.

I squat in front of her and run my knuckles down her cheek.

"Are you ready?"

She nods as tears fill her eyes. I look to my brothers, who both nod, signalling they are ready for whatever may come from this call.

Taking a deep breath, I pull up Nicholsons number and call him. When it rings out, I realise I should have done this part out of the room. It never occurred to me that he wouldn't answer. It's Boxing Day, after all; he is probably with family. I'm just about to admit defeat and end the call when it connects, and his voice is heard down the line.

"Donavon, I have just gotten rid of your arse. What do you want?"

"Merry Christmas to you too, arsehole," I sigh, rolling my eyes.

"Yeah, yeah, what do you want? I'm halfway through a very expensive bottle of bourbon, and you are interrupting my buzz." Nicholson may be an arsehole, but he has my kind of banter, which was a good thing whilst I was forced to stay with him for two days. Otherwise, one of us may have left in a body bag.

"Verity has asked me to find out what you did with Henry." The line goes silent for a moment, and seconds feel like minutes until he speaks again.

"Is she there?" his tone a lot calmer and subdue.

"She is."

Ryan's arm tightens around her further as she clings to her doll, not taking her eyes off me.

"Then let her know she will never see that arsehole again. If he had any life insurance, she could call the police and report him as a missing person. They will never find him."

"So, he's…?" I ask, waiting for confirmation.

"He's dead, yes."

Verity's eyes finally leave mine as she buries her face into Ryan's top.

"I didn't kill him; he had a heart attack before I decided what to do with him. We found him dead in the room. He has been disposed of, as we couldn't get the police involved for obvious reasons. He had a broken jaw, after all."

I take some satisfaction in knowing that he would have at least been in pain as he died. Part of me doesn't believe the story of a heart attack. But there is no way Nicholson would openly admit to killing someone. He has no reason to trust us, after all.

"Thank you, that's all we need to know," I say, standing and walking out of the room, removing the loudspeaker and holding the phone to my ear. "She needed closure, and I think she may finally be able to start coming to terms with everything. I'm sorry to interrupt your bourbon."

"Yeah, I understand why she would want to know. You thought any more about my offer?"

"I'm not working for you. Thanks for the offer, but no." He's been trying to persuade me to be his accountant since he saw how deep I got into Henry's banks and what I could do for him. Working for the people I do is bad enough, but Nicholson is a whole other board game. If I ever got something wrong, my girl would lose a husband for much longer than two days.

"Well, if you ever change my mind, you know where to find me."

"Yeah, thanks." I end the call and head back into the lounge, where the other two are holding a crying Verity.

Kneeling on the floor in front of her, I place my hand on her knee and squeeze slightly.

"I'm sorry, Sweetheart."

"Are you?" she asks, looking back at me. "You wanted him dead."

"I'm not sorry that he's gone. You don't try and force your child into an arranged marriage with a woman beater to save yourself twenty mill." Verity stares at me as I cup her cheek. "But, I *am* sorry that you are hurting. I'm sorry you had to find out what he was really like and how badly he treated you. I'm sorry any of this happened to you. You don't deserve it, as you are one of the kindest, most loyal people I have ever met. I *am* sorry I can't take this pain from you."

Verity continues to look at me from Ryan's arms for a moment, and I start to worry this will affect how she sees me. I could have done more to save him, but I didn't want to. Was that wrong of me? Possibly. But all I could see was what he had done and said to her. In my eyes, he didn't deserve to breathe the same air as her.

I move to leave her in peace with her Bear and Ethan, but she surprises me by diving off the sofa, throwing her arms around my neck and crying into my shoulder.

"Sweetheart," I sigh as I hold her back just as tight as she clings to me. "Whatever you need to come to terms with this. No matter how small, we are here for you. Nothing will ever be as important to us as giving you what you need. All you have to do is ask," I whisper into her hair while pressing my lips against her head. Verity leans back a little and looks at me.

"I want to go back to the house."

Chapter Sixty-Three

VERITY

The world flies by as Travis drives us back to my childhood home.

We pass families playing in the streets, children riding on new bikes or skateboards, or just walking hand in hand with their parents. There are so many happy families, and I see everything I longed for and never had.

Why? Why did he continue to pretend if he hated me so much? If I was that much of a disappointment and burden to him, why didn't he make me feel less loved? Was it all just for money?

I watch a couple walking down the street hand in hand, their young child rushing ahead of them on their bike. Their little legs move so fast as they peddle. I bet they think they could outrun any car with their parents cheering them on.

I don't have any memories of our family like that. I'm sure there were moments before Mum died, but I was too young to remember.

The last few days, I have pushed back all thoughts and

memories of my parents. I wasn't ready to face them and wanted to enjoy my time with the guys. Thankfully, I have years of practice when it comes to putting on a front. This time, I even convinced the guys I was coping with everything. Okay, I may not have convinced them as much as I like to think, but I'm sure there were times when they were none the wiser.

"How you doing, Baby?" Ethan's hand squeezing my shoulder reminds me that he and Ryan are sitting in the back, probably watching my every move.

"I'm okay," I answer on instinct.

"Want to try that again without lying?" Ryan asks. I turn slightly in my seat to see him watching me.

"Did I ever tell you you're starting to get the 'daddy look' down to a tee?" I tease, trying to lighten the mood slightly. It doesn't work for them or me.

"As good as Daddy's?" he asks as the cocked brow gets higher. I glance at Travis beside me, who gives me his best Daddy look as he stops to let other traffic out.

"You didn't answer his first question."

"No, Daddy's is scarier," I admit, sinking into my chair before looking back to Ryan. "I don't know how I'm doing. Better?"

"I guess so."

I can see he's about to say more, so I turn back in my seat. I'm facing forward, not giving him a chance. Travis reaches over and takes my hand resting on my lap.

"We understand you have no idea what to feel right now. Everything you have ever known has been pulled out from under you. So, when we check in on you, we aren't expecting you to know how you feel. It's more a 'what do you need' kind of question."

I open my mouth to tell him he has no idea how I'm

feeling, but then I remember he does; they all do. They lost their father ten years ago, leaving them with a mother who would put anything over her sons. Isn't that basically the same as what my father did?

"Sorry," I whisper, looking down at my hand, engulfed in his. Travis lifts it and presses a kiss to my knuckles.

"You don't have to apologise. Never apologise for being honest with us, even if you are screaming it in our faces; you are letting us know how you are feeling, which is a privilege you haven't had before."

I go back to looking out of the window, the word 'sorry' on the tip of my tongue. I don't know how to not apologise at this point. I do it without even thinking. It's a habit I'm not sure I will ever get out of, but I know I want to try.

I'm tired of being the pushover, the one everyone thinks has everything together and doesn't need help because I do. Right now, I need all the help I can get, and I know the guys are here for me.

We continue to drive in silence as Travis holds my hand, which now rests on his thigh. The closer we get to the house, the sicker I feel. When we went there the other day, I froze at the door, terrified we would find my dad or even Linda there. I guess I didn't need to worry as he won't be there ever again.

A sharp pain erupts from my chest as the house comes into view, and the realisation hits me. He's never coming back. I blink back the tears and focus on the job at hand. Luckily, the years of pushing back my feelings have prepared me for this. I know I need to cry and accept the pain that I'm keeping suppressed. But not yet.

Travis comes to a stop outside of the house and turns off the engine.

"Are you sure you want to do this now?" he asks, turning

425

in his seat to run a hand over my head. I nod, not wanting to speak aloud, as I feel the contents of my heavy stomach might decide to appear.

The passenger door opens, and Ryan looks down at me.

"Whatever you need, say. We are here for you and only you." He holds out a hand, and I take it to exit the car.

"I'm going to check Mother's not in there. The last thing we need is her causing any extra shit right now," Travis calls as he jogs to the front door, unlocks it, and disappears.

I lean against Ryan, who keeps me wrapped in his arms as I look at the house. I used to believe this place was the perfect family home and that my family was perfect, even with the pain of losing Mum and Dad being away all the time. I believed with all my heart that he would rather be with me and only worked as hard as he was to ensure I had everything I ever needed or wanted. If I hadn't heard it from his own mouth, I don't think I would have ever believed he hated me as much as he did. But here I stand, looking up at the house I have called home my whole life, and I know I will never look at it the same way again.

In what feels like less than a handful of minutes, Travis appears at the front door and jogs back towards us.

"No one's there, and I think she's lying about staying here. Just in case, I will stay outside and keep watch for her coming back."

Panic builds in my chest at the thought of being in there without him by my side.

"No, I will."

We all turn to look at Ethan as he steps beside Travis.

"I've always said I'm not Daddy material, and that's what you need in there. You go in there with your Daddy and Bear, and I'll keep watch." Ethan steps up as Travis moves to the side. "If you need me, all you need to do is say, and one of the guys can swap with me. Okay?"

I look up at him momentarily before stepping away from Ryan to throw my arms around Ethan's neck. He always knows just what I need; they all do. They have my back in a way no one ever has before, and moments like this make me realise how loved I am by them.

I step back from Ethan so I can look back at the house. I take a deep breath, push all my emotions down, and head up to the open front door. I sense the guys all following behind me and take comfort in them being close but giving me space at the same time. I know I've come to rely on them and even show them my vulnerable side. The side that needs a daddy to comfort and take care of them. But right now, I need to be the strong, independent woman I know I can be, and they are here to let me and are taking my lead for the time being. Later, when I let myself fall, I know they will hold me and let me and my younger, vulnerable self feel all the emotions that have come with losing everything we have ever known.

Walking into the house, I can feel the heaviness of the air. The comfort I used to feel from being within these walls has long gone. It feels wrong.

I stand in the hallway, looking around at the mess in front of me. I can see where Travis tidied up a bit, as there is a pile of broken glass and what may have been frames waiting to be swept up. But there is glass in the pile and what looks like a stack of broken frames on the sideboard that resides here.

"When I arrived on Christmas Eve, I found some of the picture frames had been broken, and it seemed someone had thrown a tantrum. I tidied up the best I could but didn't do it all."

I turn to look at Travis to find him watching me intently. He steps forward and takes my hand.

"I was going to hide them from you, but figured you deserved to know the whole truth, ugly bits and all."

I nod, squeezing his hand, letting him know I'm listening. Even though I can't voice my gratitude. I'm tired of things being hidden from me, and I need to know everything. Like Travis said, ugly bits and all.

"What is it you need in here, Kitten?"

"Answers," I reply before letting go of Travis's hand and walking towards the office.

I haven't been in the office for years besides the other week when Travis was here. Dad always told me not to interrupt him when he was working, so I never did.

Walking in, I find papers all over the desk and floor. I look to Travis, who shakes his head.

"This wasn't me."

"After we searched the office, we put everything back where we found it so Henry wouldn't suspect something straight away," Ryan confirms as he stands beside his brother.

"What did you find in here?" I ask, picking up some paper from the floor and walking to the desk.

"Nothing of any use. We couldn't find the safe you mentioned when I asked for your birth certificate. I didn't have time to ask if you knew where it was when you returned, as everything moved quickly."

"Do you think he would have hidden all the bad stuff in there?" I ask, turning to look at Travis, who nods. I place the papers I'm holding on the desk and walk from the room and up the stairs. The guys don't say a thing; they fall into step behind me and follow my lead.

Not allow myself to think about where I'm going; I force

myself to focus on the end goal—the safe. Ignoring how my feet have become lead weights, I open my father's bedroom door and head into the walk-in wardrobe.

I stand for a moment and picture the last time he was here. He casually packed a bag so he could leave me again. He didn't show any remorse because he had broken my heart. That's because he didn't feel any; he didn't care what damage he was doing to me mentally. I would go as far as to say he liked that he caused me pain.

"Sweetheart?"

I know if I turn around and face him now, I will break down; I don't want to cry here. I don't want this place to have another piece of my heart. Instead, I walk over to a door that looks like a standard cupboard. But, inside is my dad's safe, where he once told me he kept his most important possessions.

"Do you know the code?" Ryan asks behind me. I shake my head and kneel in front of it for a moment. I try his birthday, but nothing. I try Mum's birthday and their anniversary, but again nothing happens.

"Any ideas?" I ask, looking back at the two of them. Ryan smiles at Travis, who nods.

"Go get him."

"I always knew Henry was a cheap skate, but this safe is as cheap as they come and so easy to break into," Ethan chuckles as he kneels in front of the small safe. "I need something long and pointy." He pulls out the small safe as we look for something that matches the description.

"Hang on, if I …"

I turn just in time to see Ethan hitting the top of the safe and twisting the lock. He does it a couple of times before laughing out loud and opening the door.

"I thought those things were meant to be secure?" Travis asks beside me.

"If you spend a few quid on one, they are. A cheap one like this would have cost him about twenty pounds, and a child could break into it."

They continue discussing the different ways to unlock it, but I'm more interested in the contents of this one. Slowly, I kneel in front of the safe and pull out a small white envelope and a larger brown one.

I open the brown one first and tip the contents onto the floor. Inside are my birth certificate and paperwork for my driving license. I find myself holding my breath as I look at the parent's section, terrified I will find out who my father is. But, instead, is Henry Stevenson's name.

"It's a fake."

My head snaps to Travis, who is looking over my shoulder.

"What?"

He holds out his hand, and I pass it to him. He looks at it for a moment before handing it back to me.

"The differences are subtle; no one would ever notice. But I know it's a fake, and I could tell you who made it."

"Your friend?" Ethan asks beside him. Travis nods and rubs the back of his neck.

"When I contacted him to make up some fake ID for you in case we needed to run, I noticed he acted like he knew your name. I asked him about it, and he said it just sounded familiar."

"Stevenson isn't that rare a name," I point out. But Travis shakes his head.

"No, but when I was on my way to Nicholson's, I

contacted him again to prepare for the guys needing some fake IDs. When I was on the phone, I told him what was happening, and he told me everything. It was the confirmation I needed that Henry wasn't your father."

I look down at the paper in my hand and sigh.

"Did he ever see the real one?" I ask as I stare at the space where Henry's name is.

"I can find out, but I doubt it. He doesn't usually require any paperwork. You just give him all the information he needs."

I let out a sigh while placing my fake birth certificate beside me and picking up the small white envelope. It feels like there is something heavy inside. I open it and tip the contents into my hand.

"I haven't seen a skeleton key in years." I look to Travis, who is watching over my shoulder. "Any idea which door it unlocks?"

I look at the key in my hand and know exactly which door it unlocks.

Keeping hold of it, I check for anything else in the safe, but when I see it's empty, I take a deep breath and stand from the floor.

"Baby? Are you okay?" Ethan asks, placing a hand on my shoulder. I nod as I hold back the tears threatening to fall. I had hoped for answers, and all I got was more questions.

"Before Mum died, we used to dance in the basement all the time. It was our little studio. When she died, I couldn't bring myself to go in there. The whole place was just a reminder of her, making me miss her more." I swallow the lump in my throat at the thought of happier times. "One day, about two years after she died, I thought about going down there; I wanted to feel close to my mum.

The nanny found me by the door and told me off. She made me write lines the whole day. *I shall not trespass where I'm not allowed."*

"You can't trespass in your own home! What the fuck?" Travis curses as he steps forward. I shrug as I look back at the key.

"There were a few places I wasn't allowed to go. Dad's office, the basement, and the shed at the bottom of the garden."

"Didn't you ever try to go in there and see what they were hiding? It's the first thing I would have done," Ethan asks. I shake my head and show him a smile that is as sad as I feel.

"I was a good girl and did as her father said, remember?" I can see the anger in both Ethan and Travis's eyes, and turn to head out of the room.

Walking down the stairs, I see Ryan standing at the front door, which is open, having taken Ethan's post so he can get into the safe.

"Did you get into it?" he asks as soon as we get into view.

"Yep, piece of piss," Ethan answers as I get to the bottom of the stairs.

"Did it contain anything you wanted to know, Kitten?" he asks, reaching for my hand. I shake my head and look toward the door I hold the key for.

Letting go of Ryan's hand, I walk to the cupboard under the stairs. Where the basement door is hidden, it's one of the things that made the basement so magical to us. It was like entering our own little world, hidden from others.

I'm met with all kinds of rubbish when I open the door. There are old suitcases, shopping bags filled with clothes I no longer fit into, as well as boxes of old ornaments and pictures Linda had placed around the house at one time or another and then shoved in here when she had picked up new ones. I bet she has loved spending my mum's money, the bitch. It's all blocking the door I'm so desperate to unlock.

I reach in to pull out a box, but a hand landing on my arm stops me. I look up to see Travis frowning at me.

"The door is behind all your mum's stuff," I answer. He looks at all the boxes and back to me.

"Anything you want to keep in there?" Looking back at the boxes, I shake my head. "Then let us get it all out of there for you."

Stepping away from the door, I watch the three guys take turns grabbing a box and moving it out of the way. There is box after box of stuff; I know it all belongs to Linda. I want her things out of the house. I want to forget she ever came in here and tried to take over my mum's home.

I'm about to turn away when I see Ethan picking up a wooden box I haven't seen in years.

"Wait!"

All three guys freeze and look at me, not knowing who I'm talking to. I step towards and hold out my hand. Ryan places the box, which seems so much smaller than I remember it being.

"That was my mums," I whisper, running my fingers over the smooth chest. It's locked, but I know how to get into it.

"Dad found me with it one day when we were looking for something of Linda's. He took it from me and said Mum wouldn't have wanted me to see it that it was personal. I knew he was lying, but I also knew better than to argue with me." I start looking for somewhere to place it, knowing I need to concentrate on one thing at a time. Right now, it's the basement that I need to focus on.

Ethan steps forward and holds his hands out.

"Let me place it in the kitchen, on the table, so it's safe." He gently places a hand on the top of the box and removes it from my grasp. "No one will ever hide anything of your mother's from you again. We will search this house from top to bottom and retrieve everything that is hers," he whispers, kissing the top of my head before heading towards the kitchen.

"If you spot anything else, just say, and we will place it with that box," Ryan adds as he steps forward and retrieves another box from the cupboard.

There are only three more items I spot that I know belonged to my mum; the rest are all Dads or Lindas or things from when I was small. Finally, after what feels like a lifetime, thanks to the amount of junk stuffed in here, the door at the back of the cupboard comes into view.

The guys step back and leave me to enter first. Placing my hand on the dusty door, I remember how excited I used to be every time Mum and I came down here, sometimes with Aunty Trish. This was our favourite place; we could dance as much as we liked and never worry about space.

With a shaking hand, I push the key into the lock and turn it. It sticks a little where it probably hasn't been opened in years. But I'm able to unlock the door and open it without any issues.

"Sweetheart." Travis's hand presses against the door, stopping me from opening it further. I turn to look at him and realise he looks worried.

"Let me go in there first. We don't know why he hid the key. Or what's down there now. We also don't know the condition of the place. Are there any steps to go down?" I nod, looking back to the slightly open door.

"Wooden ones."

Travis steps forward and gently pulls me back.

"Then let me check that they are still intact and not damaged by wood mites." Travis opens the door further. "Is there a light here somewhere?" he asks, looking into the dark void.

"A switch by the door frame, I think." I can't remember where anything is from the top of my head; it's been so long —light flickers before shining brightly from within the space.

"Stay there until I say it's safe," Travis repeats before heading down the steps.

"Be careful," I call after him, praying he doesn't hurt himself.

I hold my breath as I listen to him slowly descending into the room. Each creak of the stairs makes me jump as I envision him falling to his death. If he were to hurt himself because of me, I would never forgive myself.

"It's okay, come down one at a time. Someone stay upstairs to keep an eye out," he calls. I walk to the top of the steps down and freeze. It's been thirteen years since I last went down there. Thirteen long years without my mum.

A hand on the bottom of my back snaps me from the grief that starts to overwhelm me. I turn to see Ethan giving me a small smile.

"You've got this, Baby. We are right here beside you."

I take a deep breath before slowly walking down the stairs until Travis comes into view. He holds out his hand to assist me down the last few steps. I come to a stop beside him and freeze.

"Where the hell have all these crates come from?"

Chapter Sixty-Four

TRAVIS

Looking around, I know these aren't household items being stored in this space. There are ten huge wooden shipping crates and four, nope, five, large metal-filling cabinets.

"Well, this safe is certainly bigger and more expensive than the one he kept in his room."

I walk around one of the boxes to find Ethan squatting in front of a giant safe. It's a dial one, like you see in the old movies. It's big and heavy, and I have a feeling some of the information Verity is after will be in there if it still exists and hasn't been destroyed.

"Can you get inside it?" Verity asks as she joins us. Ethan stands up and looks around the giant safe. The back is pressed against a wall, and he fails when he tries to move it. I join him on the other side, but as soon as we try again together, I know there's no chance.

"How did he even get it down here?" Verity turns on the spot, looking at all the crates around us. "And what is in all these boxes?" she asks, walking over to a large one bigger than her.

"Nothing good, I imagine," I sigh, grabbing her hand to stop her from touching them, terrified she will get injured. "Let's see if we can find out what's inside them without opening them."

Together, Verity and I walk over to the filing cabinets and attempt to open them, but as I suspected, they are locked.

"Ethan," I call, signalling for him to come and have a look.

"Yeah, yeah, I know. Pick the lock. Can't you want me for my dashing good looks or my winning personality for once?" he sighs dramatically, earning a small giggle from Verity. At least he can distract her from all her worries, even for a few brief moments.

Ethan comes over and examines the lock.

"Yeah, that's simple enough to unlock, unlike that safe. That may take me more than a few minutes, but I will be able to get into it eventually." He briefly examines the lock before digging into his pocket and pulling out a swish army knife I got him for Christmas. He finds the tool he wants, and the first filing cabinet is unlocked in less than a minute.

"You're good," Verity exclaims as he pulls open the top drawer.

"One of us had to be able to unlock Mum's alcohol cabinet. She kept it under lock and key for years," he winks before moving on to the next cabinet. "This one may take a little longer. Check out the contents of that one while I unlock it."

Verity pulls out a thick paper file and flicks through the stuff inside it.

"You will probably make more sense of this than me. It's all numbers." She hands the file to me before pulling out another one.

Flicking through the papers, I notice that most are order forms and account sheets. These are all dated from five years ago. Verity holds the other file out for me to look at, and I realise these are the same but are dated from six years ago.

"When was the first time you realised you couldn't get down here?" I ask, looking at the dates in the paperwork

"About eight years ago. The cupboard didn't used to be so full of junk. Over time, it just increased to what was there today."

I look from the paper in my hands to the large crates around the room. The hope that I'm wrong about the content of those crates is dashed when I spot some powder beside one.

Putting the files back in the drawer, I walk over to the spot of white dust and place a little of it on my finger before rubbing it against my thumb.

"Is that drugs?" Ethan asks behind me. I shake my head and stand so I can carefully look inside the crate that is open slightly.

"I think it's dust from some sort of ornament." I look at the top and see it will move easily. "Stay back there. If anything happens, get out of here as quickly as possible." I slowly push the top of the crate, which slides open. Inside is line after line of China dolls. All in different coloured dresses and outfits.

With some difficulty, I move on to the next crate and push the lid off. This time, it is filled with ballerina figures. Again, all different colours and styles.

"Did he have some strange fetish or something? Why the fuck does he need all these ornaments?" Ethan asks as he looks into the first crate I opened.

"It's not the ornaments he wanted; it's what's inside

them," I whisper as the realisation hits me. "Give me a hand to open all the crates."

Within five minutes we have each crate open. Some were harder than others, but we got through them all quicker once Verity spotted a crowbar. Each box is filled with ornaments, all different styles except two, which contain the same ballerina style. These two are the closest to the stairs and, I think, the last to be placed down here. I found a small slip of paper inside one of them that was dated three years ago.

Ethan gets the last of the filing cabinets open, and I sit on the floor going through all the paperwork inside of them whilst Ethan attempts to get into the safe. Verity goes upstairs to see Ryan and let him know what we have found, giving me space to pay attention to the information in front of me.

Each drawer in a filing cabinet relates to one of the crates. I realise quickly that there is not just one shipment of ornaments; there are hundreds. Carefully, I remove the ballerinas and realise underneath is a different type of ornament with its own folder. Each ornament is two layers deep before another ornament comes into sight. Each one is covered in sawdust and packaging paper and packed perfectly so it doesn't become damaged under the weight. Every four layers, a support shelf prevents the items on the bottom from being crushed. The bastard knew exactly what he was doing, which tells me he wasn't working alone. He was too thick to pull what I think he was off.

"She wasn't joking when she said there was a lot to sort through. Any idea what all of this means?"

I look up at Ryan as he stands over all the paperwork in front of me.

"I have a few ideas and don't like any of them." I rub the back of my neck and look behind him.

"Where's Verity?"

"Just talking to Ethan. I'm going to head back upstairs with her. I have a feeling there are a few other secrets hidden down here, and I would prefer it if she weren't present for them being found."

I nod in agreement; as I'm about to make a call, I don't want her to hear, so it would be better if she were upstairs and out of the way.

"Any sign of anything or anyone upstairs?" I ask, already having guessed the answer.

"Nothing. If Mum hasn't turned up by now, she's not going to."

"I'm half expecting Dawn to turn up instead to collect Mum's things." I point out, but Ryan shakes his head.

"There's nothing of hers here. I checked out their room quickly; it's all old stuff and Henry's—nothing of any importance. I couldn't even find any jewellery. I can't imagine they spent enough time here even to unpack a suitcase."

Just when I think I can't hate them anymore than I already do, I realise how much they did to avoid spending time with the fantastic woman Verity has become.

"Well, why don't you take Verity to her room and see if there is anything else she wants to take to ours? I have no idea how long we are going to be down here sorting this shit out. Especially if I'm right about who all of this belongs to." I wave at the boxes around us. Ryan looks at them for a moment before his jaw drops.

"You don't think?"

I nod, knowing he has reached the same conclusion as mine.

"I will know for sure in a moment. So, keep her up there as much as possible and pray Henry wasn't as dodgy as he seems to have been."

Ryan nods before heading over to Verity and speaks to her. She looks over at me, and I flash her a smile.

"You go and do whatever you need, Sweetheart. We are fine down here."

She nods as Ryan places an arm around her shoulders, and they head up the stairs. I wait for them to be out of view before standing and taking a picture of some of the ornaments I have removed from a crate. I attach the photo to a message and take a deep breath before sending it.

Travis: Does any of this look familiar?

Chapter Sixty-Five

VERITY

Two hours ago, Thomas Nicholson arrived. I'd hoped I would never see him again and had prayed that would be the end of it. Oh, how wrong was I?

Travis came into the lounge earlier and pre-warned me that Mr Nicholson was on his way and that Dad had left us one more big mess to deal with. Not only had he used my mum's favourite room for storage, but it was drugs that he was storing.

Mr Nicholson and Travis believe that for every shipment my father was in charge of going between here and the States, he helped himself to a little of it and falsified the documents so no one would know. Each figure or ornament was filled with drugs. Mr Nicholson has put Travis in charge of going through the shipments and logging how many of each type of ornament he has so they can go back through the records my father kept to see if they can work out the amount of drugs that are there and what types. I asked Travis if it had to be him, and he said yes. It could take weeks for others to do, but he can get it done in a fraction of the time. He seems as eager to get them out of the house as I am, and he does not want another reason for Mr Nicholson to be in our lives.

People are coming back and forth, and I hate it. If this place felt any less like a home, it's now. Long gone are the days when this was a happy place. That man has managed to spread his evil into every single room in one way or another.

"Little Kitten?"

I look up from my bed, where I'm hiding away from everyone, clinging to an old stuffed panda I found at the bottom of my wardrobe. It's not my doll, which is back at Travis's, but it's helping a little.

"I wanted to pop up and check on you," Ryan says softly as he sits on the edge of the bed and takes my hand. "How are you doing?"

I shrug whilst burying my face into my panda. I don't trust myself to speak. I don't even know what to say. How do you explain this kind of shit? Really, there is only one thing to say.

"I want to go home."

Ryan runs a hand over my head, and I wait for him to explain why we have to stay.

"Come on then."

I look up from the panda and frown.

"But the others?"

"They can organise another way home, or we can come back for them when they are finished." He leans in and presses his lips to my forehead. Throwing my arms around his neck, I bury my face into his neck and take a deep breath, inhaling his scent, which never fails to calm my racing heart.

"You are my priority, little Kitten. Not any of this shit

that's going on downstairs. If you want to go somewhere you feel safe, then that is where we'll go." He wraps his arms around me, giving me the bear hug I desperately need.

"Come on," he smiles as he stands and holds out a hand. I place mine in his so he can help me to my feet. Picking up the bag of things I packed to take with me, he holds my hand and walks me from my room and down the stairs.

"Everything okay?"

We turn to see Travis standing next to Mr Nicholson. I find myself leaning into Ryan, who lets go of my hand and wraps an arm around my shoulders protectively.

"Verity wants to go home, so I'm taking her." He doesn't explain himself, and from the look on Travis's face when he looks at me, he understands.

He walks forward and cups my cheek, pulling me from Ryan's arms and into his own. His warm, hard chest presses against my cheek as I wrap my arms around his waist, needing to be held.

"Take her home, and we will come back as soon as all this shit is sorted," Travis says to Ryan as his arms tighten around me for a moment longer.

"How will you get home?" I ask, leaning back. Travis smiles before pressing a kiss to my lips.

"Don't worry about us; we will make our own way back."

"I will ensure one of my guys gives them a lift."

I look around Travis and see Mr Nicholson smiling at me. When he looks at me like that, I almost forget how dangerous he is, as he's more like a man smiling at one of their children. "I promise no harm will come to either of them. You concentrate on yourself and take the time you need to heal, lovely."

"Thank you," I nod before stepping back from Travis and back into Ryan's arms.

"Go and rest with Ryan. We will be home before you know it." Travis presses one last kiss to the top of my head and steps back, smiling at me.

"Love you, Daddy," I whisper as Ryan and I start to head towards the open front door.

"Love you too, Sweetheart," he calls back. Ryan leads me to the car at the front of the house and helps me into the passenger seat. Once I'm inside, he places my bag in the back of the car, climbs behind the wheel, and drives away from the house.

I look back at it in the rearview mirror and know there is no way it will ever feel like home to me again. Turning to look out the windscreen, I take a deep breath and relax a little, knowing that we are finally on our way home, back to the place that's now my sanctuary and where I will always be loved and safe.

Ryan held my hand the whole way home. He talked to me about anything and everything except the hell that's happening where two of my guys are. I asked if he thought the others were safe, and he reassured me that they were.

"Nicholson has taken a liking to Travis and you. Plus, you have both just made him a very rich man. He has no need to hurt either of them. Even if Ethan says something he shouldn't, which no doubt he will at some point, Travis is there to ensure he stays out of trouble and does as he's told."

I know he's right. There is no reason for either of them

to get hurt, but it doesn't stop me from worrying about them.

We have been home for hours; the longer we go without the guys coming home, the more anxious I become.

"Little Kitten, you need to relax. I promise you they are fine." Ryan wraps his arms around my waist from behind as I look out the window into the dark night. "When was the last time they messaged?" he asks.

"Two hours ago. Ethan said his phone was dying and that Daddy's already had," I answer chewing on my thumbnail. He also said that the house line and internet are down. Apparently, Nicholson admitted they did it when they kidnapped my father.

Ryan turns me in his arms and removes my thumb from my mouth.

"There you go then. Stop worrying. I've made you some dinner; you need to eat."

"I'm not hungry," I answer, going to turn in his arms to look back out of the window, but he stops me.

"I haven't seen you eat since this morning. You need to eat something, even if just a few mouth fulls." He looks me dead in the eye whilst giving me a firm look. "You are going to go in there and eat some of the food I prepared for you. It isn't much, but you need to eat something."

I want to argue with him, but the second he cocks his eyebrow, I know I will lose.

"Yes, Bear," I sigh before walking towards the kitchen, where we sit to eat our meals. There on the table is a small plate of leftovers from yesterday. He hasn't given me much as he said. But I don't think I could eat any more than what's in front of me.

"Thank you," I whisper, looking up at him as he sits beside me with a larger plate of food for himself.

"You're welcome, little Kitten." He reaches over and places his hand over mine on the table. "I know you're worried, and after finding out even more shit today, I'm not surprised. But I promise the guys will be home before you know it, and together, we can start processing everything you've had thrown at you." Lifting my hand, he places a kiss on my knuckles. My heart swells as I look at this guy who's showing me all the love and support I need right now.

"You know, you are a pretty great Daddy."

Ryan's eyes shimmer a little as a smile slowly spreads across his face.

"I'm glad you think so."

Letting go of his hand, I move my chair so I can sit directly next to him.

"I do," I smile before picking up my knife and fork to eat some of the food he has warmed up for me.

Chapter Sixty-Six

VERITY

Arms tighten around me from behind as I watch the minutes tick by on the bedside clock. It's gone two in the morning, and the guys are still not back.

Ryan tried everything to distract me from the fact we hadn't heard from them, but nothing worked. I watched TV and listened to music. I even went for a light run with him to try and clear my head. That did not work, and I am *not* a runner. Nothing he did distracted me from the growing worry that something is wrong and we shouldn't have left them.

More than once, he offered to drive us back so I could see that they were fine for myself. But I was scared we would cross paths on the way, and they would be home by the time we got there. So, we sat and waited, and waited, and waited some more.

I can't do this. I can't lie in bed waiting for them to come home. I'm not tired; I'm too stressed to sleep. Slowly, I lift Ryan's arm and slide out of the bed, being sure to grab my doll as I go.

"Kitten?" I freeze at the door, my hand on the handle. "Where are you going?"

"I'm thirsty; I'll be back in a minute," I reply, turning to see him looking at me with half-closed eyes.

"You need to sleep."

"I will after I get a drink. I won't be long," I reply before leaving the room. I know he doesn't believe me, and I'm sure he will come searching for me if I take too long, but I can't stay in that bed one minute longer.

I head into Travis's room, where most of my things are, and grab my dressing gown off the back of the door. Shrugging it on, I head down the stairs, planning on having a hot chocolate with a shot of whiskey in it to see if it'll help me settle enough to sleep. Anything has to be better than worrying constantly.

Whilst I wait for the milk to warm in the microwave, I look out of the kitchen window to the front of the house. All three cars are parked together, a reminder that they have no way of getting home. My car is still at the O'Reilly's, where we left it before going into hiding. It's tucked away in one of their garages, where no one will see it. The guys offered to go and get it, but I told them to wait. This is Jasmine's first Christmas with the guys as a family. The last thing any of them want is for a Donavon turning up and interrupting their festivities.

I make up my hot chocolate whilst running on autopilot. Do I believe this will help me sleep? It's more a case of hoping. Daddy won't be happy if he realises I haven't slept.

After adding a splash of whiskey to my drink, I head into the lounge to retrieve my phone from where Ryan made me leave it. He said I wouldn't sleep because I would keep checking it. He should have realised I wouldn't be able to sleep because I *couldn't* check it.

I sit on the sofa with my doll and sip on my drink, waiting for my phone to turn back on. As soon as it comes to life, I realise I have two messages waiting for me.

Daddy: I got hold of a charger. We are both fine and will hopefully be home by four am. But don't wait up. We will see you in the morning. Xxx

Ethan: My phone is alive! Stop worrying about us; I know what you're like. We will be home by the time you wake up. Go to sleep, Baby girl. xxx

I check the time the messages were sent and realise they would have come through less than ten minutes from us going to bed. Maybe if Ryan had let me take my phone with me like I wanted to, I would have been able to sleep. Bear didn't know best on that one.

Looking at the time on my phone, I see it's twenty past two. The guys said they would be home by four. That's still over an hour and a half away. I lie down on the sofa and hug my doll to my chest, feeling more tired than when I came down. Knowing that they are really okay, I find myself relaxing as I smell the top of my doll's head, and my eyes start to feel heavy.

Travis

"What's the bet she's waiting for us?" Ethan asks as he climbs out of the car and meets me at the trunk, where I'm retrieving a few boxes of things we found at the house.

"Hopefully, she's not, so be quiet when you go in. If

she's in your bed, don't wake her, or you will have me to deal with," I warn, handing him a box before balancing the other on my lifted knee whilst closing the trunk as quietly as possible.

"Yes, Daddy," Ethan smirks. Taking the box in one hand, I punch his arm with the other, knowing he won't be able to defend himself.

"I'm too tired for your bullshit," I sigh, walking towards the front door. Before we get the keys in the lock, the door opens, and we are faced by a tired-looking Ryan. He holds his finger to his lips while holding the door to let us enter.

"Where is she?" Ethan whispers, placing a box in the corner.

"Asleep in the lounge," Ryan replies before nodding towards the kitchen. We follow him in and close the door behind us.

"Why is she in the lounge?" I ask, walking over to the sink, desperate for a glass of water.

"She wasn't sleeping; she got up around two and said she needed a drink. I found her fifteen minutes later asleep on the sofa. I saw your messages and slept on a chair so I could warn you she was down here." He looks between us as we both look towards the lounge. I have no doubt Ethan is feeling as guilty as me. We never dreamt we would be out this long. But I wanted everything dealt with.

"All done?" Ryan asks, looking between us again.

"Yep, Nicholson has all his drugs back, and I even managed to get him to buy some stuff that wasn't his. Looks like Henry had been stealing from Taylor as well. There were over four million pounds worth of drugs in that base-ment. Most was pure so the street value would have been three, even four times that. Nearly half a million's worth was from the shipment Taylor stole. It's confirmation that Henry was in on the theft."

Ryan curses under his breath. I rub the back of my neck, which is aching after pouring over the paperwork Henry had kept down there.

"So Henry was looking to become some kind of dealer?" Ryan asks.

"He already was. The safe was filled with cash, I mean filled. We counted over eight hundred thousand. There was also information on another account with over one and a half million in it. He had been selling stuff for years, but seems he was laying low for a while after stealing the full shipment with Taylor. I was thinking about going to the States and checking out their property there as I suspect they are hiding even more than what we found."

"You think Mum was in on it?"

I nod in response. Our mother will do anything to continue living a life of luxury she has become accustomed to; it wouldn't be the first time she got involved with a drug dealer.

"Then why don't we leave it for Mother dearest? Verity doesn't need any more upheaval or stress. She needs us all to be here for her. From what you have told me, she will have plenty to live off and won't need anymore." Ryan leans back against the fridge.

"We discussed that on the way home. We think we tell Mum that she can have everything that's there on the grounds she never contacts us again for anything. As far as we are both concerned, she has run off with Henry to live in the States full time."

"We found Henry's paperwork, and he has left everything to her anyway. Verity gets nothing now she is over twenty-one," Ethan explains as his hands curl into tight fists.

"We found a lot in the safe that we will need to be careful with. For Verity's sake." The three of us share a look, and Ryan knows it's not going to be anything good. I know I should tell him now, but I'm too tired. Now I am finally home and can relax; exhaustion is taking over. One look at Ethan, and I can see he is feeling the same way.

"It's been a fucking shit long day. I say we put a pin in this until tomorrow. I think Verity needs to be present for this conversation," I sigh as I push myself away from the counter I've been leaning against. "I'm going to check on her before going to sleep."

I walk towards the door and open it quietly. I know the guys are behind me as I stand at the lounge door to see our girl curled up under a blanket. Her doll is lying on the floor beside her.

"You guys go to bed. I'm going to chill out in the chair for a bit. I need to unwind before I sleep anyway."

We say a quiet goodnight before the two of them head up the stairs to their own rooms.

For a moment, I consider picking her up and carrying her to my bed. But I've learnt that she can't go back to sleep once awake, and I know she will need her rest. Especially if she hasn't been asleep long.

Quietly, I walk over and pick her doll up before placing it beside her again. Pressing a kiss to her head, I tuck the blanket around her and watch as she snuggles back into her doll before heading to my favourite chair to sit and rest my aching head.

Today did not go as planned, and I know tomorrow won't go much better. Once again, I have to tear open my girl's world and give her even more information about the man she thought was her father and the extent of what he was willing to do to ensure she didn't get a penny of her money. If he weren't already dead, I would kill him, even though I know she would ask me not to. He never did deserve her, and what I learnt today proves just as much.

Watching Verity sleep soundly for the time being helps me to relax. No matter what she learns, we will work together to give her all the support she needs and to make sure she never doubts how loved she is again. Together, we will show her she is finally listened to and respected.

Chapter Sixty-Seven

VERITY

I wake up to find Travis asleep in his recliner chair. I lay here for a while, watching him sleep soundly. If he arrived home at four as he said he would, it means he's only had two hours sleep. As tempted as I am to curl up with him so he can wrap me in his arms and tell me he's okay, I don't. Instead, I walk over to place a blanket over him. He groans slightly in his sleep but doesn't wake.

I tiptoe out of the lounge and quietly head upstairs to Ethan's room, desperate to see that he's home too. I know Travis wouldn't have left him there, but until I see him with my own eyes, I know I won't relax.

Creeping to his bedroom door, I hear him snoring lightly inside. Finally, I relax, knowing that all three of my guys are home where they belong and pray that will be the last time we are a part for a while.

I really hope everything's sorted at the house and all the drugs have been removed. I hate the idea of them being in Mum's favourite space. It's as if he's found another way to

455

taunt me and ruin something else that means so much to me.

All the misery and heartache I have felt over the years, longing for him to accept me and be the dad I wanted, was for nothing. The years I spent doing anything that would make him proud of me, for what? To be told he hates me? That he never wanted me? All of that to find out I'm not even his!

My throat starts to burn, and my eyes fill with tears at the thought of the man who raised me. I don't want to cry for him. I have given that man everything since the day I was born. Mum always said I was a Daddy's girl, and I thought he loved me. I believed that he cared.

The deep-seated pain I've been trying so hard to push down is starting to burn inside me, and I know I'm on the verge of breaking.

"Nobody wants to see you cry," his voice taunts me still. Even dead, he is belittling and separating me from everyone. Like the obedient daughter he moulded me into, I go to hide, only to realise there's nowhere to go. I look towards Travis's room and know it's not mine. All three guys are asleep, and I don't want to wake them. Every part of me wants to be alone, to hide the pain from everyone to once again do as I was told time and time again.

For the briefest second, I think about the razor I know is hidden in Ethan's room. He thinks I don't know about it, but right now, it's all I can think about. I know if I can cut myself, even just the smallest amount, it will distract me from this pain burning inside of me and let me think, just long enough to let me breathe.

My legs try to walk to his room, to the wardrobe where the razor is hidden, but I fight against the subconscious decision to do it. Instead, I feel myself lowering until I sit on the floor, leaning against the wall. Closing my eyes, I try to breathe through the panic that is building in my chest. I don't want the guys to see me like this. I know they would never judge me or make me feel like my father did. But I've shown so much weakness to them, more than I have ever shown anyone. It's so hard to be vulnerable in front of others after hiding all your pain for so long.

But as my chest tightens further, making it nearly impossible to breathe, I know I need help. Looking at Ryan's room, I see him lying in bed, fast asleep. I want to be there, in his arms.

"Bear," I gasp as the first tears start to fall. My throat too constricted to release more than a small groan. He stirs a little, but not enough to wake.

"Papa." The tears start flowing, and everything I've been pushing deep within me comes to the surface like a tidal wave.

In the space of seconds, I'm hit with every emotion you can imagine. For the first time since the day I lost her, I find myself longing for my mum to appear, just for a moment, so I can tell her I love and miss her. So she can tell me it is all going to be okay. The pain engulfs me as a sob escapes. Clinging to my doll, a sob breaks free as I gasp for some much-needed air.

I hear Ryan curse as the sounds of movement from his room get closer.

"I'm here, Kitten. I've got you." He picks me up in his strong arms as I lean against his chest and cry. Lying us both on the bed, he holds me tight.

"Let it out, little Kitten. I'm right here, and I'm not going anywhere."

"I want my Mama," I admit for the first time since the day she died as I cry hard, longing for her to come to me

457

and wrap me in her arms. The grief I've hidden for so many years overpowers me as I realise how much I need her right now.

"I know, Kitten. I wish I could get her for you." Ryan runs a hand over my head, kissing my forehead. "I would do anything to take this pain from you. You have lost so much."

I have lost a lot. First, my mum, then my auntie in her own way and now the only parent figure I've had growing up.

"He's never coming back," I say out loud for the first time. "I hate him, but he was my dad," I admit, knowing he will understand. "Why didn't he just leave? Why did he have to do all this?" I ask. "Why not just take the money and run? Why did he have to break my heart? I longed for him to love me; I believed he did.

"I knew he missed Mum, and I thought that was why he was away so much. I should have seen the signs." I look up at Ryan as he cups my cheek. "He forbid me to cry at her funeral. He told me I had to be strong for him. He should have been strong for me! I should have been able to lean on him, not the other way around."

"Fucking arsehole!" I hear Ryan growl as I bury my face into his chest. "He wasn't a man, Kitten. He was a fucking selfish prick."

"How can I hate him and miss him at the same time? It's all his fault; everything that was wrong in my life was because of him. But I wish he wasn't dead. I still want him to come and hold me and tell me everything is going to be okay. Why can't I just hate him like he hated me?" I ask as the tears fall.

"Because you are a good person," Ryan whispers into my hair. "You are far too good for him, and I wish you could see that, but I understand." His arms tighten around me as he lets out a deep sigh. "I know we aren't the same, but you know the three of us are here for you, always. No matter what's going on, we are here."

"I know," I sniff as tears silently flow.

Ryan doesn't let go of me once. He holds me close as I allow myself to grieve for my dad and my mum for the first time. He whispers words of love, affection and promises. I lose track of how many times he tells me he loves me, that they all do, and I realise I don't doubt it as much anymore.

Lying in Ryan's arms, he brushes his hand over my head and plays with my hair, helping me to relax until the exhaustion of my grief and lack of sleep starts to set in, and I drift off to sleep in his arms.

Chapter Sixty-Eight

VERITY

"She's asleep for now. I found her crying on the landing."

Ryan's whispers ease me from my slumber.

"Why was she on the landing?" I hear Ethan ask. I'm not quite awake yet, but I can hear their whispered conversation as Ryan continues to run his hand over my head.

"I don't know; I think she didn't want to wake Travis and got overwhelmed. I heard her call my name, and when I woke up, she was crying on the floor outside my room."

"Where is Travis now?" Ethan asks.

"I think he's gone for a shower. He popped in just after she fell back to sleep. I think he wants to talk to her about everything when she wakes up."

"Do you think that's wise? She's already so vulnerable."

"I do. I think she needs to hear everything to truly move forward. The fact that she called to me when she needed someone shows she's asking for help, even in her own way."

I purposely moan whilst moving in his arms, pretending to wake up. When I open my eyes, Ryan looks at me with a smile while cupping my face.

"Hey, Kitten. How you feeling?" he asks, running his thumb over my cheek.

"Like I need a coffee," I smile up at him, letting him know I'm okay, even if just for the time being. He leans in and kisses me briefly, giving me a small smile.

"Then let's get you a coffee."

Ethan helps me off the bed before wrapping his arms around me.

"I'm glad you're home," I sigh into his chest as he kisses the top of my head.

"Me too, Baby. I hated not being able to get in touch with you." He kisses me on the lips before standing straight with a smile on his face. "Travis is up; go and see if he fancies making us all breakfast. He's more likely to say yes if you ask him nicely," he winks, slapping my backside as I turn towards the door.

"Hey, that hurt!"

"Who hurt you, Sweetheart?" Travis walks to the door as I approach and holds his arms out for me.

"Ethan, he slapped me," I pout playfully. Travis holds me close as I take in a deep breath. Smelling his aftershave and shower gel.

"Well, in that case, he's cooking dinner tonight," Travis laughs as he leads us out of the room and onto the landing.

"Is everything done now?" I ask, looking up at Travis as he places an around my shoulders.

"If you mean at the house, then yes. Everything has been moved out, and you will never have to see any of the Nicholson's again."

Walking down the stairs, I can tell there is something he is holding back on saying, but I don't think I can cope with anymore yet. Not before some coffee, at least.

"How about I make you some muesli and a coffee for

breakfast?" Travis offers as he leads me to the kitchen table. I nod; while sitting in the chair, he pulls out for

"Thank you."

Travis looks at me momentarily as if he is going to say something, but he seems to change his mind.

"You're welcome, Sweetheart." He turns to the other two as they walk in, laughing together. "You can make your own food, though," he frowns as they instantly start protesting.

I watch the three of them move around the kitchen together. Ryan makes us all coffees while Travis makes the muesli. He ends up making enough for all of us, and we sit together for a moment in silence as they watch me to ensure I eat. The problem is, I know the guys want to talk to me, which is putting me off my food. I know I need to face whatever they found out yesterday and what was in the safe if Ethan managed to get into it. But I know it's going to be a lot.

"Ryan told me about this morning."

I look up from my bowl, where I have been pushing the last few bites of muesli around. Travis places a hand over mine as I shrug.

"I didn't want to wake you. You looked tired," I reply as his hand tightens on mine.

"Sweetheart, I don't care how tired I am. If you need me or any of us, you wake us up."

Taking a deep breath, I look up at Travis.

"When I first went upstairs, I had planned on checking Ethan was home and then going for a shower. But everything suddenly floored me. I don't even know what triggered it exactly. Whether it was thinking about the fact he had hidden the drugs in Mum's favourite room? Or if it just hit me that both my parents are dead. But at that moment, I wanted my mum more than I have wanted her in years. I wanted things to be like they were when I thought I had two loving parents and I was wanted."

"Baby, you are probably more wanted now than you have ever been."

My head snaps to Ethan as his mouth drops open.

"What the fuck?" Ryan yells, punching his arm.

"I didn't mean it how it sounded," Ethan instantly protests. I find myself chuckling when I thought I was about to cry.

"I can always rely on you putting your foot in it," I smile at him, watching as he visibly relaxes. "I don't know what happened, and that's the truth." I look back at Travis and find myself smiling a little. "I feel a little better for it, and I know it won't be the last time it happens. I know he hated me, but he was still my dad, and I just lost him in the worst way. I can't even really get closure as I won't be able to hold a funeral for him. He's just gone, and that's a lot to get my head around." I look from Travis to the others, focusing on Ryan.

"I didn't run to cry today. I may not have made it to your room, but I called for you. I knew you would hear me and come."

Ryan gets out of his seat to squat beside me. Taking my hand in his, he lifts it to his mouth so he can kiss my knuckles.

"I am so proud of you. You could have done anything in that time. You were alone and knew we were all asleep. Yet, you called for me."

"I thought about hurting myself, but I knew I didn't need to, not really. I promised you all I would stop, and I'm doing my best to keep that promise." My eyes drop from his as I look at how he holds my hand. I know it's time, and I think I'm ready. Looking up at Ethan, I feel my small smile fade.

"Did you get into the safe?"

Ethan nods. "There was something in there you need to see, as well as a lot of cash."

"I want to know everything. I think I need to know."

"Then let's move this into the lounge so you are a little more comfortable," Travis says as he stands. Ryan helps me to my feet, and together, hand in hand, we walk into the lounge, and I know this will change everything forever.

Chapter Sixty-Nine

TRAVIS

Ryan sits on the sofa with Verity leaning against his side, her legs tucked up underneath her. Ethan and I carry the two boxes we retrieved from the house yesterday into the lounge. I can see Verity watching them as she leans further into Ryan. Moments like this remind me why she needs all three of us. There is so much she needs to process, which affects different parts of her personality and who she is. Each of us is able to do that and be there when she needs us.

Ethan leaves the room and comes back a moment later with a chair. I thank him as I take it from him and sit in front of our girl.

"There is a lot to process in here. If you need to stop or have any questions, just say. This goes at your pace and your pace only." Verity nods as Ethan sits beside her. I pull the first box over to me and open it.

"Ethan got into the safe, and there was a lot of money in there. We are talking about eight hundred thousand pounds."

Verity's jaw drops open. "But where was it from?"

"Drugs. He had been stealing a small amount of the shipments he was in charge of and selling them for years. It looks like it started about the time your mum died." I reach out and take her hand. "You remember the money he owed for the lost drugs?"

"The reason I was being forced into that marriage?"

"Yes. Well, he knew where they were the whole time. About half a million pounds worth was in the basement. He had blocked off the room to ensure no one suspected anything. He played his part well; no one truly believed he could have pulled something like that off. He was black-mailing Taylor, the other guy involved, as he knew where he had hidden his share of the drugs. He was in the clear as no one expected that he would have the drugs and sell his daughter. He made out you were everything to him." I reach into the box and pull out a folder.

"This is a statement from the account I opened for you the other week when I was transferring the money to you. Yesterday, Nicholson transferred another two million into the bank. He took the cash and some of the drugs that were not his. He knew people would ask questions if you walked into a bank with that amount of cash, and we have nowhere safe enough to store it here. So, it made sense when he offered to transfer it over to you." I pull out a piece of paper and hand it to her. I watch her frown at it for a moment before looking up at me. Ryan looks over her shoulder and whistles.

"Damn, that's a lot of numbers."

"How much is that?" she asks quietly.

"Just under seven million. It is yours to do with as you please. I've made sure it's tax-free, so every penny of it and the interest is yours. No matter what happens, the three of us have no rights to any of it, and neither does anyone else." I pull out a piece of paper and hand it to her. "This is a contract that Nicholson signed. It states that no matter what happens now, you are not involved with the money or items, such as drugs, from the property. He has gifted you the money and can't request for it to be returned or seek you to do anything for him afterwards." I pass her a second piece of paper.

"This one states that even in the event of a separation or divorce, the three of us don't get a penny unless you offer it to us. Even then, I know I personally won't accept it." I point to the bottom of the page where my signature is. "I have already signed it; I know the others will, too." Without hesitation, both agree as Verity looks at us, the worry etched all over her face. "That doesn't mean we are looking to leave you or ever plan on it," I reassure her. "This is purely to protect you and give you peace of mind." I take the papers from her and place them on the floor so I can hold her hand in mine. "People have taken control of your money and life for too long, and we plan on helping you to take that control back. Starting with giving you the money you are owed and entitled to."

"What Travis means is that money is yours to do with as you please. You are lucky enough to have a fantastic accountant to hand twenty-four-seven. Trust me, what that man doesn't know about money isn't worth knowing," Ethan grins at her as he nudges her with his shoulder. "I should know I like spending," he winks as he gets her to chuckle slightly.

I've always thought his immaturity would be a problem, but I realise now it's what she needs. Verity has been forced to grow up so fast that the little inside her needs someone who gets them. Ethan is perfect for that and will help her in ways I know Ryan and I, who are a little too sensible some-times, can't.

"Do you have any questions about any of that? Is there anything you want confirmation on?" Ryan asks. Verity shakes her head and looks back at me.

"I think I'm keeping up. It's just a lot."

"I know, Sweetheart. But just say if you need a break or something."

"I'm okay," she replies, letting me know I can continue. I pull out another folder and open it.

"This was also in the safe. It's something we need to deal with as soon as possible." I take a deep breath, knowing this is going to break her heart. "What can you tell me about your Auntie Trish and her accident?"

Verity frowns, and I know she is trying to work out where this is going, but I wait to see what she says.

"Not much. She had a crash one evening and suffered a bad head injury. She has been in hospital since."

"What kind of head injury did she sustain?" I ask.

"I don't know. No one would give me a straight answer just that it left her confused and paranoid. She can get so worked up that they have to sedate her from time to time," Verity continues to frown as she watches me. "What's in that folder."

I look down at the documents in my hand and let out a sigh.

"This was hidden away in the back of the safe. It is a medical report that says Trish is absolutely fine, and there is nothing to suggest she has any brain injuries."

"But that's not right. I have witnessed her episodes of paranoia. She blames Dad for everything, and they said it's partially due to the grief from losing my mum. They were really close, and after her death, there was an argument between Trish and Dad just before the accident. They said the brain injury affected her memory, and to her, everything she accused dad of was actually true when it wasn't. She would say he was keeping everything from me..." I watch as the penny drops and realisation kicks in. "Oh my god," she gasps, placing a hand over her mouth before shaking her head in disbelief. "She wasn't paranoid."

I shake my head as I hold out the file.

"I'm going to get someone to look over this. But from what I can understand, Trish was injured from the crash, but nothing that was long-term. The police thought the breaks had been tampered with, but that report disappeared. I believe your father paid a doctor to falsify a report on Trish to make sure she was kept out of the way."

Verity takes the file from me and pulls out the report. I watch as she reads through it. The occasional sniff or tear slips, but she quickly wipes it away.

"That's her doctor's name. I avoid him when I go there, as he once told my dad that I had visited. It's why I only visit at weekends and sign under a different name."

"I found a long list of payments Henry made to this name. Henry had power of attorney over Trish as her only living relative. I believe if the accident had happened later in life, she would have named you. But you were still too young.

"He's been paying for her to be kept in a mental hospital, drugged up, with her own money. It wasn't only your mum who was rich; it was family money. It's not cost him a fortune like he claimed."

The anger is showing on her face.

"How do we get her out?"

"It may be a long process, as she may be institutionalised now and will need weaning off the drugs. But it is possible. We just need to move her away from her current doctor." Ethan says beside her. I had set him the task of finding out what could be done. I can see the determination in her eyes. She wants to set her auntie free, and I know she isn't going to stop until she succeeds.

"That has to be everything, right? What else could he have possibly done?"

Ethan and I share a look. Here's some of the bigger stuff.

"There are a couple of things. Most are simple, like the house and everything in it is yours, but Henry had drafted up the paperwork to have you sign it all over to him when you married. It looks like he was going to be trusting the fact you wouldn't pay attention to anything he placed in front of you."

"I wouldn't have. If he asked me to sign something, I would. He was my dad, and I trusted him completely. I never questioned anything he said to me."

I can see how annoyed she is with herself over that. Now she is seeing what he was really like; she hates that she let him get away with so much.

"That's not your fault, Baby," Ethan whispers beside her. "You are a good person; why wouldn't you trust your father? From babies, we rely on the two people who we are told are our parents. We are told over and over again that they will protect and guide us throughout our lives."

Verity looks at him for a moment and nods before leaning further into Ryan, who kisses the top of her head.

"You okay, Kitten?"

"I think so."

"There is one more big thing, but if you need a break."

"Just tell me, I want to know everything now. Otherwise, I may never hear it all."

Reaching out, I take her hand to kiss her knuckles.

"Of course, Sweetheart." I pull out another file and place it on my lap.

"This was in the safe. It contains your mother's death certificate and some other paperwork of her diagnosis. There was something that stood out." I pull the paper from the file and hand it to her.

"What am I looking for?"

"Look at the name of the doctor," Ethan points to the signature. Verity frowns at it for a moment before looking back at him.

"That's my aunties doctor."

Ethan nods but quickly holds up a finger.

"Before you jump to anything, we don't know for certain. There is a chance he and your father became friends whilst he was treating your mother. Everything on record shows your mum had a form of brain cancer. There is no way to know whether these reports are correct or not," He quickly explains.

"But there's a chance they aren't?"

"There is that chance, yes. It is something I plan on finding out," I answer. Verity turns her attention to me before shaking her head.

"No, I'm starting to believe many things about my father now, but even when we were in that office, he still claimed to love my mum. There is no way he would have killed her."

"I have to agree with Verity."

We all look to Ryan, who is running a hand up and down her arm.

"I spoke to him once about her mum and how she died, and there was no denying the pain it caused him. We all know he was a fairly good actor, but that was genuine. He loved her wholeheartedly."

I look at Ryan and Verity, who both look determined and convincing, and I believe them.

"I still plan on asking the doctor, but I think you are right."

Verity watches me for a moment and seems to relax slightly until her eyes fall on the other box we brought back.

"What's in there?" she asks, unable to look away. I can see she's scared of what it could be, and who can blame her? But I smile to myself as I pull it towards us.

"This is all good, I think. We found things that seem to have belonged to your mother. The box you found is in there, and a safe Ethan found in the large one. It appears Henry had tried a few times to get into it but never succeeded, which makes us believe it belonged to her. But there is no knowing for sure until it's opened."

"Let me see it."

Reaching into the box, I pull it out. It's not heavy, and to be honest, I'm surprised Henry never got into it because it doesn't seem the most secure.

"That's not my mums," Verity announces as she jumps from the sofa and points to the coffee table. "Put it on there, with Mum's box," she calls and rushes from the room.

The three of us look at each other, not knowing whose box it could be if not Miriams. Ethan grabs the one we know is Miriam's and places it on the table next to the other one as we hear Verity's rushed footsteps above, causing us all to look up.

"Any ideas?" Ethan asks, looking back at us. Ryan and I shake our heads as Verity rushes back down the stairs.

"I knew I hadn't dreamt the whole thing up," she

announces, rushing back into the room. Dropping to her knees and placing her jewellery box on the table.

"Whenever Mum and I used to go to Auntie Trish's house, I used to try to get into this safe. They once told me it contained fun secrets about their lives before I came along. Whenever I asked to see what was inside, they told me I would have to wait until I was older, that I wouldn't understand yet."

There is an excitement in her that I haven't seen since Christmas morning when she was like a child, soaking up all the magic and excitement of the day. I look at my brothers, and judging by the smiles on their faces, they see it too. We know it may not last, but I soak up the pure joy on her face whilst it lasts.

Verity pulls a locket out of her jewellery box and holds it up. It's a beautiful silver heart charm that shines in the light.

"My mum gave me this before she died. She told me to keep it safe, and when I was eighteen, I was to open her chest." Holding the heart in her hands, she smiles, remembering something that makes her happy. "A couple of days after she died, I realised it opened, and inside, I found this." Opening the heart, she tips it slightly, and a tiny key comes out. "I knew straight away what it would unlock, but I could never find Mum's box. When I finally found it, Dad saw it and hid it away from me again. I never told him about the key." Carefully, Verity places the necklace down and pulls the small chest towards her. She inserts the key and turns it slowly. A click sounds out, and her face lights up further. She squeals excitedly as she opens the lid and looks in.

Leaning over so I can see, I notice an envelope with Verity's name on it. She lifts it out, and I don't miss the way her hands shake slightly.

"Do you want some privacy whilst you read it?" Ryan asks beside her. She shakes her head and looks at me.

"I'm scared."

I follow my instinct and move so I can sit with my legs on either side of her as Ryan walks out of the room, whispering that he will be right back.

"Lean against me; I'm right here," I whisper, wrapping my arms around her. "No matter what it says, we are right here with you; just tell us what you need."

"Here you go, Kitten."

I look up as Ryan walks over with Verity's doll in his hand. She instantly reaches out for it and holds it tight.

"Can you read it for me? I can't see," she whispers, wiping her eyes. Pressing a kiss to her cheek, I take the envelope from her.

"Are you sure?" I ask, not wanting to do anything she might regret. But when she turns her head to look at me, I see how filled her eyes are with tears and smile softly at her as she nods.

"Please, Daddy."

I kiss her lips once with a small smile before opening the envelope carefully and pulling out two pieces of paper. Taking a deep breath, I hold the paper out so we can both see it. Verity leans against my chest.

Dearest Verity,
I wish there were a chance I would be present to witness you turning eighteen, but the Doctors say I won't see next month. I would give anything for them to find a cure so I could watch you grow into the beautiful, kind-hearted woman I know you will become. Never stop being you, Jellybean. You bring light to the darkest days, and I hope you realise how loved you are.
That being said, I have to tell you something that may come as a shock

to you. But I feel that at the age of eighteen, you will finally be old enough to accept what I'm about to say.

Henry Stevenson is not your birth father. I fell pregnant a couple of months before Henry and I met. Before that, I was in a relationship with someone else, well, a couple of someone else's. I was in a polygamous relationship with two guys. I loved both of them very much, and I had never dreamt I would find myself in that situation, but I did. We all lived in the house we live in now, and they showered me with love and affection. They worshipped the ground I walked on, and I loved them with all my heart. People asked why I didn't just choose one of them, but, well, I couldn't. They were my world, and I was theirs; I could have never chosen one over the other. But in the month before your conception, things started to go wrong for us. One by one, the guys left in the space of two weeks, which is why I'm not sure which is your father. Both disappeared with no warning.

I was sure they would come back to me; we had been so happy. But they never did. They stopped calling, and they never got back in touch. One day, Henry came around, claiming to be there for one of the guy's things. We started talking, and I told him I was pregnant and needed him to tell his friend he might be the father. Henry was so convinced that he wouldn't want to know that I became upset, which made me ill, and I collapsed in his arms.

Henry rushed me to the hospital and looked after me. He held my hand and was so supportive, promising to help me in any way he could. He showed up time and time again to check in on me and even took me to the hospital a few times for checkups. He was the perfect gentleman. He showered you with gifts when you were born and thought the world of you. I fell in love with him because of his love for you. Eventually, he became your father and asked me to marry him to make us a real family. I agreed. I wanted you to have two parents, and everyone told me it was what you needed. But I never stopped thinking about the guys who could have been your real dad.

I wanted to be honest with you, but Henry begged me not to be; he didn't want there ever to be any doubt that he wasn't your father. He said he couldn't cope with people pointing it out. As far as he was concerned, he was your father, which was the end. I believed it all and honestly believed that he would give you the best life because he loved you more than anything.

But recently, things haven't been so great, and I know things are coming to light thanks to my illness. Your Auntie Trish will tell you all about it.

Honey, I need you to know I wanted to tell you everything early on, but I didn't want to disrespect Henry. So I planned to tell you when you were eighteen and wanted to help you find your real dad if you wanted to know him. But I can't. So I'm leaving instructions for your Auntie to help you find them when the time comes. She knows them, and they will trust her. I have also asked her to keep an eye on you and told her to take you if she thinks you are in danger. Henry has told me over and over again that he loves you as his own, but something feels different. I hope and pray I'm wrong and that you and your father have a loving relationship. If not, know it's not what I wanted for you, and I'm sorry.

My one piece of advice for you is if you find love, grab it with both hands and never let it go. Whether that is with one person or twenty. Do what makes you happy, and know I love you with all my heart. I wish I could be there the day you get married and have kids.

Only you can live your life. Make it the best one possible because you have made mine complete.

All my love always,

Mama

Xxxxxxxxxxxxx

Chapter Seventy

VERITY

I lean back against Travis as he puts the letter down and wraps me in his arms. Leaning his cheek against mine, I look down at the doll in my arms as the tears slowly stop flowing.

"Sweetheart? Are you okay?" he whispers. I nod as I turn my head to smile at him.

"She wouldn't have been disappointed in me."

Loosening his arms, Travis moves slightly, and I can see the confusion on his face.

"Why would she have been disappointed in you?"

Looking back down at my doll, I run my fingers through the thick strands of yellow wool she has for her hair. I've started doing this whenever I've needed something to focus on.

"I've been worried she would be disappointed in me for being with all three of you." When I lift my head, I look not only at Travis but also at Ryan and Ethan. "She would have understood why I could never pick one of you. Why, I love you all equally."

477

Ryan squats down in front of me and cups my cheek.

"She would have understood why we could never ask you to choose between us. Like her men, we worship the ground you walk on, and there is nothing we wouldn't do for you."

"Like I've said before. You are ours as much as we are yours, Baby."

I look at Ethan, smiling behind Ryan and back to Travis. I smile as I pick up the letter and look at it.

"Is there anything you want to discuss from it? Or any questions about what you have learnt today?" Travis asks as he stands, probably getting uncomfortable from sitting on the hard floor.

"There are, but..." I look up from the letter and know if there was ever a time to ask him for something, it's now. "But I think only my auntie can give me the right answers. Would you take me, please?"

Travis holds out his hand and helps me to my feet.

"I will take you anywhere you want to go, sweetheart. All you have to do is ask."

"Merry Christmas, hope you had a good one," Kylie smiles at me as I sign the visitor's book. Usually, I put a different name, but today, I use my own, hoping my aunt's doctor knows I've been. I still need to decide what to do about that, but I know that my auntie will be out of here as soon as possible.

"Merry Christmas. It's been okay, thanks. How's Trish today?"

"She's great; she's waiting in her room for you this time."

I thank her as Travis takes my hand, and I lead him through the home, saying hi to people as we pass.

Now we are here; I feel more nervous than I did whilst I rushed around getting showered and dressed in record time.

"What do you think she knows?" I ask as we walk down the corridor towards her room.

"To be honest, other than your possible father's name, I don't think there is much else she can tell you that we aren't already aware of."

I look at him with an arched brow, and a smile tugs at one side of his mouth.

"Okay, so that's quite a big thing, and we are constantly learning more information by the day." Travis starts as we stop in front of the door with my aunt's name on. "But whatever it is, we will face it as a family." He leans in and presses a kiss to my lips. "I'm right here, Sweetheart."

"I know," I smile before taking a deep breath and opening the door.

When I walk in, I see my Auntie standing in front of her window, looking out of it in a daze.

"Auntie Trish?" I whisper cautiously, knowing better than to startle her. Her eyes fall on Travis when she turns around, and a smile spreads across her face.

"Jellybean, you've been keeping the best till last. He's one hunk of a man."

Travis laughs beside me as my jaw drops open.

"My brother said I would like you," Travis smirks as he holds out a hand. "It's good to meet you finally, ma'am."

As she did with Ryan, she knocks his hand away and pulls him into a hug.

"You can call me Auntie Trish," she winks as she stands back. "Jellybean, are you going to introduce us properly?" she asks, hugging me.

"Auntie Trish, this is Travis Donavon." I look up at him for a moment and smile. "He's my daddy."

Travis's smile turns into a proud grin as he tugs me to him and kisses me hard on the lips.

"Yes, I am."

"Oh, you lucky thing, I always wanted a daddy." The smile slips from her face slightly. "Henry won't be too happy."

"He's dead." The words are out of my mouth before I can think them through. My Auntie looks at me, shocked momentarily, before stepping back and sitting on the edge of her bed.

"When?"

"A few days ago." I take a deep breath. I walk over to the bed and sit beside her. "He upset the wrong people, and they say he had a heart attack whilst he was … under their care," I explain as I try to think of a way to explain it.

"I'm so sorry, my sweet girl."

"Don't be; he was planning to marry me off to some guy so he could keep my money to himself." The air turns a shade of blue as my auntie calls my father every name under the sun, as well as some I have never heard before.

I take my aunties hands in mine and make sure she is looking me in the eye.

"We now know it's because of him you are in here. I'm going to get you out. We found the real diagnosis paperwork and know what he's been doing. I won't stop until you are home."

Trish lifts her hand and places it on my cheek.

"There is so much you don't know, Jellybean. So many things that have been kept from you."

"We think we know everything, Trisha." Travis steps beside me and places a hand on my shoulder. "We know he's not her real father. We also know about the drugs and the money. We know about it all except who her real father is."

Travis retrieves the bag he placed down by the door and pulls out the small safe.

"Oh my god. Where did you find it?" She takes it from his hand and places it on the bed beside her.

"He had hidden it in a larger one in the basement where we used to dance," I reply, watching as she runs her hands over it like it's the most precious thing in the world to her.

"I never thought I would see it again." She wipes a tear from her cheek as she stands from the bed and walks over to her wardrobe.

"When they put me in here, your father, well, Henry, asked me where the key was. I told him he would never find it." She looks over her shoulder at me and grins. "He hated not being in control; he ensured I was out of the way. He found out what I was up to and that I knew the truth."

"What were you up to?" Travis asks.

"I could see how he had changed around you, Jellybean, and I hated it. I promised Miriam that I would take you and run if I thought you were being mistreated or used for your money. I had been planning it for a while. I was also finding out why the guys really left Miriam." She reaches to the back of her wardrobe and pulls out a shoe box. Carrying it over to me, she holds it out. "The key is in here."

Travis's hand on my shoulder squeezes slightly as I take a deep breath. I know once I find out what's in that safe, then there is no pretending it hasn't happened any more.

"You don't have to do anything yet, you know that."

My auntie looks at Travis beside me and smiles before looking back at me.

"He's right. You could take the key and the safe and deal with this when you are ready. It sounds like you have had to deal with a lot recently."

"That's the understatement of the century," Travis laughs beside me. "But she has handled it so well, and we are all very proud of her for it." he gives me that look that tells me he really is proud of me, and I feel my heart warm. His love, as always, gives me the strength to take control.

"Okay, give me the key," I say, looking at my auntie, who grins, opens the box, grabs a slipper, and holds it out towards me. My heart sinks as I realise she must have had her medication, or she really is slightly mad.

"Don't look at me like that; take the damn slipper and look under the sole."

Travis laughs as my auntie winks at him. "Well, I am the crazy aunt," she shrugs playfully before dropping the box and shoving her hand into the slipper.

"Do you remember my friend Susanne?" When I nod, she continues. "Well, I had given her this key for safekeeping. The first time she came to see me, she asked if I wanted it back, and I said yes. But I knew your dad was after it too, so I shoved it in here and never took it out again." When she removes her hand from the slipper, I realise she has the key she holds out for me. "Go on, take it. Everything that's in there is yours now anyway." Lifting the key from her hand, I look at the safe and take a deep breath before opening it.

Inside, I see two notebooks and all kinds of papers and documents.

"I don't know where to begin," I admit, looking up at my auntie who sits beside me. She reaches into the safe and pulls out the top notebook.

"This was Henry's. I found it about a month after your

mum died. It explains how he came to be there that day when they met and why he was so obsessed over her." Trish places it on her knee and pulls out another notebook.

"This holds the last known addresses I have for the guys who were in a relationship with your mum. One has moved on and married and now has kids of their own. The other never got over Miriam and has spent his life travelling. But I know they would welcome you with open arms if they were your father." She places that notebook on the other and pulls out a handful of papers, envelopes and pictures. She flicks through them for a moment before stopping to look at a picture with a huge smile on her face.

"This is your mum with the two guys." She turns the picture around so I can see it. It's slightly discoloured with age, but there is my mum. Her long blonde hair hung loosely in waves over her shoulders. She stands between two men. She looks so tiny next to them, but all three have the biggest smile on their faces.

"The guy on your mum's right, with the black hair, is Jerry. He was the first one she was with; they met at a fair and fell head over heels for each other. Miriam couldn't wait to introduce him to me, and I knew they were meant to be.

"The guy on the other side of her with the light brown hair is Dave. He was an old friend of Jerry's. He came to visit one weekend, and she fell for him as hard as she did for Jerry, and the three of them decided they would try a polygamous relationship. They were so happy together."

I look at Dave and see he has the lightest hair out of the men. There is also something familiar about him.

"Where is Dave now?" I ask. Auntie Trish takes the picture from me and smiles at it.

"He is the one who was travelling. He never got over Miriam and even tried to visit her when he heard she was pregnant and again when she was ill." Auntie Trish looks at the picture and lets out a sigh.

"When your mum was dying, your father hired the best nurses for her. We thought it was because he loved her so much, but it was also about control. He wanted to be sure no one visited her when he wasn't there. So that she wouldn't find out the truth." She places the picture on the bed beside her and starts flicking through the papers as if looking for something.

"You were probably too young to remember. But, when your mum was on bed care, there were nurses with her whenever you or I were in the room with her. She wasn't allowed visitors without someone being there to ensure she didn't let anything slip, like the fact he wasn't your dad or that we were extremely rich. That was a big thing for Henry when he realised she wouldn't survive. He didn't want you knowing about the money as he was worried you would think it hadn't been enough to save her or some bullshit like that."

"It was so he could hide from her the money and keep it for himself. The bastard had hidden it all away, and she has less than a quarter of what she should have," Travis says behind me as my auntie shakes her head.

"I dread to think what my finances look like; he has had full power for years."

"Don't worry about that, we will sort it. I'm an accountant and know every trick in the book," he winks at her, causing her to blush. I can see her looking him up and down, checking him out.

"You are obviously okay with multiple partners. Fancy another woman on your arm?" she smiles at him.

"Hey, get your own Daddy! This one's all mine!" I

protest, leaning into Travis as he laughs aloud while wrapping an arm around my shoulders.

"Sorry, but I'm a one-woman man," he smirks at her. "She's allowed me and my brothers, and that's it. We just have her, and that's the way it's going to stay." He leans down and kisses my lips, causing me to blush like my auntie.

"Can't blame a girl for trying," my auntie grins before pulling out an envelope which is bulging.

"Anyway, as I was saying, we weren't allowed to be alone together, so we devised our own way of communicating. We wrote letters to each other. Your mum would read them when everyone was in bed and reply to them. We had both noticed things we needed to share, and this was the safest way to do it."

She holds out the letters, and I take them.

"They are in order; read them that way so they make sense. But the main thing mentioned is that Henry was blocking Miriam from people. They would come to the house, and she would hear them talking from outside. They wanted to see her and you, but Henry's staff would refuse them access. Dave was one of the people she heard outside. He was demanding to see her, but the nurse kept telling him he wasn't allowed, that she was too ill, and any upset caused her pain. It was when she asked me to find out why the guys had really left. She wanted to hear the truth from them and didn't trust anyone else to do it.

"Dave came to the funeral; he stood at the back of the church and watched in silence. I tried to catch him before he left, but he was gone as quickly as he arrived. Henry was furious that he had been there. He told me that if he ever saw him again, he would kill him. But I never managed to get in contact with him directly. One of his friends told me he travelled, and that was all I could get out of them."

"If he loved her so much, why did he leave?" Travis asks.

"Henry, of course," she answers.

"But Mum's letter said he came into the picture a month after everyone left," I point out. Trisha nods and lifts the journal.

"But he had been watching her for longer."

"Henry was stalking her?" Travis asks.

"Yep. He was obsessed with her and wanted her for himself. He had no intention of sharing her with the other guys, so one by one, he made them leave her. He used his connections to scare them away. None of them would have left willingly. They really did love your mum." She places the book on my lap and taps it.

"He watched them for months and picked them off one by one. Dave was the last to break; he refused to leave, and Henry got physical. Some guys dragged him from the house and kidnapped him. They threatened the one thing he would do anything to save: your mum. They told him they would make sure she suffered if she ever saw him again. He didn't want to risk it, and when he went to the police, they didn't do anything. So he left and tried to do the right thing. But he never recovered from it. He comes back now and again to check on you."

I look down at the picture and know why he looks familiar.

"I've met him," I whisper, looking into his eyes as I lift the picture from the bed and look at it closer. "He has been at the theatre a few times. He said his wife loved to dance, and he still watches performances as they remind him of her. He's known for attending a handful of performances each time, and everyone knows him, but not his name." I look at the picture and smile. "All the times I performed pretending someone was in the audience watching me, cheering me on, and he might have been there."

"He is the one who is most likely your dad. You have his eyes and smile. You might look just like your mum, but there have been times you have reminded me of him. Your mum believed you were his too but never wanted to say in case she was wrong."

There is so much to take in, so much to read through and examine to try and decide how to process it all and how much I really want to know. I can feel myself getting overwhelmed by it all.

"Sweetheart, I won't stop you from doing anything, but I think you need to take a break for now." Travis places his hand on my shoulder and gives it a slight squeeze. When I look up at him, I can see the concern in his eyes. I can't bring myself to answer, so I nod and look at all the stuff now spread out between my auntie and me.

"Your Daddy is right. I know you haven't even told me half the stuff that's been going on with you, and there is a lot to process here alone." She starts gathering things and places them all back into the safe. "Everything in here is yours. Don't rush; go through it a bit at a time." She looks up at Travis and gives him a serious look.

"It may be best if you read the prick's journal first. There are a few bits in there that are a little graphic, and I would rather you told her the basics than have her read it first-hand."

"Of course. Is there anything else I need to be aware of?" Travis asks as he helps her to place the safe back in the bag he brought it in. Trish shakes her head and turns her attention back to me.

"I am so sorry I couldn't protect you. I tried so hard, but no one would listen to me, and the more I tried to tell you, the less you came. I knew the best thing to do was be quiet and watch from the sidelines. At least that way, you were still coming, and I could see for myself that you were okay."

I know that must have been so hard for her. She did try to tell me so many things over the years, but I truly believed she was paranoid and suffering a brain injury. I never questioned it because I believed the doctor and my dad.

"We will get you out of here," I promise as I hug her. "We will devise a plan of action and get you out as quickly as possible."

"Concentrate on getting your head around everything. I'm okay for the time being. I have it easy here now I stopped fighting them. Are you staying at the house?"

I shake my head as Travis tells her we are at his but will be looking for a house together.

"Take the house; it's yours anyway. Your mum and her men built that house for them. She wanted it to be their forever home, so make it yours. It has everything you could need, including a room each."

I promise her I will think about it as we all stand and say our goodbyes, knowing that the visiting times will end soon.

Walking out of the room, Travis places his arm around my shoulder, guiding me out of the building and towards the car.

"You okay, Sweetheart?" he asks as he opens my door. I nod as I lean up against him. He places the bag on the floor before wrapping me in his arms. "Do you want to go home or for a drive? Whatever you want, I'm here for it."

"I want to go home. I'm tired, and my head hurts." I admit as my head pounds from all the information my auntie has just added to the ever-growing pile of shit my father has left me to deal with. Travis kisses my head before stepping back from me.

"Let's get you back to the guys. I need to check they haven't burnt the house down whilst we've been gone," he smiles as he closes the door once I'm safely inside. I watch as he walks to the trunk and places the bag in it before jumping behind the wheel.

"Thank you," I whisper as I watch him putting his seatbelt on.

"What for?" he asks, frowning.

"For loving me," I reply. Travis takes my hand and presses a kiss to my knuckles.

"Falling in love with you was the best thing that ever happened to me, and I promise I will never leave you like the guys left your mum. You are stuck with me forever, if you like it or not," he winks at me as I laugh.

"I like that a lot," I reply, kissing him once. "And I'm not going anywhere either."

Chapter Seventy-One

TRAVIS

A knocking at my bedroom door pulls me out of Henry's journal.

"Yeah?" I know it will be one of my brothers, as Verity doesn't knock before entering anywhere.

"Thought I would let you know dinner is nearly ready," Ryan answers as he walks in. "How's it going?" he asks, nodding to the diary in my hand.

"Trish wasn't lying when she said it was best for Verity not to read this first. That man had a dark side to him. Listen to this.

"*Today, she almost caught me. I waited for them both to go to work and snuck into the house like I always do, knowing she would be in the dance studio she built herself. Watching her move through the hole I created in the wall isn't enough anymore. I need to be able to watch her from all angles. She moves like a goddess; calling her anything else would be an insult. Today, she wore a long, flowing white dress, which only heightened her angelic appearance. She moves with grace and poise, making it impossible not to want her. Just being within a short distance of her, I'm as hard as a rock. I couldn't stop myself from taking myself in my hand and pleasuring myself as I watched her move around the studio. The more she moved, the faster I pumped my cock, wishing it was the heaven between her legs I was fucking and not my hand-"*

"Wow! Okay, I can't listen to it anymore. What the fuck was wrong with him?" Ryan curses as he scrunches up his face.

"I don't know, but it doesn't make any sense. He was obsessed with her, and he constantly stalked her when he wasn't in the States. He kept a note of everything she did. Some pages are just him tracking her. 'She went to the shops and brought bread and milk. Then met with her sister for a walk around the park before going home and cooking some exotic dish.' I don't think this is the only notebook because it's full, and I can't imagine he just stopped once he got rid of the others." I rub my face as I'm tired. It's been a crazy couple of weeks, and tomorrow, I plan on just trying to relax, even for a little bit.

"If he was so obsessed with her, why did he keep returning to the States when he finally had her?" Ryan asks the big question that's been burning in my mind, too, which is why I want to find the other journals.

"The only thing I can think of, without asking Nicholson straight, is that he was in some kind of deal with him that meant he had to go. From what I've read of the notes Trish and Miriam passed to each other, Verity told me he didn't usually go for long. It wasn't until Verity started getting older and Miriam became ill that he started going for a couple of weeks at a time. Before then, it was a week there and three weeks here. By the time she died, it was two weeks there and two here."

"What was it by the end? One week here, three months there?" Ryan asks through gritted teeth.

"He wasn't even here a week. Verity would be lucky if he spent more than a full day with her." I lean back against the headboard as Ryan's jaw clenches.

"I'm so glad that fucker is dead. I know I shouldn't be. Verity is grieving for him, but I hate what he did to her."

"It makes me wonder if Dave knew what was going on with her. The fact he is still around and has apparently been watching her tells me he thinks he's her father. Has she said anything to you guys about it all?"

Ryan nods as he rubs the back of his neck.

"Yeah. She thinks she wants to meet him and ask. But not yet; she wants to come to terms with everything first, which I agree is the best move here."

I nod in agreement, as I've been thinking the same thing.

"What about the house?"

"She's thinking about that too. She won't talk about it yet, though, as I'm sure it's a lot to consider. I think she wants to keep it deep down, though." He lets out a sigh and heads back towards the door. "Just to warn you, she's moody. I think she is over-tired and needs an early night. Dinner's in five; don't make me send her up here to get you," he calls, walking out of the room.

Looking back at the diary in my hand, I let out a sigh and finish the entry. I now know how he persuaded the first guy to leave.

Jerry had been working in the large back garden when Henry cornered him. Henry managed to knock him out and drag him to a nearby woods. He left him tied up for days, only popping back now and again to give him water and food, left to the cold and wet elements. By the eighth day, he was broken. Henry warned him that if he ever went anywhere near Miriam again, he would kill him next time and take her where no one would ever find her. Jerry agreed and left, but apparently, just over a week later, Henry saw him going to the house and leaving a note. Henry took the note and then faked a reply to Jerry from Miriam saying that she couldn't and wouldn't forgive him, and they were done. I know things were different back then, as very few people had mobiles or the internet. I can see why persuading him to leave via letters would have been easier. There is still so much that doesn't make sense, though, and I don't know if I will ever get the answers I want.

I place the diary in the top drawer of my bedside cabinet where Verity won't see it. She may walk around this house freely, but she doesn't like going in our drawers or wardrobes without checking with us first. I don't want her reading it; what I read to Ryan is just the sexual side of it. There is also the way he threatened the guys Miriam was dating to leave. It took a lot, as they obviously loved her, but I still can't believe Jerry left as he did.

I know there isn't anything in this world someone could do to make me leave Verity. I remember the way I felt when I had the gun pointed at my head, and Verity was freaking out. I didn't care that it was me who was about to die. I was more concerned about what they would do to her if I weren't there. If they had said to me, walk away, or they would kill her, would I have walked? I think I would, but I wouldn't have gone far. I would have waited in the shadows and grabbed her at the first opportunity that arose. There is no way I would leave her in anyone else's hands but my brothers. I certainly wouldn't leave, meet someone else and move on. That's why I think this Dave is her father. He couldn't move on because not only did he lose the woman he loved, but he lost his daughter as well.

Climbing off the bed, I stretch and click my neck, which

is stiff from yesterday. Spending a full ten hours on the floor looking at paperwork has crippled me. I'm getting too old for this shit.

"Daddy, Bear said dinner's ready," Verity announces, walking into the room. "He told me to tell you if it goes cold, it's your fault." She's smiling, but her eyes look tired, and she's pale.

"You feeling okay, sweetheart?" I ask, approaching her. She nods before closing the distance between us and leaning against me. "What's bothering you?" I ask, running a hand over her smooth hair, hanging loose rather than in the ponytail she wore earlier.

"I just have a bad headache, which is getting worse. Bear said I'm to have some food and water then an early night." She looks up at me through her eyelashes. "He's becoming bossy."

"He's doing his job as your Papa Bear. I agree you need all those things, and I will ensure you listen to him. He's in charge tonight, and what he says goes," I smile as Verity huffs and walks out of my arms.

"You are meant to take my side," she huffs again before walking out of the room with that adorable pout she gets.

"I'm not taking sides; I just agree more with Bear than you do now. You need to rest," I answer, walking out of my room and heading down the stairs after her.

"That's the same as taking sides," she calls, storming into the kitchen, where I can hear Ethan and Ryan talking.

"Who's upset you, Baby girl?" I hear Ethan ask. I walk into the kitchen just in time to see him pulling Verity onto his lap.

"Daddy and Bear are ganging up on me," she strops.

"We aren't ganging up on you; I just said I agreed with

Ryan," I sigh, heading over to the side where Ryan is dishing up tomato, pasta, and vegetables.

"Which means you are ganging up on me!"

Ryan and I both look in her direction at the same time as Ethan whistles. I've always wondered if there was a little in there, and now I see it. Verity told me the other day that when she is tired, she gets stroppy, even more so when she hasn't cum in a few days, which I know she hasn't. Not since Christmas Day night when she was in with me. Too much has happened since for her to want anything sexual.

"Little girl, carry on with the attitude, and you will be going to bed sooner than you think," Ryan warns beside me, and I have to stop myself from smirking when Verity crosses her arms over her chest and pouts harder. She's getting bratty fast, and it's fucking adorable.

"She's all yours tonight," I say to my brother as I pick up two plates, purposely leaving the smallest one for Ryan to bring over, knowing it will be Verity's.

"Best sit in your chair, Baby. Bear isn't messing," Ethan points out, tapping her hip. Verity climbs off his lap and sits, looking pissed off.

Ryan walks over and places a plate before her as he sits to her right.

"You can sulk all you want. You are exhausted and need to relax and have an early night." He holds out her fork, and she takes it from him without a word. "Good girl, now eat your dinner, and I'll run you a nice bath."

I watch as Verity starts eating her food, only occasionally throwing a dirty look at Ryan as she does. Oh, he's in for a fun night with her.

Chapter Seventy-Two

RYAN

My senses are overcome with the scent of her apple shampoo. Opening my eyes, I find Verity still curled up beside me as she rests her head on my bare chest.

After a painfully tense dinner, I had run her a bath as promised and encouraged her to have an early night. She had tried to tell me she wasn't tired but then burst into tears as she argued with me. She soon lay down on the bed, curled up in my arms and cried until she fell asleep.

I know there was more to the tears than the fact that she was tired, but it was a big part of it. She's exhausted physically and mentally, and her body and mind need to rest.

I glance at the clock on the chest of drawers to find it's just gone seven in the morning. She has slept for ten hours, and I don't think she has really moved in that time. For the briefest second, I panic that she has died in my arms, but then she moans slightly, and my heart starts to beat again.

After she had fallen asleep last night, I had considered sneaking out and speaking to my brothers. But the more I relaxed, the quicker I realised I also needed an early night.

We are all exhausted. It's been a crazy few weeks, and none of us have had time to sit and reflect, so that's what I did last night. I lay here with my woman safely in my arms, and let myself breathe, and truly relax.

Verity moans in her sleep as she repositions herself slightly, pressing further into my side. I smile, pressing another kiss to her head, causing her to do it again. I notice that she's rubbing her legs together as she moans, and it dawns on me she hasn't had sex for a couple of days. Our girl has proven her sexual needs really are as intense as she said. Not that a single one of us is complaining; we love nothing more than giving in to her every need.

I reposition us slightly so I can pull my left arm from underneath her, and she is on her back. Smiling to myself, I slide down the bed to position myself between her legs. She moans slightly but can't see if she's awake or not. I know the perfect way to find out, though.

It might be dark under the covers, but I could find this woman's pussy anywhere. It calls to me like a siren to a sailor. I know she has no underwear on, as I helped her get ready for bed last night while she cried. I always planned on rewarding her for going to bed early last night, and I think this may be the perfect way.

Running my finger through her slit, I feel how wet she is already, confirming that my girl needs some attention. Unable to hold back any further, I slide my tongue through her plump lips and start licking her clit. Her body tenses underneath me, and I know she can feel me licking up her sweet juices.

She moans whilst grinding herself against my face. I hear her gasp as I lean an arm across her stomach, applying pressure in the right area as I continue to assault her clit with my tongue. Her breathing becomes heavier as I slide one and then two fingers into her.

"Bear."

The sound of her gasping my name as she gets closer to her first release of the morning has my cock digging into the mattress underneath me, desperate to be where my fingers are.

As I continue to lick and finger her just the way she likes, I can hear and feel her moans as they radiate through her body and into mine. Every time she gasps or cries out my name, my cock digs harder into the mattress. Occasionally, I grind my hips into it a little, just to take some of the pressure off. The need to sink deep within her is unbearable. But I will always put her needs above my own. Judging by the sounds my girl is making as I pleasure her, tells me she needs this more than me right now.

I can feel her body tensing around me before she cries out, and her orgasm vibrates through her, sucking my fingers deeper within her as she screams my name. I don't let up licking her clit and rubbing her g-spot, trying to drag out her ecstasy as long as possible.

It's not until she begs me to stop whilst wiging away from me that I lift my head and press kisses up her stomach until I am out from underneath the covers.

"Morning," I grin down at her as she gasps for breath. Her hair flared out around her head on the pillow, and her cheeks flushed after her orgasm. I don't give her any warning before finally pushing my cock into her sweet heaven as slowly as possible, knowing it will stimulate all her sensitive spots. When I hear her whisper my name whilst lifting her hips from the bed, trying to get me deeper faster, I grin before placing a hand on her hip to steady her.

"Stay still; I'm far from finished with you yet," I whisper

against her lips, pushing my cock so deep in her I swear I hit resistance.

"Bear," she cries out as I push harder again. "Don't stop."

"Oh, I don't plan on it, Kitten." Grinding my hips into her, I can feel her pussy already tightening around my cock. "I want to hear you purr." The sound she makes next takes my breath away as she orgasms whilst crying out my name and looking deep into my eyes.

"That's it, little Kitten. Look at me as you cum around my dick. I love the way you clamp it so hard I can't tell where you start and I end."

Something feels different this morning. I can't put a name to it, but I feel closer to her than I have before. We keep eye contact as I move within her, bringing her to the edge before changing the rhythm. I love the sound of frustration and need in her voice, the way she looks so deep into my soul and hers.

I make love to my girl in a way I haven't before, and it's perfect. Every kiss, touch, and word we exchange feels like we are claiming each other in a whole new way. I might share her with my brothers, but when it's just us in a moment like this, I know she is as much mine as she is theirs. I know I will fight heaven and hell to give this woman everything she desires.

"I love you." The words are just a whisper on my lips, but I feel her body react to them. "I love you, all of you, never doubt that." She looks up at me for a moment before throwing her arms around my neck and kissing me with a passion that heats my whole body. Nothing else exists for a few moments, just the feel of her lips and her silky skin as our bodies become one, and we come together in every way possible.

As we come down, breathing heavily, I hold her in my arms and breathe in her sweet scent as I try to find my way back to earth.

"I love you, Papa Bear."

She's never referred to me as *Papa* before; I've always wondered if I wasn't doing a good enough job to earn the title. But hearing her calling me now fills me with a sense of pride I've never experienced. Christ, this morning is far more emotional than I planned.

"Not as much as I love you, little Kitten," I whisper into her hair as I kiss her head.

"I'm sorry for arguing last night."

Running my hand over her head, I smile to myself.

"You were a bit of a brat."

"I think you were right; I needed to sleep." Verity leans back in my arms so she can look at me. "I do appreciate it when you look after me the way you did last night. If I ever tell you otherwise, I'm lying."

I chuckle whilst hugging her tighter to me.

"I'm sure there will be times you will hate me for making you put yourself first. It's not something you are used to doing, which is why you fought me so hard last night."

Verity shakes her head, leaning back in my arms again.

"I'll never hate you; I love you too much."

Pressing a kiss to her lips, I smile as I'm overcome with emotion again.

"Every time I think I can't love you anymore, you say something like that, and I fall even deeper in love with you." Leaning in, I kiss her again and show her in a whole other way why she is my absolute world.

Chapter Seventy-Three

VERITY

Hugging my hot tea between my hands, I sit on the bench in Travis's garden and look out over the field in front of me. After the most amazing wake-up call, I came downstairs for a drink while Ryan held an online fitness class. Time for myself is what I need to try and digest everything I learned yesterday.

I think of the guy, Dave, and how often I have seen him at the theatre and talked to him about his wife and her love for dancing. That whole time, he was talking to me about my mum, and I didn't even realise.

But why would I? As far as I've been concerned, my parents have always been in love, and there was never anyone before them. But to find out that she had not one but two lovers before my dad had made me doubt how happy she really was.

I can't imagine the pain she must have felt when the two men she loved left her as they did. I know when Travis left that morning, it broke my heart. The pain his absence caused me is difficult to put into words. Even after reading the letter and knowing he planned to come back if he could, the pain was still excruciating. How did my mum manage? When did she stop loving them and start loving my dad? Did she ever truly love Henry Stevenson? Or was it the family unit she loved?

I know I could never move on if any of my guys left me. I certainly wouldn't cope if I were to find out I was pregnant. Was it my fault she let him into our lives? If I hadn't been born, would she have seen how he was manipulating her? Did he really love her? Or was it just about the house and money? There are so many things that I wish I could have answers for, but I know I only have the information presented in his journal, which Travis doesn't think I should read. He said he would explain more when he finishes it, but the stuff he's read isn't great.

I let out a sigh as I sip my tea and miss my favourite spot in the garden back home. I used to love sitting out there like this. I would see the horses in the next field and look out over the low fog on cold mornings. It was a spot my mum loved, too; I would often find her out there first thing in the morning or late at night when the sky was clear. She loved the garden and the house, making me reconsider what I wanted to do with it.

"Hey, what you doing out here, Baby?"

I turn to see Ethan leaning against the back door with a smile.

"I just fancied some fresh air," I reply, forcing a smile.

"Have you found her?" I hear Travis call from inside.

"Yeah, she's in the garden," Ethan calls over his shoulder before rolling his eyes at me. "You had your daddies worried."

"We weren't worried, just … curious," Ryan answers, coming into the garden with Travis quick on his tail.

"I'm fine, just enjoying the peace and quiet ... or I was," I tease, looking at the three of them before glancing back out over the garden.

"Do you want us to leave you alone?" Ryan asks, standing next to the bench I'm sitting on. I shake my head, so he sits beside me. I lean against him, instantly feeling a little better.

"No, I was about to come in anyway," I lie, leaning my head against Ryan's shoulder and looking out over the field.

"Is there anything you want to do today?" Ryan asks, pressing a kiss to the top of my head. I shrug at the same time as I answer in my head. But I can't bring myself to say it out loud, as I'm not sure if the guys will agree or not.

"Your face is saying something different," Travis points out as he steps forward and squats down in front of me. "What have we told you about voicing your opinion? We want you to be honest with us and tell us what you want to do, not what you think we want to do."

I look from him out to the field again and wish I was in my favourite spot.

"I want to go home," I whisper before looking back at Travis.

"For good? Or for the day?" he asks, taking my hand.

"I don't know," I answer honestly. I look at all three of the guys as I voice what's been going through my head. "There is a lot to consider, which we all need to decide."

"We know, Baby. We were just saying the same thing. It's one of the reasons we were looking for you."

"How about this? We go to the house, take an overnight bag in case we stay the night, and we talk about what we all want to happen. We take the next couple of days just to be together and try to avoid any drama whilst we come up with a plan we are all happy with," Travis suggests. I look to the others to find them nodding in agreement.

"Sounds like the best idea to me," I answer. Travis stands and holds out his hands for me.

"Come on then, let's get a bag packed, and we can hit the road within the hour."

This drive feels different from the one we made a few days ago. I *know* my dad won't be there this time, and I have accepted that. The hatred I'm feeling towards him after everything he has done is overpowering my grief. Will it always be that way? Right now, I think it might be. Hearing what he has put my auntie through and that he is the reason I don't know who my real father is just goes to show how evil he is.

"Do you think your mum has been to the house?" I ask Travis as I turn in my seat to look at him. Travis is driving us again, but I've noticed he has slowed down a lot.

"She may have. I have no idea where she is or what she is doing, and I don't care to be honest," he answers. I turn to look at the others behind us.

"Have either of you heard from her?" When they shake their heads, I realise I'm not fazed. I never really had any feelings for Linda, neither kind nor otherwise. But I know I don't want her in my mum's house. Would I kick her out if I found her there? Yes, I would. The way she spoke to the guys and me the other day just confirmed we don't need her in our lives. I would have made sure she was okay and had everything she needed, but not now. No one treats my men like that and gets away with it.

As we pull up outside the house, I climb out of the car and look up at it, seeing it in a different light.

"Do you think he changed much of the house when he moved in?" I ask, looking over the car to Travis and Ethan as Ryan steps beside me.

"I don't know. Trish would be the best person to ask, I guess," Travis answers. I nod in agreement.

"I need to make a list of things to ask her. There was too much to remember yesterday."

"That's a good idea. I'm sure she will happily answer anything you ask," Ryan says, taking my hand in his. "Are you sure you want to be here?"

I turn to him and nod before looking back at the house.

"If you change your mind, just say the word, and I will drive us back to mine, no matter what time it is," Travis calls as he walks to the trunk of the car and retrieves our bag. Ryan and Ethan both have a backpack with them.

"Thank you," I whisper as he comes to a stop beside me.

"You never have to thank me for looking out for you, you know that, Sweetheart."

"Doesn't mean I can't show you how grateful I am," I smile at him. He watches me for a moment before leaning in and pressing a kiss to my lips.

"Come on, let's get inside before it starts to rain."

We walk up to the house and stop. Even though I know each of the guys has a key, they step back to let me unlock the front door.

When we walk in, I look around and see how nothing looks any different but feels like a completely different house. I don't know if it's because no one lives here or if everything I now know has changed my views on the place.

But one thing is for sure: this doesn't feel like home anymore, and I hate it.

"I used to love this place. No matter what, it was home and somewhere I was safe."

"You are safe, Baby. No one will ever hurt you again," Ethan says as he places an arm around my shoulder and kisses the top of my head. I lean against him as I turn to Travis.

"Are all the drugs gone?"

He nods, and I let out a sigh of relief.

"I checked in the loft and every other room I could think of for anything that looked suspicious. But other than a couple of ornaments in his office cupboard, there was nothing which shouldn't have been here."

I nod as I step away from Ethan, look at the lounge, and then towards the stairs. Letting my feet carry me, I slowly walk up the stairs and head to my father's room. I remember the last time I was in here with him and how much he hurt me. Never again will that man make me feel worthless and pathetic. He made me feel like I was a burden to him, and now I know why.

I walk into his wardrobe and look around it.

"My mum and her men built this house for them; they designed it for their needs," I say, looking around the wardrobe. "They would have built this space for all three of them, yet now the only thing left in here is his and your mum's shit."

I walk to the first rack, grab an armful of clothes, and pull them from the racks.

"Sweetheart?" I can hear the worry in his voice. When I turn around, I see all three of them looking at me.

"I want his stuff out of this house. I don't care if you take it to a charity shop, to the recycling centre or burn it.

But, I want it out now." I grab another arm full of stuff and throw it onto the pile by my feet.

"Are you sure that's what you want?" Ethan asks as he approaches me.

"Absolutely, get his shit out of my mum's house!" I don't mean to snap, but the need to get his stuff out of this house is overwhelming.

All three step forward and help me empty the wardrobe of Dad and Linda's things. We end up throwing them out of the window, and Travis moves them into the car. As soon as it's full, he takes them to the recycling centre, where there is a charity bin which accepts clothes and shoes.

With every arm full of stuff leaving the house, my heart feels a little lighter, and I realise I want to take back my mum's home.

Chapter Seventy-Four

VERITY

While Travis is out, we go through the rest of the house, removing anything I want gone. The guys don't ask questions. They just take things from me and place them outside in the relevant piles. By the time Travis returns, the house is almost empty, and the front garden looks like a dumping ground.

"Is there anything left?" Travis laughs as he walks into what was Dad's office.

"Probably not," I reply, climbing to my feet from where I had been looking under the desk. "Ethan phoned a skip guy, and he is bringing around a large one tomorrow. Everything that can't be donated can go in there. We will take the rest to different places tomorrow. I just need to get rid of everything they ruined." I lean on the edge of the desk, and Travis stands beside me. He takes my hand and holds it between his own. I love how small I am in comparison to him. Having a bigger man, or three, beside me gives me the confidence to do what I want and not what others expect.

"I promised I would check in with you now and again. So, how are you doing?"

When I look at his face, I can see the concern in his eyes. But as I smile, I realise it's not a fake one I'm hiding behind.

"I feel a little better," I answer honestly. "I know I still have a long way to go, but I like that we have removed him from this place. It's like undoing some of the pain he caused." I look at the desk and smile. "Although I'm considering keeping this just for the memory you and I have with it."

Travis stands and spins me around in one move, forcing me to bend over the desk. He steps behind me, pushing his hips forward as he grabs me around the throat. Causing my sex to flood instantly.

"I'm more than happy to reenact that little scene any time." He moans into my ear in that deep, sexy voice. "Daddy's always willing to give his kinky little girl just what she needs." He grinds up against me again, coaxing a moan out of me. "But not yet."

Travis steps back and pulls me with him before catching me in his arms. "We need to speak to you first; come on." He takes my hand and marches from the room, dragging me behind him.

"Where are we going?" I laugh, rushing to keep up with him as he leads us past the stairs and into the kitchen.

Ryan and Ethan are sitting around the table with plates of food in front of them. There are two places set for Travis and me as well.

"I grabbed food whilst I was out, so sit down," he orders, pulling out a chair. I frown at him before doing as I'm told.

"You know, you are getting very bossy," I sigh, rolling my eyes.

"That's the way you like it, Sweetheart," he teases as he sits beside me. Well, I can't really argue that, can I.

I quickly pile Chinese onto my plate, and we start talking and eating like it was any typical day, not that we've had many of them. For a short while, I forget everything we have been through, and I focus on the fun we have together. Travis had picked up wine to go with the food, and we all have a drink and relax further.

The conversation flows easily as it always has with us, and we tease each other and playfully bicker like our world hasn't been turned upside down in the last month.

"We want to discuss something with you," Travis says as I lift my last forkful of food to my mouth. I freeze my fork still in the air and look at them all cautiously.

"What's happened?"

"Nothing, we just want your opinion on something," Ryan says from across the table. I place my fork on my plate and look at them all.

"Okay," I answer slowly. The three guys all smile at each other, but it's Travis who takes my hand in his.

"We want you to consider keeping this place."

I open my mouth to speak, but Travis holds up one finger.

"Wait and hear us out." I nod as his hold on my hand tightens. "This house is perfect for us. There is plenty of room, plus room for development. There are enough bedrooms so we can all have our own space, and it is close to the dance school. Your life is here, all the positive things, not just the past."

"Your mum built this house for her and her men, and

we think she would like it if you were to take over it with yours," Ethan adds, placing a hand on my thigh.

"Can you honestly say you don't want to live here?" Ryan asks.

"But your work and everything is there; you can't just pick up at move because of me. It wouldn't be fair to ask you to do that," I point out.

"We can easily relocate our businesses. We travel for a few clients or work from home," Ethan answers. "Plus, to be honest, this place is more central to where we travel, making life a little easier."

"And you aren't asking us to move, we are offering," Ryan adds. "To be honest, I already have another reason to move here anyway."

We all focus on Ryan, who rubs the back of his neck.

"Sean is looking to start managing fighters and has asked me to be his first client. I'm seriously considering it. I love fighting, so why not make some money out of it."

"Why didn't you tell us?" I ask, jumping from my seat and rushing to sit on his lap. "That's great news."

Ryan chuckles as I hug him tight.

"We have had more important things to think about than a few fights. I didn't want to add any pressure to you all."

"I think you should do it, bruv. You always kick ass when you fight," Ethan laughs, slapping Ryan on the shoulder. We all look at Travis as I find myself holding my breath. The tension between him and Christian may have eased, but is he willing to put his brother's life in the hands of an O'Reilly?

Travis looks at his brother for a moment; as he clenches his jaw. I think he's going to tell him he shouldn't do it. But instead, he lets out a deep breath and nods his head.

"If he can promise to look out for you, you should do it."

A huge grin spreads across Ryan's face as he looks at his older brother.

"You think I'm good enough?"

"I haven't seen you fight for years. But I think you should go with your gut." Travis turns his attention back to me, and I turn on Ryan's lap to see him better.

"I want you to do something for me," he starts. "Close your eyes." I frown at him momentarily, but he gives me his best Daddy look and I do as I'm told. "Now, forgetting everything Ryan just said, where do you see us all in five years?"

"Together," I answer, not really having to think about it as I imagine it easily.

"What do you see around you?"

A smile spreads across my face as I see everything clearly.

"The three of us, surrounded by toys and kids."

"How many kids?" I hear Ethan ask as my smile gets bigger.

"Lots. I want as many as you will give me."

"Now focus on the surroundings; where are we?" Travis asks. I look around the vision in my head, and my heart swells.

"Here, where my mum would want us to be. I can feel her watching over us as we achieve everything she dreamt of and more." I open my eyes to find all three guys smiling at me. "I want this to be our home. Where we raise our kids and find our happily ever after."

Travis moves his seat closer and takes my left hand as Ryan's arms tighten around me.

"Then let us make that wish come true. We can move in

here, re-decorate the whole house and make it ours. Between us all, we could completely re-renovate the place, and you wouldn't recognise it." He presses his lips to the finger his grandmother's ring sits on. "Soon, we are going to make this official, and we are going to make every single one of your dreams come true because it's what you deserve and so much more."

"Are we really going to do this? Are we going to move in here together, no matter what?" I ask, looking around at my guys.

"No matter what happens, as long as we are together, we can deal with anything, Baby," Ethan says, placing his hand back on my thigh.

"I love you, all of you," I whisper as tears fill my eyes, and I feel happier and positive for the first time in weeks.

"Not as much as we love you, Kitten," Ryan whispers in my ear. "There are three of us and only one of you," he adds with a smile. I grin as I press my lips to his as I answer.

"Just the way I like it."

Bonus scene

RYAN

One month later

Grabbing my pencil, I make a quick note on the papers in front of me.

"You still messing with that?"

"I want it to be perfect," I answer, not looking up as I hear Ethan sitting on the new sofa.

"You are designing a dance studio for her. No matter what you do, she'll think it's perfect," he sighs. Looking at the floor plan in front of me, I know he's right.

Verity loves the studio space downstairs, but now she has more knowledge and experience dancing; she's noticed how uneven the floor is and that it's not fit for purpose, so I'm working on making it perfect for her.

"The twins gave me the number of the guy who created Jaz's dance studio at theirs, and he's coming round on Monday to check it out."

It's been a month since we all decided to move into Verity's childhood home. Between the four of us, we have decorated and refurbished every room, except the basement and the room Travis has always used as his own. His is now in Verity's old room. It only seemed fitting that Verity should have the master bedroom, and she took great pleasure in redesigning the whole room. She has the largest bed on the market, so all four of us can sleep comfortably if she wants us. We probably spend more time in there than in our rooms. Verity has wanted us close as she came to terms with all she has learnt.

As soon as the Christmas season was over, Travis contacted a therapist who she has been seeing twice a week. She has done amazing to handle everything and has come out of it stronger than ever. We couldn't be prouder of all she has achieved in the short time since her world was turned upside down.

"Have you heard from her at all?" Ethan asks as I drop my pencil onto the plans, knowing there isn't anything else I need to do with them.

"Yep, she sounds like she's having a good time. I'm expecting her to be pretty drunk when she gets home."

"It's a hen party. Of course, she's going to be drunk. She planned it after all," Ethan laughs.

I check the time on my phone and see it's just past one. I have no idea what time she'll be back, and I don't want to message her to ask. This is the first time she's been out in a long time, and she deserves to enjoy it. They spent the whole day in a spa, where they relaxed and were treated to champagne and anything else they wanted, followed by getting one of the O'Reilly clubs VIP section to themselves.

"She's on her way, Layton just called. It seems they are all partied out," Travis calls as he walks into the room and heads for his favourite chair.

"Where have you been hiding?" Ethan asks, frowning at our brother.

"In the office sorting some of Trish's accounts. The bastard has done a number on them, that's for sure." Travis rubs his face, but I don't miss the way his jaw clenches as it does every time someone mentions Henry. We rarely refer to him by name; it's usually some form of insult. Verity seldom mentions him, and we try to avoid the topic, knowing how much it still pains her.

"How is Trish? Has she settled into her new home?" I ask, picking up my bourbon and taking a sip.

Trish was finally discharged from the mental health facility after being imprisoned for seven years. The doctor Henry paid to falsify her diagnosis and keep her medicated was found dead in his home the same day as we took all the relevant paperwork to the police and the health board. It seems he knew he wouldn't survive in jail and killed himself. We are disappointed that he won't pay for his crimes, but I don't think Trish and Verity wanted to deal with the courts and everything that would come with it.

Sure, Trish still has to go to court to fight for justice after what happened to her, and some people need to pay for everything she has been through. But they have all pleaded guilty to malpractice, and it seems they didn't want to speak up against her doctor because he was known for his temper and for making life difficult for those who questioned him. Trish is looking at a hefty payout, but no amount will ever truly compensate for the years of her life she has missed or the pain she has endured, physically and mentally.

"She's doing well. I went over earlier to help her with some furniture she wanted built. I thought she would be slightly unsettled after everything, but she is doing great. I think having the house to concentrate on is helping." Travis looks at me with a grin. "I think she's seeing someone."

"I thought she was still pinning over you!" Ethan laughs. Travis shakes his head and sips his drink.

"She was eager for me to leave tonight, and another car arrived as I was pulling away."

"Go, Auntie Trish!" I laugh, turning to look at the window as headlights shine through it.

The three of us share a grin and head to the front door to see what state our woman is in.

"Fifty quid says she has to be carried to the front door," Ethan laughs as Travis opens the door to reveal Layton about to knock.

"They weren't joking when they said you looked like you went ten rounds with Anthony Joshua," Travis laughs when he takes in Layton's black eye, split eyebrow and bruised cheek.

"How did you hear?" Layton asks, frowning. Before hissing as his eyebrow slits back open a little.

"Logan, he said everyone looks about the same. Sound like the stag do was a bit of a blood bath."

"Wait until you see Terry. He's even worse. Poor guy has two broken ribs as well as a bruised collarbone. He refuses to take a day off, though," Layton sighs, handing Travis a small suitcase Verity took out with her before stepping back and holding out an arm. "You might want to retrieve her; she's a little worse for wear herself."

"Called it!" Ethan laughs as I head towards the limo.

"I'll get her," I sigh, chuckling. Terry walks around to the door and attempts to smile at me. "Damn, did anyone get off lightly?" I don't think there is a part of his face that isn't swollen, bruised or cut.

"I'd laugh, but it hurts," he sighs. "Thank god, they

decided on a combined stag do. I don't think we would survive going through that four times."

"That bad?" I ask as I come to a stop beside him.

"Put it this way: It's a good job they own the club, and everyone there knows to keep their mouth shut. It's been a long time since I saw Christian lose control, but he lost it big style, and I think he's made a few enemies for life."

"I'm glad Ethan and I left when we did."

"Yeah, you missed it all."

Only Ethan and I showed our faces at O'Reilly's bachelor party. Travis decided to avoid it and stayed home before picking Verity up from Jasmines. It was probably for the best, as he and Christian may have buried the past, but there will always be a little hostility between them. Too much has happened for there not to be. But they are happy to try and put it behind them, for the girls at least.

"Do you think there will be repercussions?" I ask. Terry nods, letting out a sigh.

"The security has been tripled for the wedding, as well as Jasmine's personal guard. By the way, she doesn't know everything other than a fight broke out and security dealt with it." In other words, don't say anything to Verity. I make a show of zipping my mouth and winking at him before turning to the limo door.

"Do I want to know what to expect from inside there?" I ask with a grin. Terry rolls his eyes as he places his hand on the door handle.

"Expect anything; they are wild."

He opens the door, and the music, which had only been a slight hum outside, bellows out, followed by the sound of screeching women, some singing along to the music, some laughing. It sounds like they are all having a great time.

I lean into the door and look around for my girl. The

back is flashing with different-coloured lights, and they are all dancing in their seats while singing along. I don't even think they have realised the car has stopped.

"Somebody orders a big, strong man to pick them up?" I call out over the music. Verity turns to look in my direction, my smile getting bigger when I see the look on her face.

"Papa Bear!" She attempts to walk over to me but nearly bangs her head on the roof of the car. She stumbles over and smiles as the others all laugh at her. I look down at her slick black fitted dress, which stops halfway down her thigh.

"Kitten. Where are your shoes?"

Verity looks down at her bare feet and briefly looks confused before shrugging her shoulders.

"Hold on," I sigh, lifting her into my arms, bridal style.

"My bag!" she calls, reaching towards the limo.

"Here you go. Thanks for the best day, Verity!" Jasmine calls out as she passes a bag out of the car. Jasmine is wearing a short white dress, a costume veil, and a tiara.

"You look beautiful, Jaz."

"Thank you, Ryan. Her shoes are here somewhere. I will give them to her next week." Jasmine moves away from the door and blows Verity a kiss. "Love you, Verity!"

"Love you too, Jaz!" Verity calls back as the door closes. "Thank you, Terry," she adds, smiling at the O'Reilly bodyguard.

"You are very welcome, Verity. You did her proud today. Jasmine is very lucky to have a friend like you."

"I'm lucky to have her," Verity replies, leaning her head against my chest as she shivers.

"Come on, little Kitten, let's get you out of the cold."

"Bye, Terry!" she calls over my shoulder as we walk to

the front of the house, where Layton is walking back towards the limo.

"Later, Verity. Hope the hangover isn't too rough!" he laughs, jogging past us.

"Bye!" she calls back before looking forward to where the others are waiting. Looking stern, Travis crosses his arms while Ethan grins like the joker behind him.

"Oh, don't look at me like that. You knew I was getting drunk," she smiles at Travis as we walk past him and head to the lounge.

"Where are your shoes?" he asks as I hear the front door close and the locks being put into place.

"In the limo. I think. I'm sure I had them on when we left the club."

I can't help laughing at the perplexed look on her face.

"It's a sign of a good night when you can't remember how you left the club," Ethan laughs. I go to place Verity on the sofa, but she tightens her arms around my neck.

"Don't put me down. I plan on doing some very naughty things to you," she smiles up at me with her gorgeous fuck me eyes.

"Oh really? Do you want me upstairs? In your room? My room? On the sofa?" My dick instantly comes to life as I move closer to her ear. "Just me or all of us?"

"All of you," she gasps as I take her earlobe between my teeth. "Here. Now."

Sitting on the sofa with her back against my front, I slide my hand up her thighs, pushing her dress up to allow her legs to open.

"Ryan, stop."

The command surprises me because it doesn't come from Verity; it's Travis. I look up to see him glaring down at our girl.

"Do you want to explain yourself?" he asks, stepping forward.

"I don't know what you mean, Daddy?"

Oh, I know that tone; our girl has gone into brat mode and done something only those in front of me can see.

"Oh really?" Travis asks, closing the distance between them. Ethan steps beside him and looks down at Verity. I watch his eyes widen with shock.

"Oh, Baby girl, I hope you haven't been like that all night?"

"What's our little brat done?" I ask. Noticing that my two brothers are staring between her legs. I run my hand up her thigh. I expect to find the material of her underwear, but instead, I feel nothing but her plump pussy.

"Kitten, you had better explain yourself quickly," I warn as I cup her sex and squeeze before removing my hand.

"I didn't want to have any panty lines on my dress," she answers, trying to sound innocent.

"That is not a reason to go out without any on!" Travis answers firmly. "Open her legs wider, Ryan."

Taking hold of Verity's thighs, I spread her legs wide on my lap. Travis reaches forward, and I feel the effect his touch has on our girl.

"Not only were you completely bare, but you are also soaking wet."

"Well, I am horny, Daddy. What do you expect?" she answers back, all innocence leaving her tone. "You can't expect me not to be aroused when I can feel Bear's cock digging against my ass," she adds. She starts to wiggle on my lap, which heightens my arousal.

"What do naughty girls get, baby?" Ethan asks as I grip Verity's hips to keep her still.

"Punished, Sir." The little minx planned on it; she loves it when the three of us dominate her, and she gets to be the naughty little girl she craved being for so many years.

"I think you enjoy being a brat a little too much these days," Travis says, taking her chin between his finger and thumb to lift her head. "Are we making your punishments too fun? Maybe we need to try something else."

"How do you want to punish me, Daddy?"

"I think it's time we try something different," he answers before nodding for Ethan to follow him. "Come to her room."

Lifting Verity as I stand, I look at her face and find her biting her lip.

"Not feeling so cocky now, brat?" I ask, giving her the daddy look I've spent the last month perfecting. Verity sinks into my arms and tries to appear vulnerable.

"You wouldn't let him hurt me, would you, Papa Bear?" Rolling my eyes, I carry her up to the room. She has started calling me Papa Bear whenever she's bratting, and as adorable as it is, it's also a sign that she wants to play.

"Punishments aren't about hurting you. They are about teaching you lessons, you know that."

Walking into the room, I see Ethan and Travis standing beside the bed.

"Place her on her feet there," Travis orders, pointing to the floor beside him. Once she's standing, the three of us surround her as she looks at each of us while chewing on her lip.

"Into position," Ethan orders.

Verity looks around us all, then quickly slips out of her dress, revealing that she is completely naked under the dress. No one says anything as we watch her drop to her knees and sit with her hands behind her back like an obedient little sub.

I reach over to the bedside cabinet and grab a hair tie before passing it to her.

"Thank you, Bear," she whispers as she ties up her hair. Watching her now, I can see she's nervous, but I know she trusts us not to hurt her. This isn't the first time we have disciplined her together, and it won't be the last. She knows it, which is why she likes to push her luck.

I look at Travis and see he plans to take control tonight. We decided as a family that all discipline would be controlled by one of us at a time. That way, there is less chance of her getting hurt accidentally. He steps forward and squats down in front of her to ensure she is looking at him.

"Do you understand why we are doing this?" he asks. Verity looks at him for a moment and nods. "I need you to use your words tonight. So, I'm going to ask you again. Do you know why you need to be punished?"

"Yes, Daddy." Her reply is so quiet that I can only hear it.

"Why are we punishing you tonight?" Travis watches her as she answers.

"Because I didn't wear any underwear today."

"That's right. Anyone could have seen between your legs." He reaches out and tilts her head back using a hooked finger. "Who does that pretty little pussy belong to?"

"You three, Daddy." Verity looks him straight in the eye. I can see her trying to work out what's coming next. There again, so am I because I have no idea what he has planned.

"That's right. It belongs to us. But I think you need reminding of that." Travis stands, forcing Verity to look up at him from where she is kneeling.

"Here's what's going to happen," he announces, crossing his arms over his chest. "The three of us are going to remind you who owns that pussy. We are going to fuck you in any hole we see fit. We are going to fuck you until we fill you with our cum." Verity's face lights up, but I know Travis hasn't finished. "But-" With that one word, the smile drops from her face. "But, you are not allowed to cum. You have to take what we give you, but you are not allowed to find your release."

"Daddy! That's-"

Travis cuts her off by holding up a finger.

"You are in no position to argue. If you don't like the punishment, then maybe you need to stop being a brat."

Oh, he's good. He knows just how to push her buttons and knows the one thing she loves more than sex is the feeling she gets after an orgasm. Take away one of her favourite things, and the rest becomes less exciting.

"But how am I meant to stop myself from cuming?" she asks, staring up at her daddy in disbelief.

"It's possible, and you need to learn quickly. There will be consequences if you ignore the rules." He steps back and pulls his t-shirt off over his head. "Every time you cum, you will be spanked ten times."

"Ten!" she cries out, lifting on her knees. "But Daddy-"

"Don't 'but Daddy' me. You knew what you were doing when you didn't wear any underwear when out tonight. So you have two options: you take your punishment like a good girl, which will end in you being treated like a good girl. Or, you refuse the punishment, and we leave you in bed, and you go without sex from any of us for a week."

"A WEEK!"

"Yes, a week! During that time, one of us will be with you at all times to ensure you don't pleasure yourself either.

So, what will it be, Sweetheart? Are you going to be a good or naughty girl for your men?"

Verity watches him for a moment before sitting back on her heels and nodding her head.

"Okay, Daddy."

Travis nods once before stepping to the other side of the room. Ethan and I quickly follow him, leaving Verity where she is kneeling on the floor.

"Are you sure this isn't pushing her a little too hard?" I ask quietly. "I'm all up for dominating her, as she asked, but that sounded a little too close to how that prick used to speak to her. Is it too soon?" One glance at Ethan tells me he is on the same wavelength as me here. Travis looks back at our girl and shakes his head.

"This is what she asked me to start doing. She told me the other night that she never doubts that we love her and knows we will be here for her no matter what she does. With him, love wasn't unconditional; it had to be earned. She knows that if she said her safe word, we would stop instantly and shower her in love and comfort until she felt better. He would have used her weakness against her. Those are the differences she sees between us and him. She knows our love is not whether she is a good or naughty girl; those are just terms that are kinks. All of this is just about her getting a thrill, experiencing the side of her she thought no one would ever accept, not like we do."

I look at him momentarily, and it all feels different, more fulfilling for her and us. I feel proud that we have shown her that we love her no matter what and that all of this is what she wants.

"Damn it, how am I meant to fuck that woman now you've thrown all that emotional shit into the mix?" Ethan curses under his breath as Travis and I try hard not to laugh.

"By remembering that she still went out with no underwear on, and we need to make sure she doesn't do it again," Travis grins.

He turns around and opens up the cupboard we have moved any sex toys into. He pulls out a couple of things and winks at us before turning back to Verity.

"Lie down on your back in the middle of the bed."

Verity climbs to her feet and does as she's told without saying a word. Travis stands at the bottom of the bed to crawl between her legs.

"What are your safe words?" he asks, kneeling in front of her sweet pussy I know will be soaking wet.

"Orange and black. If I can't speak, I tap a shoulder or a thigh three times," she answers, looking into his eyes.

"Good girl, remember to use them no matter what," he reminds her.

"I promise."

Travis leans in and presses a kiss to her lips.

"Good girl," he whispers as her pussy clenches before my eyes. There is no way she is going to avoid cuming she is always too sensitive and comes alive with the right stimulation.

"Ethan is going to start us off by fucking any part of you he likes, except your ass. That is going to be filled with this." Travis holds up a butt plug for Verity to see. "This will be staying in until it's my turn because then I'm going to teach you that every hole in your body belongs to us; no one else gets to so much as look at them. Do you have any questions?"

"No, Daddy," she replies before chewing on her lip.

Travis leans in as if to kiss her, keeping his hand between her legs.

"You are very wet for someone who is being punished. Do I need to be harsher?" he teases. I can't stop myself from looking between her legs from the bottom of her bed.

"Spread her legs, Travis. I want to see what you are doing to her." Travis moves so he is now beside her, looking down at her sweet pussy.

"Open those legs, little Kitten."

I hear her reply as she shows me everything. She's glistening in the dim light where she is so wet. Travis starts sliding the plug between her lips to cover it with her juices. Verity moans slightly, and Travis slaps her clit, causing her to cry out with shock more than pain.

"Do not cum. You know the rules."

I expect some backchat; it has become common with her, but she knows she has pushed her Daddy a little too far this time.

Travis continues to tease her with the plug. He alternates between rubbing it between her folds and inserting it into her sweet pussy; occasionally, he will tease her back entrance with it until, with no warning, he pushes it into her. I'm not even surprised when she cries out with pleasure as she cums. Her back passage is so sensitive, and he knows it.

Travis clicks his tongue in disappointment as he moves from the bed to stand beside it.

"I'm sorry, Daddy. I tried, but it was too much." I can hear the pleading in her voice, but I also know how much she enjoys being spanked.

"Hands and knees, facing the end of the bed." Travis's instructions are precise and Verity knows to do as she's told when he gets that tone.

"Ethan, do you want to preoccupy her mouth as I administer the punishment, or would you rather we swap positions?"

"I'm doing the spanking," Ethan declares, stripping off in front of us before climbing onto the bed and positioning himself behind her. "There is nothing better than turning this ass a sweet shade of pink."

I look at our girl there on her hands and knees, just like that first time with Ethan and me, and my whole body comes alive with the need to feel those lips around my cock.

"I'm taking her mouth," I announce, stepping forward as I pull off my clothes. Travis gives me a knowing nod and steps out of the way. If he wants her ass, that's fine. Seeing her like this always turns me on to the point I can't hold off, and I know what will happen here tonight. It may be quick, but it'll be amazing at the same time.

I tilt her head back and look down into those beautiful blue eyes framed with winged eyeliner. Her lips are bright red, and I am filled with images.

"I want to see that lipstick on my balls. Lower your head so you can take them in your mouth," I order.

"Yes, Bear," her voice lifts a little higher as Ethan lands one slap onto her ass cheek.

"One," she cries out, and I can already see it's going to be torture for her. There is no way she will avoid cumming again, especially whilst being spanked with a butt plug-in. Travis really did know the best way to punish her.

"I'll count them; you do as Ryan asks," Travis calls from the seat beside the bed. He loves to watch the three of us together for a while before he joins in.

For the next five minutes, I take great pleasure in using Verity's mouth as Ethan fucks her whilst spanking her. I can tell how close she is to falling over the edge and cumming, and I know that Ethan is edging her more than he ever has before.

"Ten."

I feel the relief flood through Verity as Travis announces the last one. It couldn't have come at a better moment because seconds later, I found myself releasing stream after stream of thick cum down her throat at the same time as Ethan finds his own release. Verity's body is shaking as she tries desperately not to orgasm as she always does when one of us cums.

Travis stands from his chair as I step back from our shaking girl.

When he tilts her head back, I can see the sweat and tears streaming down her face. Her eyes always water when she gives her head, but for a moment, I worry we are pushing her too far.

"Are you still with us?" Travis asks, looking into her eyes as she nods.

"Yes, Daddy. Can I cum yet?" she pleads.

"Not yet, but you're doing so well." His praise causes her eyes to light up, and a smile spreads across her lips. This is what she loves, the praise she gets from us. This is why we shower her with love at every opportunity, making up for all the years she chased it only to be left wanting.

Whilst Ethan moves off the bed so Travis can take his place, I step forward to kiss Verity.

"Bet you won't be going out without underwear any time soon," I tease as my lips brush across hers.

"No, Bear." Her voice goes up a couple of octaves as Travis pulls the butt plug from where it's been for a while. She looks over her shoulder, her eyes wide. "Warn me next time!"

Travis gives her his best Daddy look before grabbing her

hips and thrusting into her in one move. She cries out as her eyes nearly roll into the back of her head. How she manages to stop herself from cumming I don't know. Verity has the most sensitive asshole. If we want to make her cum that is the quickest way to do it.

"Don't," Travis warns as she cries out in frustration.

"Please, Daddy! I'm sorry! I won't do it again!" she cries out as he grinds against her. I watch her face as she cries out again.

"What did you learn, Kitten?" I ask, forcing her to look up at me.

"My body belongs to the three of you. No one but you can see it!" she cries out as Travis edges her again. Bringing her right to the brink of an orgasm before pulling out of her.

"And if they do?" Ethan asks, stepping beside me.

"Then you will punish me."

"Oh no, Baby girl." Ethan tips her head back so she has no choice but to look at him. I notice Travis waiting for him to finish before no doubt edging her again. "We won't just punish you. We will find every single person who sees what is ours and kill them. We will make sure that everyone knows not to even look at you," Ethan declares before kissing her hard as Travis thrusts into her.

Verity cries out to the point I think she is about to cum when Travis pulls out of her again.

"I'm sorry! Please! I learnt my lesson. My body is yours and yours only!"

"Glad you are finally on the same page as us, sweetheart!" Travis growls as he slowly slides back inside of her. "You belong to us, every part of you." He starts thrusting into her, and I know he's about to send her over the edge. "Now be my good girl and cum."

Verity cries out as she orgasms instantly. I love watching the way her body shakes. She is the most beautiful woman in the world, but there is something about the way she looks and sounds when she orgasms that makes me love her even more.

I climb onto the bed next to where Travis is still fucking our girl and reach underneath her. Not giving her a chance to recover from her first orgasm, I start rubbing her clit, bringing her closer in another way. She is soaking wet, and I know she can still cum a few more times before she becomes overstimulated.

"Don't stop," she cries out as Travis's grip on her hips tightens, and he picks up speed, no doubt chasing his own release.

"We don't plan to," Ethan answers. I turn my head just in time to see him push his dick into her mouth whilst taking one of her breasts in hand as she swallows him deep into her throat. The three of us continue to stimulate her in any way we can, giving her orgasm after orgasm until I start to worry she is going to safe word. Travis must notice, too, as he nods for me to stop and runs a hand up and down her back.

"One more, Sweetheart. Give your men one more," he coaxes through gritted teeth, and I know he's close. I never thought I would be so intoned to when my brothers are close to an orgasm or not. But the three of us sharing the same woman has made me aware of many things I never thought I would want to know about them.

I step back and watch as Travis and Verity find their release together. As always with the two of them, he instantly removes himself and pulls her back to cradle her in his arms. I grab the blanket off the chair and place it over them before heading into the bathroom to get a flannel to clean her up and a glass of water to rehydrate her.

Considering I was initially worried about taking on a daddy role with our girl, it has come naturally to me. There is nothing I wouldn't do to make sure she has everything she needs. I now seem to know what that is before she does.

As I return to the room, I see Travis and Ethan pulling on their boxers. Verity is now curled up in the middle of the bed, and I have no doubt she will want all three of us to be with her.

I pass the flannel and towel to Ethan, who helps Verity clean up before Travis hands her the glass. I take the time to pull on my boxers and gather up our clothes, knowing we won't want everything to be a mess in the morning.

"Do you need anything, Kitten?" I ask as I place our clothes on the chair.

"My phone is almost dead," she answers as Travis climbs into the bed and holds her as Ethan climbs in on the other side of her.

"I brought her bag up; it's on her dresser," Travis adds.

Standing in front of her dresser, I open her clutch bag to pull her phone out. Instead, I find something else in there.

"Umm, Kitten. Do you want to explain this?" I ask as I let the object hang from my finger whilst turning to face the bed. Verity giggles as Travis stares down at her.

"You didn't really think I would be commando all night, did you?" she asks, leaning into Travis.

"You little brat," Ethan growls through his teeth as he pounces on top of her, causing her to screech as he tickles her.

"I don't know why I'm even surprised," Travis sighs as I laugh at the two of them. I should have known better than to think our quiet, sweet Verity would do something as risky as spend her evening dancing with no underwear.

"I think you are getting very brave, little Kitten. I don't know what we are going to do with you." I shake my head while placing her phone on charge. By the time I climb onto the bed, Ethan has stopped tickling her, and she rolls over him to land in my arms. Pressing a kiss to her forehead, I tighten my arms around her.

"You all love me when I play the brat," she smiles at me.

"And you know it," Travis sighs from his spot.

I look down at our girl as she lies in my arms, looking breathtakingly beautiful. Her smile lights up the whole damn room, and I can't stop myself from pressing a kiss to her lips.

"Did you have a good time today?" I ask, tucking some hair behind her ear.

"It was perfect; almost everything went according to plan," she announces proudly.

"Almost?" Ethan asks behind her. She lies on her back to see us all as she nods.

"Jaz's friend Abbi got drunk early on, so we had to call someone to pick her up. That scary guy McIntire collected her and didn't look too impressed."

"I bet he didn't," Travis sighs. We all know how McIntire has been helping the Youngs since Geralt's death a few months ago. I have heard that his daughter Abbi hasn't been taking it well, and McIntire has had to intervene a few times to relieve the pressure on the rest of the family. Personally, I think he feels he needs to because the Young family were meant to be under his protection.

"So, did it give you any ideas for your own hen night?" Ethan asks. Verity shrugs.

"Not really. We haven't discussed it properly yet, so I've not thought about it," she points out. I realise she's right; we haven't discussed the engagement ring she has on her left hand. "I mean, you never really asked me. We said we would discuss it once things settled down," she adds, looking at us all.

"Funny enough, Ryan and I spoke about it at lunch today," Ethan says, smirking.

"What were you talking about?" Travis asks. I look at him and smile.

"We think you should be the one to marry our girl legally. It makes the most sense," I answer before looking at Verity. "He is your main daddy. He is the one Gran gave the ring to, and he is the eldest of us all. It makes sense for him to be your legal husband."

Verity looks from us to Travis, who is staring at me.

"You would really do this? You would let me marry her?" he asks. I nod before responding.

"We can do what the O'Reilly's are doing and have our relationship blessed after your legal wedding. We know that your relationship isn't any different from ours, but you have proven time and time again that what you two have is special, and it's what Verity needs."

"I need you all."

I look down at her in my arms and smile.

"And we all need you."

"We are all here for you, Baby. We always will be, but it makes sense for you to marry Travis over us two," Ethan adds before looking at Travis with a grin and climbing between him and Verity.

Travis moves closer to her and cups her cheek lovingly.

"Is that what you want? To be legally married to me?" he asks, gently stroking her cheek with his thumb.

"You know I do, but do you want to be legally married to me?" she asks, chewing on her lip.

"Sweetheart, I would be honoured to be your husband, legal or not," he whispers, leaning in to brush her lips with his own.

"Does this mean you are going to propose properly?" she teases with a smile. Travis looks at her momentarily before rolling so he is on top of her. Placing his arms on either side of her head, keeping her in place, he looks deep into her eyes.

"You are the most important person in my world; I love you more than I ever thought it was possible to love anyone. I want to spend every day showering you in love and encouragement until I breathe my last breath." He leans in and presses one small, slow kiss to her lips.

"Verity, the love of my life, the other half of my soul, will you do me the honour of becoming my wife?"

Verity wraps her arms around his neck as she nods, a single tear rolling down her cheek.

"Yes, Daddy, I will marry you." She kisses his lips before looking around at Ethan and me, and we smile back at her.

"After your two are married, how do you fancy having a blessing ceremony with us? Because Kitten, there is no one else in the world we would want to be with. I know I speak for all of us when I say we love you more than life itself." I take one of her hands and kiss her knuckle.

"I want to be married to you all as soon as possible." She answers, smiling.

"Then we need to start planning because, baby, I have no plans on waiting around to marry you," Ethan chuckles behind Travis.

"I want to be married soon. I don't want a big wedding. Nothing else matters as long as I have the three of you."

I lift her hand to my lips and kiss her knuckles again, and the three of us look at our woman.

"Then it's a good job that as long as we have you, nothing else matters to us either."

Four Fiancé's & I: Chapter One

JASMINE

"Please tell me this is the last one," Layton whines beside me as we make our way down the busy high street. "Why couldn't you have brought your fiancé, who loves to shop? That would have made more sense than making me deal with all these people. I hate people."

Count to ten, Jaz. Daddy and Terry will not be happy if you stab your security.

"Because I'm shopping *for* Jason, so he couldn't come," I point out, rolling my eyes. "And yes, this is the last one, so stop sulking. Otherwise, I will tell Daddy you threatened to shoot me." I warn, but looking at Layton, I know he's not threatened.

"He would ask what you did to annoy me," he points out. "They are all surprised I haven't done it yet."

I open my mouth to argue with him, but as I turn to do so, I see the way his eyebrows have disappeared under his hairline, daring me to try and prove him wrong.

"Yeah, fine. I'll give you that one," I sigh, shaking my

head. "Why don't you put the bags in the car, and I'll meet you there. I will only be in here for ten minutes."

"Yeah, like that's going to happen," he laughs, shaking his head.

"I won't tell anyone you left me. It will be our secret."

"Please, you can't hold your own piss when it comes to the O'Reilly's. Do you really believe you won't let it slip that I left you unsupervised?"

"I'm not that bad!" I argue, turning back towards the jewellers I have an appointment with. I notice the security signs and smile. "See, you can watch me go in and leave. I will be perfectly safe." I turn back to Layton and can tell he's assessing the situation.

Honestly, he's not the only one fed up, but I have to get the last Christmas gifts today, or I risk not having anything for the guys. Performances only finished yesterday, and with everything that's been happening with Verity, who is still hiding with her men, I am stupidly behind. It doesn't help that the constant worry of them being found has left me exhausted, thanks to being unable to sleep properly. I'm terrified she will be forced to marry the prick like her arsehole of a father has arranged behind her back. Thinking about it makes me so angry that I force myself to concentrate on everything around me.

Turning to Layton, I see him eyeing the multi-storey car park before us. The car is on the third level, and would only take a few minutes to get to it. If it weren't for the fact that I still need to find Christian a Christmas present, I would be demanding Layton take me home.

"Come on," he sighs, reluctantly walking to the door of the jewellers. He knocks on the door, and a gentleman in a suit appears.

"Do you have an appointment?"

"Yes, under the name O'Reilly," Layton explains. The gentleman's eyes widen when he recognises, and his whole persona changes.

"Of course, Mr O'Reilly, please do come in."

"I'm their security team, she…" Layton nods at me, "Is their fiancée. You are to treat her with the same respect as you would them. Is that understood?"

"Yes, of course, sorry." The gentleman smiles nervously as I watch him tremble slightly before turning his attention to me. "Congratulations on your engagement, Miss …"

"Connors. Thank you for seeing me at such short notice, Mr …"

"Cooper, but please call me Trent."

"Mr Cooper is fine," Layton warns. He can sometimes be a little overprotective, even more so when he is tense, tired, hungry, or all of the above.

"Layton," I say through gritted teeth whilst trying to force a smile. "Why don't you sit outside while I get what I need from here? You will be able to see the door and will be only a call away should I need you."

Layton stares at me momentarily before looking down at the bags, which I know must be hurting his hands. I offered to carry them myself, but he went all macho man on me and told me I was being ridiculous.

"Fine," he sighs, walking towards the door. Mr Cooper quickly steps around and opens it for him. "I'm going to drop these bags off at the car and come straight back. Do not leave this shop until you see I'm out there," Layton snaps at me before rushing towards the car park.

"Feel free to grab me a coffee on the way back," I call out while giving him a little wave. I can see him muttering under his breath, no doubt calling me every name under the sun. I smile, stepping back as Mr Cooper closes the door behind him and turns to me nervously.

"Let's try this again without the hangry guard," I say with a relaxed smile. "Hello, Mr Cooper, I'm Jasmine Connors, but please call me Jasmine." Holding out my hand. His body visibly relaxes before he reaches out and shakes my hand.

"It's lovely to meet you, Jasmine. Please, call me Trent."

"Thank you, Trent," I reply happily before turning my attention to the display cabinets around me. "The O'Reillys all speak very highly of you and the quality of your products." I spot Trent's chest expanding at the praise. "I know you know their style, so I need to find something special to gift Christian for Christmas. I also need something for each of the brothers as wedding gifts. The wedding is in just over a month, so I want to order them now. Do you have anything unique that can be personalised?"

His face lights up as he almost skips around the counter, holding up a finger.

"How about I show you a few options, and you can decide if any would match what you are looking for," he declares, walking over to a cabinet.

"That sounds like a great idea," I reply, hoping he will have something to fit the bill and show my men just how important they are.

Fifteen minutes later, all wedding gifts are picked and ordered, and Christian's Christmas gift is hidden safely in my bag. I look out the door to see if Layton is back, but he's nowhere to be seen. But I spot two people I haven't seen in a very long time, and my heart jumps into my throat. My old best friends Sophia and Amber sit on a bench giggling together. I have conflicting feelings seeing them. Part of me wants to hide away, remembering the last time we saw each other, but another is desperate to make peace whilst we can. I don't know if it's because I'm missing Verity so much or if it's because I still think of the girls regularly, when I decide to speak to them and put the past behind us.

"I'm going to wait for Layton outside," I declare as I walk to the door. Trent quickly rushes out from behind the counter and places a hand on the handle as if to stop me.

"I think you should wait here until your security comes back," he says nervously, looking around.

"I promise I will be fine. Layton is probably just waiting in the queue at the coffee shop and will be here any minute," I reassure him. Sometimes the whole 'save the little lady' attitude pisses me off.

"Then please let me stay with you until he returns." He doesn't realise that I am better equipped to defend myself out of the two of us. Sean has trained me every other day since I was recused.

I open my mouth to point this out but am interrupted by someone calling my name. I turn to see Amber and Sophia walking towards me, both smiling. I wave and turn back to Trent.

"My friends are here and will wait with me. But thank you for everything, and I look forward to coming to collect the other gifts when they're delivered." Before he can reply, I step away from the shop and hug my old friend.

"Where the hell have you been? We haven't seen you in months!" Sophia yells as she hugs me tight.

"Here and there, you know how life is," I answer with a smile. I know I should be pissed with them; they abandoned me when I needed them the most. But I've changed, and I'm sure they have, too.

"Did you just come out of that jewellers? Do they sell anything in there for less than a grand?" Amber asks.

"Yeah, it's not cheap. I think I just spent a huge chunk of my savings," I start but stop myself from saying any more. I don't know how much of my life I want them to know right now. I also don't miss the way they smile at each other. "What are you two doing with yourselves?" I ask, hoping to change the topic of money.

"Nothing much; going out, enjoying life, same old," Amber smiles before looking me up and down and then at the shop I had just walked out of. She has noticed that my outfit is designer, as Jason only buys what he classifies as 'the best' for me.

"We should go out and catch up. You can tell us all about what you've been up to."

"Definitely, it's been so long since we had a night out like we used to," Sophia chimes in. "We were just saying the other day how much we missed you and how much fun we used to have on weekends together."

I'm nodding in agreement when I hear someone shouting.

"Jasmine! What the hell did I tell you!"

I spin around and see Layton storming towards me, holding a take-out cup of coffee. He doesn't pay any attention to the girls, but I notice the girls are paying plenty of attention to him.

"I told you to stay inside the shop until I got back!" he snaps, stopping in front of me and thrusting the coffee cup into my hands.

"I'm fine. Don't get your panties in a twist," I sigh, rolling my eyes.

"Is this your boyfriend?" Amber asks, checking Layton out.

"What? Hell no!" Layton and I respond in unison. If it wasn't Layton, I would probably take the look of disgust personally. But with him, the feeling is mutual.

"Good to know," Amber grins with that look in her eye, which she gets when she sees something or someone she likes. "Hi, I'm Amber. Single and always up for a bit of fun," she declares, holding her hand out for him to shake.

Layton looks at her for a moment and obviously thinks better of commenting as he rolls his eyes and turns back to me. Sucking my lips between my teeth, I attempt to ignore the look of disappointment on her face.

"Maximus just called to see if you had finished. He said he would meet us here."

"What? Already?" He's meant to check out a new property for a potential club. He had asked me to go with him, but Christian gave him a list of things to do first. I was expecting it to take him the majority of the day.

"Your stepbrother?" Sophia asks excitedly. I'd forgotten how obsessed she was with Maximus. She was determined to have at least one night with him and would throw herself in his direction whenever she had the chance. I hated it then, but now it leaves me feeling protective as well as jealous. Layton looks from me to her and back again.

"Who are these girls?" he asks, nodding towards them. This is what I love about Layton, he never pretends to like someone. He shows it if he doesn't deem you important or worthy of his time.

"They used to be my best friends; I've known them most of my life," I answer, sipping my coffee. Layton's eyebrows disappear under his hair before looking back at them.

"The ones who left you the night Maximus offered me the job?"

I nod, knowing what night he's referring to.

Layton got his job as my bodyguard after Maximus saw how well he looked after me one night. I was so drunk I couldn't stand and was throwing up everywhere. He had been a bouncer at the club, and the girls had left me to chase after some guys, leaving me with the moron I was dating at the time.

"Who is this if not your boyfriend?" Sophia asks, watching Layton and me.

"I'm her bodyguard," he answers, standing tall beside me. Amber and Sophia look at each other and burst out laughing.

"What the fuck do you need a bodyguard for?" Amber laughs. "Thinking very highly of yourself, Jaz."

"It's to keep her safe from lowlifes like you."

My heart skips a beat as Maximus steps into view in his jeans and black shirt, looking like a god.

"Max!" Sophia screams and goes to launch herself at him. He growls as he stops her before she can touch him.

"For the last time, it's Maximus," he growls.

"But Max will be so much easier when I moan it," she smirks, causing me to choke on the coffee I was sipping.

"Oh shit!" Layton gasps as he looks at me. I'm staring at the girl who has the audacity even to suggest my man would touch her.

"Shorty never has any issues moaning my name," he replies, wrapping an arm around my waist and tugging me close to him before kissing me so hard that it takes my breath away.

"You're sleeping with your stepbrother!" Amber yells before laughing again. I smile at Sophia as I lean against my man, leaving my hand resting on his chest. I can tell she's put out that I have what she has always wanted.

"Oh, this could be interesting," Layton mutters under his breath, unable to hide the massive smirk on his face, as Maximus chuckles in my hair. The girls seem oblivious to the fact, and the guys are trying, but failing, to hold it together.

"I always thought she would end up with that stuck-up fucker Christian," Sophia adds.

And just like that, all the humour from the situation has gone.

"What did you call him?" I demand, stepping out of Maximus's arms.

"Oh, come on, he was always telling you what to do and that you should stay at home and be a good little girl," she answers, rolling her eyes.

"Maybe he was looking out for me as he could see I was on a slippery slope and was going to end up throwing everything away," I point out, annoyed.

"You wouldn't have thrown everything away; you were just trying to have fun. He was a killjoy, and you know it."

I step forward and close the distance between us a little. I hear Layton asking Maximus if he should intervene, but he knows, as well as anyone else, that this is overdue.

"At least he helped me when I hit rock bottom. He didn't force me out onto the streets with nowhere to go or money to eat."

"We didn't force you out; we gave you a couch to live on. You're the one who disappeared in the middle of the night without so much as a word!" Amber snaps, taking a step forward.

"Because I couldn't afford to stay! You wanted two

hundred pounds a week from me!" I yell, throwing my empty hand up in the air.

"It was to go towards the rent and bills," she screeches back.

"Yeah, the whole amount! What were you going to pay towards?" I ask. "I heard everything you two said that last night when you thought I was still at rehearsal—laughing about how you were going to get me to pay for everything so you guys could enjoy the free ride and have more money to spend at the weekends. You figured you would get more money out of me that way, not like you ever paid for the nights out anyway; it was always me. You even said it was the only reason you kept my sorry ass around." I had been so hurt hearing how my best friends didn't really care about me, and it was always my generosity they loved.

I leave out how I heard they would try to get money from the O'Reillys for putting me up. I can already sense Maximus's anger radiating behind me. I don't need to add fuel to that fire. Feeling him there reminds me that I don't need them anymore. I have more than they ever will.

"Let's face it, you were always well off and could afford it! You would have asked your stepbrothers for help eventually." Amber shakes her head and looks at the guys over my shoulder. "You did fine anyway. You bagged a millionaire, and I'm sure stick-up-his-arse Christian still has his say over what you can and can't do."

I jump forward, all anger taking over. I feel an arm slide around my waist, holding me back as someone takes the coffee from my hand. Maybe lashing out wouldn't be the best thing to do right now, but I will not let anyone talk shit about my man.

"Say one more thing about my fiancé, I dare you," I

snarl, desperate to teach her a fucking lesson once and for all.

"Fiancé? I thought you were with him," she frowns, nodding to Maximus behind me.

"Oh, I am," I reply, grinning. I stand tall and look her dead in the eye. "I haven't just got one fiancé; I have four, and in less than two months' time, I will be Jasmine O'Reilly."

A grin spreads against Amber's lips as she shakes her head.

"Who would have thought the fridged bitch would become a slut."

"Watch your fucking mouth," Maximus growls behind me, but I place a hand over his, which rests on my stomach. I sense Layton standing closer to me and know he will be just as furious as Maximus right now. Layton and I call each other every name under the sun, but if anyone else does it in front of him, he reminds me why he's my security.

But I realise I'm not angry; I know these girls, and I expected nothing less than them becoming nasty bitches when they found out about me and the guys. So, instead of getting irate, I lean back against Maximus smugly.

"It's okay, let her say what she wants. She's just jealous. I have four men who love me, whereas she's always struggled to keep a man longer than a few months."

"I never thought you would turn out like her, but here we are. Both of you are unable to keep your legs closed and happy to take whatever dick is offered as long as you get something out of it. Like mother like daughter." The smug look on her face tells me all I need to know. She wants to hurt me, and in many ways, she has. The one person I never want to turn out like is my mother, but with the guys' help, I have realised I never will. So, I smile instead of letting her think she's getting one over on me.

"If you had said that a few months ago, it would have destroyed me to be compared to her," I start, taking a step forward to close the distance between us as I stare my child-hood friend in the eye, refusing to let her get to me. "But now I know I will never be that bitch. I will never abuse my children, and I certainly won't ever let someone touch them or try to sell them. You can say what you like about me, but I can hold my head high, knowing that I have not one but four men who love me more than anything in this world, and there is nothing they wouldn't do for me, as I would do anything for them. I have the love and stability you could only dream of." Taking a step back, I lean into Maximus's arms.

"You know, I've actually missed you. Even after every-thing I heard, I've been thinking about reaching out. But you just reminded me why I'm better off without you and my bitch of a mother. I'm stronger, wiser and loved in a way you will never understand. You once told me you felt sorry for me, but how the tables have turned." I resist the urge to punch her, and instead, I take my coffee back from Layton and sip it as I watch the two of them.

Sophia looks like she's trying hard not to cry, and Amber looks furious. I can feel the two guys tensed and ready to intervene if they have to. But they won't without my say-so.

"You can sugarcoat it as much as you like, but it won't work. You still think you're better than everyone else, but you're not. Let's face it, no one wanted you, so you had to settle for your stepbrothers like the desperate whore you are," she snarls whilst staring at me.

"That's enough!" Maximus shouts as he steps around me and gets into Amber's face. "You need to watch your fucking mouth because I will not stand by and watch you trying to upset my fiancée when you have no idea what she has been through. And you," he turns his attention to Sophia. "When will you get the picture that I'm not interested? It's pathetic how you throw yourself at me every chance you get. Why would I pick someone like you compared to the woman behind me."

"Fuck you, both of you," Sophia yells before grabbing Amber's arm and dragging her away.

"Nice seeing you both; we will have to catch up again," I call cheerfully as they flip me off.

"Well, that was unexpected," Layton sighs beside me. I turn to face him with a smile on my face.

"You are so fucking hot when you stand up for yourself," Maximus growls before pulling me against him and kissing me hard.

"I'm ready to go home," I point out, smiling as the two girls hurry away. "Are you finished with whatever you were doing?" I ask, hoping to go back with him and show him how much I love him.

"I've got her from here," he tells Layton, not looking away from my eyes once. My whole body has come alive with need. I want this man inside me now.

"But Christian wants-" Layton starts, but Maximus stares in his direction, daring him to keep arguing.

"I will deal with my brother if he gives you any hassle. Now go." Layton doesn't say another word. I catch him nodding once and walking away. Maximus looks back at me and grins.

"Daddy needs some alone time with his Shorty. You

fancy a short weekend break?" he whispers in my ear as I nod, grinning from ear to ear. "Good." He kisses me once on the lips, takes my hand and marches towards the car park as I giggle, trying to keep up.

Four Fiancé's & I: Chapter Two

JASMINE

Maximus starts tapping away on his phone as soon as we're in the car. Pulling my coat off and throwing it in the back, I ask what he's doing, but he flashes me his devious grin and tells me to wait and see. I playfully try to look over his shoulder to peek at his phone, but he just looks at me with one sexy arched brow.

"Brat, don't think I won't pull you over my knee and spank you in this car in front of everyone," he warns. My thighs clamp together as my sex throbs. Is it wrong I want that?

Maximus looks down at my lap, slowly letting his eyes roam up my body. He stares deep into my eyes as I chew on my bottom lip. "Behave." The deepness of his voice makes me want to do anything but behave. He reaches over and takes my chin between his thumb and forefinger.

"Put your seatbelt on and do as you are told for a little while. I promise it will be worth it." The way his eyes burn into mine, I know he's about to blow my mind. "Are you going to be a good girl?" I nod slowly, unable to look anywhere but at him. "That's what I thought," he winks before kissing my lips and returning to his phone.

We sit silently for a moment as he grins at whatever he's organising. As soon as he's finished, he connects the phone to the car and pulls up the number for the house phone. It starts to ring as he pulls out of the parking space and heads for the exit.

"O'Reilly." Jason's voice calls out through the speakers.

"Hey, it's just me," Maximus starts. "Just giving you all a heads up that Shorty's with me. We won't be home until tomorrow evening," he explains whilst swiping his card at the barrier, allowing us to leave.

"Where's Layton?" he asks.

"I sent him back. We don't need him; I've got her."

"No worries, I will give him the day off if he can't get hold of Terry to see if he needs him for anything."

"Are Terry and Daddy still away?" I ask. Christian was only meant to be gone for a few hours the other day, and it's now been three days. I've hardly heard from him, which is very unusual as he always makes a point of calling me at least three times a day when he's forced to be away. But I've had nothing this time besides three very short text messages.

"Yes, Jazzy. Don't worry, though. I spoke to Terry less than twenty minutes ago, and everything is fine. He reckons they will be home tomorrow evening, so don't worry about them. Concentrate on having a good time with just the two of you. I will see you when you get back. Love you."

"Love you too," I answer with a smile as Maximus reaches over and places a hand on my thigh.

"Have fun, you two, and try to stay out of trouble," Jason laughs.

"Where's the fun in that?" Maximus laughs, his hand sliding further up my leg. I can't help grinning as I slide my butt closer to the edge of the seat, giving him better access to the part that's throbbing for his touch. Knowing what I'm after, he grins but removes his hand and winks, leaving me aching for his touch.

"You okay after seeing the two bitches?" Maximus asks as we head out of town.

"Yeah, I am," I answer with a smile. "It sucks to know that our friendship meant so little to them, but I'm happier than I've ever been, and I don't need them in my life." Maximus lifts my hand to his lips and kisses my knuckles.

"You have come a long way, Shorty, and I know I speak for all of us when I say we couldn't be prouder of you." Leaning my head against his shoulder, I close my eyes and smile.

"Thank you, Daddy."

Maximus kisses my head before I sit up, letting him concentrate on driving.

"You're welcome, Shorty. Now, why don't you sort some music out? We have a thirty-minute drive ahead of us."

I don't need telling twice, especially as I know Maximus will have my favourite band ready for us to listen to. As much as he sighs, just as he is now, I know he would never stop me from listening to them.

Nickelback starts playing from the stereo, and I place my hand on his thigh as he drives and tells me about the building he visited this morning and his plans for it.

Thirty minutes later, Maximus pulls off the road and heads down a smaller one. I look ahead, hoping to get some idea of where we are heading; it's then that a huge hotel comes into view.

"Where are we?" I ask excitedly.

"Somewhere I've wanted to bring you for years," Maximus grins as he stops outside the main entrance. A guy around the same age as me jogs down the steps to the car and stops beside my door.

"Open that door, and I will break your legs," Maximus warns as he climbs from behind the wheel. The guy instantly jumps back and looks like he is going to soil himself, stumbling over an apology. Maximus storms to my door and opens it as the guy jumps back further, wanting to put as much distance between them as possible. The door opens, and he holds out his hand to help me out of the car.

"Was that really necessary?" I ask under my breath. He places a hand on the base of my back and leads us up the steps, chucking his car keys to the trembling valet.

"For the first time in weeks, I don't have to share you with anyone. So yes, it was necessary. No one will touch you except me for the next thirty hours." It takes everything in me not to stumble as my heart rate skyrockets and my body shakes with need.

Until I moved in with the guys, I had no idea they could be so ruthless or that I would like it as much as I do. At some point, every single one of them has shown me just how dangerous they can be and why everyone who knows the name O'Reilly understands what will happen to them if they get on the wrong side of the brothers. Well, everyone but me. I know that the guys would never hurt me in any way. Nothing will ever come between us again; people have tried and failed. Our parents included.

Maximus leads me through a beautiful entrance hall to a reception desk where a woman is smiling. I don't miss how she looks at him, and only him. I can see the lust in her eyes, and I don't like it. Maximus may be drop-dead gorgeous, but he's also mine.

As we come to a stop at the desk, I lean into his side and place my left hand with my large engagement ring on his chest to ensure she knows he is taken. I feel, rather than hear, Maximus chuckle under his breath as he kisses the top of my head affectionately. The woman does a double take at the ring and then quickly looks at me as she introduces herself and welcomes us to the hotel and spa.

"Mr and Mrs O'Reilly, I booked online half an hour ago," Maximus announces. I smile as warmth rushes through my body. I love it when they guys already refer to me as their wife. I'm rarely introduced as their fiancée, and I will never get bored hearing it.

"Of course, I have already made sure everything is ready for you in the suite," the receptionist smiles as she types something on her keyboard before lifting a key card and placing it on the desk on top of some papers already there.

"Here is your key and all the information about the facilities available. Do you require someone to take your bags?"

It suddenly dawns on me I have nothing with me, not even a hairbrush or change of underwear. But as I'm about to point this out, Maximus's hand slides around to my hip and gives a quick squeeze.

"They aren't here yet; my brother will drop one off in about an hour. His name is Sean O'Reilly. Give him a key card, and he will drop them off in the room before returning the key. No one else is to enter unless we say so."

"Of course, Mr O'Reilly. Is there anything else you need? Would you like to book a table for dinner?" she asks, but Maximus shakes his head.

"No, we will eat in our suite."

"That's absolutely fine," she smiles and notes something on the system. "Do you have any questions?" Maximus shakes his head and picks up the paperwork and key card.

"Okay, if you go to the end of the hall, you will find an elevator. The suite you booked is on the third floor. The elevator opens, facing the door to the suite." The two of us thank her before Maximus takes my hand and leads me in the direction, she pointed us towards.

We stop in front of the elevator, and Maximus presses the button. He looks at me with a devious smile on his face. Leaning in, his lips stop just before they touch mine.

"I've wanted to bring you here for so long," he whispers as his lips brush against mine.

"Why haven't you?" I ask, leaning forward to close the distance between us, but he moves back, grinning further.

"Things get in the way, like you not knowing how I felt, brothers, arsehole parents and work." The door opens in front of us, and we step inside. The second, the doors are closed, and Maximus presses the button for the third door; he walks me backwards until my back is pressed against the mirrored wall.

"Give me your phone, Shorty," he demands, his hand held before him. Retrieving it from my handbag, he takes it from me and unlocks it before turning it off.

"As I said outside, I'm not sharing you for the next thirty hours. You will not be contacting any of your daddies until I say so. Is that understood?" When I nod, he arches one brow in warning.

"Yes, Daddy," I answer quickly. It's usually only Christian who demands I always use my words. But when the others are feeling particularly spicy, they demand the same thing. It's their way of reminding me to use my safe words if things become too intense.

Maximus leans closer so his whole body is pressed against mine, sandwiching me between him and the mirror behind us.

"I can't wait to spend this time just you and me. No interruptions or having to share you." He grinds up against me, rubbing me in just the right spot through my jeans.

"Daddy?" I gasp, my eyes rolling back as he rubs against me again.

"Yes, Shorty?" Maximus whispers against my neck.

"I need you."

Maximus lifts his head and grins, a look I've come to associate with him being ready to blow me wide open.

"Where do you need me?"

"Everywhere!"

I barely get the word out as my whole body tightens with desperation. His hands leave the wall behind me as the door pings to signal we have reached our floor.

Grab your copy...
vinci-books.com/fourfiancés

About the Author

D.E. Bartley lives in Wales, UK, with her husband, three feral boys, four cats, and a budgie.

To say her home is a madhouse would be an understatement, but she wouldn't have it any other way.

When she isn't running around after her tribe or driving her husband up the wall, she can be found reading and hoarding books like a dragon.

Nothing is as important to her as time with her family, and she loves her trips home to Cornwall with them more than anything in the world. What could possibly compare to sitting on a Cornish beach, with a glass of Cornish gin in one hand and an authentic Cornish pasty in the other, while the monsters, I mean children, play and bodyboard in the sea?

Absolutely nothing.

Acknowledgments

I don't even know where to begin. Never in my wildest dreams did I think I would be able to write full-time and give up my job, but that's exactly what you guys have made possible! Just before the release of Three Stepbrothers Save Christmas, I handed in my notice. After twenty years working in various areas of the healthcare sector, I am now a full-time author, and it's all thanks to each and every one of my readers! You have turned my dreams into a reality, and I couldn't be more grateful for each and every one of you.

I want to thank my husband and kids, who have always supported me 100% and never let me give up. Without their support, I would have been completely lost. I love you all, always and forever, and that will never change.

To my besties, Clare, Lorraine, and Gemma, there are no words to describe my love for you all. I know I don't show it anywhere near as often as I should, but I try. You guys have laughed and cried with me through so many different life events, not just with my writing but with life in general. You listen, never judge, and keep the drinks flowing when we need them most. I love you guys to the moon and back! xx

To Rochelle, you have been one of my biggest supporters and one day, we will meet face-to-face. The world will not be ready for the trouble we will cause. Your friendship means so much to me, and I hope you know how much you are loved. Xx

To Sarwah, without you, there would be no O'Reilly Fight Club, and I would still be working nights at a job that was killing me. Thank you for all your support and for encouraging me to step out of my comfort zone. We need to organise that spa day, as it's long overdue. Xx

As always, I can't have an acknowledgement section without mentioning my amazing friend Karen. As always you have listened and guided me through writing yet another book. I don't think I have a book you haven't been a big part of, and there are no words to describe how much your support means to me. I know I say it time and time again, but there would be no D. E. Bartley without you and your guidance. From the bottom of my heart, thank you. Xx

All that's left to say is a huge thank you again to each and every person who has picked up one of my books or supported me in any shape or form. You have no idea how much it means to me that you are all part of this journey.

I love each and every one of you.

Thank you for being you! Xxx